NO TAME CAT

J. HARDCASTLE
1931

No Tame Cat

An HBC Captain's Voyages between London & Victoria
1865–1885

Robert J. Harvey

GRANVILLE ISLAND
PUBLISHING
GranvilleIslandPublishing.com

No Tame Cat

Cover Design: Alisha Whitley
Maps: Jamie Blackmore

Library and Archives Canada Cataloguing in Publication

Harvey, Robert James, 1927–
    No Tame Cat : An HBC Captain's Voyages between London & Victoria 1865–1885 / Robert James Harvey.

ISBN 978-1-926991-03-0

    I. Title.

PS8615.A7739N6 2009   C813'.6   C2009-902525-6

The painting on the cover of this book is by the noted marine artist Jack W. Hardcastle (1881–1980) of Nanaimo, B.C. It depicts the Hudson's Bay Company barque the *Lady Lampson*, which Captain James Gaudin sailed on nine roundings of Cape Horn 1869–1878. Contrary to the depiction, the *Lady Lampson* did not cross skysail yards; nor did she carry the weight of covering boards at the bows.

Granville Island Publishing
212 – 1656 Duranleau Street
Vancouver, B.C., Canada V6H 3S4
www.granvilleislandpublishing.com

Printed in Canada

The writer dedicates this book to the memory of his late father, Robert Oliver Dunsmuir Harvey Q.C. (1900–1958), who placed great stock in his Gaudin and Anderson connection.

Gaudin Family Portrait

c.1904 photo in Victoria
Standing left to right: James S. Harvey, Miss Kate Gaudin,
Mrs. Mabel Harvey, J.R.P. Gaudin
Seated left to right: Mrs. Marie Wilby, Capt. James Gaudin,
Master Bobbie Harvey, Mrs. Agnes Gaudin, Mrs. Beatrice Bond

CONTENTS

Agnes Anderson (Mrs. Gaudin)

Captain James Gaudin

Robert Harvey was born in Duncan, B.C. in 1927. He currently lives on Denman Island, one of the Gulf Islands on the Pacific Coast. He graduated from Oak Bay High School on D-day, June 4, 1944, at the age of 16 and graduated from the University of British Columbia Law School in 1949. Relying on his own sense of the sea gained in teen-age years on coastal towboats, he wrote this story following retirement after 54 years as a courtroom lawyer.

AUTHOR'S NOTE

For the factual basis of the passages at sea the author relied on over 600 pages of the official logbooks of the Hudson's Bay Company barques *Ocean Nymph* (late 1868) and the *Lady Lampson* (1869–1873) from microfilm records in the Government of Manitoba Hudson's Bay Archives in Winnipeg and on Captain James Gaudin's Service at Sea records from Apprentice Seaman in 1855 obtained from the Record Office of Shipping and Seamen at Cardiff, Wales.

For his latter-day service as Master of his own barque, the *Rover of the Seas* (1869–1885), old newspaper records in Victoria enabled the author to piece together a fuller account of the voyages out of Victoria, which ended with her sinking off the Falkland Islands on December 15, 1885.

For his sense of the conversation between Gaudin and his father-in-law, retired HBC Chief Trader A.C. Anderson, the author relied on his own family history and on his near-60-year study of B.C. history, including that of the Maritime Fur Trade, 1788 to the late 1830s; and also research extending to the logbook of the HBC brig *Dryad* (1834–1835) on microfilm in Winnipeg and that of the *Lama* (1834–1835) at the B.C. Museum.

CAPTAIN GAUDIN'S VOYAGES

• Whitehorse
• Skagway

Victoria
• Vancouver
• Seattle

• San Francisco

Pacific Ocean

Montreal

• New York

• Valparaiso

Cape
Horn

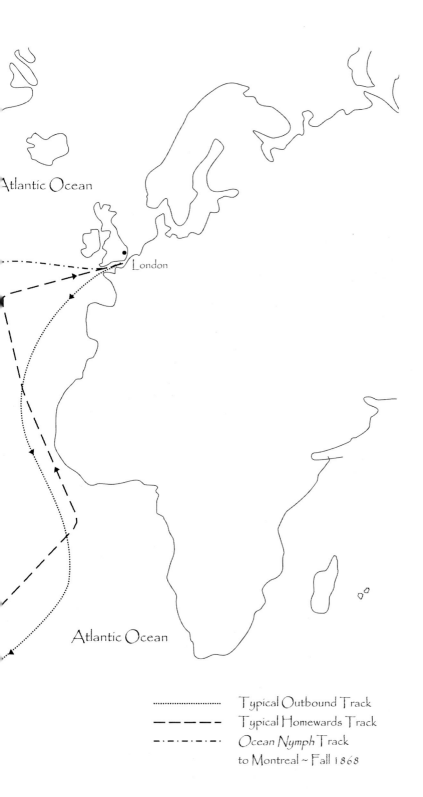

Atlantic Ocean

London

Atlantic Ocean

.... Typical Outbound Track
— — — — Typical Homewards Track
—·—·—·— Ocean Nymph Track
to Montreal ~ Fall 1868

GULF OF ST. LAWRENCE

For his first ship command, Captain Gaudin sailed the HBC barque *Ocean Nymph* from London to Quebec City and Montreal in the late fall of 1868, returning before ice came to the St. Lawrence River. After sailing over 2000 nautical miles across the North Atlantic to pass Cape Race, Newfoundland, the barque sailed to Cape Ray, across to Cap Gaspé and to Pointe-des-Monts, where it entered the river to pick up the Quebec City Pilot.

Local steam paddlewheel tugs towed the barque 150 miles up the River to Elgin Basin in Montreal Harbour and back down the River to Quebec City. On the return, north winds and snow hurried her out to sea by November 30 for storm winds to carry her to London by December 23, 1868.

ENGLISH CHANNEL

Like many of his Jersey brethren, Captain Gaudin built his sea time for command on commercial vessels by sailing out of the Port of London. He began as an Apprentice Seaman in 1855 at the age of 17.

Hired by the HBC to sail as Chief Officer of the *Prince of Wales* on two roundings of the Horn from London to Esquimalt to gain Cape Horn experience, he rose to command of the new HBC barque *Lady Lampson*. He sailed her around Cape Horn from London until she was stranded off Victoria in a sudden storm in January 1878.

Captain Gaudin then travelled to England to buy his own ship to sail the same run. He bought the British barque *Rover of the Seas* in 1879, which he operated in the dying days of Sail out of London and Victoria, B.C. On the return of one voyage to London, he picked up his wife and children in Jersey to sail back as a family to settle in Victoria.

Royal Navy Capt. James Cook named Cape Flattery when bound for Nootka Sound in 1778. He did not see the ten-mile-wide opening of the Strait of Juan de Fuca in poor visibility. Adverse weather caused him to turn away.

Less than 100 years later, aided by the American lighthouse at Cape Flattery, HBC sailing vessels ended their 20,000 mile voyages from the London Docks by entering the Strait to sail the final 50 miles to their destination at Esquimalt Harbour.

STRAIT OF LE MAIRE TO CAPE HORN

When rounding Cape Horn, strong ocean currents driven by westerly storm winds predominated. This made westing into the Eastern South Pacific a struggle against the elements. Experience showed it best to turn at Cape San Diego and take a 120-mile slant through the Strait of Le Maire, rather than to slip south past Staten Island into the mountainous seas of the Great Southern Ocean and chance being driven back.

Against boarding seas that swept rigging and decks clear, crews struggled with icy ropes and heavy canvas sails to help their ship turn north into the Pacific. The risk of colder temperatures and drift ice increased the farther south the Captain drove the ship to find a southwest wind to take them north.

Falkland Islands

In 1885 the Falkland Islands comprised sparsely populated sheep-farming settlements totalling 1,800 persons, not yet connected by telegraph cable to the rest of the British Empire. These settlements relied on a mail schooner to bring mail 800 miles from Montevideo, Uruguay.

The islands had a Governor appointed from London, a detachment of Royal Marines, a Government Dockyard, a Chief of Police with a force of constables seconded from the Royal Irish Constabulary, a Magistrate, a Gaol, a Church of England and a Government in London that consistently ignored diplomatic notes from the Argentine Republic claiming ownership of the lands it insisted upon naming the Malvinas.

1

BLACK NIGHT

At two o'clock in the morning of 9 January 1878 the Second Mate George R. Ferey caught sight of the Captain bursting up on deck in his bare feet. Presenting an awkward sight as he strained to keep his footing, the Captain rushed up the slant of the wet deck wearing only his long underwear. With his right hand cupped to shield his eyes from the driving wind and rain, he scrambled over to the binnacle to take the compass bearing on the light he knew would be shining from the lighthouse on Fisgard Island, but he could see nothing in the thick and violent windstorm that held the vessel heeled over in its grip.

The hours since sunset the previous evening had passed in good cheer aboard the ship despite the need to maintain silence on deck. The *Lady Lampson* will set a new 122-day record for the passage from London unless unforeseen events prevent it. Some sailing vessels strain to make the westbound passage from London around Cape Horn to the Pacific Northwest in eight months, but now many can make it in 135 to 140 days.

Ferey knew the captain pronounced his surname as *Go-Dan* with emphasis on the last syllable and the N almost silent. English people tend to mispronounce it as, *Gaw-din* or *Gow-din*, but some get it nearly right by saying it, *Go-din*.

Ferey, muscular and short in stature with a red beard, pug nose, and a ready smile under his moustache, knew he'd made a success of himself on this passage. The crew respected him and his Captain could do no wrong. The respect for that man began when he followed him up the rigging to climb the masts before moving out on the yards to check the lines and gear before the vessel made her Ninth Annual Departure from Blackwall Dock in the London River last September. Ferey worshipped the man from a distance, the Captain, ten years older. Both were far from home and family on the Island of Jersey in the Channel Islands off the coast of France. They called themselves Channel Islanders but would not object to others referring to them as Jerseymen. At sea the Second Mate often climbed the masts leading the men to reach the highest parts of the rigging to see the Captain's orders for sail carried out, but the ship's Chief Officer (or *Mate*) Mister King did not expect to be called on to leave the deck to go aloft, because that's the way it was aboard ship.

At the root of silence on deck lay ship's discipline. Otherwise how could crew pay attention for orders? Or indeed, how could the captain listen for the sail's flutter and creaks and groans of the ship's timbers, which would enable his ship to speak to him? Seamen were to endure the weather at sea and not talk about it. In sole command of the ship and her movements the captain took counsel from no man. Even the mates obeyed the unwritten rule: no one pursue conversation with the captain on the subject of the current weather or what turn it might take. To stress that requirement officers left the captain to stand alone on his windward side of the quarterdeck where he would have the better view of the weather coming. In the result no one spoke to the captain without first asking him, *May I speak, sir?*

Of course, a captain could initiate talk and then the words will come from tongues eager to speak.

A ship's captain and his mates were not to be distracted from their duty by chatter on deck, nor by common street whistling, not even to rustle up a wind. The Captain told Ferey he grew up in a family that could not abide men or boys whistling. Women and girls, of course, never would even try to whistle because that's the way it was in Jersey.

A rule going back to the days when necessity dictated forestalling mutinous talk aboard ship, the demand for silence applied also to the men aloft in the rigging but some older and more experienced hands knew how to get away with it.

Ferey watched in fascination as Captain Gaudin chose the time to turn into the Strait of Juan de Fuca at Cape Flattery. He had timed to make the entrance to coincide with low tide water in the ocean off Cape Flattery. The incoming tide from the ocean will flow into the 10-mile wide Strait and push into river mouths inland at the heads of navigation as far as gravity will allow. In the next six hours the inside waters of Puget Sound and the Strait of Georgia fill two-fathoms deeper before turning to ebb back out in a broad stream by gravity to the ocean.

With the flood tide soon to begin he gave the order to turn the *Lady*

Lampson to take a new heading to steer up the Strait to her destination. Less than six-hours of sailing with this wind and tide will take them through the harbour entrance at Esquimalt with the last of the flood tide current.

Ferey mused over the learning Gaudin taught him that no Tide on earth runs for more than six hours before turning to run in the opposite direction. It spoke to him of some arithmetical design to Creation neither could fathom.

Scuttlebutt, which gave a chance for men to speak to each other, spread the story that Gaudin often refused offers from tug captains for a tow in from Cape Flattery in his keen pride to sail all of the way into the destination at Esquimalt Harbour without a pilot. Some other company captains of sailing vessels of similar tonnage made landfall too close in to the rocks in summertime calms and fog. They ran the risk of the running tide current putting their vessels into the rock shallows beyond help. The sight of kelp and rocks emerging close aboard on an unruffled lazy ocean swell gave them early warning of the nearness of danger but without any means to resist the pull of the tide current. Tugs coming from Puget Sound and British Columbia hoping to find a sailing ship to engage often found easy pickings.

Scuttlebutt had also spread the word that their captain had often faced adverse winds out of the east in the Strait on previous passages to Esquimalt, but that had never stopped Gaudin from turning into the Strait to gain entry. He sailed the *Lady Lampson* on 15-mile or more boards to work the distance up the Strait from Cape Flattery to Race Rocks Lighthouse with the tide, tacking from one side of the Strait to the other against the wind, sending spray flying to leeward. In that condition, the barque sailed heeled over by the wind on her sails aslant to impart the miracle of forward motion on the ship. But for a dramatic end to this passage from London the wind blew from behind in gusts varying from out of the west and the southwest to make it a violent romp.

Sailing downwind this night brought on a new and different sensation, that of the wind in gusts catching the ship up in a dangerous but exhilarating wild ride with the wind pushing from behind. In that state the helmsman fights the tendency of the ship's design to make it want to turn back into the wind, which came as a necessary but unintended consequence of making the ship sail so well to windward.

Ferey, off-watch, and wearing layers of woollen sweaters under his jacket to keep warm in the cold wind, came on deck at dusk on the late winter day keen to catch a glimpse of the landfall landmarks at Cape Flattery afresh. He had able-seaman-time sailing in these waters. Now a ship's officer, he felt the need to imprint the lay of the land on his mind. Ferey felt the force of a fresh southwest wind on his cheek as he stood at the side of the ship to check his ship's passage by Tatoosh Island and Juan de Fuca's fabled rock pillar abeam to starboard lit by the rays of the setting sun shining through rifts in the cloud.

Now the studdingsails added to the exhilarating run up the middle of the Strait with them set outboard of the square sails to bring added speed. Free of watch-keeping duties until later at midnight, he stood at the side of the main deck to gaze at the sight of the specks of foam and pinnacles of light spangled among the phosphorescence sliding by alongside to slip into the wake, an hypnotic sight for any man free to spend time looking down at it streaming aft.

Ferey resisted looking for too long and lifted his head to catch glimpses through low cloud of scarcely discernable snow-covered trees on hills and mountains on both sides of the wide Strait.

The men on deck heard the sound of the water rushing by, pushed aside by the ship. No one said a word. Men on watch stood as if entranced by the moan of the wind in the rigging and the creaks and groans from the ship's hull timbers below and from the blocks with rope line running through them. The men of the Mate's watch came to wash the decks, tidy up, and put all ship-shape and glistening for port. They did their work in silence. Ferey lifted himself up into the lower rigging to keep his trousers and soft leather boots out of their way. The ship, now shining, could slip along in the dark like a woman dressed up to be seen by others.

As the ship came farther up into the Strait Ferey looked to see if he could catch a sight of the Olympic Mountains lit in the light of the moon, but the cloud kept the view hidden. He caught himself as he remembered knowing the Captain favoured the American side coming up the Strait to pass Pillar Point 40 miles to starboard, and that the lower hills and mountains lying between the peaks and the shoreline barred the sight of the Olympics even in the best of weather.

Gaudin's time as mate in the *Prince of Wales* had made him wise to Pacific Northwest weather. The *Lady Lampson's* extended maiden voyage return to London from Victoria by early summer 1870 allowed him to time his later departures from London to be off Cape Flattery inbound for Victoria in season to turn the winds of winter into a blessing. His vessel, he would say, is a creature of the wind. If the wind blew, he could sail his ship.

After over three hours of fast sailing Ferey noticed the ship's passage falling to a walk as the wind dropped off. No stars showed through the overcast sky. A light rain fell and only a breath of wind filled the sails. Water passed by the stern with a pleasant contented sound. The wind soon freshened to a cold breeze out of the east of southeast to make the foretopsail flutter. Seeing the barque headed and stopped from sailing in that direction, he turned to hear the Captain and the mate talking on the quarterdeck, but could not make out their words from where he stood. They must have been talking about what he saw happening next without an order calling all hands on deck. On signal seamen came running to haul on the ropes called the braces to make the yards swing to enable the wind now coming from a different angle to fill the sails. He saw the ship swing her long bowsprit off the wind to turn north to her destination, the harbour at Esquimalt.

The new patent windlasses on deck, kept well greased, eased work involved in hauling. The ship responded in an instant by heeling to port. After a moment's hesitation the sails filled and she picked up speed through the water again in the new direction.

Ferey made his way aft in time to stand his Middle Watch from midnight to 4 a.m. He heard the Captain calling to Steward Samuel Powder to lay out his going ashore clothes and to be ready with hot water for him to wash and shave. His Steward often helped him do this when in port, but never before the ship came to anchor. Ferey heard the Captain speak with a note of irritation.

"Yes, despite the hour, I will land on the shore as soon as we anchor."

What on earth had got into the Captain? Ferey knew he had been champing at the bit to drive the ship to make an early arrival in Victoria. No trouble existed concerning the record, now certain. Knowing the passage had gone very well, he expected to see his Captain's face beaming with the same pride felt by everyone else. Perhaps something other than the time record drives him. What can it be?

In the passage down the South Atlantic the Captain did not let up in his determination to drive the ship to hit a favouring tide to pass through the Straits of Le Maire and strike southwest into Sir Francis Drake Channel to get past Cape Horn. And once in the Pacific Ocean, to Ferey's mounting excitement he drove the ship north using Maury's

Book to choose a course to avoid calms south and north of the Equator. The sharp American Clipper the *Flying Cloud* did likewise in the mid-1850s to set an 89-day time record on a passage from New York to San Francisco in Southern Hemisphere winter weather at the end of July. The welcome and unexpected wind out of the east and northeast at the Horn sustained swift passage for the *Flying Cloud*. That same wind came again this time to cut days off the *Lady Lampson's* passage.

With eyes now accustomed to the darkness Ferey reported to the quarterdeck with the seamen of his Middle Watch standing at their stations on deck. At the turning of the hourglass at the change of watch he saw the Captain's dark black eyes look troubled and distant as he turned to report the watch to him.

"Hola! Mister Ferey," Gaudin called out in a firm voice. "Do you see where we are? Can the ship weather Race Rocks Lighthouse from this position?"

Ferey did see two lighthouse lights to steer by, one abeam and the other 10 miles ahead. He nodded as he said he agreed, and he listened to the Captain speak again.

"As you can see, Mister, the studdingsails have been taken in and we are now making way under all plain sail in a light air from the southeast. The wind dropped off a half-hour ago. The tide is still flooding for another two hours before the ebb will put the ship in danger. Race Rocks lies on our port abeam. If it pleases you, Mister, you will now hold the ship's course *North 1/4 West* to head in for Esquimalt distant ten miles ahead. The Fisgard light points the way. Steer for it. I intend to sail right in to anchor in Esquimalt Harbour. We will not wait for daylight or for the local Pilot."

By the light of the binnacle Ferey saw the Captain frown in anger as he spoke.

"By God's blood, damn Pamphlett and his slow-up ways. I have matters to attend to in my cabin. Mister King stands by to take the conn with All Hands on Deck when he decides to take it from you. You will then stay on deck to follow his orders. He knows the way in."

"Aye, aye, sir!"

Seamen on the Middle Watch stood forward on the main deck in silence at their stations. Ferey checked the compass heading the helmsman steered in the direction of the light at Fisgard Lighthouse, seen blinking through the masts and rigging. He knew the light stood at the western side of the narrow entrance into the harbour and that he should keep it to port in entering the channel. No lights lit the other side of the entrance, which lay in darkness to the north and to starboard.

In the shelter of an inner waters shoreline to port the ship slipped along in silence under a low dark overcast sky. The Mate's off-watch crew stayed awake in their quarters forward on deck, told to be ready to participate in the imminent All-Hands-on-Deck arrival in port. Just enough wind filled the canvas sails to move the ship through the water at a steady pace. Two hours passed in a rain shower and with a light wind coming in from the southeast on the barque's starboard quarter.

No one had seen a patch of usable land since sighting the green peaks of Madeira, and no ports of call since London. Even Ferey had the itch to have a run ashore when the Captain gave leave to go into town.

Other sailing vessels lay lamped out at anchor in Royal Roads. The *Lady Lampson* swished by them without a word exchanged. Ferey could see no lights on either shore ahead except that from the dim flashing light at Fisgard Lighthouse. The rain had started to fall there, too, but the ship would soon swing on her anchor in the harbour, he said to himself as the ship made way through the water in near silence.

The Captain remained below in his cabin. The Chief Officer Mister King came up to stand at the weather side of the quarterdeck to take the conning of the ship through the dark into the entrance to Esquimalt. All hands now stood in silence on deck at their stations with no shouted command to bring them there. Ferey stood at the foot of the lee gangway to the quarterdeck within sight of Mister King on the far side of the quarterdeck. Neither Ferey, nor the Mate knew what the other was thinking, this being another unintended result of the legacy of the requirement for silence on deck. The southeast wind began to rise in strength to lift the ship forward. More rain fell.

Ferey grew uneasy when the cloud lowered and he lost sight of the Fisgard light in a heavy wind and rainsquall. Minutes passed and moments later he heard the crash and felt the thud through the deck. The ship faltered and heeled, the wire rigging on both sides twanging and shaking as if struck by sledgehammers. In the same instant Ferey heard the Captain's bellow come from below deck.

"God's Teeth! What's that?"

Gaudin had the razor to his face when the ship struck the rock. At the lurch, he cut his cheek.

The ship glanced off whatever it had hit and would have gone on into the dark had Mister King not shouted the order to let fly the topsail halliards and run to stations to brail up the fore and mainsail, which relieved the ship from being blown down by the force of a blast of a much stronger wind that turned the ship broadside-to. The squall screamed through the masts and rigging as it hit with a terrible noise and with such force that the ship presented much of her bottom side up to the wind. The *Lady Lampson*, no longer moving like a vessel under command, lay heeled over in the turbulent water with her lee rail under. The wind gusts lashed her lines and rigging, and the seas washed over her weather bulwarks to drench everyone on deck. Against the screaming wind in the rigging came the sound of hard wet canvas slatting and flapping against wood and wire rope sounding like crackling gunfire.

****

Gaudin's cheeks felt the sting of cold salt spray blown by icy winds off the waves. Men on deck stood waiting for him to do something to save the ship. He sensed an air of despair taking hold.

He knew the seas would be breaking on a near shoreline, but he could see nothing. The *Lady Lampson*, he thought, must have slid off one of the many rocks along the long rocky shoreline he could not see in the dark between Saxe Point and Duntze Head at the eastern entrance to Esquimalt Harbour. Gaudin knew enough of the ship's predicament to sense that the ebb tide current will edge his ship onto a lee shore in the dark.

In the words of next morning's Colonist newspaper, by that time the wind had increased to a *howling tempest*. Three other sailing vessels, the *Locksley Hall*, inbound from San Francisco with cargo consigned to Welch, Rithet & Co of Victoria, the *Two Brothers*, and the *Ocean Gem* rode out the storm at anchor at the nearby Royal Roads roadstead waiting for the weather to improve for Pilots to come out to them next day.

The Mates stood their ground as best they could on the slanting deck. They did not avert their eyes when Gaudin turned to them to speak. The Captain cupped his hands and shouted to Ferey who was close to tears.

"The southeast breeze I left you with has freshened into a whole gale of wind and driving rain! Why didn't you call me?"

Gaudin didn't wait for an answer and turned to look around him. The anchors might yet save the ship. Yesterday, with Cape Flattery in sight he ordered the Mate bring up the anchor cables from storage below decks and secure both anchors to the catheads ready for use. He could now think of letting go the anchors. The Mate lay forward without delay to work the hands already in the bows in anticipation of the order coming, but time stood still on deck. Finally, the order came.

On the Mate's order to the Carpenter to strike his heavy maul against the chain stopper holding the first anchor at the port cathead, the sharp ping of the Carpenter's Iron sounded through the rain, jarring nerves. The second anchor from the starboard cathead followed in moments that lasted an eternity. The crew's loud cheer of relief soon came as the ship's bow turned swinging into the wind on the anchors taking hold.

Gaudin's order to the Second Mate came in an instant to clew up the loose and flapping sails to make the wind find less to blow against and to end the distraction and heart-rending noise of the wind making a bedlam of high-pitched cracking sounds. The ship now held her position against the wind and the seas, but the sound of the wind in the masts and rigging remained to make Gaudin remember former times of threat and danger.

Instinct told him to send Ferey to sound the wells for water in the hold. He came back running up to call out a warning.

"Sir, I have sounded the wells to find the water rising fast, twelve feet of water now. The ship is filling, sir!"

Gaudin and Ferey knew the cavernous cargo hold, though strengthened with iron frames, had no bulkheads to hold back a leak filling the hold. Not a moment to be lost. No time for the ship's pumps to have any effect. Unless he could now put the ship aground, she could fill with water and plunge to the bottom at the harbour entrance. Everyone knew wooden sailing vessels, unless kept pumped clear, can become too heavy to remain afloat when filled with seawater.

Gaudin could not delay giving his next order to the Mate.

"Mister King, if it please you, slip the anchor lines, now."

With a quick salute and an aye aye, sir, the Chief Officer moved on the run to give the order to let the chain run out overboard. The order to slip the cables presupposed urgency with no time to be lost trying to bring in the anchors. Gaudin could now gauge how the wind and seas moved the ship in relation to the light at the Fisgard Lighthouse.

The Captain's Steward came running up to him with his long coat, boots, and cap. With a show of vigour to belie his jitters, Gaudin gave a shout.

"Oh, that's good of you, Sam!"

And now warmth came back to him when he put his arms out to pull the heavy coat over his shoulders.

Hurried compass bearings on now visible Fisgard light told him the end near; the wind and tide had carried the *Lady Lampson* westward into the shallows off the Esquimalt Lagoon Beach. Held in the grip of the storm, he could not sail his ship out into the Strait. But, with the tide now turning to ebb after high tide, he could use the ebb current to help the ship come aground in a spot where it could remain upright in the mud when the tide went out.

Gaudin turned to face a question from his Steward.

"What are we going to do, Sir?"

"Sam, I'm going to let the waves beach the vessel as close as I can steer to where the stream comes out of the Lagoon. The ship may find a deeper place there to lie aground when the tide goes out."

"Don't let her sink, sir! Precious few of us can swim," Sam Powder whispered back.

The *Lady Lampson* drifted ashore in the dark to fetch up with her deep keel on a bottom of mixed sand and coarse gravel at the end of the Esquimalt Lagoon beach by the stream. Lying stern-to, the next rising tide lifted her for the waves to pound her hull around at an angle to the surf. The storm mounted an attack with waves breaking high over the ship, drenching everyone cold and wet. By morning's light all hands could see the ship lying grounded four cables southwest of the Fisgard Light. Gaudin could see now how close they had come to making safe arrival in the harbour. How fortunate the tide had begun to ebb out from the harbour entrance when it did, otherwise the ship would have perched up on the rocks beside the lighthouse to become the ultimate spectacle Gaudin would never live down in eyes of all mariners. Especially those now anchored in Royal Roads would have seen the wreck at low tide as a testament to the need for a ship's captain to wait for a Pilot to enter Esquimalt Harbour.

By mid-morning on 9 January 1878 the southeast wind and rain drove low dark cloud in to afflict the entire southern end of Vancouver Island with even greater force than the previous night. The *Lady Lampson* lay hard aground on the shallows, heeled-over with the waves sending spray high over the masts aslant. Half full of seawater, she listed toward the land as if turning her head away to ward off the pounding of the surf.

The surf worked to build up drift sand on the outer side to hold the *Lady Lampson* in its grip. No lives now were in danger, but the wind continued to moan a distinct and chilling sound. Gaudin gave orders for the men to bring down the weight and windage of the upper yards and top sections of the masts to ease the pounding and waited for the help his rockets of distress signaled.

To the east in daylight Gaudin could see the waves at low tide breaking on Scrogg Rock on the other side of the Esquimalt Harbour channel entrance. No other, that's what they must have hit last night, but ship's discipline continued to rule out chatter on deck about it.

In a lull in the storm Chief Factor Charles sent out the company steamer the *Beaver* with a party of experts consisting of the Lloyd's Agent Roderick Finlayson, Captains Devereaux and Nagle, and Robinson, a master ship's carpenter. They carried a note from the Chief Factor offering assistance. Gaudin took the inspection party below to make a survey of the vessel's condition for report back to shore.

Not wasting the opportunity, Gaudin sent the *Lady Lampson's* three forlorn paying passengers, the Pearse brothers and young Master Harry Innes with their baggage in a boat to the *Beaver* in a stirring display of dipping oars and boat handling. The *Beaver* then took the passengers into town before coming back for the three experts.

With a chance to talk to them while waiting for the steamer's return, Gaudin lost no time in finding out what they were thinking. The four men stood talking on the slanting deck holding on to whatever came to hand.

"Do you have anything to say about my plan to repair the ship?"

Captain Devreaux spoke for the three. "You have already brought down the upper yards and upper masts as we would be recommending," he said. "They should now be put overboard in the water to lighten the ship and towed into town by the *Beaver* when she comes back out. In my opinion the vessel as she lies now is not sufficiently strained to injure her framing or to warrant her being condemned. You lost your two anchors and chain in the storm. Now, she requires an anchor with 60 to 80 fathoms of chain laid out to the southeast and hove taut to prevent her from worsening her present position or being driven inshore."

The others nodded and stated their agreement.

"I will send back a note with you to the Fort making the requisition."

"I hear the Hudson's Bay Company has a warehouse full of casks containing 75,000 gallons of whale oil from the West Coast and the

Strait of Georgia," Mister Finlayson said. "If the weather holds, perhaps that's your cargo to London."

"That's the best news I've heard, sir," said Gaudin. "I am hoping the Company will allow me to sail her back to London when she's ready. In the meantime we will stay on board to see her brought into town to be hauled out for you to make a full inspection on the ways."

The *Beaver* returned to the wreck in several hours to take the inspection party back into town. Captain Devereaux made a final remark as he stepped down to the boat the *Beaver* sent out.

"We can only hope another January storm does not come up," he said, "to do its worst, Captain."

Two days later, the seas calmed for Gaudin to take a steamer-ride into town in the *Beaver* to talk to Chief Factor Charles in his office. Curiosity gnawed on Gaudin's mind: he had to find out what Charles was thinking about him and the whole sorry mess he had caused. Charles met him at the door.

"Gaudin, you will be pleased to know that the survey report says the *Lady Lampson* should not be condemned, not sufficiently strained, as they put it. All depends on how quickly you unload the cargo to float her off. Then we can bring her into town to be hauled out on the ways for a full survey."

"Will you tell me, sir, what the Company intends to do about claiming on the insurance?"

"That would be premature. I cannot throw up my hands and simply call on the Underwriters in London to pay the claim if the possibility remains open that men can bring her in for survey. The Marine Insurance Underwriters will rely on the Hudson's Bay Company fulfilling its obligation to lessen its loss by acting under the Sue and Labour clause in the Marine Insurance Policy even though thereby they oblige themselves to pay the ship owner the full amount of all reasonable costs and expenses incurred by the Company to save the vessel, which may include such an item as the cost of running the *Beaver* back and forth to the *Lady Lampson*. In that category also comes the money the Company has agreed to pay under the contract I have signed with Messrs Pamphlett, McQuade, and Spratt for them to salvage the cargo to lighten the vessel. Then we can tow her off and bring her in for survey."

"And for repair?" asked Gaudin, but Charles said nothing.

"The contract will prevent them from making claim for salvage of the ship, won't it sir?"

"Yes, that may be so, Gaudin, but whatever may be the case, I want you and the crew to stay in control and take no step to abandon the vessel until the seas no longer permit you to live aboard." Gaudin waited for Charles to talk about the insurance on the cargo, some of which included cargo carried on his own account. After he had checked some papers, Charles began to speak again.

"The position of the Ship and Cargo claimants is in the hands of a General Average Adjuster, who will be in touch with you to obtain a statement. Vessels that strand purposely to avoid sinking is one thing, but vessels that strike a rock and begin to leak, damaging cargo, and then strand for the purpose of lessening the damage to ship and cargo may be another. The Cargo Insurance Underwriters, as opposed to the Ship Insurance Underwriters, will claim they should not contribute to the cost of salvage of the vessel when done to enable the vessel to be floated off. The lawyers and adjusters will work it all out."

Gaudin asked if Charles had sent a letter off to London to tell them of the stranding.

"I should tell you London already knows. My short dispatch by cable telegram went out the same day."

Charles showed Gaudin The Anglo-American Telegraph Company telegraph message pad and a copy of the short message he had written on one of its pages.

"This copy shows the short cable I sent for transmission to London to explain the critical situation. I followed up to the Company Secretary Armit in London the same day with a letter with full information. In the letter I told him your vessel arrived at between 2 and 3 o'clock in the morning, and while sailing into Esquimalt Harbour unfortunately struck Scrogg Rock, off which she got free, but now lies hard aground and nearly full of water: and that Her Majesty's Ships *Opal* and *Rocket* promptly rendered every form of assistance possible but found they could not tow her off. And a severe southeast storm wind has been blowing all day to prevent lightening the vessel by offloading cargo. And marine surveyors would go out the next day. And the cargo may be considered a total loss. And the vessel remains in a very precarious position."

Gaudin told Charles the letter spoke well of the Navy, but in fact no navy vessel came out to provide assistance until after the storm died down.

"If they had come before the tide changed, the Navy might have pulled us off. Likely they could not get steam up in time to come out to help us. I have embarrassed them."

"I must have been misinformed about the Navy's part," Charles said, "but I can do little about that now."

Gaudin remarked that Charles must find the telegraph connection useful for company business, and he asked how Her Majesty's Mail now gets sent to London.

"Yes, Gaudin, the cable connection with London perhaps more useful than we know. I followed up on the cable to send my letter to Armit same day in the company mail pouch on the steamer *City of Panama* to San Francisco for onward carriage by railroad across to Boston or New York and then by trans-Atlantic steamer. It will get to London within a month."

After a long pause Gaudin brought up a new subject.

"I am happy to think we may repair the *Lampson* and sail again, sir."

"You cannot be sure of that, Gaudin," Charles shot back. "Go back to your ship now and work with the contractors to lighten the vessel. The steamer *Cariboo & Fly* and the schooner *Bonanza* will be bringing out a steam donkey engine with a crane to help lift cargo onto scows they have at their disposal."

Gaudin went back out to his ship, but he refrained from calling it a wreck. Another storm struck. The seas broke over the vessel for days, during which she remained prey to a succession of winter storm waves coming in on a fetch of forty miles from the southeast. Captain and crew, cold and wet, held on silently to handholds wherever they could find them, stunned by the sight and sounds of the wind's raging, which kept returning in one howling tempest after another.

The contractors finally found spells of weather when the seas calmed for them to bring out their two steamers to lie alongside with their own lifting tackle to bring up boxes of cargo from the hold. Then they steamed into Esquimalt to unload the salvaged cargo for storage. The work proceeded at a slow pace with the winter weather threatening to worsen. Next day Charles sent a message to Gaudin to come to his office to report on the present situation. The *Beaver* came out to pick him up and steamed into town to drop him off at the Company wharf in the Inner Harbour. He walked up to Charles's office to find himself not kept waiting. Charles came out of his Office to greet him.

"Sit down Gaudin and tell me what is going on out there. Of course, from here, I cannot see how the contractors are doing."

"I have kept my crew aboard to prevent breakage and plunder whenever the contractors' men and vessels come to lift out our cargo, but I fear yet another storm will force us to leave the ship to save our lives. Against that possibility I have obtained permission from the Navy Storeskeeper to occupy an empty wooden shed on shore at nearby Gotha Point, which the Navy uses to observe gunnery practice on targets being towed in the Strait. From there, we can be aboard ship whenever we spy the contractors' men coming out of Esquimalt Harbour to do work."

"I imagine you enjoyed the opportunity to remove yourself from the misery on board, Gaudin."

"Yes sir, little cheer on board in the wet and damp."

Gaudin walked down to the wharf to await the return of the *Beaver* to take him back to the wreck. Improving weather allowed him to keep the crew on board to maintain a watch on the contractors' men whenever they came out to work. But a series of violent southeast gales over the next ten days prevented the contractors from going out for more than two or three days at a stretch before they had to flee to shelter in Esquimalt Harbour.

In the morning of 28 January Gaudin made a quick trip into town to confer again with Charles on progress of unloading.

"Gaudin, would I be correct to cable London to say the *Lady Lampson* remains aground with about 100 tons on board, but the poor weather conditions have continued to prevent the contractors going out?"

"Yes sir, that says it true."

"I am adding that you have built a bulkhead at the forward part of the ship for you to place the two pumps powered by the contractors' steam donkey engine. Weather permitting, steam-powered pumps on the *Cariboo & Fly* will continue to pump out the hold. Can I write we hope in a few days, at most, we shall be able to tell whether or not we can save the ship?"

"Yes sir, that's true, but I hope our chances are better than that."

"Gaudin, in truth, I am beginning to fear she will stay on the beach as a wreck."

With the weather looking to worsen, Gaudin went back out to the *Lady Lampson*. Only 100 tons of cargo remained in the hold for unloading when another great storm came up in early morning darkness on 29 January. The contractors stayed in Esquimalt, but Gaudin and the crew continued to live on board in misery. The seas washing over the decks made it impossible for them to use the ship's boats to go ashore to land on the beach to occupy the nearby shed for shelter.

In the next morning's light and at the height of the storm Gaudin ordered another distress rocket sent up. The Navy replied by flag signal to ask if it were possible to render assistance. Gaudin sent a reply in the affirmative. But by the time Navy whaleboats arrived more than two hours later, the tide had turned to make the sea too dangerous for the boats to come alongside. They returned to base.

Later, during a lull in the storm another whaleboat did come alongside. The young Navy Officer in command asked permission to come aboard. He scrambled down into Gaudin's cabin to hear him make a firm statement: he would not give up on his plan to avail himself of the shed building on shore. He must decline being taken off in the Navy boats and seen to abandon ship.

"I will send off three ill seaman with you, Mister," Gaudin said. "I cannot abandon the ship. To make my position clear, I will hand you this note asking Captain Robinson to allow me to use the shed building. It stands only 100 yards away for me to lodge the crew close by the ship in a position to come back quick if the contractors come out to work."

The next act in the drama came later the same day when Jack Tars rowed out another whaleboat flying the Royal Navy White Ensign to the stricken *Lady Lampson*. Another Navy Officer, a full Lieutenant in rank, asked permission to come on board. He came to deliver a copy of a letter of complaint dated 31 January 1878 from the Senior Officer at the Royal Navy Base. The Mate took the letter from him and carried it up to Gaudin who held on to the weather mizzen shrouds on the slanting deck. Gaudin held his breath as he broke open the seal to get past the short covering letter to scan the biting words of the copy of the Report addressed to the Board of Trade in London in plain round handwriting of a captain's secretary-writer for the signature of a *Captain F. C. W. Robinson*.

Gaudin knew the Board of Trade in England had jurisdiction to make an inquiry, the outcome of which could be a report that might end his career in command of a ship. The covering letter also stated Robinson had sent a copy of the complaint report to the Secretary of the Hudson's Bay Company in London c/o Chief Factor Charles.

Gaudin's heart sank and his head spun as he picked out the words from the formal complaint against him, but in a moment of calm he realized it did not mount an attack on him for his seamanship in striking the rock; instead the words focused on his eventual decision to refuse to abandon ship after having signaled a necessity to be taken off.

The letter from Captain Robinson came addressed to **Mr Gaudin, Master of the British Barque _Lady Lampson_**. Smarting under the insult implicit in the manner of address, he wrote his reply to the letter the next day from the room he had taken at the St. Nicholas Hotel in town. Gaudin told himself he must keep his head about him. He dated the letter 1 February 1878, and asked Charles to send it to the Naval Base.

Captain Robinson, I have the honour to acknowledge the receipt of your communication of 31 January. In reply to your inquiry I state as under, leaving it to yourself to bring the matter before the Board of Trade or otherwise act as you may see fit. When on the morning of the 29 January I signaled for aid I did so under the apprehension that owing to the increasing storm there was danger for the lives of my crew. After my signal and until the tide turned, an interval of about two hours, there was no danger in approaching my vessel on the port or lee side to rescue my crew and to perform an ordinary act of humanity. After the turn of the tide, your prudence having prevented you from giving me assistance, the circumstances changed. The roughened sea owing to the change of tide and the increase in the storm during which my last remaining boat was swept away from the studs made it impracticable for me to receive the desired aid that then came offered from your boat lying off. I have however to thank you in the warmest terms for the assistance afterwards rendered by your people to my crew and me. I have the honour to be, Sir; your obedient servant, 'Jas Gaudin'.[1]

Gaudin and Charles, each bundled up with warm clothing for the winter weather, soon met at the company wharf in Esquimalt for more talk about the unloading operation.

"Wait no longer," Charles said. "Keep to your room in the hotel in town and send your mates and crew to room and board at the house we talked about earlier. I have already put them on notice for a guaranteed two-weeks' board and lodging with chance of further if suitable. We can't do better than five dollars a week for each man."

"The southeast wind still blows to keep the contractors on the shore," Gaudin replied. "I will be able to bring the crew into the wharf in Esquimalt Harbour. They can walk from there to the house."

Charles mounted his horse to ride back to town. He turned to see Gaudin's nod of agreement when he made a statement for Gaudin to confirm.

"Though lacking the convenience of being able to keep a lookout from the Navy shed on the shore, you have told me you have the comfort of an agreed-on working arrangement with the contractors to be notified whenever their men go out for your crew to be there with them."

For ten days Gaudin remained at this hotel in town and the working arrangement with the contractors held, during which more of the cargo came to be removed piece by piece whenever weather permitted under the supervision of the Mates. Charles had made it clear he desired reports of progress in writing as a prelude to meeting to discuss. On Monday morning 11 February the new week began with Gaudin hearing a voice calling from the street to his hotel room.

"Captain Gaudin come quick! The '*Cariboo Fly*' is bringing in the wreck of the *Lady Lampson*."

Gaudin hurried down to see the *Lady Lampson* listing in an ominous manner to starboard. Captain Spratt's side-wheel steamer the *Cariboo & Fly* led the procession. In her newly constructed length and bulk, the *Cariboo & Fly* loomed larger and higher than the prey at the end of her short towline. The *Bonanza* tied to one side appeared to hold the little *Lady Lampson* wedged up from sinking. Smoke streamed straight up from both smoke-stack funnels in the calm weather, but no sound of any of the activity made it to shore. Thin lines of silent Victoria citizens stood on the shore to see the stately little black ship brought in like a child taken by the ear for punishment.

"No crew aboard, so they must have abandoned her, leaving her open to a salvage claim."

"They're paying a lot of attention to the shouts of encouragement from some on the shore and not minding their business."

"They look very pleased with themselves, don't they? '*Little Jack Horner stuck in his thumb and pulled out a plum and said, What a good boy am I.*'"

That resulted in a good *Ha! Ha!* all around, but Gaudin didn't think it funny.

No brass bands played. No applause came from any quarter. No one came from the Company to greet the ship, now being laid to rest in shallow water. Gaudin looked on in disbelief as the *Beaver* steamed out from her berth in the harbour to take over to nudge the *Lady Lampson* in closer to the shore where she would lie high and dry on the mud at low tide. He then went back to his hotel on silent streets. Gaudin and the marine surveyor met by arrangement to take advantage of a near-zero low tide in the early hours of the winter morning to walk out onto the mud to make an inspection of damage to the hull by lamplight.

Charles sent a note to Gaudin to come into the office at 10 a.m. next morning to make a report. On his arrival Charles held a copy of Gaudin's letter dated 14 February[2] in his hand to explain the sequence of events leading up to the *Lady Lampson's* present state and condition.

"Thank you, Gaudin, I have your report," he said. "I sent your letter to Captain Robinson for delivery to him at Esquimalt. For my report to London I have your letter to say that you did not give permission to the contractors to bring in the vessel to Victoria Harbour. Is that correct?"

"Yes sir. The contractors towed the *Lady Lampson* into Victoria without any notice to me. Neither my crew, nor I, was onboard at the time. The day previous I was on board when the contractors notified me they would not work that night. At 4 p.m. I left the vessel, leaving the Second Mate in charge. At 6 o'clock the contractors steamed off to Esquimalt after informing the Second Mate they would not work that night. All hands then left the ship, rather than stay aboard without provisions. In the night the contractors' people came back to the ship to keep the pumps at work. When the tide came in the vessel lifted off. They must have slipped the anchor chain and the stern moorings to begin the tow. Previous attempts on my part to float the ship on a high tide had failed. I had been unable to lift her lee bilge from the sand on each occasion. A heavy swell continuing and the ship lying on her beam ends, I considered it imprudent to try to get her off until more of the cargo had been taken away from the starboard side lest the ship capsize as soon as the China pumps sucked dry."

After an awkward silence Charles spoke again to change the subject.

"I have acted on your statement to the effect that in consequence of the dangerous position of the ship with water coming into the cabin to submerge all the beds and bedding and to destroy all the perishable stores, you judged it unsafe for the crew to live on board. That justified me to hire the room and board in Esquimalt. The contractors were lucky the ship didn't capsize on them to starboard anywhere along the route of the tow. I am sure we will be finding just enough weight of cargo remained down in the hold to keep her from doing just that. Being secured tight by rope to the *Bonanza* likely kept her upright until she got put on the mud_____. I have a note you engaged a navy diver. What was that about?"

"Sir, I had the diver from H. M. S. *Opal* for two days, but he was unable to get to the whole extent of the damage. The ship is slightly hogged and badly strained all over. I shall call for a survey as soon as I can get the ship up on the ways to be examined."

After a long silence Gaudin added, "I have done what I could to keep down expenses."

After writing notes on paper, Charles spoke again to say he couldn't imagine the trouble had the *Lady Lampson* capsized and sunk in the entrance channel to the Inner Harbour, and he asked Gaudin if he had anything to add to his letter of report.

"I may not have covered some of the happenings before the con-tractor *rescued* my ship: I focused on explaining why none of us was onboard at the time. The contractors took a great risk in moving her, sir. I do not know which one or more of them breached the working arrangement. They had told us they would not be going out to the *Lady Lampson*, but they did. My Mates and crew remained asleep at their lodgings in Esquimalt and missed them leaving the harbour."

"I called in the contractors to get their version before I called you in, Gaudin. I found they realized the danger too late and had to scramble to put on more lines when *Lady Lampson* nearly got away from them twice during the tow. In their talk to me they were shame-faced about it. They now await your instructions to go alongside *Lady Lampson* in the harbour at tides that will permit you to supervise the unloading of the remainder of the cargo, and make up a final tally report for me. You will be in touch with the shipyard to arrange to take the vessel up on the ways for the marine surveyor to make his report. You will discharge the crew and go to your hotel to write your report to explain stranding the company vessel. You did not direct your previous report to making an explanation of that."

2

REBUKES BEGIN

Gaudin rarely showed his face on the street except to make his rounds of hotels at night in the exercise of a citizen's legal right to open hotel guest register books to see if he could find the name of Consuelo Cochrane as a registered guest. With a raised eyebrow, his old friend, the Victoria Colonist newspaper reporter, told him he had never heard of a woman of that name.

The company office in Victoria had no mail or messages for him. Two days later Gaudin convinced himself that Consuelo had not come to Victoria from San Francisco as she had written in the letter addressed to him c/o of the Company Office in London to say she would.

Never before in all his years of sailing had he been ordered off his ship and told to stay in his room to make a written report about anything. He wanted time with Charles to speak of his own eagerness to sail his barque back to London with local repairs done with ship's crew not yet dispersed from their lodgings in Esquimalt. With his permission he could move soon to gather the crew and re-constitute the ship to sail with company cargo. Gaudin dashed off a letter making this request, and he walked to the company office to deliver it and asked to speak to the Chief Factor.

The man at the front desk told him wait while he inquired.

"Captain Gaudin, I have handed your envelope to the Chief Factor. He has told me to tell you your orders remain the same. You are to stay at your hotel for word to be sent to you to come to the office."

Turning on his heel, not wanting the man at the desk to see his cheeks flushing in anger, Gaudin returned to his room at the St. Nicholas Hotel. He sat alone at his table writing out his report to deliver to the company office. He did not make a copy of it, but on recollection, his last attempt ran much like this: -

On the pages attached please find my report of the incident whereby I stranded the Honourable Company barque Lady Lampson at two a.m. on 9 January last. I can declare the necessary Protest document under oath for underwriters when you tell me the name of the solicitor in town you wish me to attend for the purpose. Please give favourable consideration to my request to resume my command to carry out the refit of the vessel to make her seaworthy again and resume service. I understand the Honourable Company has 75,000 gallons of whale oil in casks waiting in warehouses to load. My crew and I can carry out the refit with minimal assistance from the shipyard and carry the load homewards. On arrival the vessel will stand ready for whatever disposition may seem appropriate in a wider market than here. I have the honour to be, sir, Your humble and obedient servant.

To his embarrassment and rising annoyance, weeks passed before he could get an appointment to be heard. With the Mates sent back aboard to keep watch, the *Lady Lampson* lay on the mud at low tide close enough to the shore for little boys to come to the beach to jeer and throw stones at. Each issue of the local newspapers paraded the wreck of the ship in yet another notice of advertisement for the sale of items salvaged from the *Lady Lampson* in good condition and now in the hands of retail merchants in town at bargain prices.

A week later his father-in-law, the redoubtable Alexander Caulfield Anderson rode his horse into town and took a hotel room. Anderson knocked on Gaudin's door and came inside. Gaudin spoke in a manner that reminded himself of sheep bleating on the farm and regretted it as soon as he spoke.

"I don't know how I am going to come out of this. I am thousands of miles away from my wife and family, and I must have lost my employment. I would have set a 122-day time record from the Downs."

Anderson did not respond to any of that.

"Gaudin, you look exhausted, flushed, and drawn. You are drinking far too much, if I may say so. This room reeks of whiskey."

"You don't understand, sir. Hear me out, please. The Navy sent a formal letter of complaint against me making adverse comments on my conduct to the Board of Trade."

"What has the Board of Trade got to do with any of this? Are you out of your mind?"

"I am not, sir. The Board of Trade in England can rule on the conduct of ship's officers on all British registered vessels_____."

Gaudin continued, labouring over the pronouncing of the initials of the man's name.

"Royal Navy Captain F. C. W. Robinson," he said, "wrote the letter on his warship in Esquimalt, the H. M. S. *Opal* dated 31 January 1878 to the Secretary of the Honourable Company in London, with copies shown to have been delivered to Chief Factor Charles at Fort Victoria and to me on board the *Lady Lampson*. With each letter came a copy of his Report to the Board of Trade. Here, sir, you read this copy of his letter. No, I will read out his Complaint from H.M.S. *Opal* aloud to you. He calls it a *Report*.

'On the 9th January, the Lady Lampson entering Esquimalt under sail at night struck one of the Scrogg rocks, and from there drifted on to the beach, a little to the S.W. of the entrance to the salt water lagoon. From the 9th to the 27th January several S.E. gales rose, but the crew of the Lady Lampson voluntarily lived on board the vessel. Severe gales followed on the 28th and 29th January. At 0930 that morning the Lady Lampson signaled she wanted assistance and the crew wished to abandon ship. After much difficulty, two boats from H. M. S. Opal went out to her, but brought off only three of the crew, the master and the remainder of the crew then not thinking it necessary to leave the vessel. I was surprised that the master of the Lady Lampson, after having for three weeks neglected to provide himself with means to leave the ship, should have allowed his apprehensions to make him so considerate of his own position (at the worst, one of doubtful danger) as to make him fail to perceive the great danger he asked that other men might be placed in order to relieve him.3 '"

Gaudin continued to speak after Anderson picked up the letter to read.

"I can tell you, sir, Captain Robinson's lecture strikes fear in my heart as to how London will react. Look how the son-of-a-bitch ended the account in his so-called Report. I don't know what I ever did to him that would justify this stab in the back. Late at night on the next day in town I sat down at the table in my hotel room to make an answer to explain my position. The weather and tide conditions during that time would have allowed his boats to approach, but by the time his boats came out, the tide had turned, making the sea conditions impossible for them to make an approach. Much later when the boats finally came alongside, they did so in a lull in the storm. The emergency no longer existed, and I decided to stay aboard. I informed the young naval officer in charge of the party my duty to the ship owner required me to remain with my crew to assist the contractors in unloading the cargo to

3 HBCA A.1/101 folio 160 at seq and HBCA A.1/89 folio 353

take into town. That must have ignited Robinson's anger. I delivered my reply and copies of both letters to the Office of Chief Factor Charles with the request he send my letter on to Captain Robinson and copy to Secretary William Armit Esq. of the Honourable Company in London. I am told he did so. I am pleased to know London may now know my side of the story."

Anderson spoke again after a long silence.

"Rumours have been flying around town. Never mind them. How did you happen to run on the rocks? You told me long ago that Lloyd's of London considered Esquimalt Harbour to be the safer destination, and that marine insurance policies require vessels to proceed there instead of Victoria's Inner Harbour."

"That Lloyd's have such a requirement I can understand. In answer to your question: the ship struck Scrogg rock at 2 a. m. on the date in question but glanced off without sinking. The rock lies unlit and unmarked by a beacon. Captain Robinson does not mention in his Report that a fierce southeast storm came up suddenly that night. It laid our ship broadside-to and heeling over under the force of the squall, dead in the water, adrift and ready for the storm to put her ashore."

After the silence that followed Anderson spoke again.

"That doesn't tell me why it happened. I know the ground out there. Esquimalt Harbour lay close ahead only a mile in from Scrogg Rock. Against the weak ebb tide current coming out the harbour, you had only to pass Duntze Head on your right and Fisgard Lighthouse on your left. Your ship had come off the rock: why didn't you steer to sail with the wind, straight ahead into Esquimalt Harbour?"

He waited a time for an answer, but on Gaudin remaining silent, Anderson spoke again.

"I am told you could have slipped in with the wind pushing from behind for the mile or so that remained for you to get into the Harbour," he said. "Instead of doing that I hear you tried to anchor in the rough sea outside the harbour entrance where the Navy prohibits vessels to anchor, obstructing navigation."

"The anchors did hold," Gaudin said, "but I had no alternative than to give an order to slip them when Mister Ferey sounded the well and came to me with the report the ship filling with 12 feet of water already in the hold. I had only moments to steer to assist the wind and tide to beach the vessel in the best position for recovery."

"Gaudin, you don't answer the question. Why didn't you sail the ship straight ahead into Esquimalt?"

"That, sir, presupposes I knew the *Lady Lampson* had hit Scrogg Rock. I didn't know what rock we'd struck_____. I did not know that until later_____. Yes, I could have easily made the ship sail downwind into Esquimalt Harbour if I had known in what direction the entrance channel lay. All caution made me reject any thought that setting sail offered any solution to the ship's difficulty."

"Could you not see any lights along the coastline, east toward Saxe Point?"

"I could see nothing of any shoreline in the storm, not even the light from the lighthouse at Fisgard. I did not know where we were when I came up on deck."

"I have heard stories you were below in your cabin when the ship ran on the rocks. What explanation can you possibly give the Chief Factor?"

"The newspaper's report praised my seamanship in dealing with the emergency, but everything I did became necessary because I had been such a damn fool not to appreciate the danger for anyone trying to conn the ship into the harbour at night in what I ought to have known were worsening weather conditions."

"Did you have any cargo on your own account aboard?"

"Yes I had a whole lot of it. I had the wit to insure my part of the cargo. That will put some dollars in my pocket to help me come out of this. The ship did take in some water, which will have damaged most of my freight, but my 122-day record-breaking run from London around Cape Horn went up in smoke because I neither completed the passage into harbour, nor the second half of the voyage back to London _____. I am at my wit's end. I am dreading the meeting with the Chief Factor. What can I possibly say to him about the stranding? I have met the man, but please tell me more about him."

"Not quite 10 years older than you, Gaudin. Charles spent time in recent years away from the office in Victoria to carry out added oversight in the Interior, but this winter he has kept to the Victoria office, now bustling and linked to much of the outside world by telegraph cable. He has come more and more to the notice of the Committee of the Honourable Company in London. Himself, the son of a chief factor, Charles grew up in the far northern parts of Canada. He worked in the Service in the fur trade at remote posts in the Columbia Department and advanced in rank and salary as the company acknowledged his abilities as a manager."

"Can I find any hope in the Birnie family connection?" Gaudin asked almost under his breath.

"Certainly not," Anderson shot back. "He married one of my wife's sisters, but his long service in the company will have taught him the Committee in London respects officers who make hard decisions unaffected by sentiment or by family considerations. You must consider Charles to be a man of promise with yet higher rank lying ahead. He has not yet reached the pinnacle of success and salary. He will have in mind his own prospects against his assessment of the circumstances of the company's business in the West. Even though he may consider you a friend, I doubt he will do anything to help you."

"Yes sir, I understand. And I know I face an unbroken line of disfavour shown by the Committee in London to captains who strand their vessels."

"In 1848 Captain Brotchie sank his Company barque *Vancouver*, the most recent of those three unluckily-named company sailing vessels carrying the same name. A schooner, a brigantine and a barque, I think I have named each of the rigs correctly."

After Gaudin merely nodded and made no comment, Anderson went on to speak.

"And Brotchie, after taking time for leave, with an unbroken line of success in command, applied for a command, but the Committee, despite circumstances that called for sympathy for his position, turned him down on the ground he had lost a company vessel in his charge."

Gaudin spoke to say he feared the Company will take steps to declare the vessel a total constructive loss, allowing the insurance underwriters to sell the vessel, and make a claim to be paid money under the policy of marine insurance.

"Sir, the underwriters in London can elect to sell the ship by public auction, as is, where is," he added, "to cut their own outlay of funds when they pay the company's claim under their contract of marine insurance. The buyer will do the same repairs my crew and I could have done, load her with coal at Nanaimo, sail her to San Francisco, and sell the coal to pay expenses before selling her at auction for top dollar to a buyer who will carry out a total refit at the shipyards there. Then they will put her in the profitable South Pacific trade to and from San Francisco, Honolulu and Sydney Australia."

"I can tell you this, Gaudin: the mere presence of the local Rithets firm at the auction with their banker's money behind them will discourage any others from getting into a bidding war. They can be confident they can buy her for not very much. Even if you had money in your hands to bid, you would lose out to them."

"Can you imagine it, sir, my fine little *Lady Lampson* being sent to carry COAL to dirty her deck? My crew will be discharged and on the beach. I must try to get work for them before I leave town."

"Gaudin, you must know Charles will be using the telegraph to ask the Committee for instructions. You must count on those instructions coming to throw the responsibility for decision onto the local man, the Chief Factor himself. But let us talk of happier matters."

"Yes sir, let's do that. I did not miss that Agnes found a fresh happiness when I took her aboard in the late summer 1874 to bring her back from Jersey to you at the farm. After only one year in Jersey she wanted me to bring her back . I made a mistake in thinking she would take to the life in Jersey."

"Had you any inkling of her unhappiness when you left her there for the first time at the end of August 1873?"

"No, not really."

"Yes, and you told me you made your next annual passage, departing London by a date in September and arriving here in January 1874 with no thought of trouble back at home in Jersey?"

"Yes sir. That's right."

"But you had a bad time getting in past Cape Flattery on that occasion. That winter proved not much better than the year previous, Gaudin. I'll not forget your story of the struggle at sea you had getting into position to enter the Strait of Juan de Fuca at the end of January 1874. I have kept the newspaper clipping of the report you gave to the Colonist Reporter who published it in the newspaper. I have it here with me. Perhaps you will be pleased to have me read you the gist of it with emphasis on the weather you encountered at this end of the passage. You departed London in early September 1873. A tug towed your vessel in two stages to the Downs off Deal by 3 September, landed the Pilot the next day, sailed for three days in the English Channel to make a departure from the Lizard Point light on 7 September. From Land's End onward in the Atlantic the ship sailed in fair breezes and fine weather. Crossed the Equator on 2 October and passed through the Straits of Le Maire between Tierra del Fuego and Staten Island on 30 October. You made good time and had a mild passage past the Horn, passing it on 31 October, followed by Islas Ildefonso, on one side, and

Islas Diego Ramirez, on the other, the next day. On rounding the Horn, you began the counting of the number of days it would take to run from 50 degrees South latitude in the Atlantic to the same latitude in the Pacific. In this instance the time came to only 17½ days due to fair weather and a fine crew."

"Very good time for such a small vessel, sir, but I ask you to understand the late return to London from Chile and Peru in May 1870 permitted a change in the timetable for *Lady Lampson's* annual voyages. Thenceforth we could sail westbound past the Horn in Southern Hemisphere summertime weather. We avoided the misery and damage we would sustain in winter when torrents from breaking mountaintops of water in a succession of storms could sink us. But please go on to read the clipping."

"The newspaper reported you met a succession of gales from the northwest for three weeks, which delayed progress, and threatened to send the ship toward the rocks on the Chilean coast. Then you picked up the South East Trade Winds. Calms encountered crossing the Equator in the Pacific on 17 December. You then met calms and a succession of light winds from the north for 12 days from 40 degrees North latitude until making landfall on the North American coast. From then on your ship met strong winds and heavy seas and low barometer readings. When the wind and seas abated the ship entered the Straits of Juan de Fuca with a flood tide 137 days out from the Downs at noon on 17 January 1874. But in the night you were driven back by strong gales coming out of the Strait from the east."

"Yes, sir, 137 days would have been a good time for the passage from London had the storm not come up to prevent us from making it in to Esquimalt with the tide that next morning."

Anderson continued his editorializing of the newspaper reports of the Great Storm in January 1874.

"I gather from the newspaper report the wind and seas kept you out beyond the western entrance to the Strait for 10 days under shortened sail. During this time you kept track of the ship's position by working the ship back and forth between Cape Beale and the lighthouse at Cape Flattery as the wind and seas permitted. By 2 a.m. on Friday, 27 January the wind shifted to come from the south and from the southwest. That enabled you to steer your ship to slip in with a flood tide to re-enter the Strait with daylight soon to come."

"The ship's compass and running bearings on the light at Cape

Flattery gave guidance it was safe to proceed into the Strait in the dark."

"With a strong wind coming on her stern quarter to hurry her along your ship arrived in Esquimalt Harbour at 10 a.m. on Sunday 29 January."

"Yes sir, a fine sail in clearing skies with studdingsails set."

Anderson continued to speak with the clipping in his hand.

"To get the flavour of the weather at the southern end of Vancouver Island on the weekend of your arrival at Esquimalt see the next day's Colonist Tuesday 30 January 1874. I have the clippings: First, under the heading of THE GREAT STORM: –

'For at least ten years there has been no such storm experienced as that of Saturday night, Sunday and yesterday. The wind on Saturday night was almost too much. The storm blew down trees, fences, barns, and sheds. In some instances pedestrians were carried off their feet. A barn fell, killing a mule valued at $300. At Port Townsend in Washington Territory several small craft were driven ashore when the wind was coming from the southeast and spray dashed clear over the warehouses. At Bellingham Bay the storm raged with great fury and the barometer fell very low.' The reporter wrote he feared the wreck of some vessels near the Straits would be reported in a few days. And under the heading of ROADS BLOCKED: –

'The storm that raged Saturday night covered the roads with fallen trees. The snow on the ground lay six inches deep, slushy and soft, causing travelling to be tedious and heavy.' And see the item in the next column: PUT BACK IN DISTRESS: –

'The barque W. J. Parke, outbound laden with Nanaimo coal encountered a storm when 20 to 30 miles off Cape Flattery. In a short time her deckload and water casks were swept off. Several of her sails were torn to ribbons and two or three of her small spars carried away. The ship's carpenter had a heart attack and died. Flying signals of distress, she reached Royal Roads on Sunday 28 January 1874. The W. J. Parke had sailed from Victoria's outer harbour on Saturday last 27 December.'"

After a long silence Anderson continued.

"At that time, Gaudin, the same easterly storm wind that favoured the W. J. Parke's departure out of the Strait had been holding the Lady Lampson out off Cape Flattery? Did you catch sight of that vessel?"

"No sir, we didn't see her in the storm. We keep a sharp lookout to avoid collision in storms."

"More by chance and happenstance, I suspect. The news report of your vessel's arrival included a particularly sad item, which I will read out to you: –

'On Friday 15 December when first approaching Cape Flattery in heavy seas, the pitching of the vessel threw a Norwegian seaman, Henrich Hansen, at work in the bows of the ship, off balance. He lost his footing, and fell overboard. He was seen for a moment, floating. The mate threw a lifebuoy to him, but he did not reach it. A boat was lowered to rescue him, but on the boat being lowered alongside in the water, the force of the seas stove in the planking of the boat in an instant. In the meantime the man disappeared and was not seen again.'"

"A crewman truly loved by the crew, and fine seaman," said Gaudin. "We put a boat overside with men who volunteered to go out to find him, but they had to scramble out of the boat in the nick of time when the seas threw it and them against the side of the ship, the boat ending up smashed to pieces. Sadness gripped the ship for several days as we endured the storm that forbade us entry into the Strait. On the return passage to London with the noted Robert Burnaby aboard as a patient, the weather proved to be unremarkable in the same waters."

Anderson then persuaded Gaudin to go out for a walk warmly dressed.

Sitting on a park bench with Anderson, Gaudin began again.

"Agnes welcomed me back with warmth and good cheer when I returned to Jersey for the summer 1874. But on our first night together I was thunderstruck to hear her say she was not happy with her year at the Gaudin family farm. She asked me to take her back to Victoria."

"I knew you had taken Burnaby aboard in stricken condition and confined to his stateroom. I suspect you would have taken on some oversight of the patient on the passage."

"Yes, sir, that may be true to some extent, but Mister Burnaby paid the company for the passage with an able-bodied person as a nurse to care for him. The gift his family made to me on returning him to London in July 1874 went far beyond what anyone would have thought necessary. But to get back to Agnes: she had her way with me about getting back to Victoria. She didn't say much else why, other than to read out parts of your last letter telling of the problems you faced."

"How did you explain Agnes' decision to your father and mother?"

"I told them her father needed her help. As you know, we all arrived back in Victoria in the dead of winter in January 1875 with little Marie, and Agnes three-months pregnant on the passage. With the previous honeymoon voyage experience in '73, this time Agnes knew what to expect in the ocean passage."

"Well, Gaudin, I certainly do remember the day you arrived here to drop them off to stay with me to help look after the house and family during my long illness after the election campaigning four years ago. I knew tongues would wag, but Agnes kept her head up. She spoke well of you and your people in Jersey, which helped still the gossip."

Gaudin remembered hearing that Anderson had fought a good campaign in British Columbia's first General Election to elect a Member of Parliament in Ottawa. He came close to winning the Vancouver Riding, which then extended south to include North Saanich and north to Nanaimo in the 1874 Federal Election. Gaudin heard newspapers reported on his campaign speeches at Nanaimo and Victoria. Audiences gave him warm applause even when he spoke at length. Also that one newspaper in Victoria wrote an editorial, which Gaudin remembered reading to the effect that although many good things can be said in his favour, his father-in-law at 60 was in no sense a politician and being advanced in years not likely to achieve much distinction in the political arena should he be elected. The editor added words to list the items of favour to be taken into account, an old and highly esteemed resident of the district, and a gentleman of considerable ability, and not a word can be said against his character.

Gaudin decided to say nothing about the election and to change the subject. Instead, he would talk about matters that would give the old fellow some happy memories.

"Agnes' return must have enlivened everyone in the farmhouse."

"Yes, Gaudin, all of that, especially when Agnes gave birth to Mabel at the farm in June of that year."

"By that time I had the *Lady Lampson* in the North Atlantic off the coast of Ireland nearing the end of a record passage of only 113 days. I remember my happiness to know all was well with her here when I picked up the telegram in London announcing Mabel's birth."

"Of course, you went home to Jersey for that next summer."

"Yes, I did that. I hastened there to settle things up with my parents. They missed their grandchild Marie, whom they adored. They could not understand why Agnes had not been content to live with them on the farm. I could think of little to say to them about that."

Anderson spoke again after another long silence.

"I find it helpful to run over the sequence of your voyages to keep

things straight in my old mind. Please forgive me for going back over
what we may have talked about: you returned a year later, two years ago,
in January 1876 to tell Agnes the tragic story your widowed sister Marie
Renouf had been killed in a horse buggy accident. Her young daughter
Nan had been injured in the same accident, but her son emerged unscathed."

"Yes and as soon as he became old enough to do a man's job I had no
trouble persuading him to come with me to Victoria for you to take him
under your wing and set him on his way. I signed him on the ship as
a supercargo, but he jumped at the opportunity to learn a sailor's work,
filling in as an apprentice seaman. You, sir, took him in hand to give him
a steer to get more schooling to enable him to find good work at Burrard
Inlet's Hastings Mill."

"Yes, Gaudin, but bear with me as I continue to put the pieces together. You came in January 1876 to persuade Agnes to go back to
Jersey with you. She would return with you on the footing she would
have a new place to live in Jersey to bring up Nan with Edwin's help for
at least the first year_____."

"I told you, sir, of the necessity to keep the Renouf property intact
and unsold until Edwin turned 21 for the sale of his inheritance carried
out."

"Edwin told me all about that when he came here to stay with us,
Gaudin. He told me he does not want to go back to Jersey. As heir he
would rather see the property sold for money to advance himself in this
Province, perhaps in the hardware business in this growing town."

"I must say Agnes showed a lot of pluck in going back to Jersey, sir.
I know she was moved to help by the sense of gratitude she owed my
sister Marie for her friendship in Jersey more than by any wish to return.
Also I must say that Agnes insisted on my promise to bring her back to
settle in Victoria when the Renouf property can be sold."

Before Anderson could speak Gaudin turned to talk of Edwin again.

"He has been helpful to me with funds from time to time, which has
kept my head above water. But to get back telling you of the voyages:
Agnes with Marie and wee baby Mabel sailed with me from Victoria
departing 23 February 1876, and I landed them in London at the end
of June. Agnes found great excitement in seeing London again and
crossing the English Channel to St. Helier on the fast steamer ferry
from Southampton. I know she wrote you to say how much she enjoyed
the ocean passage, the excitement of the fast train ride from London to

Southampton and the ferry ride to Jersey, although rough the day we went."

"I know from her annual letters to me, Gaudin, she has been enjoying her new little boy, Jimmy."

"Yes, I am a proud father of that son, another Gaudin child born in Jersey, and this time in October 1876 with me away at sea again."

"I can tell you it brought me a father's joy to see Agnes' face brighten when she knew she would be living in the new house you told her about, named Number 2 Isla Villa. She remembered the situation of that property from her earlier time in Jersey."

"Your letters to her in Jersey since then have been a great comfort to her."

"Gaudin, that's almost two years ago. Is Agnes really happy there now?"

"Yes, she really is. The children and Nan and your Arthur have been doing well at the new place."

"The sale of the Renouf property will bring you all to Victoria, is that correct?"

"Yes, without that promise from me in '76 she said she would not go back to Jersey. She always wanted to make our home here in Victoria. In fact, you likely know Agnes wanted me to make a home for her in Victoria from the first days we talked of marriage."

"Yes, Gaudin, I know that. I am not sure why you didn't leave Agnes in Victoria when you married her."

"Nor I today, sir, but such a step did not occur to me then."

A long silence ensued as the two lit the tobacco in their pipes again. Anderson spoke to end the silence.

"The 1858 Gold Rush has come and gone, but the place is bursting at the seams to bring work and employment for willing and energetic men."

"That bodes well for those of my crew who now seek employment. I remember my father telling me that a man will know where his future lies when he reaches 40. I am now that age. My crew know I want to repair the ship and sail back to London with casks of company whale oil freight waiting in warehouses here in town, but that does not seem to be likely. I have a family to support. What can I turn my hand to? I am not a landsman. I am a Master Mariner in Sail, and proud of it. How will I ever be able to bring Agnes and our children back to this coast as I promised?"

"When you do bring Agnes to make a home here," Anderson said wthout any hesitation, "I am confident that you will find a ship to sail out of Victoria, but perhaps not a sailing vessel. The port of Victoria bustles with vessels powered by steam raised from stoking boilers fired by Nanaimo coal. Sailing ships from England and Europe arrive and depart almost every day. The cities of New Westminster and Nanaimo begin to rival Victoria to provide industry and employment. You might take to Steam if you have a chance to talk to Captain William Irving who runs stern-wheel steamers on the Fraser River with his son John."

Anderson did not pursue the subject further and a long silence ensued before Gaudin spoke again.

"I feel hard done by the waiting the Chief Factor puts me to. How much longer must it be?"

"Cheer up, Gaudin, I have connections in Ottawa as a result of running as a candidate in the '74 Federal election_____. Yes, I know I was a defeated candidate, but even defeated candidates may have a say in Federal Government patronage appointments. Something, I know, will come up for you, but it may take time."

3

WIFE IN JERSEY

Chief Factor Charles in Victoria sent a cable telegram to London as soon as he heard the *Lady Lampson* had been shipwrecked off the beach at the Esquimalt Lagoon, but all aboard safe. London sent a note by messenger to Gaudin's wife at her home in Jersey to tell her of the wreck without any mention of the storm that had played a part in it. The children ran to comfort her when they saw their mother in tears.

Bundled up in warm clothing and composing herself with all of them clustered around her, Agnes sat on a bench in the garden in low winter sunshine, filled with worry about how it would end for her husband. The Honourable Company would end his employment with her miles away from him. They would not dismiss him from his employment: they would say they had no other ship to send him to; and that would be that. She remembered how it all began between them. She cast her mind back to when she first saw Gaudin in Victoria, remembering it as if yesterday. Agnes caught first glimpse of him from where she stood outside a shop window in mid-December 1865. Seen across the wide muddy street, he stood tall in grey slim-legged trousers under a black half-open cloak and a black vest and jacket in a group of men talking and smoking pipes, some with cigars. His Mariner's cap and his smooth black leather half-Wellington boots, easy on and easy off and often seen worn by naval officers, made him stand out from the others as no landsman.

A woman beside her noticed her looking at him and whispered in her ear,

"That man, his name is Gaudin. He is the new Chief Officer of the *Prince of Wales*. This is his first time in town. He must have a way of walking that keeps the mud off his boots. They do look so clean."

That evening at the dinner table her father made a special point of mentioning Gaudin's name, saying his manner made a good impression on everyone in town.

"They all call him Captain to his face even though he is only the Mate of the *Prince of Wales*. He has his Master's papers and is not married."

With a change in pitch of his voice and a glance toward Agnes he went on to add, "Some say he is looking for a wife who will live in Jersey."

Agnes lost no time in speaking when she realized all at the table were looking at her. "Papa, I did catch a glimpse of him across the street in town," she piped up, cheeks flushing, "I did not see him up close enough to see his flashing black eyes ablaze, which some say *mesmerize*, and look so big_____. Yes, that's what I heard. People I know have brown or blue eyes."

Her father said her fair skin and blue eyes could be classed as mutations, at which her mother got up from her chair and went to the kitchen.

"Oh Papa, that's nonsense," Agnes burst out. "How can you say any such thing?"

He shrugged his shoulders, shook his head, and got up to stand behind his chair.

"Agnes, you suffer from sunburn," he said, "but your mother with Cree in her Métis blood strain does not. She may be more the norm than you or I."

Agnes knew what the word mutation meant. He had touched on the subject of genetics in the case of farm animals and the human species as part of what he thought she should know, and he had gone on to expound on the subject of Physiognomy and Phrenology, which he and fellow fur trader friend Doctor Tolmie thought they knew a lot about from books sent from England.

"Papa, you can't tell about people's character by how they look. I think this teaching to look at people's faces and the shape of their noses and the position of their ears on their heads leads you to misjudge others before you know them."

"Yes Agnes, perhaps, but perhaps not. I have little doubt I have been right."

Agnes drew in a breath and raised her voice so even her mother in the kitchen would hear.

"From what I could see Gaudin has such a lively expression on his face," she said. "A fine figure of a man as tall as I am, and he tends a fine black beard. I do like the look of his boy's nose. Even at a distance, I could not resist a smile when I saw him smiling."

Her father came back to sit at the table.

"Yes Agnes, I can understand why you liked the look of the man. He dresses in keeping with his station as a company captain-in-waiting. I heard someone ask him why he wore a black silk foulard neckpiece instead of a coloured one as some do. With a grave expression on his face Gaudin said wearing black shows respect for souls who have been lost at sea. It shows the measure of the man that instead of leaving it on a sombre note he picked up on it with a funny tale and in a moment had everyone laughing."

Agnes' mother overheard this. She came back to sit at the table.

"A seaman lives a life full of risk and danger," she said. "When you say good-bye to a seaman you must be thinking he may never come back. You should think twice before you wed such a man, Agnes."

"Oh Eliza, don't say that in front of Agnes. Men in all walks face danger in their work. But let me say men at the company office tell me Gaudin not yet 30, so not much more than ten years older than you, Agnes. He has good prospects if he can resist the temptation to answer a call to captain another owner's ship. He must remain patient for his promotion and for the pay and emoluments that will come with it."

"Oh Papa, what are ee-moll-you-ments?"

"For a captain it may include a right to carry cargo on his own account and become a wealthy man, Agnes."

A long pause followed.

"I haven't even met the man, but if he found another vessel to sail, he might never come back to Victoria and I might never see him again. Come Mama, let's do the dishes."

Agnes soon heard stories about the swath Gaudin cut in town. Some Chief Officers saw their shipboard duties in port as time-consuming and burdensome, but Gaudin seemed to have a light touch and still get his work done. He left the ship to come ashore often to be seen on the street and to be invited by families with unmarried daughters to parties. No one invited her to come into town to any. After all, she said to herself, half believing it, she had turned only seventeen in October.

Her father did not let the subject of Gaudin being the kind of man Agnes should marry rest, and he could not resist bringing up the subject again.

"Perhaps he will want to live in Victoria, Papa?"

"Not likely," said her father.

"I will tell him I want to live in Victoria."

"Don't throw away the chance to marry him if he insists on a life for you in Jersey, dear girl."

"But that would take me to live far away. Sister Eliza now lives in New Zealand and we will never see her again. For me to live in Jersey would take me to the far end of yet another ocean."

"You cannot think of that, Agnes. Your mother and I will do just fine. She has not been well but I will look after her. We can be happy living in this climate on the coast. The other children can help."

After another long silence Agnes spoke with tears in her eyes.

"How terrible that the distance between you and your father and mother has prevented you from going back to Lake Simcoe to see them. They live thousands of miles east of the Rocky Mountains. I have never seen those grandparents."

"Yes Agnes, 30 years ago they left England to live at Sutton on the south shore of the lake that lies north of Toronto. I never had the money to travel to see them, and they are too old to make the journey to see us, but we do keep in touch with letters."

"Papa, Mama told me you and your brother James as an officer in far northern posts of the company sent money to them to help out from your earliest times here when each of you could ill-afford it. Mama says you insisted on doing your 'filial' duty. That's what you told her."

"Civil Society demands children owe a duty to support their parents, Agnes. I found satisfaction in sending what little I could."

With that he got up and left the room, and that ended the discussion.

That night at dinner Agnes decided to speak her mind.

"Papa, you have often spoken in the past year about Gaudin as the man for me to marry. I find this quite maddening because you do nothing about getting someone to make the introduction. Gaudin and I have never met. I cannot imagine why we are talking about him in this way. You say *when he returns*. I say IF he returns. How can you keep talking to me about him? We should be talking about other men for me to marry."

"Agnes, gentlewomen do not pursue men to the point of being seen to importune them."

"Oh Papa, that doesn't help me understand anything any better. I don't even know what that word means but it sounds like something I would never do."

No one said anything more about Gaudin even though everyone expected the *Prince of Wales* to be back with him again in mid-December.

A tangled thought came clattering down in her mind one morning: Gaudin and her ravishingly beautiful older sister Eliza would have been of an age for each other. In a dark mood and sobbing she went to her mother alone in the kitchen.

"Why didn't Papa use his connections with the company at Fort Victoria to arrange for Gaudin and me to be introduced a year ago when he came into town the first time? We talked around the dinner table about hardly anyone else. And why can't he see to the introduction being made now that his ship will come again this December? I know I have freckles and am not as pretty as sister Eliza. Can Papa be ashamed of me?"

"Agnes, don't keep thinking about Eliza. You saw her as a beautiful bride when she married. But you're a tall girl. You have a fine body and such rosy cheeks. With your fair complexion and long auburn hair you are now like a yearling colt. The time was not right for you last year. Not the right time for your father who went through a difficult time himself last winter. No, I won't go into that."

Both fell silent for a moment before Agnes spoke quiet words with a difficulty that must have been evident to her mother.

"I know Papa is such an independent person he won't allow himself to feel beholden to anyone, which he imagines might happen if he asked someone to introduce me to Gaudin. That's why he won't, Mama. He is such a sensitive person. He won't run the chance of a slight from being ignored or laughed at behind his back."

"Perhaps, Agnes. I know he sees slights where no one intends them."

Agnes remained in thought at the table when her mother left the room. She knew her father approved of Gaudin. He did not approve of other young men in town mentioned. The Royal Navy maintained naval vessels and dockyards at nearby Esquimalt Harbour and at other parts of the world, Halifax, Jamaica, and in Ceylon as part of Queen Victoria's British Empire foreign policy. The Army Garrison and the Royal Navy played an important role in the life of the town, not least for those with marriage in mind for their daughters. But her father remained set against them all.

One day, out of the blue, Agnes heard him speak about it.

"Agnes, it pleases Mama and me," her father said, "you have not become enamoured with some of the English newcomer dandies I have seen in Victoria."

"In truth, Papa, you have frightened the lot of them away. None of them will come to visit me here."

"You shouldn't regret that. No good can come for you to marry any of them."

He walked out of the room to end the discussion.

Months went by without any further mention of Gaudin at the supper table, but a day came when Agnes heard talk in town the *Prince of Wales* had come back into Esquimalt. Yes, people had seen him back in town again.

She suspected her father knew more about what Gaudin had been doing in town when he came before, and also now, but thought it wise not to ask. She thought Gaudin no tame cat and she felt a sense of excitement she had not known before when she thought of the man so much older than she and experienced in the ways of the world.

What could she do to get an introduction to this man before he went out of her life forever? She could not throw herself at the man. But her father might be moved to help. She cornered him working with a spade to drain away water from his garden.

"Papa, Gaudin has come back and is in town now. Please ask him to come to visit us on the farm before he goes. How will I ever meet him if no one introduces me to him? I don't know how long his ship will be staying in port."

She didn't remember what her father answered. Whatever he said made no sense. He seemed distracted, so she went to her mother in the kitchen to say it all over again and to make a plea.

"Mama, you married Papa when you were much younger than I am now. I will end up an old maid unless he does something to help me meet Gaudin."

"Leave it to me, child, I will speak to Papa again."

Agnes went to her bedroom that night buoyed up with an unreasoned sense of optimism for the first time in many days. By supper the next night she learned that her mother put the plan to her father, and he did what she suggested to slip away from the farm to ride into town to put himself forward to Gaudin before the *Prince of Wales* sailed back to England before Christmas.

Agnes, outside chopping firewood and burning winter windfall tree limbs and branches, saw her father come riding up the road. He put his horse in the barn and hurried over to the house, not seeing her at the other side. She called out to him, but he did not hear. Agnes put down her rake and turned to chop firewood into smaller chunks. Soon her father and mother surprised her by coming outside together to approach her. Agnes stood clear of the smoke and sparks from the fire to greet them.

Her father spoke in jagged sentences, which Agnes took as meaning he had seen Gaudin. He sails before noon tomorrow. He will come to see us next year.

Agnes cried out.

"He will come to see us *next year!*"

Her mother chimed in, "All for the best, child."

"It's hard for me to imagine that. Yet ANOTHER year is long for me to wait. Oh Papa! You married Mama when she was only fourteen. On my next birthday I will be nineteen years old, and I will never marry."

"Times have changed, Agnes," her father said. "You should not be in a rush to marry."

Agnes said nothing as she listened to the sound of the wind in the trees and the fire crackle and spit. She turned to look at them hearing her speak.

"I am so sad. I just know the time was right for me to meet him now, but what else can I do _____. I'm going out in the woods for a walk."

When Agnes settled herself down she came back into the house to find her father at his desk.

"Please tell me what you and Gaudin talked about, Papa."

"Let me get to it by telling you what I did. I left here before any of you had awakened and rode into town with the light of the moon leading me on. I walked my horse to the waterfront hoping to see the *Prince of Wales* at the company wharf or at anchor in the Inner Harbour, but the wharf and the bay clear and still. Thinking I had missed my chance to see him, I put my horse in the livery stable, and went to find a place open to order an early breakfast. At the company office I asked if the *Prince of Wales* had departed. The answer: a company steamer towed her out and around into Esquimalt. She had lain alongside the company wharf in Victoria's Inner Harbour for over a fortnight. She now lay at the company wharf in Esquimalt topping up cargo and loading ballast.

I decided to pay for a message to be sent to the vessel for Gaudin."

"Oh Papa, thank you for doing that."

"I felt my dilly-dallying might have ended your chances of ever meeting Gaudin. I waited in town to watch for him even though I knew his duties on board could keep him from coming. Early in the afternoon Gaudin came striding through the waiting room door to enter the office intent on ship's business, which he attended to straightaway. He then came back into the waiting room calling out for me. We met and stood talking for a short time before he left to go back to his ship."

Agnes knew the building. She could picture the scene in her mind: some men sat on benches and other men stood waiting, her father and Gaudin standing in the office's unheated outer lobby. She could imagine the sight of her father, his weathered and wrinkled face, and his nearly worn-out Hudson's Bay Company buckskin officer's jacket, fringed at the shoulders and cuffs to make the rain run off. She loved to see him in this get-up, which he did not often wear. Her own fringed and coloured-bead embroidered jacket, much newer, resembled it. As if in church he would have been carrying his hat when he entered the company office. The jacket gave him an impressive cachet, which made her proud to be his daughter. The other men in the outer office would not find it easy to ignore her father's presence in the room. Only 53-years of age but made to appear older by his physical ailments, he would stand out.

"I stood as Gaudin entered the waiting room and I went up to speak to him. I will tell you exactly how the conversation went if you wish."

Agnes, anxious to hear every detail, told him to please go ahead. She knew of her father's ability to recount conversations as if he had been a person listening and taking notes of it.

"I told him my name, and asked him, 'Did you get the note I sent you?'

'Thank you for the invitation, sir, but I must return to the ship to make ready to sail with the tide in the morning.'"

Agnes knew her father would have kept back his look of dismay. Though disheartened when he learned he had come too late, he would have put on the inscrutable look he prized. Her mother entered the room to sit beside Agnes as her father continued with his account.

"I asked him, ' Please tell me where is your home, young man?'

'I come from a farm on Jersey, sir.'

'Who have you left behind on the farm, if I may ask?'

'My oldest brother is working my father's 25-acre farm with a hired hand and my older sister Marie married a man named Renouf and lives on a farm close. My father and mother live not far away at their own house. My other brothers and I have gone to sea.'

'Captain, you speak as if you had some good schooling if I may say so. Did you have a school in Jersey?'

Gaudin replied, 'Yes, sir, my father sent me to school until I was seventeen. I never took to farming. Do you live in town, sir?'

'No, Captain, we did for a time after '58 but I did not like life in town. My wife and family moved in '62 to live 20-miles north on over 300 acres of forest and land we are in the process of clearing. Will you be coming back to Victoria again?'

'Yes sir, I should be back next year at the same time if the Honourable Company doesn't send me in another vessel.'

'As you saw the day you arrived, Gaudin, we do get dumps of snow and cold northeast winds from the Interior at this time of year. We cannot move on the roads then. That is why I could not come into town to invite you to come earlier. I hope you will come to visit our place in the country. Perhaps the next time you are in port.'

'That would be most pleasant, sir. I hear you have a fine looking daughter. I hope you will introduce me. I am sorry I cannot come now.'"

Agnes gasped. Her father carried on without a stop.

" 'Very well, Gaudin. Good sailing to you.'"

"Agnes, I have told you the conversation *verbatim*."

She knew what the Latin word meant. Her father read his bible in Latin.

"I like to hear a man who does not speak pretending he is a highborn Englishman," he said. "He pronounces his surname as '*Go-dan*' with the accent on the last syllable and the N half under your breath. I have heard people in town mis-pronounce the name."

"Papa, does the name Gaudin show Old Italian origins?"

"It may, Agnes. It all depends. I cannot be sure. The family name in Jersey may have come from an early influx of refugees or religious minorities who dispersed through Europe to find safety from persecution. Also I will ask him if the Gaudin Family has some connection with the Dispersal of the Knights Templar on the Pope taking action against the Order 500 years ago. Other minorities at different times going back to the time of the Celts found sanctuary in the Channel Islands away from the Continental Shore."

After a long silence relieved only by the ticking of the clock on the wall her father spoke again.

"I overheard him speaking French to someone in the street. He does not speak like any Frenchman I have ever known in the fur trade west of Montreal."

Struck with a sudden thought, Agnes interrupted her father.

"Oh Papa, in the morning please take me to see the ship sail out of Esquimalt. We can start early and ride our horses and get there in time for noon."

By next mid-morning father and daughter in farm boots, heavy cloaks, and thick cold-weather mackin_aw_ jackets, led their horses from the road to a rocky point of land swept by a strong wind out of the east. Steeped in the history of the French and English in the fur trade in Canada and the place Michilimackinac had in it, her father knew how those old names were to be pronounced, so he insisted on calling them mackinaw jackets, just as he spoke the name of the Micmac Indians as Mick-maw, an Algonquin name, he said.

On the way to the shore Agnes called out over the wind.

"Papa, I spy a white clamshell beach by the water. Let's go there out of the wind. I will gather some dry driftwood and light a fire to warm us by."

The two figures huddled under a tarpaulin to keep dry in the pouring rain of a morning cloudburst. After an hour or two passed they heard the sea shanteys across the water as the barque *Prince of Wales* weighed anchor to come barreling out of the harbour with sails set and drawing tight. Agnes stood in the wind at the water's edge and waved but she saw no one on board looking in her direction. She could see the figure of the man she fantasized over standing on the deck but she resisted the temptation to keep looking at him as his ship drew away. The Anderson family paid attention to a bundle of superstitions, one being : *Look at a friend drawing away in the distance while the looking is good, then turn away if you want to see the person return.*

She did not look for too long. Struck by how quiet it had become, she turned to her father.

"I'm glad he can't see me in this bulky clothing," she said. "I must look a fright."

"Agnes you do look like a farmer's daughter dressed for the cold, but your cheeks are rosy and your eyes sparkle. I can tell you he would be delighted to see you up close."

4

SUSAN MOIR

Only yesterday afternoon London sent the note to Agnes to say her husband had run the *Lady Lampson* aground attempting to enter Esquimalt Harbour, but no lives lost. This morning, after tossing in bed all night with the nightmare of her husband a captain of a river steamer running up the river to a new home for them in Hope, she awakened with the firm belief the shipwreck will prove the dream true. But how would she ever get back from Jersey to be with him? Her jangled thoughts lit on Susan Moir, whom she loved as a close friend for the time they knew each other ten years ago. Susan married and went with her husband to live a hard life, Agnes thought, beyond Hope and over the mountains in the Interior. She longed to have someone to talk to again. Susan's tonic of good cheer and joy of living brought back some happy memories. She had come to Victoria in the spring of 1865 with her mother at the invitation of Agnes' Aunt Mary Charles for an interview by her sister Amelia Wark for Governess in the Wark household. Agnes and she soon met and became good friends.

Amelia's husband, John McAdoo Wark had seen his wife needed assistance to bring up the children in this new and rude town. The Warks lived in a large house, one of several clustered outside close to the protection of the fortified Bastion at the entrance gate to Fort Victoria. Brimming over with joy at her prospects in staying on with the Warks in the new town, Susan asked her mother to return by steamer to New Westminster to pack and send all she would need.

Mary Charles and Amelia Wark were younger sisters of Agnes' mother, Eliza Anderson. The three sisters grew up together in the Birnie family at distant fur trade posts on the North Coast and in the Interior on both sides of the Forty-Ninth Parallel. All three, Eliza by far the oldest, now lived with their husbands in or near Victoria, the capital of the new Crown Colony of Vancouver's Island. Agnes' father retired early from service with the Hudson's Bay Company in the autumn of 1851 to settle with his family at Cathlamet on the banks of the Columbia River in Washington Territory, U.S.A. Seven years later he decided to sell his business interests and holdings in Oregon, lock, stock, and barrel, and move the family to the new Crown Colony at Victoria in pursuit of a new dream of prosperity. But the Andersons did not take their eight-year-old daughter Agnes with them. She stayed on in Cathlamet to help her grandmother Birnie care for her ailing grandfather Birnie, whom Agnes adored.

Agnes made one short visit to her parents and siblings to be flower girl at her older sister Eliza's wedding in Victoria in May 1860. The reception in the garden at the house in town with spring flowers and blossoms, she thought, must have cost her father a pretty penny. Some time later her father sent a letter to her at Cathlamet informing her in the midst of other items of news that he had sold the property. Agnes knew of no need to sell the house and garden on the eastern edge of the townsite in the midst of Garry oak and wild flowers growing in the grass on high and well-drained land. In fact, her father had bought and paid for the property in North Saanich several years earlier with what in mind he never said. He never explained why he made the move from town. She decided her father's reasons for selling the house in town to Mister Pritchard must have had to do with the place being *far too close* to a town with muddy streets for *far too many* months of the year, with *far too many* barking dogs, and *far too many* nosy newcomers with manners and speech her father could not abide. That pretty well summed up the story Agnes learned from the insight of her Grandmamma Birnie.

Agnes traveled north seven years later to rejoin her family at their new home 20 miles out of town. Aunt Amelia Wark did not let the month of June in the year 1865 go by without inviting Agnes to come into town from the Anderson Farm in North Saanich to stay over at her fine house to meet Susan Moir, the pretty and vivacious blue-eyed fairhaired new governess for her children.

Despite the nearly four-year age difference between Susan, the elder, and Agnes, the two became close friends. Agnes with her long auburn hair and tall figure looked older than sixteen. As their friendship grew she and Susan appeared to be young women the same age seen talking endlessly together. On leave from the Warks Susan Moir visited and stayed over at the Anderson farm during the next two summers. Not yet comfortable with horses, Susan told Agnes she envied her for how grand she looked on horseback.

Susan took special pleasure in helping Agnes launch her Indian dugout cedar canoe and make it skim through the water for picnics in the warm sunshine at white shell beaches on small wooded islands in the waters nearby. One afternoon in August in the first of their summers together Agnes' brother Alex drove the horse and carriage with their camping gear to Canoe Cove for the women to take Agnes' canoe to her favourite island, Pym Island, which the Navy had named after a young officer when it surveyed and charted the Saanich offshore island channels ten years earlier. With Alex's help to rouse the canoe out of the bushes the two young women launched it into the water to paddle only a mile to the island's steep white shell beach.

At high tide, bare-skinned and screaming with delight that no one could see them, they ran into the tingling clear saltwater to swim. The small island with its white shell beach that shelved off into deep water enabled them to make a quick plunge into the water before striking back to the shore to lie in the sun.

Susan compared this beach with those in Ceylon where she had lived as a child with her parents.

"So very different from the warm tropical beaches. The cold water here makes me catch my breath. I think it quite icy. The tingling skin begins as soon as we have dried off. Then we feel warm and good with ourselves."

They put on their clothes after sitting in the warm sun to dry off and followed Susan's suggestion to walk and explore the little island. Finding no undergrowth or bush to impede them, they circled the island in the trees to end up where they began. Sitting on a smooth weathered log to eat their picnic supper, they made tea from a kettle on their little driftwood fire and watched the sun set.

With blankets over their shoulders to keep warm they talked for hours under the stars. Agnes mentioned the wild animals in the woods of North Saanich.

"We can sleep here in peace with no wild animals to keep us awake, and not a living soul in sight."

"Why are there no wild animals here, Agnes?"

"None live on these little islands, only birds and insects. The wolves and the bears will not bother swimming across the salt water to search for prey to catch and eat. The animals have a special sense of knowing where they will NOT find prey. Must be that scent carries a long way in the wind. Nor will panther make the effort to swim such a distance from Saanich only to find nothing to capture."

Susan gasped at the mention of panther.

"Yes Susan, I thought you might know them by that name. Papa likes to call them *Puma*, but everyone else here calls them *Cougar*, a kind of mountain lion. They may sleep all day and come out to hunt at night. They can be dangerous to humans if surprised at first light and at dusk. A cougar killed some of Papa's cattle the first night after they got settled behind their fences. He brought in the beginnings of a herd from the American side on a steamer to drive ashore on the beach a few miles away from the farm."

"Oh Agnes, do you mean to say we might see a cougar at your farm?"

"They come only when hunger for deer meat drives them. They do not bother us, and we keep out of their way. They live in silence in the woods and will not attack unless they have become desperate; and more often at dawn or dusk, as I have said. They keep themselves out of our sight. We won't see them."

Earlier the two had begun to talk as they worked to build a bivouac filled with the scent of cut young green fir branches laid over a lean-to frame made from lengths of dry, bleached-by-the-sun driftwood. They would sleep together that night in bedrolls on thick green moss.

Susan must have thought it time to broach the subject of Race.

"I have heard in town," she said, "that you are from a half-breed family."

Agnes knew she winced. Even the seagulls stopped keening their calls.

"I won't say yes to that," she whispered. "I am sure you didn't mean it as a slur but many people do."

"Oh Agnes, of course I didn't mean it as a slur."

"I know you didn't, Susan. My father will never speak the words half-breed, but I need you to know my great-grandparents Beaulieu came from Red River on the far eastern side of the Prairies, and their daughter Charlotte, who became my grandmamma, was born at Red River in 1805. She so declared in the first U.S. census of Washington Territory a few years ago. Have you heard anyone speak of Red River, Susan?"

"Yes, I have and I know it is a place a thousand miles east of the

Rockies and south of Lake Winnipeg. I have heard it has a population of Indians and *Frenchmen* who left Quebec years ago. You will notice I did not say half-breeds."

"Yes Susan, Grandmamma's father was a Frenchman, Joseph Beaulieu, and her mother was a Cree Indian woman whose name only came to be recorded as *Josephte Cree*. She crossed the Rockies with him and with two-year old Charlotte on her back. Many in the fur trade pronounce their name as BO-lee-O, close to the true French BOWL-lee-yew, or something like that, with the lips pursed to make the sound."

Susan interrupted to ask why Beaulieu left Red River to come across the Rockies, and found Agnes eager to answer.

"Papa tells me this: a big man in the North West Company named Alexander Henry the Younger traveled on snowshoes in the winter of 1805-1806 to recruit Beaulieu, who had his own fur trapline on the banks of the Sâle River, south and west of Red River. Henry hired Beaulieu for his canoe experience as a *voyageur*. David Thompson needed men like him for his party planning to gather at Rocky Mountain House to explore the Kootenay Country west of the Southern Rockies."

Agnes went on to tell of the story told by her father: Beaulieu and his wife dallied to sell his traplines and spend a last summer with family and friends. Beaulieu, never thinking it befitting to be seen to be in a rush over anything, delayed decamping until the next winter's early snow. With daughter Charlotte and their five dogs they began their trip to Red River with the dogsled his wife had made. The express waited with orders not to delay past a certain date for them to arrive. Just in time, the Beaulieus joined the westbound Winter Express, which had started from North West Company headquarters at Fort William on the shores of Lake Superior, bound across the Prairies to Fort Augustus. With his dogsled running at the end of the train he could be left behind to fend for himself or freeze to death were he to fall off in the snow.

"Fort Augustus?"

"A North West Company Post near where the Hudson's Bay Company established Edmonton House. You must know where Edmonton is located?"

Susan nodded. Agnes continued.

"They were off on a long journey in stages over frozen prairie on North West Company business. The leader stopped the train for necessary sleep or to feed themselves and the dogs with hunted game-meat stored frozen in caches or in pits at fur trading posts on the banks of the frozen North Saskatchewan River."

"Perhaps they ran the dog teams at night?"

"Yes, and under the Aurora Borealis Lights. The winter cold opened up the opportunity to run the light load express sleds on snow, but if the snow got deep, the men had to find the energy to tramp out a trail on snowshoes for the dogs to run on."

"Can you imagine the demands for strength that would place on the men doing that kind of work, Agnes?"

"Grandpapa Birnie told me of the enormous amount of meat all of them ate every day the winter he came west in 1819. In the dead of winter the snow surface stayed firm much of the time. The leader saw to them avoiding snowdrifts. Frostbitten faces became a common complaint. I never had to contend with frostbite, Susan. I cannot imagine how my great-grandmamma Beaulieu managed on the passage west. The express dogsled team did not carry freight, only the mail packet, a parcel or two, and bundles of belongings. Thin birchbark fastened to sled frames kept everything in, and the snow and ice out. Papa explained Beaulieu working as a *voyageur* with his woman increased his value to David Thompson's Party."

"Yes Agnes, I am sure she had the satisfaction of knowing her skills as fur trade wife made her a person of great worth." Susan spoke again to tell she had heard stories of the northern Eskimo dogs and that they find a better life held in a kind of captivity because their masters feed them to keep them doing what they like best, pulling to compete with the dog beside them.

"I doubt they could survive in the wild against packs of wolves that would have given them no quarter, Susan."

Agnes continued to speak, recounting stories she'd heard that the men valued their women for their ability to gather nuts and berries, build fires, snare rabbit and other small animals to eat, and to carry out many other tasks, stitching bark and pitching or using tree gum to stop leaking canoes. She went on to tell more of the tale her father had told her: the Beaulieus traveled over 1,000 miles from Red River to join Thompson. They wintered with his party at Rocky Mountain House on the higher bank of the North Saskatchewan River. At low water in 1807 all of them departed upstream in canoes loaded with trading goods to be accounted for on return. After being guided up a wrong river and delayed, they returned downstream to drag their canoes up the fork of a river coming from the south by this time in spring flood. With loads on their backs, they tramped onwards on foot through a pass Thompson's men knew from the year before. On the other side they found a river flowing north they didn't know was the Columbia. Moving south, Thompson's party mapped the Kootenay Country, trading with Indians they could persuade to set up trap lines and bring in pelts to trade for blankets, pots, pans, knives, and rifles.

"Agnes, I'm interested in your story about the Birnies. What happened to baby Charlotte and her mother?"

"Let me tell you the rest of story. Before you go back to town I will show you on one of my father's maps where the exploring party spent that year and the next. West of the Rockies the party chopped down trees to build a log cabin without windows, naming it Kootenae House to sleep in and to store their trading goods. In December winter 1807 Beaulieu and the party's mountain guide Bercier carried a letter report from Thompson to the North West Company north back over the mountains to the North Saskatchewan River and on to Rocky Mountain House. In the dead of winter Beaulieu and his wife marched both ways on snowshoes with little Charlotte on her mother's back over what later became known as Howse Pass."

"You mean to say his wife and child went back with them?"

"Yes, they would have been a hindrance to Thompson's party crowded into the cabin at Kootenae House. Beaulieu might not survive to return, and if not, the exploration party would be left with too many mouths to feed. She would have gone with her husband without any discussion about it."

"What a hard life for them, Agnes."

"Yes Susan. Opposition from the Blackfoot kept the Thompson group to focus on exploring and trading west of the Rockies over several winters. During that time they took their pelts to Spokane House, which the North West Company had established early on in their trade south from New Caledonia to compete with the American Astorians at the mouth of the Columbia River. Papa has firm ideas about the character of my great-grandpapa Beaulieu. As he tells it, Beaulieu, a young man, finally tiring of the group, settled his family at a stream nearby to Spokane House. Everyone in the Thompson Party called it yet another *Beaulieu's Brook* for his continual good-natured threat to take leave of the expedition at some likely looking spot to become a Freeman fur trader in the new land. He and his wife knew how to survive alone, and they ended up doing exactly that."

"What happened then, Agnes?"

"Beaulieu bid adieu to his fellows to become a Freeman when Thompson left the party in 1810 to go east of the Rockies for a time. Beaulieu prospered from the pelts he took in for trade at the North West Company's Spokane House from his own trap lines. To his own take in pelts he added pelts he gained in wide-ranging trade as a middleman with distant Indians who preferred not to travel to the trading post at Spokane House."

"He and his wife ranged across all of the Kootenay Country?"

"Yes, that's what Papa tells me. Thompson hadn't been able to persuade him to keep on going with the rest of his party to the mouth of the Columbia River to find the Americans already there in the summer of 1811. On his return up the Columbia, Thompson hired Beaulieu to repair his cedar-planked canoes before heading north on the Upper Columbia River to Boat Encampment before crossing the Rockies over Athabasca Pass to avoid going back through Howse Pass only to encounter Blackfoot, who were angry at them for having traded rifles to their enemy, the Kootenai Indians, who used the rifles to raid buffalo herds east of the Rockies."

"Where does your grandfather Birnie fit into this?"

"Not until nearly ten years later. Grandpapa Birnie told me the story. I want to tell you all about it. Perhaps I should tell you tomorrow. I am sure I am falling asleep as I speak. The Sandman makes me want to close my eyes."

"Agnes, it is getting late, and I am falling asleep, too. Let's talk in the morning."

They awoke talking. After an outdoor breakfast they walked to the south point of Pym Island to sit on a blanket spread on the dewy grass, and put hands up to shield eyes from the morning sun in the eastern sky.

"I imagine some of the islands in the distance stand on the American side," Susan began, "but please go back to tell me more about your Birnie grandparents."

"Yes, the island a dozen miles to the east with three high humps in a row is American. Papa at Fort Nisqually entertained the Captain Wilkes U.S. Navy Expedition in 1841. He showed Papa a chart showing it named as Stuart Island after his clerk aboard the U. S. S. Active. But yes, I do want to tell you more about the Birnies. Someone in the family from Aberdeen had a coat of arms. A framed drawing of it hangs in our house. I will show it to you. But as Grandpapa not the first son,

Scotland remained a homeland that offered him no hope of ever going back. He told me his own entré into the West over the Prairie came much in the same way as Beaulieu came from Red River. Grandpapa came by canoe express from Montreal to Fort William at the western end of the Great Lakes more than ten years later in the autumn and early winter of 1819-1820. Dazed by the speed of travel over an un-known country, my grandpapa doubted he could find his way back over the rocks and rivers had it been necessary. He traveled by the winter dogsled express carrying the mail and new arrivals to Fort Augustus. Papa says Birnie's orders had him avoiding the places of murderous rivalry in isolated northern parts between the North West Company and the Hudson's Bay Company pre-1821. Instead, the North West Company sent Grandpapa Birnie with an express party across the Rockies on their established route over Athabasca Pass and on into the Columbia country as soon the weather permitted."

"What a terrible life for the packhorses I hear were used from Ed-monton House to the Athabasca River and more of them from Jasper's House to gain access to the path to Athabasca Pass, Agnes."

"Yes, Susan, the trail named *Le Grand Portage*. Pack horses from Edmonton House to Fort Assiniboine on the Athabasca River, where they took the loads off the horses to load into boats to line or track upstream to a point where horses sent from Jasper's House met them. Every place in the fur trade in this wide expanse of the country lies many days travel from the nearest next."

Susan remarked that, unlike the dogsled dogs, which ate game meat, the horses must have gone hungry.

"Yes, Grandpapa says the horses relished the pasture at the side of the braided river channels part way up. When the men took off the loads to carry on their own backs, a man with a rifle and a musket from Jasper's House stayed behind to meet the next upcoming party from the *Columbia*, the man to guard horses against animal attack. Papa says he can imagine the quiet descending on that pasture when the men disap-peared into the trees singing fur trade songs as they marched away to the heights of the Pass. Beyond at the foot of the steep slope they called *Le Grand Côte* lay Boat Encampment, where men from Spokane House met them with their boats carrying mail and, often, men on return east who hauled their baggage up the steep slope to gain the summit and go on down to find the horses in the wilderness pasture for the next stage of their travel east."

Agnes told the tale of Birnie's travel to go down the Columbia River, and how they returned the boats 400-miles or more down the dangerous rapids in the Upper Columbia River at low water. After carrying the boats in a portage around Kettle Falls, they ran the boats downstream to the place where the Spokane River fell into the Columbia near Fort Okanogan.

"They found horses in the large *parc*," Agnes said. "Grandpapa Birnie left the boats to ride on horseback on a trail above the winding banks of the Spokane River to Spokane House to report to Chief Factor Haldane, who was the officer in charge there over the winters at the time."

"How soon did your Birnie and Charlotte meet?"

"Perhaps not right away, Susan. I don't know. Grandpapa worked for two winters there before the news came that the Hudson's Bay Company had taken over from the North West Company. During that time his orders sent him east from Spokane into the Kootenay Country. Also orders sending him south into danger in the wooded western parts of the extensive river basin called *The Snake Country* under the command of an early North West Company leader with a Scottish name like Mackenzie from Fort Walla Walla over the Blue Mountains to a place they called Boisé at the western edge of the Snake Basin."

"I know some French, *bois* for woods."

"Yes Susan, Frenchmen in the fur trade gave it that name, but let me go on. That particular *Snake Party*, not the first nor the last of many, trapped for fur pelts south over the Blue Mountains. Grandpapa Birnie told me their lives were in danger on account of unfriendly Indians who stole their horses and killed some of the party."

"What a disturbing name," Susan interjected. "I mean to say, for land to be called *The Snake Country*."

"Oh Susan, the name does not refer to snakes, but to the Snake Indians, a western branch of the Shoshone Indians. Papa says the Blackfoot and the Sioux Indians in times past drove the Shoshone west as they did with the Kootenai Indians from the Plains into the mountains. But much of it IS rattlesnake country, as is much of the Southern Interior of British Columbia, which you say you like so much."

"Enough to that, Agnes! Let me get you back to where I asked you, Where does your grandfather Birnie fit into the Beaulieu family?"

"Grandpapa Birnie had come west over the Rockies with the North West Company to Spokane House in 1819. There he met Joseph

Beaulieu, now an older man and wealthy enough to dress his family in the finest fur trade fashion. He had held off all suitors and kept his daughter Charlotte unwed until the right man came along. She, then 16, would have believed the tall handsome young man of 23 to have a future far beyond any other man in the country. They wed in a great fur trade feast and ceremony at Spokane House. Fiddles and bagpipes played, men and woman danced, and everyone drank too much strong liquor. Governor Simpson ordered all Hudson's Bay Company Posts to stop buying fur pelts from the Freemen unless they signed on as engagé employees, but Beaulieu refused to do any such thing. He only did what he enjoyed doing. I'm going to have to tell you more about Papa's ideas about Beaulieu's character now. My father taught me the new word *ungovernable* to describe Beaulieu's independent Métis temperament. Papa told me he not surprised by the refusal to sign on as an engagé with the new company. Many Whites in the fur trade viewed Beaulieu as having the normal and expected Frenchman's unwillingness to take direction from anyone in authority. As I remember Papa saying it, Beaulieu had an *insubordinate* turn of mind."

"What happened to the Beaulieus after that, Agnes?"

"Beaulieu turned his wealth from furs into horses, which he could sell in a ready market on the other side of the Rockies, perhaps on the American side. We heard talk of a younger Beaulieu daughter, Josephine, who married a Rondeau in Minnesota."

"That's over forty years ago now, Agnes. Taking that pack of horses across the Rockies to the Prairies would make a story wouldn't it?"

"Yes, Susan, what a sight to have been able to see. Papa says he must have gained passage for his horses through the Southern Rockies. The Indians on the other side, the Blackfoot, must have regarded him as a friend from his earlier days in the fur trade and let him pass after parting out a number of horses, which he gave to them after a long parley. Grandpapa said Beaulieu had a wonderful herd of Appaloosa horses gained in trade from the Nez Percé Indians."

"Agnes, tell me, did you ever know the Beaulieus?"

"No, my parents never did see them, but at Fort Vancouver Papa met the man he believes to have been their son, named Joseph after his father. Papa says that man crossed west of the Rockies in 1832 to work at Fort Vancouver as an experienced canoe man. He went with the so-called *Southern Parties* trapping and exploring south into the Humboldt River and Northern California. A Roman Catholic priest married him to an Oregon woman named Betsy Tillamook, but I never did meet them."

"With the fur trade history in Canada going back many years, do your Beaulieu ancestors in Quebec go back to the days of Samuel de Champlain?"

"Oh no, I cannot say that, Susan, but he may have been one of the earliest French *voyageurs* and *coureurs de bois* who poked their way into the West in the last days of New France in Quebec."

"Perhaps you do look a little French, Agnes?"

"That doesn't worry me, Susan. I suspect many of the newcomers from England have foreign blood in their veins, but won't admit it. Papa has told me my great-grandfather Beaulieu's ancestor came west in the decades before the English under General Wolfe defeated Montcalm at Quebec. Papa says those early men coming from Quebec before the French Revolution named the North Saskatchewan River as the Rivière Bourbon after the old French Royal family, and they used that river to gain access to the headwaters of what is now called the Mackenzie River. They found it rich in beaver. No one could ever say those waters flowed into Hudson Bay, the preserve of the Hudson's Bay Company. And they not being trespassers, the pelts were free for the taking. Papa says some of them never went back to Old Quebec but settled in the North, but others like our man Beaulieu preferred to live and work in the southern parts and come and go to the Red River region."

"Perhaps he aimed to please his wife, who liked it better there? But why do you go into all of this old history?"

"Perhaps you are right about his wife making the decision to live closer to her kin. Why am I telling you all of this history? I am trying to show you what my lonely father knows despite his years in isolation. Newcomers in town do not pay him due respect, which makes him frosty to strangers. When we get back to the house I will show you on a map the travel route of the *voyageurs*. Papa traveled up the North Saskatchewan and the Athabasca Rivers on his way to Oregon in July though November 1832 and again ten years later in 1842. Grandpapa Birnie did it in 1819 and 1826. In 1806 Beaulieu and his young family took the North Saskatchewan River all the way to Rocky Mountain House. They did not get themselves north to the Athabasca River or Athabasca Pass when they crossed the Rockies in 1807."

"And now it's 1865," Susan said. "But don't tell me any more history. I am much more interested in your canoe trip up from Puget Sound."

"Before I tell you about that and before I forget to say it, I will tell you the story of the big Birnie canoe. Please let me, Susan?"

With mock enthusiasm Susan agreed.

"Yes, tell me about the BIG canoe."

"Grandmamma Birnie took charge of the Birnie family's annual clam digging, fishing, hunting, and wild berry-picking expedition to the coast in the autumn before Grandpapa died. For this last time he insisted we leave him behind and that I go with her in her big West Coast cedar canoe. I mean to say, it was *her* canoe because Grandpapa made a present of it to her long ago. Eight Wahkiakum Indians on each side paddled and chanted while we sat in the back like royalty as we charged downstream from Cathlamet with Grandmamma in command. I hadn't expected to see how much respect the Indians and their chiefs showed her everywhere we went."

"How long was the canoe?"

"Perhaps 40 feet, Susan. We passed through the territories of several Indian nations on the way down the Columbia and portaged over the low land north at Baker's Bay to the wetlands and saltwater lying to the north at Willapa Bay. The men lifted the remarkably light cedar canoe over the portage."

Susan remained silent for a time.

"Please tell me the story about _your_ West Coast Indian Canoe, which I just love the look of."

"Grandpapa Birnie gave it to me a year before I came north. He traded with the Chinook Indians who traded with a tribe to the north, the Quinault, who in turn traded with the Makah Indians at Cape Flattery, who in turn traded with the Indians across the Strait of Juan de Fuca at Nitinat on Vancouver Island. The best cedar trees grow there in the heavy West Coast rain. The builder likely built it to order. I remember when Grandpapa limped through the rain to his boat shed to show it to me and tell me it was mine. I was excited to see its shape upside down high in the rafters in the dim light. The Indian who made it painted it dark red and black with a trim white Indian design at the front on each side of the high prow. The design will not be overpowered by a sea wave, but rise into it to keep the water out of the canoe. Turning my head over on its side to imagine it, I saw it slipping through the water even when standing still. I got it launched in the water the next morning and gave my canoe a name, but in the Indian ways I learned at Cathlamet, I have never told anyone the name. This is special between the canoe and me."

"Please tell me the name. I won't tell anybody."

"No, I will not, Susan. After Grandpapa Birnie died I stayed on with Grandmamma for the winter to help her. The people at Cathlamet gave me a send-off in May to bring my canoe here. My older brother Robert rode his horse to guide me, driving a horse cart with my baggage and my canoe as just so much overland freight from Cathlamet to Fort Nisqually. He left me there in the care of Papa's friend Doctor Tolmie. Do you know where that place is located?"

"Yes Agnes, a Hudson's Bay Fort not far north from the new town of Olympia on the American side."

"Yes, I stayed as a guest of the officer in charge of the Fort, Mister Huggins, and his wife Letitia, a daughter of old Chief Factor John Work, until the Indian guides came down from the north in their own canoes. My grandmother Birnie arranged for them to go south to Puget Sound to lead me to my new home."

"How remarkable that, she, your grandmamma, a woman, could make the up-coast Indians heed her."

"Well, Susan, in truth, the local Indians made the connections for her with their northern kin over the winter. Over 40 years she and her husband won and held the admiration and respect of the Indians. She showed no fear of any man."

"How wonderful for you to see. Clearly she respected them and their territories. Please go on. Tell me about your canoe trip north from Nisqually." Agnes then told the background of the story. As a favour to Agnes's father Doctor William Fraser Tolmie of the Hudson's Bay Company made a special trip to the fort to go down to the beach to meet the guides to become satisfied they understood where they were taking Agnes.

Doctor Tolmie spoke in the Chinook language to the Indian guides, one older than the other. They told him they planned to take her part way and then hand her over to their kin to continue on to where *Mister Anderson* has his house. The Indians knew Papa from his earlier years at the Fort, and they knew where he moved to live. Doctor Tolmie asked them to draw a picture in the sand to show him they understood the plan.

"Could you keep up when your guides started off?"

"That WAS funny, Susan. They did charge off at a great rate. They thought I was a headstrong white girl and I wouldn't be able to keep up.

But my canoe and I were too good for them. My canoe, far lighter, did not sit as deep in the water. I had no trouble keeping up to the first stop. Afterwards they slackened off and I had a chance to look around to see where we were going."

Agnes told Susan a newspaper on the American side later wrote that Agnes Anderson had been the first white woman to cross the Strait in a canoe, but Agnes knew she had simply followed the guides and the Continental shoreline up from Puget Sound with tides and back eddies to help, paddling for most of four days.

"Grandmamma Birnie arranged for the guides to lead the way to the San Juan Islands. From there, a third pair of Indian guides came to make a convoy to slip across Haro Strait before the wind got up in the afternoon. We paddled through a narrow deepwater passage between islands on the Canadian side of the new International Boundary to land me at the cove my Anderson family soon named Canoe Cove. My older brother Alex camped at the cove for a week waiting for me to arrive. I saw him on the beach as soon as I steered my canoe around the point of the island at the entrance to the cove. I waved but said nothing out loud to break the spell of the still afternoon as our three canoes slipped into the cove."

Agnes told Susan she jumped out onto the beach to embrace her brother Alex, who rushed down to meet her.

"He turned to give money and tobacco to the guides. The Indian canoes then slipped out of the cove to go back the way they came. I helped my brother lift the canoe and carry it through the grass to stash upside down in the bushes. Alex loaded my bags and packages as I heard the happy clattering cry of a Kingfisher bird greet me."

Agnes described how Alex drove his horse and carriage on a wide path along the edge of the trees and deep into the forest to get to the farm.

"I took the high-pitched keening call of a bald eagle above in the trees as welcoming me to this place," she said. "Soon followed a scene of a great family feast and jubilation, but I am sure my father and mother found it painful to begin getting to know me again after such a long time. I found it difficult to get to know them again."

Susan spoke to break a brief silence that followed on Agnes ending her story,

"And not long after came your Aunt Amelia's idea she invite you to come into town to meet me, and I will never forget how awkward I felt trying not to patronize you, not to seem better than you. I had come from a different world."

"But Susan, from the start I wanted to be like you if I could. I knew I didn't look Indian and might have a chance to be like you and have everyone with eyes only for me when I come into a room, like the men have for you."

"Oh Agnes, don't talk like that! Begin thinking you are a catch for any man. You have long legs and a fine body and such good posture: we both have that."

Agnes remarked her own father, fastidious in all things himself, had taken special care to see she, a farm girl helping her mother run the farm, kept her hands and fingernails spotless. And as a tall girl, she knew all too well he insisted on her holding herself erect when sitting or standing or when riding her horse. He told her not to slump. She would look better to others, especially to men if she paid attention to her posture and held her chin high.

"But he didn't need to say much about it because Grandmamma Birnie persuaded me to think of my shoulders helping me to stand and sit straight. Said it would show off my figure, too."

Agnes saw Susan move her shoulders back and forth, lift and turn her chin and heard her say, "Yes, it does that, doesn't it."

Susan broke the silence that followed. "You knew, didn't you, some people in town left you off invitation lists to parties because of Indian blood in your family?"

Agnes remained quiet for a long moment before she replied.

"Oh I sensed that, but you are the first person to talk to me about it," she whispered.

"I knew from what I had seen in New Westminster that girls known to have some Indian blood simply were not invited to parties given by many in the Colony. That prevented them from being introduced to eligible young men, and vice versa. Looking as white as you do made no difference. And I know it is the same in Victoria. So, I will be your friend and tell you of the plans I want for my life without any of that nonsense. I will found my own dynasty somewhere else and you should think of doing the same. I tell everyone I am looking for a husband to take me to live a life in the Interior. The sight of wild animals in their wilderness world fascinates me. That will discourage faint-of-heart dandies!"

"Oh Susan, be careful, you might get your wish. No, that's not for me. Cougars live in the mountains in the Interior where you keep saying you want to go, and you may have to keep them from attacking your small children to eat."

"Oh what a terrible thought," Susan cried out.

"My father and mother hated the *privations* of living in the Interior, *de-privations* he said a better word. They really hated life there. Their health suffered from the cold, and at some places it was too damp. Papa constantly blinks his eyes as if the glare of the winter sunlight on the snow damaged them. Also he has had much difficulty with his legs, which even today he must bind with cloth to lessen the pain he feels."

After a long silence Susan changed the subject.

"Agnes, I will have my husband build a fire for us to keep warm_____, but hasn't your father ever talked to you about *ostracism* in this new town society? It must anger him."

"I know what the word *ostracize* means, Susan, but Papa has never spoken to me about it. I am sure that's because he doesn't want my mother to feel a sense of guilt for me being at disadvantage. People in town did not ostracize my older sister Eliza. But in such a small population, no one, apparently, dared to leave such a shining beauty off the invitation list."

"Where is she now, Agnes?"

"She found a handsome husband who had been posted to work for the Hudson's Bay Company at Fort Nisqually before he found himself better employment working in a banking office in Victoria. He took Eliza away to live and prosper in New Zealand. I saw him when I was a little girl. Likely we will never see her again. Do you want me to tell you about her wedding?"

"Oh, please. Agnes, I'd like to hear about it."

"The story, Susan, begins with the help given to my father by his old friend Chief Factor Douglas in charge at Victoria in 1858. His retired company officer status entitled Papa to buy land in town at a good price. He built a fine house facing south for warmth in winter in a park-like setting among Garry Oak trees. A carpet of gorgeous blue camas wildflowers with wild white lilies sprinkled in the green grass. And Papa knew how to plant an orchard of cherry trees with grafts to the native wild bitter cherry."

"Yes, I know about that. Everyone in town says your father knows so much about gardens and trees."

"Eliza sent a letter to ask me to come to Victoria to be a flower girl at her wedding. I stayed in that first house in Victoria only for a few days before and after the wedding. My brother Robert, who now wants to go by the name James, eight years older than I am, escorted me up from Oregon on the passenger steamer *Eliza Anderson* from Olympia, so named by an admirer of my sister."

"Agnes, what do you know about your sister Eliza's early life with the Anderson family in the Interior?"

"Papa told me she had been born in the north at Fort St. James in 1837 and moved with the family to all of his later postings as the oldest Anderson child. I wasn't born until 1849, so I don't actually remember any of what I am going to tell you now, but I do know Papa took her and my older brother as young children on horseback on the 1851 Fur Brigade from Fort Colvile on the Upper Columbia over the Hope Trail to Fort Langley. He sent them in canoes to Victoria to go to the new school in the Fort. Papa returned up the Fraser River to Hope to round up their horses to carry loads of trading goods freight back to Fort Colvile over the Hope Trail. At Colvile his friend Chief Factor Ballenden arrived to bring his replacement and to tell Papa he must turn the post over to that man and return down the Columbia River to Fort Vancouver with no new orders."

"What does that mean, no *new orders?*"

"It meant Papa had no new posting or promotion, Susan."

Agnes continued after a long silence.

"With Papa and Mama and the rest of us aboard, Ballenden led us all down the Columbia River in late October to Fort Vancouver. I was only three years old at the time of the move down from Colvile but Mama tells me the sun shone every day in glorious autumn weather, which made her health and spirits rise. I remember none of it, but Papa tells me Mama's health improved by the day on the way down in the sun. But to get back to the wedding in the month of May 1860: Eliza and I had been apart for such a long time. Papa sent her and my brother Robert to school in Victoria before I can remember. I caught my breath to see such a beautiful bride. I got caught up with all of the preparations for the wedding reception in the garden. I carried back vivid memories to Cathlamet to tell grandmother Birnie. She didn't come to the wedding and didn't tell me why: I think she stayed away because she knew she looked 'too Indian' for this town."

"How cruel, but perhaps she could not leave your grandfather Birnie in his condition?"

"Oh I think she could have left him there."

"I have often thought of a summer wedding. Perhaps, Agnes, each of us can have one?"

"Perhaps, but perhaps not, Susan," said Agnes.

As she spoke Agnes thought of Gaudin's sailing timetable to arrive in Victoria in late winter of each year.

By this time the two young women had returned to the beach to decamp and launch the canoe to take them back to Canoe Cove to meet Alex who had come for them. Susan went back into town the next morning.

The night after Susan returned to town Agnes dreamt a nightmare of her wedding in the dark of winter, a stark gothic scene of a cold storm wind shrieking through bare limbs of the Garry Oak trees at the farm. After the dream came a second time she told her mother about it.

"And the groom was missing," she said. "Not even a church in the dream, only the sound of moaning."

Looking troubled, Agnes' mother told her she should get out-of-doors more often.

"Go ride your horse and get some fresh air into you," she said.

Agnes thought her friendship with Susan had come to an abrupt end in late September 1867 when Susan came to announce her departure.

"Now that I turned twenty-one a month ago, I have been paid my inheritance money from England. I have been able to leave my position with the Warks and will return to New Westminster as soon as I can."

"Oh Susan, I will miss you."

"And I you," said Susan.

"The money is not much, but it will be enough for my mother and me to live at the new settlement in Hope. She and I will leave New Westminster to start a school there next spring. We will travel up the Fraser River to Hope on the stern-wheel steamer."

"Yes Susan, I know the distance is close to 100 miles. Papa says a steamer also goes farther upstream to a settlement and a church at Yale."

"I daresay I will marry a good man there someday, but I meant to say also the steamer to Hope stops half way up at a place they call *Tschillee-whack* to take on wood to burn to run the steam engine. Often, especially when the river is in freshet, I hear, the steamer lets off the passengers to spend the night at an inn close to the riverbank. For now and for the winter my mother and I both will enjoy the dances and social whirl in

New Westminster. The garrison of lively young Royal Engineer officers will be eager, I know, to fill my dance card. Who knows, perhaps I shall find a good man there, but I expect most of them will want to go back to England. I don't."

5

SUSAN AND AGNES

Agnes remembered she had groaned when her father told her the news. The men in the company office in town reported the builders delayed the launching of Gaudin's new barque until the end of the year for some reason not explained. She groaned because Gaudin will be sent in the meantime to take the old Hudson's Bay Company barque *Ocean Nymph* on a voyage to Montreal. He would return to London in time for Christmas 1868, but that meant he could not return to Victoria until the middle of next year at the earliest.

She went to the barn, saddled up her horse, and took Blackie for a long ride through the high maple trees in yellow autumn foliage. Agnes came back into the house in tears.

"Oh Papa, Gaudin may get stuck in the ice in the river at Montreal," she burst out, "or be delayed in some other way in Quebec. Another captain may be given the new barque in his place. He may never get a chance to return to Victoria. Even if he does get back from Quebec in time, the delay means I won't see him until the middle of summer next year. He will be away now for a whole year and a half. I am getting too old to marry."

"Agnes, think for a moment. Gaudin's earlier sea experience had him sailing to the Gulf of St. Lawrence and to the Maritime Provinces. Here, I will show you on a map. He will be sailing the *Ocean Nymph* in waters long familiar to him. This will build up his self-confidence in command."

"Oh that doesn't make me feel any better, Papa. I have a horrible feeling I will not see him again."

Her mother came into the room to catch the last of this.

"I am quite sure he will come," she said, "and Papa will bring him out here for the two of you to meet. If you have a hold of yourself by that time, you will dazzle him. That's the word you have used when talking about Susan: why not you?"

"Yes, why not you, my daughter?" chimed in her father.

With such encouragement Agnes found comfort in pleasant thoughts of what might yet be. But she did not know Aunt Mary Charles intervened last December to invite Susan Moir back to Victoria for Gaudin to be introduced to her on his first visit to the Pacific Northwest in the *Prince of Wales*. Her husband Chief Factor William Charles arranged for the two to meet when Susan made a quick trip before Christmas. Susan did not stay over in town. She returned to New Westminster without delay on the steamer in time to dress up for Christmas parties.

Life for Agnes on the farm played itself out month after month. She stayed at home in North Saanich helping her often-ailing mother bring up the Anderson children: Walter 12, Rose 10, Alan 8, and Arthur 4. Rose would be a better help when she grew older. Her older brother Alex, 23, did the outside work on the farm. Another, James, 27, with more schooling, found employment in Oregon, but said he planned to return to Victoria to open a bookkeeper's office; and big red-headed Henry, 25, made his way somewhere in the Northern Interior. No one knew exactly where, and he did not send letters. Years earlier, underage for enlistment at 16, young Henry joined the U.S. Cavalry to ride their fine horses. Not taking to the Army discipline, he absented himself without leave and faced execution for desertion. Agnes' father rode from Fort Nisqually to intercede with a U.S. Army General to stay execution and to substitute a painful discharge from army service on the ground of his nonage.

In the evenings with her day's work done Agnes read books her father brought home from the officers' library at the Fort. Forty years ago he and his old friend Doctor Tolmie agitated to set up a lending library for officers. Agnes found great enjoyment in reading and talking to her father about the books he brought for her.

She often spoke fur trade French with her mother and father. Some men knew him to be a scholarly person and a contributor to such publications as the Journal of the Royal Society in London. He composed and wrote letters in his plain clear handwriting for other retired officers of the company who asked for help in writing important letters.

Agnes enjoyed riding her horse into town to stay with friends who were happy to have her visit. But no one replaced her friend Susan who now lived many miles away up the Fraser River in another world entirely. Would she ever see or hear from her again?

Her mother did talk with her about Gaudin and what life would be like in Jersey if she were to marry him.

"It must be such a lively place, Agnes, with so many neighbours close-by and so different from living here so close to the forest."

"Mama," she said, "I cannot imagine life on that ancient Island of Jersey. People have been living there since long before 1066. Living in this new rough country on the Pacific Coast where nothing is old does not prepare me to live in such a place. If the truth be told, Mama, I have never liked cows. Perhaps he will find us a place to live in the town Papa told me about on the south side of the island, the one with the pretty sounding name, St. Helier?"

"Your father says Jersey has a warm climate. More sun than the England he knew, so that would help, wouldn't it?"

"Yes, he told me Jersey lies in the same latitude as Victoria, but I do wonder whether I will be able to ride a horse over the countryside like I do here. Perhaps the roads only narrow paths? And all of the farms are walled off like chequer-boards with laws against trespass."

"Perhaps the farm is a large one?"

"I will have to ask him about that. I think I'd like living in town much better."

Agnes received a letter from Susan in May of the next year. She found her mother working in the pantry to tell her about it.

"Susan has written to say she and her mother plan to make a trip from Hope," she said. "Her mother will stay at a hotel in town and Susan hopes she might come to stay over with us. She wants to talk to me about the simply wonderful man who is courting her. He has given her a fine horse and has taught her how to ride in the same way she had seen me ride. She always wanted a husband to take her to live in the wilderness. This man offers her such a life, but she worries whether she should pay attention to a man almost 20 years older and only a prospector living in a tent. She wants me, of all people, to tell her what to do."

"I am sure we all here will welcome her. She made your father's eyes light up. Do tell her to come. You and Alex can pick her up in town."

With her brother Alex riding escort, Agnes drove her father's horse carriage rig to meet Susan at the hotel on the morning after her arrival. Susan remarked on the jacket Agnes wore that day.

"Oh Agnes, I have seen a jacket like yours, but never on a woman, only on some Hudson's Bay Company Officers. But I must say you look good in it."

"Thank you Susan. Englishmen in town won't wear any such garb because it has not come from London. Of course, women in town want something more in style."

"My John Allison will see I get a jacket like yours when I tell him how good you look in it. On a lovely summer day I went on a picnic all by myself. On the other side of the stream came a Hudson's Bay Company horse brigade nearing the end of its travel at the outskirts to Hope, laden with furs. The officer in charge wore such a jacket. He rode up to me on his fine horse and doffed his wide brimmed cowboy hat. We spoke to each other. He did look wonderful wearing such a jacket. I think he had never seen a young white woman with blue eyes, blonde hair, and fair skin."

Susan led Agnes over to talk to her splendid horse, which had spent the night in the livery stable on Broad Street. With Susan's horse on a line, and Alex on his horse leading the way, Agnes and Susan drove off from town to the Saanich Road. Susan told Agnes about her marvelous two-day-trip from Hope, first on the Fraser River in the *Reliance* to New Westminster, followed by passage in the larger stern-wheel steamer the *Enterprise* steaming through open water on the Strait past the Gulf Islands to Victoria. She said the excitement began in Hope.

"We bought our tickets from the Purser. Some kind young men carried our baggage aboard. I settled my mother in the room called, if you can believe it, the saloon, which provides a sitting room for passengers; and I went back to the shore. I led my horse down from the riverbank to a stall on the lower deck of the *Reliance* with men on the shore cheering me on. Can you imagine it? I had delayed the steamer in its departure, and I was embarrassed I was holding everyone up. I am sure my cheeks blushed red, but I put all the men in a merry mood. The captain tooted the steamer's whistle to the cheers of onlookers lining the riverbank. People came from a distance to see the departure. It ranked as the main event of the day for the town."

"Please tell me about the trip."

"The current took hold when the bow swung out from the shore, and we swept off down the river. I stood comforting my horse on the way down to New Westminster, making sure she had hay and that she was not spooked by the glow of flame whenever the stoker opened the fire door, or frightened by the ugly thumping noise made by the steam engines making the turning motion of their cranks in plain sight on the main lower deck. I made friends with crewmembers who liked my beautiful horse and spelled me off at times as the steamer swept down the bends of the river. I lifted my skirts to climb the companionway to the upper deck to meet the Captain and the other passengers. And two days later we came on to Victoria aboard that wonderful big stern-wheel steamer the *Enterprise*. I put my horse in a stall on the lower deck. But I had to dress for the occasion. They had built the lower deck open to give the wind, which her speed through the water makes, free passage through. Little housework to slow the vessel. Yes, *housework*, that's the proper word they told me for the cabin space below the level of the top deck. I could look out to see the small wooded islands we were passing in calm waters. I have a good sense of direction. I looked to make out Pym Island where we camped in the summers we spent time together."

"That was so much fun, Susan, and not another person in sight when we took off our clothes to swim in the water so cold that we came out covered in goose bumps, but our skins were left tingling as we dried ourselves off in the sun."

"Yes I remember. I was excited to be invited to climb up from the windy deck to speak to the captains on both steamers. The *Enterprise's* captain, incredulous I would have known the name of Pym Island. Speaking to the other men in the wheelhouse to hear, he said, '*You're right about that, Miss Moir. How did you know?*' So I told him I had been there, sir, in summertime with Agnes Anderson who knew the name of the Island. Both captains seemed to me to be happy men. Captain Irving on the *Reliance* has a tall and up-and-coming son John working with him, but the son is much too young for either of us, even though he does show sign of becoming one of the handsomest men in the Colony, but I did not come to talk about him. John Allison DOES have such an unfortunate middle name, Fall, F-A-double L. I do think I could love the man with a passion if only I could see a future for us."

Agnes waited for her to say more.

"Almost twenty years older than I am, John Allison prospects for gold and precious metals in the mountains far beyond Hope. I am not trying to be funny: I intended to say *in the mountains far to the east of Hope*. Farther than walking distance from Hope, a four-day ride with horses. He immigrated with his parents to Illinois in the U.S. of A. but left them behind to join the 1849 Gold Rush to California. Prospering there, he says he sailed north to Victoria in 1858 to join in the later stages of the excitement of British Columbia's Fraser River Gold Rush, but on the advice of Governor Douglas, he chose to head east from Hope over the mountains instead of north with the crowd to the Cariboo Country."

"Perhaps you like the man because you see he knows what he is doing, but are you worried he is an older man, Susan?"

"I am not sure about that, Agnes. I do like a man who knows what he is doing. But I must tell you I DO enjoy the company of other men in this new place named Hope. They pay a lot of attention to me on social occasions. Promising young men arrive on the boat from New Westminster every week. Agnes, you should think of coming to live in Hope. You could find work with my mother and me to add a school classroom. You could find a good husband."

"Oh Susan, I have told you I am not interested in living in the Interior."

"You would love it, but before I forget to mention it, I must say that my mother and I did enjoy an excursion party day trip from Hope by steamer up the Fraser to see the new Alexandria Bridge, which crosses the river upstream of a wee little place with the excrutiatingly funny-sounding name of Spuzzum."

"Oh Susan, I know that name Spuzzum!"

"Do you, really?"

"Papa climbed over the mountain lying to the east of Spuzzum to by-pass the terrible canyon whirlpool at Hell's Gate when he came south from New Caledonia in 1847 to explore for a horse brigade trail to and from the Cariboo. In the year following he led the Fur Brigade from New Caledonia to Fort Langley by much the same route, coming and going."

"Oh Agnes you are droning on with more of your father's history in the midst of what I am telling you about my simply wonderful fun time in Hope. I find the newcomer Englishmen arriving every week so much fun to be with. They are a sorry lot in Victoria, but those who have gone on from that place to Hope jolly me along in a most amusing way."

Agnes did not know what to say and an awkward silence followed.

"I started off telling you about my John. I have seen no other with the quiet force and strength of character as this man, John Allison, who is courting me. He is quite beside himself I made this trip away from his attentions. I do miss him, but should I pay any more attention to him? Other men do interest me, too."

The two young women rode their horses over all of the Anderson property in North Saanich during the short time they had together again. Agnes thought both of them astride their mares made for a fine sight as they cantered along the paths and trails. Agnes did not wear her buckskin jacket this warm June morning. Susan and Agnes wore loose shirt tops and lighter clothing to ride. In a quiet moment at the side of the trail Agnes talked about the hat and boots she wore.

"My Birnie grandparents gave me these hand-tooled Spanish riding boots and my uncle Robert Birnie sent me this black flat-brimmed Spanish hat from California."

"Where in California does he live?"

"He ranches with his Mexican wife in a valley south of the Spanish Settlement at Martinez and east of a settlement named *Pinole* on the eastern shore of North San Francisco Bay. People in Cathlamet say in earlier years he went by a Hudson's Bay Company brig to Hawaii and on to California to work as a cowboy driving cattle north to Oregon. That done, he returned south to live. But Susan, let's talk about his mother, my grandmother Birnie. She said men have a liking for shapely legs and ankles."

Susan laughed.

"I am sure she is right! What else did she say about that?"

"Grandmamma told me enough about men to know that the sight of the two of us astride our horses with our hair streaming behind us would stir a man."

After a long moment of silence Susan spoke.

"You have such a strong and active body, Agnes. Each of us is fortunate: I like being a woman. I think you do too, but I do worry about how you are going to find a husband stuck out here in the countryside. You MUST change your thinking about moving away to live at Hope."

Agnes flushed and felt herself tongue-tied and did not know what more to say about Hope. She would not respond to any more of Susan's talk about it. Nor would she mention her crush on Gaudin or that her father met him last December to invite him to come to the farm his next time in town. She planned to keep it to herself.

At one point during the last morning ride the two dismounted and sat together on a log under a large green-leafed maple tree to talk. Susan said something about the unmarried men in Victoria. Agnes, thinking about something else, did not listen, but her ears pricked up when she heard the name *Gaudin*. Susan said she had traveled to Victoria last

December to meet him! Agnes could scarcely breathe, let alone speak.

"I did make a quick trip back to Victoria at the instigation of your Aunt Mary Charles after I left the Warks and before my mother and I moved to Hope. I had no time to be in touch with you. Your aunt asked her husband to introduce me to Gaudin, 26 and still a bachelor. He had come into town as mate in the *Prince of Wales*. Would I come to Victoria to meet him before the ship departs? She could not have known he looked for a wife to take back to live in Jersey. He asked me if I knew you, Agnes."

Agnes held back her gasp, feeling a hot flush to her cheeks. Her mother's sister, the Chief Factor's wife: why hadn't she thought of introducing her to Gaudin? Perhaps she meant to exclude her? The moment passed in a long pause.

"I can't imagine why he would ask about me," Agnes whispered,

"Gaudin told me he'd heard *Agnes Anderson* could be one for him to look for. She is a ripe one for marriage they told him, and she lives with her father and mother 20 miles out of town."

Agnes' face flushed again and she drew in her breath. She had seen Gaudin only from a distance, but he had been on her mind ever since. A *frisson* followed by a tingle stirred down her back and she felt the tips of her breasts flicker at the thought Gaudin had been thinking of her.

"I told him I knew you well. Did you ever meet him?"

"No, Susan."

"Such a waste of time for me to come over to meet him. Your Aunt did not know that no man could ever take me away to live in Europe. A question did cross my mind why your Aunt Mary would not have put him on to you instead of me. Would you want to go with him to live in Jersey, Agnes?"

"Perhaps. Not possible for me to say, Susan."

"Let me tell you the rest of it lest you be mistaken."

Susan said she and Gaudin met in the room Chief Factor Charles provided in the Company Office. He closed the door behind him, leaving the two talking. The awkward beginning did not improve. Gaudin confirmed he aimed to find a wife to marry and take back with him to live in Jersey.

She told him she could not imagine any young woman here having ANY desire to live anywhere other than this beautiful new country in the Northwest. She wouldn't.

"That response did not stop the man. The conversation took a bad turn. I can only put it down to him having been away so long at sea. He stood very close to me. I could tell he did not have alcohol on his breath."

"What happened?"Agnes asked almost under her breath.

In a tone of voice to indicate her disapproval, Susan spoke again.

"He said he'd been much taken with me and that he saw me as a *lively* one. Can you imagine how forward a man can be. He said he admired my long blond hair and he had seen my lips as *inviting*. And then he said that I had a *saucy* nose. Wasn't that just the limit?"

Agnes, wide-eyed, spoke not a word. Susan continued to talk.

"From the look in his eyes and the way his hands keep moving to touch my shoulder I saw that he would have been happy to have me out of my clothes in a trice, as if I was one of the willing women he calls on in London and Montreal. Perhaps he HAD been at sea for a long time, but I was astonished the man couldn't see I would not have been interested in him."

She told Agnes of the shocked expression on his face when she spoke in a whisper that may have seemed more like a growl. I told him, she said, 'You are much too forward sir. I don't like the look in your eyes.' And I added, ' I am not sure Agnes Anderson would not reject you too, but since you did ask me about her I will see you are introduced so she can make up her own mind about you. You would find Agnes most attractive I am sure; whether she'd like you is quite another matter.' At that, I stood, turned and walked out of the room. That pretty much ended that, don't you think Agnes?"

Agnes did not answer right away and both remained silent as the western screech owls above them made their muted calls in the trees.

"You are so quiet, Agnes. What would you think of such a man?"

"I think I might have handled it differently and spun it out a bit."

"Oh, with what in mind, Agnes?"

They rode their horses in a slow walk through the trees lining the trail.

Agnes said nothing for a long moment. Finally, the words came.

"To get him talking a bit more, Susan, to show me what kind of man he was."

"To get him talking a bit more to show you what kind of man he was, you say! How could getting him to talk more help you make up your mind?"

"Somehow I might have seen a chance for me to avoid what happened to my mother and my grandmother Birnie if I kept him talking."

"What do you mean by that?"

"I am sure they became ill and old before their time as a result of having too many children when they weren't ready to have more."

"How would marrying him and going to Jersey prevent that?"

"I may be wrong but we would not be spending our lives living all of the time at home together every night. Perhaps my chances to live a long life in good health would be better."

"How ridiculous! From what he told me of his ship's timetable I can see he would have you frolicking and rolling in the hay every summer for a month or more. How would that stop you from having children by the dozen?"

"Perhaps it wouldn't, but I think I might have a better chance of good health over there. My grandmother Birnie told me when I was fourteen about men who make such talk as you described Gaudin's *sally* to get you interested in them. Papa taught me that word and also *gambit*, which could be a better word: Gaudin gambled, and made himself vulnerable to your rebuff. But, getting back to what grandmamma told me: how men talk to you will help you decide whether you want them."

Susan dismounted and stepped over to Agnes's side to look up at into her eyes.

"I know what those words mean," she said, "but what WOULD you have said to him?"

Agnes lowered her eyes and hesitated before answering.

"I'm not entirely sure," Agnes whispered, "but I don't think I would have ended it as you did."

Agnes found she could speak now with more strength than before.

"My grandmother Birnie put some ideas into my mind about how to handle men," she said. "It must depend on the man and whether you decide you want him."

Susan mounted her horse and they rode on together for a time. At a turn in the trail they came down off their horses to sit on a log and continue talking.

"My grandpapa hung on to her every word after years of marriage. She must have done something right, Susan."

"Mercy! What does a married woman have to put up with? I am not sure I can find a husband who will hang on to MY every word. Let's hurry back. It's getting late for lunch at the farm."

Agnes, having regained her composure, now felt relief she had not made a fool of herself by confiding in Susan about her inner passion for Gaudin after Susan had spoken so ill of him.

"Let's ride into town this afternoon and put our horses in the livery stable for overnight, Susan. The three of us can meet for supper at the hotel. I will stay at Aunt Amelia's overnight and see you and your mother off in the morning on the steamer."

"Yes let's do that. I will leave instructions at the stable for my horse to be taken down to the steamer wharf tomorrow morning. I want to be there to put her in a safe place on the main lower freight deck with hay for the trip. My mother will be so pleased to see you_____. I have told her so much about you."

****

True to her word that she would send Agnes a letter, Susan sent a note at the end of September 1868. The wedding took place in a *wee* church, she wrote. She and her husband will set out in the morning to ride their horses to reach their new home on the other side of the mountains at Vermilion Forks in four days of travel through mountain meadows and wild flowers. She married the man she had told Agnes about: the man who gave her the horse and taught her to ride, and she was thrilled about being John Allison's wife.

Another letter followed in which she described how Allison came on horseback over the mountains from the Similkameen River valley in the British Columbia Interior, where they will settle to make a home and start to ranch. Agnes read the letter aloud to herself in her bedroom,

He did not come alone, but with a string of fine horses and three young Indian cowboys to go on ahead to hunt for game and to make camp and light campfires for us to follow up on. Of course, he and I had light moments together when we fell behind on purpose. John put one of the Indians in charge of the horses, calling him a wrangler to denote his responsibility for the horses. He could ride like a madman if he had to, but most of the time he talked to the horses in a quiet voice, and the horses did what he told them to do. Such wonderful food the young Indians cooked for us to eat around the campfire: pots of strong tea with fish and game they caught, bacon, and a new kind of bread to me roasted on the fire. The Indian who did most of the cooking also led our little party on the trail in the wild with a bell sounding to warn off bears that could be dangerous if startled and taken by surprise with cubs nearby. The snow on the ground had all gone. In no hurry to end the journey, I did not count the days and nights we rode on ridge trails and across mountain meadows and camped in the midst of a wilderness of late summer wild flowers blooming in the green grass until we wended our way down from the heights to the place we will make our new home. I am glad I did not continue to hesitate over John's proposal. His plan to ranch at Vermilion Forks where the Tulameen runs into the main Similkameen River lit the spark for me to see a future together. We intend to raise cattle for the New Westminster market with horses, cowboys, and an annual cattle drive to the steamers at Hope. Perhaps he will let me come, too. John talks of bringing cattle up from California to strengthen the stock of our herd, and he says we can make money mining in the nearby hills. I see him as a simply wonderful man to start an empire of our own with.

Keeping in touch with friends in town in Victoria and local gossip, Agnes heard not a word linking Gaudin with anyone, least of all Susan, which made it all the more possible for her to keep dreams of a life with him dancing in her head.

6

GAUDIN DELAYED

Gaudin never doubted his decision to ship out again on his first day ashore in London after a year away at sea. On that day in May 1865, three years ago, Captain Herd said to him: 'You come with your last captain's recommendation after six years sea-time as Mate in the barque *Josephine*, and before that as Mate in the *Ocean Bride*. My Congratulations Gaudin! Learn everything you can from Captain Adamson.'

Jumping at the opportunity to step up, he stowed his kit and gear in the finest ship's chief officer's cabin he had ever seen. He would be away for yet another year at sea, now as the Mate in the Hudson's Bay Company Flagship the *Prince of Wales* equipped with nothing but the best in men and ship's gear. Over the next three years he sailed 100,000 miles or more on two voyages around Cape Horn to the British Crown Colonies in the Pacific Northwest, thereby adding to his sea-time and experience. Captain Adamson enabled him to find shore time in the town named Victoria where he made many friends, perhaps a fine young woman there to marry?

On the return of the *Prince of Wales* to London in June 1868 a messenger came from the office with a message for Gaudin to proceed forthwith to the office of the Marine Superintendent. Captain David Herd sending for him this second time could mean a promotion to command a company vessel, but perhaps not? Although Gaudin confident he had done his job well and would have had his captain's recommendation, he could not be sure he not being called on the carpet on an allegation of some misdemeanour from his time in Victoria. But, no rebuke dealt out when they met. Herd told him of his promotion to command the new barque.

"Captain, you will be pleased to know the Committee of the Honourable Company has accepted my recommendation. You will take charge of the new barque not yet launched."

He knew the culture of the Honourable Company required him to show a degree of humility to speak his thanks, which he did with heartfelt gratitude. No doubt Captain Herd, himself, acted so when addressing his superiors at the Committee.

"Her name has not yet been decided," Herd said. "I will call you back from Jersey when she's ready for you to take charge. Fitting out with wire rigging will be a demanding job of work."

Charged with energy and optimism, Gaudin left London on leave to spend most of summer 1868 at his mother and father's house named Croix au Maître. First-born sons stayed to run farms in Jersey; other sons went to sea. As a 10-year-old destined for the sea he imagined voyages to the Far East when he joined the crowd lining the shore to see the Chinese Junk *Key-ying* out of Hong Kong anchored in St. Aubyn's Bay on her way to London from New York and Boston in March 1848. Now back again on leave he rode his horse to the quays in the harbours to renew friendships with men of the sea he had known since childhood. Called back to London early Gaudin listened as Herd said the launching of the new barque delayed, but in the meantime he would take charge of the company barque *Ocean Nymph* on a passage from London to Quebec City and on to Montreal. He should return in time for Christmas.

Gaudin's heart sank at the complications of this unexpected turn of events flashed in his mind. He had set his heart on getting the new ship, not such a battered old barque as the *Ocean Nymph*. Such a black joke to name that burdensome old vessel after the sprightly mythical young woman whose insatiable desire for physical union with yet another man left behind the littered wreckage of seamen by the score, spent. He knew fellow captains coveted the command of the remarkable new barque, much improved in design and blessed with the newest kind of deck machinery and appliances to enable a seaman to do the work of many with ease. Lady Luck could desert him in the next three months if others whose opinions mattered deemed his shiphandling of the *Ocean Nymph* open to criticism. And even if his run to Montreal and back brought him plaudits, an early readiness of the new ship to sail could have him returning to find the new barque gone to sea without him.

Gaudin knew Herd must have seen the look in his eyes. Neither spoke for a long moment. Herd broke the silence. "You may not know the Committee authorized me to buy the *Ocean Nymph* fresh off the builder's stocks at Quebec City in 1862," he said. "I know her as well as any man. I had her hull strengthened for ice, which made her ideal for the work the Company planned in northern waters. I called for commodious crew's quarters forward to be built in the 30-foot long foc'sle housework on deck for the demanding conditions in the Arctic. Seaworthy and strong, even though she will be a wet ship on deck at sea."

"Yes sir. I gather from all reports she is that."

"I took charge of her on voyages to Labrador in 1863-1864. Afterward the Company used her to make annual passages to York Factory and to Little Whale River on the eastern shore of Hudson Bay. Here, I will show you the chart in behind Belcher Isles. Then the Company sent her on a whaling expedition to Marble Island to winter in the ice with the crew living like Esquimaux clad in seal furcoats. Here, I am pointing to Marble Island in the upper northwest corner of Hudson Bay."

Putting on a wan smile, Gaudin knew he must make the best of it.

"I know how you spell *Esquimaux*, sir." Gaudin said. "Passing strange isn't it the Royal Navy took the Indians near Victoria to be calling the place where we anchor as ESQUIMALT Harbour. No connection at all, only a corruption of the local Indian place name as they speak it. But to get back to the *Ocean Nymph*, I am happy not to have spent time trying to sail through ice, sir."

"I was always able to depart York Factory in time to avoid being required to spend the winter there, hauled up on the shore to avoid ice damage. You may have icebergs to watch out for in the North Atlantic off Newfoundland, but you will not run into ice in the River or in the Gulf of St. Lawrence coming back if you depart Montreal in time. I am asking you to take the command."

"Where does she lie now, sir?"

"The mate and most of the crew are aboard loading the cargo in Shadwell Dock. You will have an experienced crew to help you over a rough spot. I sense the old crew will be eager for an itinerary lying farther south than the ship's usual haunts in the north. Your chief officer will expect you to hand in his Journal of the voyage to discuss with me on your return."

Gaudin captained the *Ocean Nymph* back to London three months later on 23 December 1868. He hurried to hand in the Journal[4]. The clerk at the Company office desk told him the Dover Watch Tower sent word the *Ocean Nymph* had passed inbound flying her number and that Captain Herd had left this note for him.

1-Captain Gaudin will remain in London.

2-The new barque *Lady Lampson* will lie at Blackwall shipyard for his inspection on 28 December.

3-Captain Gaudin will go aboard to begin to see to her fitting out.

Gaudin stayed at his lodgings at #5 West India Dock Road in town over Christmas. He wandered down to Blackwall Shipyard where men let him through the gate to see the tug bring in the *Lady Lampson* from the North Sea to lie alongside the wharf. Gaudin felt overcome by emotion in the magical moment the two of them saw each other. To himself he said, *Only a seaman will know what passes between us now, dear girl. You and I will get to know each other.*

Back in his room at his lodgings that night he began to write out a letter to send home to explain why he would not be coming this Christmas. Pulling out the desktop of his heavy mahogany ship's desk, he sat to write a long letter with pen and ink to tell his father of his new command : -

'*Dear Pater, I cannot be home this Christmas. I made a success of a stormy North Atlantic passage to Montreal and back in the barque Ocean Nymph. The Company has entrusted me now with the charge of a new wooden barque, which has been christened the Lady Lampson. She is built with iron frames, wire rigging and the latest sail handling mechanical winches for a smaller crew to sail the ship. Survey enabled Lloyd's to class the vessel A1. I have orders to stay in London to take charge of her fitting out and to make her ready for a 20,000-mile voyage around Cape Horn to the Pacific Northwest and back. Without taking into effect the outstretch of her curved bow and long bowsprit and the sweep up from the water aft of the quarterdeck, she runs 121 feet in the length of the waterline of her black-painted hull. The Chinese Junk the Key-ying, which you took me to see at St. Aubyn's Bay in 1848, extended for a longer length, but the Lady Lampson will be a much more usable vessel with less windage to hamper sailing to windward. I am much pleased to have command of her. A prominent long bowsprit jib boom will soar high ahead when I order it up and installed after departure to enable jib sails to be set on stays leading forward to it. The design called for expensive teak woodwork on deck. At the stern counter, which sweeps up aft from the rudderpost, those who find themselves astern of her will see emblazoned in gold-coloured letters: Lady Lampson, and under the name, her port of registry, London. My time and experience as Chief Officer in the Prince of Wales under Captain Adamson should allow me to have a fast passage in the new ship. I made two voyages in the Prince of Wales to the Pacific Northwest. I am now 31 and have been at sea for 14 years. I am no stranger to this part of the London River and know how to handle vessels in the London Docks. I do have a friend to spend Christmas with in London, but I am champing at the bit to go aboard to take charge of my new command. I have lost track of where my four brothers would be sailing now. I have not seen them for years. Have you any news of them? Have they married yet? I am hoping to meet and marry a wholesome young woman on Vancouver's Island and bring her back to live in Jersey. Perhaps you and Mater and family will help me find a place for her to live and raise a family and you all will welcome her. Your affectionate son, James.'*

Captain Herd called him to his office early in the New Year to talk about the Chief Officer's Journal he had been told to keep on the voyage to Montreal. Both had already been on board the new *Lady Lampson* after Christmas to confer on lists of matters remaining needful to be done. Herd came free of other pressing matters, and they soon met to talk about the voyage to the Gulf of St. Lawrence and Montreal in the *Ocean Nymph* during the last few months.

Gaudin heard loud voices coming through the walls to the outer office where men spoke in whispers. Ship's officers in the Hudson's Bay Company Marine Service knew this could be a long wait.

Warm memories came flooding in of his life since Captain Herd gave him the boost to join the Hudson's Bay Company Marine Service in May 1866. Unattached to any woman, Gaudin felt mounting pressure from his mother and sister Marie to marry and settle down, to settle down as much as a seaman away for a year at a time could.

The routine of his annual voyages from London to the Pacific Northwest allowed him the perquisite to spend a month each summer on leave at his parents' home on the island of Jersey off the coast of France, an English possession having a unique history of Independence from the English Crown_____not a Crown Colony by any stretch. Going home during parts of the summers of 1867 and 1868 had not landed him any closer to finding a woman to marry. His experience with the fleeting smiles of the young daughters on the island left him with a sure sense they remain distant, stolid, and without a fire to kindle. Perhaps they knew better. Perhaps he didn't have the spark to kindle their fires, but that he doubted. He knew some men at sea content without a woman waiting for them, but the mere sight and scent of some women he had seen elsewhere and the way they walked and dressed made his senses rise to lingering peaks of desire. He decided to keep on with his plan to bring a bride home to Jersey as a prize to show everyone the kind of woman he could catch.

This meeting with Herd would take time. More than mere conversation, this serious piece of business might last well into the afternoon and extend past the midnight hour at Captain Herd's house. Gaudin knew he could end up sleeping on a couch under a blanket and staying for breakfast the next morning. Captains in the company knew old Herd found enjoyment bringing back memories re-living his early days in Sail by having his captains come in and talk about the voyage they'd returned from. These meetings with his captains also gave him the opportunity to better judge the character and temperament of those he put in charge of vessels in the company fleet. Gaudin counted on taking advantage of the opportunity to keep Herd thinking well of him. Why not paint a good picture of myself, he thought as he waited. He could keep up his end of a conversation.

The door to Herd's office opened and men of business filed out in silence. Herd came out to greet Gaudin in good cheer and asked him to come into his office. A steward knocked on a side door and carried in a large silver tray laden with food and drink for a mid-day meal of slices of cold roast beef, hot bread rolls, chutney from India, and boiled coffee laced with rum.

On the way into the room Gaudin reported he had ordered tugs to move the *Lady Lampson* from the shipyard to lie alongside in the unique wide circular basin in Blackwall Dock and that the Chief Officer and crew have been working to load the cargo for the Pacific Northwest.

Herd nodded to indicate his satisfaction.

"Before you go ahead with your account of the passage to the Gulf of St Lawrence, tell me, do you like Command?"

"I like it sir! For the first time aboard ship I felt a real sense the Mates and the crew stood on the *que vive* with their eyes alight and minds alert, waiting, nay expecting, me to be giving orders. I felt free for the first time in my life to make my own decisions. I make my ship sail as I want and *May the Devil take the Hindmost*"

Herd laughed.

"Yes Gaudin, but not everyone can handle the responsibility. I found it best when no one was telling me what I should be doing, particularly someone from the shipowners' office."

"But in truth, sir, I enjoy talking to someone who is interested in what I have to say about the voyage."

Gaudin followed Captain Herd into the adjoining room with a long table. They stood looking down on marine charts, rolled out and held down flat with dull brass weights the Navy would have kept polished. They took to nearby chairs. Captain Herd lit his tobacco pipe and invited Gaudin to fill his pipe from the urn of tobacco on the table at the side of the room.

With entries in the journal to help him string the recollections together Gaudin began his account.

"Some of this you already know, sir. You came on board with Captain Adamson for the departure and stayed aboard until we put you ashore at Gravesend."

"Yes Gaudin, I have a note you took the *Ocean Nymph* out from the Shadwell Entrance to the London Docks on 4 September 1868 at 2 p.m. high water into the bend in the Thames named the Pool, which lies downriver of the Tower Bridge, upstream of the more recent additions to the London Docks. The ebb about to begin, the tug began to tow you down the London River. Adamson and I came aboard to show our support of you to the crew. Scuttlebutt had settled it: this is your first command, but you had lots of sea-time, the most recent as mate on our long runs to the Pacific Northwest."

"Yes sir, I knew that, and I appreciated your support. The mate dressed the ship with all signal flags. The company house flag flew from the maintop."

"Yes, Gaudin, a fine sight to show the other vessels in the Basin and also on the River until you ordered it down. Do go on to talk to me about what you had your Chief Officer write in your ship's journal. From now on I will have you make the entries in the ship's *official logbook*, not a journal, a far more seamanlike a name."

Gaudin picked up again with his account.

"The paddlewheel steam tug *Macgregor* put up a line to the men at the bow to pick up and bend to the towing hawser. The Thames River pilot Mister Irvine stood on the quarterdeck with us. A slow trip down the London River followed in thick fog."

Herd said he remembered.

"Four hours later Adamson and I left the ship to go ashore in a boat I hired to come out from the south bank of the River at Gravesend.

Sitting in the stern sheets, he and I turned to look back to see the *Ocean Nymph* at anchor disappear behind in the fog. Please go on, Gaudin."

"On the way down the River I had the crew rig out the jib boom from the stemhead."

"Yes, Gaudin, and you brought it down again coming back into the London River on the homeward passage from Montreal to save tie-up charges at the dock. The Basin charges by overall length, as you know."

"Yes, sir, and we did the same before handing down the hawser to the tug taking us under tow at Quebec City to lessen chance of collision in a close quarters situation during the tow upriver to Montreal. I could see little of the low Thames estuary shoreline lying distant to the north and south. By 10 p.m. the next evening tug and tow arrived off the sandbank named the Mouse and we anchored. I am told a small low island named the Cat lies near but I have never seen it. Maybe this a joke played on novices to spend time looking out for the Cat. Either I have been passing it in the dark or it has been foggy."

Gaudin told Herd they anchored to wait for the next tide, and he continued.

"I mustered the crew to set the two Deck Watches, Port and Starboard, and I asked the mate to set an anchor watch. At 3:30 a.m. I roused up all hands to weigh anchor. With no wind to set sail I ordered the tug to tow our heavy and well laden vessel past Margate and make the turn into the English Channel at North Foreland. Not enough wind yet to dismiss the tug, so I gave the signal to carry on close to shore in the deepwater channel between the shoreline of England and the Goodwin Sands."

Herd interrupted, "The fog would now have cleared to show smokestack smoke rising in the still air from other steam tugs towing sailing vessels in both directions. I remember well such a sight. By morning you would have been passing many vessels at anchor in the Downs within sight of smoke rising from the chimneys of houses in Deal. Many a seaman in that lot anchored there had not seen home for a long time and must have been longing to go ashore."

"That says it true, sir. The *Macgregor* towed us down the channel inshore of the Goodwin Sands."

"Did you know an island named Lomea under the lordship of the last Saxon Earl Godwine of Wessex stood there before it disappeared under the sea in a great storm in the years before the Norman Conquest?"

"Yes sir, I stayed in school until I was 17. My schoolmaster told me about Lomea and that its remains now form the large sandbank in the Channel with the shelter behind it in the roadstead named the Downs for ships to anchor. We know it as a splendid anchorage for outbound sailing vessels to wait for tide or weather. Inbound vessels know it a safe place to wait for a berth to come clear."

"Now please go ahead with your account, Gaudin. I interrupted you."

Gaudin went on to describe how the tug kept chugging on into the English Channel past the point of land named the South Foreland to reach a position off the town of Folkestone before passing the White Cliffs of Dover with no wind yet for him to order sail to be set.

"But by 11 a.m. on 6 September the wind came up for me to send Mister Irvine off in the *Macgregor*. The tug put him on a pilot boat seen in the distance coming out under sail from the shore. I found my new voice of command beginning to speak in conversational tones to my mates. I gave my orders to set sail in the light wind that had risen out of the east. Instead of calling out as I did when I was mate with a voice that could be heard at the masthead, now as a ship's master, I give my orders to the mates in normal tone of voice. They know I expect them to make it happen as I have ordered. Wearing the white cloth gloves of a Hudson's Bay Company ship's command, I kept my station to weather on my quarterdeck; and the mates moved forward on the deck to work the crew."

"Yes Gaudin, a ship's captain does not go forward except to deal with terrible trouble and even then not until necessary. The foredeck belongs to the Mate, who can resent interference. Please go on from where you left off."

"The crew you provided me knew how to sail the ship. I gained confidence when I saw them on deck and up on the yards carrying out my orders with skill and enthusiasm. Entering or leaving harbour requires all hands on deck, as does tacking ship in strong winds or wearing ship in mountainous seas that could poop us. In that state I had the Mate forward and the Second Mate midships and all hands on deck to handle the sails. I found my old voice of command again."

After a pause Gaudin picked up to say he gave orders to anchor the *Ocean Nymph* off Folkestone when the wind out of the east fell off to a calm by noon.

"The incoming flood tide in the Channel would have driven us back had we not anchored," he said. "The tide current began to let up by 5: 30 p.m. We heaved up her anchor with sea shanteys to ease the work, and I gave the order to make all plain sail."

Gaudin described how the *Ocean Nymph* made her way west along England's southern shore with lower and upper sails set to fill and harden in the light wind from behind. Gaudin's adventure in command began with the coast of England close at hand and the coast of France on the other side of the Channel scarcely visible, low through haze.

"At midnight Dungeness Point lay off the starboard bow distant four miles."

"Yes Gaudin, I can see it all now, thank you. Your ship is moving well under sail."

"Yes sir, early next morning 8 September found the ship sailing in fine weather. I ordered the foretop and lower studdingsails set outboard of the rest from the yard ends to catch more of the light wind coming out of the east. By 9 a.m. we passed Beachy Head and 12 hours later we passed the lighthouse at St. Catherine's Point."

"Sighting that point on the Isle of Wight on an outward passage and leaving it swiftly behind proved always to be a good omen for me, Gaudin."

"At midnight I could see the lights on the shore at Portland. The next day came on with more of the same good sailing in a fair breeze with the South Coast of England remaining visible in pleasant hazy weather. Such a joy for me to see the *Ocean Nymph* passing Prawle Point, Eddystone Rock Lighthouse, and also the light at the Lizard in quick succession by the time darkness of night fell. The tide aided by the following wind hustled us past all three of them to clear where I calculated Land's End would be. I could not see it in the haze. The ship rode the ocean swells by midnight when we sighted St. Agnes' light on the Scilly Isles. I took a compass bearing on it, calculated our distance from it at 10 miles, and drew an -X -on the chart to mark the point of my departure."

Gaudin did not need to tell Herd he converted the compass bearing to a true bearing to mark on the chart, nor say that up to now this had been no more than coastal piloting. Nor did he need to say from here onward each day would begin at noon when the sun reaches its highest point in the sky for the noon sextant sight. Marking the time as shown by the ship's chronometers set for time at Greenwich and making a calculation of the difference between noon local time and Greenwich time, he can proceed to calculate the ship's position at sea beyond sight of land and set the course to be steered.

Gaudin continued without further interruption as Herd listened with close interest.

"Our *Ocean Nymph* sailed on a total of 73 miles to her noon position on 10 September with studdingsails remaining set to good effect and to make the most of the light winds out of the east," he said. "This worked out to an average speed of 6 knots since midnight to begin to cross the North Atlantic on a track of *North West by West ½ West*. This deep beamy little sailing vessel cannot really sail much faster without big waves and a gale pushing from behind."

"This old vessel I put you in charge of must have made a housefull of creaks and groans you had not heard before?"

"Yes sir, and it reminded me of one more reason for silence on deck, which is to let the captain listen to his ship speak to him in the only way she knows how_____. The grizzled old Mate told me he had never seen such a good beginning for a crossing of the North Atlantic."

"Your story may say something about the advantage to be gained by leaving London in early September, and not in February."

"Yes sir, I expect a stormy time of it when I take the *Lady Lampson* out to sea in the New Year."

"The Committee cannot stand for your new vessel to be tied up to wait for a better season to sail. Go ahead with your account."

"Yes sir, of course. By next morning the light wind continued to blow from behind in fine weather. By noon my calculations showed the ship made good 99 miles on a track of *West ½ North*, but the wind hauled around to northward and began to blow a fresh breeze out of the north-north-east. I took in the studdingsails. The ship sailed on a close reach to the northwest with the freshening breeze keeping the decks heeled over to port as we punched through heavy swell. The ship began to lurch, knocking spray to windward, which came back to drench us. Waves came aboard to sweep the deck, shipping huge dollops of the sea frantic to find an exit over the side through the scuppers, washing knee-deep on deck. High bulwarks please the passengers, but they keep shipped seawater on deck for longer than we like before it all runs overside. By midnight the ship ran in a cross-sea with the wind still blowing fresh out of the north-north-east, rolling from side to side in slow movements to bring seas aboard at the end of each roll. I ordered the Royals brought down to ease the motion of the ship and to lessen the amount of the water being shipped aboard. By 2 a.m. on 12 September I came on deck to order all light fore-and-aft sails brought in lest they be blown out in the rising wind. At daylight I ordered the t'gallant sails brought down, leaving the ship sailing with topsails and main and foresail, but the ship did not slow her steady *pacing* west through these seas. The word pacing scarcely the word to describe the ship's movement in the seas as this old vessel shouldered her way through, refusing to be denied passage. Reminded me that the square cut sails, the main and the foresail, and the topsails, the t'gallants and the Royals each set flying above each other on the main and the foremast, derive from the wind a force that *lifts* the ship along. The fore-and-aft sails help in other ways, but they do not lift."

"Yes, Gaudin, we often talk about driving a sailing vessel through rough seas, but we forget to mention that the square rigged sails tend to keep us up on top of the waves by their lifting effect_____. You described the way in which she *shouldered* her way through: indeed, she had a mind of her own at times when I had her."

Turning a page of the journal, Gaudin continued with his account.

"Seven days out found the ship sailing on a close reach in fine weather," he said. "By noon I calculated a near seven-knot run of 164 miles noon-to-noon on a track of *West ½ South* with the wind continuing to come hard out of the north-north-east, but soon we were running under reduced sail in drizzling rain. By nightfall, the wind having moderated, I gave an order to set all possible sail, and we sailed westward across the North Atlantic into the darkness of night."

Gaudin turned a page to continue.

"13 September found the ship sailing on a close reach in fine weather steering a course of *West by North* in a wind blowing out of the north," he said. "What a wonderful change in the sea! We made 124 miles noon-to-noon heeled over to port. Now we are cutting through the waves with little disturbance and no rolling_____. Daylight on 14 September presented with the ship facing a freshening wind blowing variably from the west or west-south-west, which helped us to sail northwestward."

"I remember that kind of morning, Gaudin. Keeps the helmsman on his toes to keep the sails full and the captain alive to the course being made good. You are no steamer steering a set course, day in and day out."

"My sextant sight at noon showed the ship made 120 miles since the previous noon. The seas rose to make the ship heave and pitch. I decided to bring down the Royals again to ease the ship's motion. With daylight ending we sailed into a more troubled sea under lowering dark cloud and squalls of wind and rain. A big storm began to make up. We can always expect the worst weather in March and September in equinox time wherever we are in the temperate parts of the world."

"Do not forget to include December, Gaudin."

"Yes sir, that's correct, of course. How can I ever forget the storms the barque encountered on our return from Montreal in December. Before I get to that, I have more to say about the passage westward. After midnight on 15 September, nine-days out from the Downs, I found the ship pushing against a strong head sea and making scarcely any way through it. By the early light I discovered the t'gallant part of the foremast had carried away under strain. I gave orders to go aloft to dismantle the wreckage and send down the yards for the ship's carpenter to make a new foretop while we made little headway under reduced sail."

At noon Gaudin calculated the ship's position at 49°29' North and 22°52' West, which showed how much distance remained to cross the North Atlantic.

"Through the evening and into the night the ship lurched into a strong head sea and shipped much water on deck," he said. "By next day's evening the carpenter and I conferred to decide the adequacy of the repair. I gave the order to send up the fore t'gallant mast replacement and the t'gallant yard, which would be held in position on the mast by chain link. The repair done, the wind changed direction to come in a moderate breeze out of the north. I set the course for the helmsman to steer *West-North-West* in hazy weather with all plain sail set. But the wind fell off by noon, at which time the sextant sight showed we had come in the right direction for a distance of only 93 miles."

"I remember your Journal stated the repair did not hold."

"It did not hold, sir, nor did the lighter wind and clear weather, which ended in a freshening wind showing sign of becoming a strong gale out of the north. A slanting wind-driven curtain of dark cloud and rain hit the ship by noon on 17 September, 11-days out from the Downs. All Hands on Decks coped with the condition as the helmsman bore off to put the wind behind us, which took the force of the wind off the sails to allow the men freedom to hand them in."

Gaudin spoke again after a long moment of silence.

"The noon sight showed we made only 72 miles to the southwest noon-to-noon," he said. "The afternoon ended with a terrible noise on deck. To my surprise the wind in a squall tore down the repaired fore t'gallant mast, which only yesterday the ship's carpenter had built to my satisfaction. And the yard broke in the slings. I ordered men to go aloft to send the whole mess down to deck so we can work on it when the seas coming aboard permit_____. A cold wet piece of work."

Gaudin then spoke of the wind having made large waves form on the surface of the ocean with darkness beginning.

"The wind continued to rise in strength, the wave crests being blown off in streaks of foam running on the surface of the sea," he said. "The sight prompted me to give orders to send men aloft to take down the Royals and all fore-and-aft light sails lest the force of the wind blow them out. The wind out of the north rose from Beaufort Scale Force 6 to freshen into Force 8 by the time the men returned down to the deck. The sails remaining set could not bear this burden, so I gave orders to bring in the main t'gallant sail and the main topmast staysail. My next order followed to send hands aloft out on the yards to reef the topsails and foresail. By 8 p.m. the ship tossed and lurched in squalls. High seas, not visible until close aboard and threatening, marched in on us from all directions. I gave an order to bring in the mainsail, the jib, and the spanker, leaving set only reef'd topsails and foresail. Violent squalls came down on us through the night, the ship making bad weather of it with the decks awash. In the driving rain I gave the order at 1 a.m. to send hands aloft in the dark to bring in the foresail and furl the upper topsails to their yards to lessen the strain on the ship. The storm continued for the rest of the night and into the next day, 18 September."

"Amazing that more men are not lost overboard, Gaudin. I know the picture of the ship rolling and lurching in heavy sea, and the hands knowing they must keep working the ship or they will become casualties at sea."

Turning a page of the journal to mark the beginning of a new part of the story, Gaudin continued with his account.

"At first light, 4 a.m., with the wind screaming out of the north in low dark clouds, the apparition of a barque close aboard flashed in front of us," he said, "sailing to eastwards under only close-reefed topsails. I could see mouths open on deck bellowing at us, but no sound of voices made it through the noise of the storm. We were close enough aboard to make out the faces of the men on the other deck, but in an instant all was gone from our sight. Their first glimpse of us would have been our bows close aboard plunging into the seas, throwing sheets of spray to loo'ard_____. I cannot say we would have seen each other in time to avoid collision had we met in worse visibility. I say this notwithstanding the vastness of the ocean and the lookout we keep in the dark, alert for the loom and lamp of other vessels closing fast. I am sure some ships reported missing have gone down in a storm by collision at night with seas closing over them to bring a blessed silence."

"The landsman cannot know the sounding noise on the deck of a sailing vessel in the hours of a storm at sea," Herd said, "much of it being moans and screams from the masts and rigging standing up to it all. And how quiet the time that comes afterwards."

"Yes sir, that is so. By noon I calculated we made good only 67 miles from previous noon. As the gale lessened by 4 p.m., I ordered men sent aloft to set the foresail again and to set reefed upper topsails on the main and on the foremast. By 5 p.m. in even better conditions I could set the spanker sail again, and the jib, and the mainsail. By 8 p.m. the wind lessened again, so I ordered men sent aloft to take the reefs out of the upper topsails and to set the main topmast staysail and the main t'gallant sail to keep up the ship's speed. Such *busy-ness* keeps men tired and cranky."

Captain Herd sat still as he listened and said nothing. Gaudin knew he might be re-living his times at sea in the same part of the grey North Atlantic.

"The wind lessened further again by midnight," Gaudin said. "The ship sailed on to the west-north-west, dropping her bows into a heavy ocean swell and rolling from one side to the other, which kept the decks awash. At 6 a.m. on 19 September in improving conditions I gave the order to set all possible sail."

Gaudin turned to another page.

"The next noon sight showed the ship had come 137 miles in the right direction over the last 24 hours," he said. "Late afternoon with the ship's heading steered to the northwest, I gave orders to set additional sail consisting of the foretop and lower studdingsails to catch more of the wind now coming up out of the east-north-east _____. A schooner with dories piled on her deck standing to the southeast made a sudden appearance out of the haze to cross our bows. The rain and scud cloud came down to take her out of sight in two blinks of the eye. The next day, 20 September, two weeks out from the Downs, presented in the morning with light winds and continuing haze that reduced visibility. Slow progress now even though we carried all possible sail. The noon sextant sight showed the ship had come 103 miles in the last 24 hours to reach a position in the North Atlantic far off the Newfoundland coast at 47°14' North 33°40' West. In the afternoon with a shout from the lookout, *Sail ho! Close off the starboard bow,* another barque loomed up to cross our bows and pass out of sight to the north in several blinks of the eye. No time to speak her. I cannot tell you anything about her."

"It takes a knowledgeable person to know what you mean when you say you could not *speak* another vessel," Herd said, "or what you mean when you say passing vessels *spoke* in the past tense."

"Yes sir, people may think we are calling out to each other by speaking tubes, so as to be speaking to each other. Sometimes that does happen, but most of the time we do not want to lose time by stopping with decks rising and falling in the swell, sails flapping, and the wind blowing in the rigging for ship's masters to call out to each other. Such a meeting on the vastness of the ocean might seem a blessed occurrence in the turmoil and tedium of an ocean passage, but a captain won't want to take the time. We fly signal flags showing our ship's number and the name of our port of registry to be passed on to the Lloyd's Agent at the other vessel's destination for owners and all of the marine insurance underwriters who have an interest in knowing we remain afloat. The acknowledgement flag in response tells us we have spoken to the other as we pass at speed for each to soon see the last of the other, topsails-down on the horizon."

"Do go on, Gaudin, I have interrupted you again."

"Yes sir. The next day 21 September brought about a big change in the weather for the better even though followed by fog that stayed with us for days."

Turning pages of the Journal as he spoke, Gaudin explained that four days later in fog upon nearing a position calculated to be a safe distance off Cape Race, the southeast tip of Newfoundland, he turned the ship to head west to enter Cabot Strait, shaping a course to slant past the southern coasts of St Pierre & Miquelon Islands, 22-miles off.

"During the next few days with the fog lifting, the ship carried all possible sail and we made good time westwards with a fair wind in light seas," he said. "The carpenter made chafing battens. Taking the opportunity offered by the light seas and the fair wind, I ordered crew to go aloft to put seizing on the battens and repair rigging. But the thick fog returned on 24 September and a light wind came up out of the west to oppose us. We cast a lead line at 47°02' North 47°57' West to find sandy bottom at 67 fathoms. A blanket of thick fog descended all around us again on 27 September. We continued to run in fog with a freshening wind, which did nothing to disperse it. By noon the wind rising in strength required me to bring in the Royals. On the fog lifting we soon caught a glimpse of a barque passing eastward under reefed topsails a little too far away to speak her. I reckoned our noon position at 47°11' North 50°06' West, a position distant 122 miles from Cape Race. We continued to tack westward with all possible sail set. By afternoon the wind and slanting dark walls of rainsqualls hit us hard out of the north. I brought in light sails and the fore t'gallant sails. The *Nymph* now lurched into a strong swell, shipping much water on deck. Next day 28 September found us lessening wind. Set all possible sail and ran in heavy rain. Spoke the British Ship *Wabino* bound for Miramichi. Noon position at 47°26' North 53°14' West showed 141 miles made good since yesterday on a track of *West by South ¾ South*."

Herd remarked many shipments of lumber from New Brunswick have been coming by Sail out of that Bay named Miramichi.

Gaudin nodded and carried on.

"Next day 29 September the thick fog returned in the dark of the early morning hours. Sailing on a course of *North West by West* took us onward to a noon position of 46°35' North 56°40' West, which showed 134 miles made good. Cast the lead in the morning and hauled it up to show a bottom of shells at a depth of 35 fathoms. On a course of *North West ½ North* the depth continued to show the same on casting the lead again. No wind of any consequence_____. Next day a noon position at 46°27' North 57°44' West showed we made only 46 miles since yesterday. We tacked westwards in light northerly wind, but on the wind changing to come out of the west in a strong breeze, we switched to tack northwards from a position I calculated to be distant 95 miles from Cape Ray, Newfoundland and 128 miles from the lighthouse on St. Paul's Islands. I intended to say Cape Ray, not to be confused with Cape Race many miles to the east on the south coast of Newfoundland."

"Fog would have made this an anxious time for you, Gaudin, as you closed with the Maritime Provinces shoreline."

"Yes sir, it was that. The next day ended with us making little distance in a strong gale of wind with squalls of rain and hail. The ship lurched into a heavy sea out of the northwest, making bad weather of it. Handed the jib, furled the courses and reefed the topsails to ease the motion of the ship. On the gale ending I ordered the mainsail and jib set at 4 a.m. Two hours later I ordered men sent up the masts to take out the reefs of the topsails and set the t'gallant sails to maintain speed through the water, but by 2 p.m. we found ourselves becalmed. This lasted into all of next day with the ship rolling on a sea surface that would not remain still."

"How did you keep the crew busy in the calms?"

"I kept the people re-bending sails throughout and reeving upper topsail spilling lines, and I had the carpenter nailing copper to the rails and wedging up the rudder head rendered somewhat ajar from recent hard sailing. May I go on sir?"

"Yes, of course."

"No land in sight during this period of calm. Cloud prevented a noon sight to establish position, but dead reckoning showed ship's position distant 53 miles to the southeast of Scatarie Island Lighthouse on an estimated true bearing of *North West by West.*"

"Yes, Gaudin, I know the Light, which lies north of the headland named Cape Breton and north again from Louisburg, which stands farther south down the coast of Nova Scotia."

"You say correct, sir."

Gaudin continued.

"The wind got up again on 3 October, 28-days out from the Downs, just after dark on sighting the light at Scatarie Island Lighthouse clear enough on a bearing *West-North-West* estimated 12-miles distant," he said. "In the morning I could fix the ship's position at 10 a.m. by cross-bearings on Scatarie Lighthouse and Flint Island Lighthouse, both now visible to me in daylight, each compass bearing adjusted to *True* to draw out on the marine chart to mark our position. I tacked ship to eastward to gain more sea room to cross Cabot Strait."

Herd asked about the wind for the crossing.

"This day we had brisk breezes from northward," Gaudin replied. "We tacked all the way across Cabot Strait on one board to make landfall on the coast of Newfoundand at La Poile Bay, then turned about to make Westing on the next board. We tacked ship again and again, night and day, back and forth from one side of the Strait to the other against the wind to gain entrance into the Gulf of St. Lawrence. I might be excused for thinking the St. Lawrence River pushed out this far to sea,

but I found the river not to blame: the wind and tide stopped us getting past the new revolving light at St. Paul's Islands, which stand in the
middle of the entrance to the Gulf of St. Lawrence between Newfoundland and Cape Breton Island."

Gaudin described the prolonged zigzag track of the vessel, which
he referred to as *long boards*, by which he sought to get past St. Paul's
Islands to enter the Gulf of St. Lawrence. He turned another page of
the Journal before continuing.

"Just imagine my frustration, sir. The next landfall on the north side
of Cabot Strait at Cape Ray showed us having made good only 50 miles
to the west from La Poile Bay where we had been two days ago. We
turned about again and headed southwestward. On 6 October we were
still not into the Gulf of St. Lawrence. For two days the *Nymph* made
ponderous lurches to windward into a strong swell and a freshening wind
out of the west. Handing in the mainsail and upper topsails did little
else than ease the ship's motion. On 7 October I ordered in the foresail
at 2 p.m. on the ship making bad weather of the wind and sea that made
up in clearing weather. Four other Sail spaced out on the horizon in no
better a position than we were. Cape Ray in sight, but now bearing to
the *North East*. On the wind lessening in strength we set all plain sail
and tacked again. On 8 October we sailed in light variable winds on
a course of *North West ½ North*. A light southwest breeze sprang up at
7 a.m. Clear weather gave us a bearing on Cape Ray 10-miles distant
to the north, which gave proof we had made headway the previous day
bashing forward into the seas. We turned about again_____. By
4 p.m. we sighted St. Paul's Lighthouse to the *West-North-West*. By 10
p.m. we passed the light at Bird Rocks_____. Early next morning 9
October the wind surprised us to came on strong out of the southwest
to send us in the right direction. But it did not last: overnight the wind
left us, and the next day 10 October presented with light weather off the
Gaspé Peninsula. By 6 a.m. the wind freshened over rising seas to make
me bring in the main t'gallant sail and send men scrambling to reef the
topsails and hand in the mainsail. On the wind easing off and hauling
to northward I ordered men up to take out the topsail reefs, and we set
the main t'gallant and the mainsail. But the wind fell calm in sight of
Cape Gaspé, now closer at estimated 12 miles to the northwest."

"That unusual land formation always a remarkable landmark."

"Yes sir, it is that. We drifted in a calm all night, the silence broken
only by shipboard creaks and groaning sounds. Next noon a light air

from southward came up. After passing seven miles off Cape Rosiers in company with a fleet of sailing vessels bound up to the entrance of the Gulf of St. Lawrence with us, we stood away from them to northward, tacking across the Gulf to the west of Anticosti Island in light airs. We could not gain entrance for several days, often becalmed when the wind fell off completely."

"I know that sea condition, which leaves the sails slatting loose on their yards. You must have wondered how the fleet of ships you saw bound up at Rosier would fare close in the South Shore?"

"Sir, they may have found wind, but they will have been facing the full seaward thrust of the St. Lawrence River running the strongest. For us, you will understand the fitful winds for the next six days provided no rest to the crew as they sail-handled the ship to catch zephyrs on one short tack after another to gain advantage. Following which, for much of two cool days the *Nymph* lay in haze in the water alone on an empty flat calm sea, ruffled with occasional light airs from one direction and then another. At 8 a.m. on 12 October 1868 we stood northward in a fresh breeze to fetch the red earth banks on the shores on both sides of Pointe Jambon at noon before the wind dropped off again. A fresh breeze came up in the next day's afternoon. Under cloudy skies we tacked every hour against the wind in the Gulf of St. Lawrence between Gaspé Peninsula and Point de Montes Lighthouse. We sailed an open sea, free of ocean swell and without landmarks. Later we found we had made progress to windward along the North Shore of Quebec toward where the channel will narrow to a 25-mile width. In the night I climbed the masthead to sight the Point de Montes light over the horizon and the lamp lights of six ships inshore of us plying to windward under the North Shore. They'd been looking for an offshore night wind to help them up into the narrowing waters that will take all of us into the inner waters leading to the St. Lawrence River. Next day we tacked through waters thick with small fishing boats from the villages marked on the marine chart without names. At nightfall we had Pointe des Montes light in sight, this time closer, about 10-miles distant. The wind dropped off to a calm on 16 October, but the flood tide carried the ship drifting mid-channel, making the distance to anchor closer in to shore, there to await the next flood tide or a good wind. After passing Point des Montes on 17 October a fine sailing breeze sprang up from northwestward to allow us to ease the yards and sail free on a slanting reach to southwestward. The fair wind continued to allow us to take full advantage of the tide. Before day's end we sighted Point au Père, which we know as Father Point on the Quebec South Shore. On 18 October, 42 days out from the Downs, we picked up Mister Dumont, the Quebec Sea Pilot in the outer approaches to the 5-mile wide narrowing inner parts of the Gulf of St. Lawrence downstream of Ile Verte, or Green Island. With the Pilot aboard to show the way for the next 90 miles to Quebec in thick fog and on a port tack off Iles de Kamouraska, we soon hit and cut down the English brig *Louisa* and sank her. The islands lie off the southern shore of the Gulf of St. Lawrence and upstream from the place Pilot Dumont calls Rivière du-Loup. We left the brig sinking after we picked up her captain and crew. They told us they were heading outbound from Quebec City to Labrador."

"The collision must have come at slow speed for both of you?"

"Yes sir, she'd sunk US had she been larger. I recollect we had been making slow progress in the silence and dampness of thick fog at night. We did not suspect another vessel to be in the vicinity. With a knot in my stomach today I remember the shouts of alarm at the same moment from the lookouts on both vessels, which came too late to turn the vessels away from each other. Our much heavier vessel sank the other, fortunately with no loss of life."

"Gaudin, although often in wide waters not another vessel in company, sound signals in fog must come to be customary for all sailing vessels."

"Yes sir, especially to say what tack the sailing vessel is on to warn another vessel to stand clear and give the right-of-way to the vessel on a port tack. Our ship's hulls are built of wood but when heavily laden, the vessel goes down fearful quick, often by the bow. What a terrible end to be trapped below decks and go down in a ship collision."

"Marine Insurance may have to pay part of the claim of the *Louisa's* owner."

"Yes sir, I understand Admiralty Court judges come into court with a mind to share fault and apportion losses according to the degree of fault on both sides of a collision_____, sounds like Jersey Law. The English Common Law provides no remedy in claims for wrongs done to another on land if the claimant has been partly at fault. In our case we sustained no damage that could not be repaired by the ship's carpenter. We lay at anchor all day on 19 October upstream from Ile-de-Kamouraska swept by a strong gale before the wind direction changed to enable the pilot to show his mettle. He took us sailing 75 miles with the flood tide in the dark of night with little I could see to guide him through the Chenal du Nord and onward past the long southern coastline of Ile D'Orleans to anchor off the Custom House at the foot of the flickering lamps and house lights of old Quebec City."

Gaudin told Herd he spent two days in Quebec City to unload part of the cargo, take on a cargo of spar timbers for London, and go ashore to make an official declaration before a notary public, a *notarial note of protest* setting forth the facts of the collision for marine insurance purposes.

"I hired the steam tug *Hercules*, almost as long as ourselves, to tow the *Ocean Nymph* night and day for 100 miles or more up the narrowing bends and channels of the St. Lawrence River to an anchorage short of the last Rapids in the River east of Montreal. A high, populated shore lined much of the land on both sides. I don't know of any major seaport so far inland as Montreal."

"I am thankful I reminded you to insist the tug did the towing at standard towing rates approved by ship owners last year, Gaudin."

"Yes sir, it helped me to know that. The company agent in Quebec City made a good selection of spar timbers for us to load on the way up to Montreal for shipment to London on our return. I carried them as a deckload. The tug came alongside to pick up our towing hawser at low water on 24 October. We weighed at 10 p.m. to get underway with the tide coming in on the surface of the River. By 2 a.m. snow came down with a biting wind to make life on deck miserable, but the tug chugged on. I welcomed the stop to anchor at Port-Neuf to wait for the next tide to assist the tow upstream as far as Trois Rivières where the incoming tide no longer makes an appearance against the force of the river current. The crew stand watches on deck when being towed, ready for the worst. A dreary business with nothing to do, even in daylight, had us watching strange landmarks passing for hours as the tug does what she knows best to move us upriver using range lights and buoys to mark the navigable channel, narrow in many places. On dark nights navigation must become a Black Art. The snow stopped and the weather showed clear at 5 a.m. on 25 October. We weighed and the tug carried on towing us across Lac St. Pierre through which the River makes a narrow channel to the beginning of the upriver channel at the western end. Some insist on calling it Lake St. Peter. We stopped here to anchor on 26 October. The *Hercules* took leave of us at 7 p.m. after the Pilot advised us to anchor to await tugs coming to tow us through the rapids in the channels upstream to Montreal. Lamped out the ship and set an anchor watch. Next morning I hired three Montreal Harbour Tugs to come to throw lines out for our large stock of towing hawsers. Your provision of them made me look well prepared, sir. Tugs do not provide their own towing hawsers except at a price."

Gaudin explained two tugs ended up coming alongside to put on their lines. Two of them pushed and the other tug pulled from station ahead to take the *Ocean Nymph* the last 50 miles up against the strong flow of the St. Lawrence River to Montreal Harbour.

"On 27 October they pushed the *Ocean Nymph* alongside a wharf in Montreal's Elgin Basin at 10 a.m. I had the people unbending sails and preparing for discharge of cargo, using ship's tackle to lower onto the wharf. Next morning, 28 October presented with strong wind and rain. We started unloading at 2 p.m.. The carpenter carried on making a new jib boom from one of the fresh spars. The old one had suffered strain on the last part of the passage in the Atlantic. The carpenter told me he'd find a use for the old one."

"Please go back and tell me more about the tow up from your last anchorage to the wharf at Elgin Basin."

"Sir, the crew found great excitement being towed literally uphill against the current all of the way to Montreal Harbour. I had long shipped the old jib boom. We looked forward past the bow stem to see the tug in the lead straining to pull the ship up into the Harbour to a position where all of them could come to push us into the wharf at the basin, which in no way resembled any of the London Docks. Until they got us into the wharf my vessel acted like a horse being led to where it did not want to be going, tugging this way and that in the river current on her towline. The bows moved from one side to the other as if caught in strong tiderips in shallowing water off a point of land. The River seemed to be objecting to my attempt to enter and to be trying to tell me to turn back. But of course I could not do that."

"Did you find time to get into town in Montreal, Gaudin?"

"Yes sir, I took a good hotel room for the three weeks there."

Gaudin felt no call to explain too much here. He'd made money for the company on this voyage. Now a captain, he found he could draw money from his salary and expense account at the Company Office in Montreal to live well in port. The town stood close to Elgin Basin and within walking distance off nearby Commissioners Street. Never before had he as much money in his pocket. New doors opened to him and he found new faces and enchanting feminine voices with a French accent to take delight in. As a Jerseyman who could speak French he enjoyed an abiding sense the persons he met saw him as a lively companion with stories to tell.

He spoke to Herd of the urgency he began to feel to make his departure from Montreal. December fast approached with all that meant in terms of ice on the River and weather to be expected in the North Atlantic Ocean.

"The days flew by," he said, "but I could not avoid taking the time to hire men from the shore to line the cargo holds with dunnage to protect the cargo of oats and peas when it came in for the return passage to England. But rain fell to delay my departure after that work had been done in the hold. The mate suspended loading at times on account of rain. Any rain falling on the cargo would cause it to swell inside the hold and provide no end of trouble at sea. I became quite philosophical. I did not fret about it. I decided to leave the loading to the Mate and play the hand fortune dealt me."

"How did you manage to stop the peas and oats from taking on dampness from the wood in the spars?"

"With difficulty. We separated the cargo and placed a cover over the spars. Opening the hatches not possible for much of the homeward crossing, but I doubt the spars secured on deck fared any the worse."

"You did not get away until late in November, which can be a late date."

"Yes sir, we stay moored at the wharf in Elgin Basin until we departed on 12 November with a full cargo of oats and dried peas and the spars we took on at Quebec City_____, also rock ballast. The weather stayed fine until late afternoon. Then it began to snow, building fast. I gave orders for a tug to tow us to anchor at the foot of the Lachine Rapids to wait for the large tug to arrive to begin the long tow down to Quebec City next morning. The steam tug the *John Bull* came alongside in the dark at 5 a.m. to begin the tow in alternating snow and sleet, such that even when daylight came I could not see the shore. The riverbanks downstream on both sides narrow to form the navigable channel. It's a river, not an estuary, quite different from being towed down in long sweeping river bends in the London River. Steam tug whistles sounded at times to warn other traffic in the river with us, coming in and departing. With the assistance of the swift downstream current we passed the lights of the town of Trois-Rivieres in early darkness; and by 9 p.m. the same day came to anchor, the pilot told me, off the village of Batiscan. The tides from the Gulf flood in to this place and ebb out from here. At 5 a.m. next morning we weighed anchor in calm weather for the tug to tow us the distance to anchor at the Custom House at Quebec City to await the next ebb tide to sail onward. The Montreal Pilot left the ship to be replaced by the Quebec Sea Pilot Felix Caron, a man who could charm the birds out of the trees and quieten my concern about the delays we encountered in the next several days. He came aboard at 6 a.m. on 15 November in light airs and fine autumn weather to take charge by asking me to weigh anchor at 2 p.m. high water. With the tide beginning to ebb, we made way under sail, but the Pilot called for a stop 15 miles along the Quebec South Shore. We anchored off Saint-Vallier Church. I became quite impatient to be making such a slow departure. With a better wind rising to fill the sails we weighed anchor at 6 p.m. to proceed under sail. Anchored at midnight off Cruise Island. We sailed on again at 6 a.m. on 16 November. We plied to windward against a light easterly wind, but with the tide current and clear weather favouring. Came to anchor off the Pillars at 3 p.m. Here a strong northeasterly gale blowing in our teeth kept us at anchor for two days in clear frosty weather."

"Yes Gaudin, I know where you mean."

"Finally, at 1 p.m. on 19 November a light wind and an ebb tide enabled us to set sail to beat through the Traverse until the tide forced us to anchor at 3 p.m. to wait for the tide to change. At 3 a.m. on 20 November we got underway again until forced to anchor in 10 fathoms when the wind fell off in blinding snow. At 2 p.m. we weighed and sailed on in a light wind until forced by snow and fog to anchor in nine fathoms to the west of the Pèlerin Light, which we all know as Pilgrim Light. Eleven other vessels anchored nearby. Brandy Pots Lighthouse visible at times when the snow dropped off. We got under way again at 10 p.m. in a light wind and snow to sail on into the night. Next day presented with snow carried by a strong northeasterly breeze, dead against us again. On the snow falling off and the wind hauling more northerly, we weighed to ply downriver as far as Green Island. By the end of the day the wind kept blowing light northerly on our port side to assist us out toward the Gulf. The sky turned clear at midnight. We landed the Pilot after passing the Baguette Lighthouse and sailed on into the dark night. Dim lights on the shore and an occasional dog barking on the beach to object to our passing warned us of the nearness of the shoreline whenever we closed with the South Shore. The next day presented with fine clear weather. The wind freshened from the southwest by 9 a.m. to enable us to make distance down the River to pass Father Point on Gaspé Peninsula. At 8 a.m. on next day's morning we crossed the channel to pass well off Pointe des Montes light on Quebec's North Shore by midnight, making best speed with a fresh westerly wind."

By this time Herd suggested they stop to eat. Later Gaudin went on with his account.

"Next day the northwest wind took us across the wide channel west of Anticosti Island to sight Cape Rosier north of Cape Gaspé bearing 20 miles to the *South-South-West*. Breezes in clear weather followed by gales of wind and snow harried us on our way out through the Gulf into Cabot Strait past St. Paul's Islands by 28 November. Never had I such a feeling of being chased out of a place by the wind."

Gaudin turned pages to pick out items of interest.

"By the last day of November we were in the Atlantic with the barometer going down fast," he said. "By midnight a violent gale presented. I set only two sails, my small Spenser trysail abaft the foremast and the lower main topsail to cope with our inability to steer a set course through peaks of jumbled seas and harrying blasts of winds from one direction and then another. By morning I thought I'd be excused were I to log it as a *complete hurricane*. The sea was more white than grey. Driven sea spray on all sides ended any possibility of seeing another vessel in the same waters. The helmsmen could do no more than shake the rain out of their eyes and try to keep the rags of sail I had left set filled with wind to prevent the ship being blown over or backed down to break the rudder off its rudderpost. The wind and seas will take the ship where they will under these deplorable sea conditions. The cabins on deck were filled with water up to the berths from waves sweeping over the decks from all sides. By noon on the next day, the first day of December I could set a course to steer to the east-north-east and run with the wind pushing us from the west-south-west. Spoke the brigantine *Pearl* from Quebec City destined for Liverpool. She had lost two men overboard in the recent gale. One mast down, yards askew, and sails in tatters, but she required no assistance, sir."

"Yes Gaudin, if only to fend off salvage claims a ship's master is often unwilling to admit his difficulties. I often think a ship's master sends away help offered when he should not."

"Yes sir, too often an element of pride intrudes. The gales continued with constant sail handling by crew and manning of the pumps. As
you recommended the men manned the pumps hourly at times. Not a
watch went by without attending to the pumps to keep the ship afloat
and the cargo dry. You warned me to do that and to make log entries
to record. Thunder and lightning and frequent squalls of wind and rain
filled most of the days as we were driven homewards. On 14 December
more squalls of wind with cold rain beyond belief hit us from lowering
dark cloud with thunderclaps sounding at the masthead and strikes of
lightning all around us. We sailed on in a heavy sea, which carried away
some of the starboard side t'gallant bulwarks, leaving splintered timber
ends at both sides of the gap, which the lifelines didn't hide. At midnight we caught a glimpse of a rag of sail showing a ship hove-to with
her bow to the side, riding the storm waves and not in any apparent
difficulty as we shot by in moments, homewards. At 4 a.m. we shipped
two high seas, which set everything on deck adrift, washed away the
compass binnacle, unshipped the spindle of the steering wheel, and
filled the cabin with water. I ordered the hands to haul up the foresail,
clew up the foretopsail, and hove the ship to. Kept the pumps constantly
going. I had my left hand crushed in an attempt to secure some items
back on deck but I am now recovered."

"Gaudin, I am taken with the new pocket time-piece you bought
with your captain's pay. You just move it back four minutes a day for
each degree of longitude to the west you have gone to tell you the time
of day where your ship is sailing."

"Save's a lot of figuring, doesn't it, sir? And coming back the other
way, four minutes ahead for each degree of longitude."

"You are going to get the *Lady Lampson*, Gaudin. For you to bring
the *Ocean Nymph* back through North Atlantic storms as you did before
Christmas showed me and everyone else you knew what you were doing.
I hear the scuttlebutt. The crewmembers were more than ready to size
up the new captain and spread the word."

"I get the same thought coming, sir, and I am thankful for it, but as
you know, no one on board says any such thing to me."

"Yes Gaudin, the command of ship brings a lonely time. No one
speaks to the ship's master unless spoken to first. And the master dare
not become too friendly, lest it be misunderstood and ship's discipline
suffer."

7

THE NEW BARQUE

Two hundred years after a King of England named Charles ran his spaniel hunting dogs in the vacant wild wetland, the north bank of the Thames downstream from London rang with the sounds of commercial shipping activity in a newer section of the London Docks.

Gaudin hurried out the front door of his lodgings at #5 Wellington Place on West India Dock Road in East London to board his new ship now in final stages of loading at Blackwall Basin. He carried the latest marine charts, books and other publications for navigation, packed heavy in the leather portmanteau Company Marine Superintendent Captain David Herd handed him late last night after they talked for many hours about Gaudin's recent voyage across the North Atlantic to Montreal and back in the *Ocean Nymph*. Their meeting ended with remarks touching on the steps taken by the mates and crew to make the new barque *Lady Lampson* ready for her maiden voyage to the Pacific Northwest, which would begin this morning. Before returning to his lodging Gaudin ordered a steam paddlewheel tug to come in the morning to the Basin to pick up the *Lady Lampson's* heavy rope towing hawser and tow the new barque down the Thames to the English Channel.

Gaudin knew navigation on the London River through experience. Recently turned 31, he had often crewed sailing vessels to and from the Port of London over the 14 years of working his way up the ranks from apprentice seaman. Now he held in his hand orders that filled him with pride. He would take the spanking new Hudson's Bay Company barque out to sea on her maiden voyage of 20,000 miles or more around Cape Horn to Esquimalt Harbour on Vancouver Island, one of the new Crown Colonies on the far distant Northwest coast of North America.

Lloyd's of London and all marine insurance underwriters familiar with the experience of vessels transiting the Strait of Juan de Fuca waters leading to the new town of Victoria on Vancouver Island insisted the passage from London should terminate at the safer destination of Esquimalt Harbour and make the return passage from the same place as a condition of insurance coverage. The shipowner who wished to use Victoria's Inner Harbour to unload and take on cargo must undertake the risk and expense of hiring a tug to tow his vessel from the one place to the other. The Hudson's Bay Company used their steamers as tugs to tow their vessels the six mile-distance past the hazardous rocky shoreline off Esquimalt to Victoria, choosing their weather to make the tow in safety.

Jones, his short wiry porter, an old man, carried Gaudin's bags as they tramped through the thin fall of snow the short distance to the gated entrance to Blackwall Basin. Gaudin turned to look back through the early morning smoke and haze to remember the scene of the tops of tall towers and church spires in London Town in the near distance he will describe to Agnes Anderson in six-months' time. They have not yet met but someone pointed her out in town. He liked what he saw, and he is confident she will agree to marry him and live in Jersey. The city scene she will see on the way to a new home on the old Island of Jersey will be a pleasing change from the life she faces in the Colonial Society in the dark little town with wide muddy streets.

Even though people in the town had been good company, he would not want to raise his children in Victoria or in the only other town of size on that part of the coast, New Westminster.

The guard beckoned him to pass through the portal to enter with his porter. Inside, Gaudin stepped into a scene of two-dozen sailing vessels tied to the wharves all around the pool of the wide circular Basin and men working in the cold air to move boxes and sacks of cargo. A kaleidoscope of sights and sounds with loud voices, yells, and shouts, some in foreign accents. The *Lady Lampson* lay alongside a cable's length away, 600 feet, as seaman learn to estimate distances at sea in multiples of the number 600. They call out visible distances at sea in *cables*, rather than yards or feet.

The large red harbour ensign with the Union Jack in the inside top corner, too large to flutter, flapped and rolled with pride in the light wind, as if to say, *Look At Me*. All of the ship's signal flags flew from on high to celebrate the impending departure. The precious Hudson's Bay Company embroidered House Flag, not yet arrived, will fly displayed from the maintop. Only the men on other vessels and on the wharves in the Basin would see it. He would bring it down soon to avoid tarnish from the coal smoke in the air from the river traffic and from factory chimneys. The over-riding regulation of his conduct as ship's master required him to keep it safe and dry at all other times.

The guard at the portal did not allow family and friends to pass through to see a ship sail. This rule made for lonely departures with men paying attention to their duty.

Other vessels lay moored around the circular basin with their long bowsprit jib booms unshipped and taken down out of the way. Every vessel had ropes with wooden collar guards to bar rats seeking another home.

His new ship lay alongside waiting for the tread of his soft leather sea boots again. Hardly a day had passed since Christmas without competent shipyard workers and seamen aboard ship doing the difficult work of splicing the wire rope rigging or without him coming aboard to search below deck and to climb the masts and rigging to decide on work to be done to make ready to sail south around Cape Horn. Two days earlier he put out a ship's boat to take him to the far side of the Basin. His experienced eye enabled him to give orders across the water to set the slant of the three masts in harmony with each other. Pleasant thoughts washed over his mind as he told himself how pretty his new vessel looked. Not yet loaded down to her depth marks inscribed to indicate how much water she floats in, newly applied copper sheathing on what will become the underwater part of the hull shone in the cool cloud-filtered sunlight as if polished.

Wearing a black suit, jacket and hat, the Mate came to the gangway to meet him, saluting. Crews know the Chief Officer on all vessels at sea by the name of 'the Mate'. Gaudin bounded up the gangway, carrying the leather portmanteau in a firm grip. He wore a low flat-visored captain's cap, white gloves, a black topcoat and trousers, and ankle-length smooth black leather boots. His porter followed close behind with his bags.

Stepping aboard his ship, Gaudin hailed the ship's Chief Officer on deck.

"Hola! Mister Mate! Our *barkee* presents a pretty sight."

"Yes sir, she does that. You told me to load to draw 15 foot of water forward and 15 foot 6 inches aft. She will meet your specification when I have finished loading, sir."

"Please show me the loading diagram for the additional cargo you are now putting aboard."

He put down the portmanteau and laid out flat the mate's paper to see a diagram of how he had arranged for the loading of cargo in the hold.

"This looks good to me, Mister. Now let's go over the crew list to see who is coming with us."

"Aye, aye sir. The steward and cook came on board yesterday. As you can see Mister John Farrow signed on as Second Mate, sir. He comes with good recommendation from his time as Able Seaman in other barques. Bright mind you might say, sir. He sat early in his time for his examination certificates."

"I see him now working with the men in the bows of the ship. I have seen him before and I remember him."

"I took Mister Farrow over the vessel as soon as he came aboard, sir. He now knows it from stem to stern."

"Send him to me in my cabin when he finishes that job. I will want him to come up with me to check the gear. He and I will climb the masts to inspect the rope lines and rigging you have set up for me. Call me when you are ready with the crew assembled on deck, but first, let's go over the other names of the men who have signed on_____. I see none I know."

"Aye, aye sir. Eight of the men are able seamen and have been aloft handing sail on the yards in many a gale, sir. We are lucky to have them to show the apprentices."

Gaudin nodded and went below to his cabin aft under the quarter-deck to talk to his steward.

Mister Irvine, the Thames River pilot used by the Honourable Company, came through the gate in morning's early darkness to board the *Lady Lampson*. He will stay on board to advise on navigation in the River until Gaudin drops him off later to a pilot boat coming out for him. Retired Captain Adamson and Captain David Herd, patrons for Gaudin's promotion to command the vessel, boarded early enough for Gaudin to offer them the courtesy of a hot breakfast, which neither had time for on shore, followed by an inspection of the new vessel with the ropes and gear on deck, neat, clean, and tidy.

Captain Herd handed Gaudin the newly made Hudson's Bay Company House Flag with the mysterious words *Pro Pelle Cutem* embroidered on it. He asked Gaudin to set it flying at the maintop for the departure from Blackwall Dock and to call all hands to salute the flag hoisted for the departure.

To the sound of the feet of sailors running with evident purpose about the deck the three master mariners and the pilot waited in the cabin below decks with mugs of hot coffee laced with rum to drink to the success of the maiden voyage. The vessel began to stir as if to show she sensed she would soon swing on her tug's towline in the Basin and move out through the Blackwall Entrance to the River. Gaudin found himself imagining a glimpse from above of his washed and glistening vessel being turned by the tug in the Basin. He decided next time to adopt a buff and dark green colour scheme for the masts and outer sides of the housework on deck. As ship's captain he will decide on such a matter. But he will keep the white taff-rail around his quarterdeck for its appearance, and because the whiteness provided an incentive to the Mates to keep the ship clean.

Knowing the bluff and taciturn ways of his two patrons, Gaudin tried to think of words to say to thank them for all they had done to advance his career without demeaning himself or embarrassing them. He ended up saying nothing and instantly regretted it. The tug *Macgregor's* distinctive whistle signal sounded to end any thought of further chat. All four of them knew enough of the River and its tides to feel tension in the air: the tug came into the Basin late for the tide, which today had already begun to turn for a short *run-out* before turning to come in again. Tug and tow will get down no farther than Gravesend before the flood tide and fog will require them to tie up to a buoy in the River. Gaudin will order the tow to continue at next morning's turn of the tide.

Although late, the tug *Macgregor* had no difficulty in bucking against the water oozing slowly out through the 40-foot width of the gate opening. Everyone could see the water in the Basin had begun to flow out into the River without the push of an incoming tide to keep it back inside.

"This will make for a quick exit," Gaudin remarked to the two senior captains as he gave the order to the Mate to let go the lines to the wharf and bring them back aboard. While that was being done he took in a deep breath and felt a sense of exultation to know he was making it all happen. How lucky to be in control of his own destiny. But he stopped his reverie when Captain Herd said something to make him decide to take the steering wheel on the quarterdeck himself and send the helmsman to take station midships.

The *Macgregor* steamed into the Basin with a small stream of hot water issuing from a pipe at the side and paddlewheels moving slowly, then at idle, to slip alongside in a peculiar silence that Gaudin found ominous and foreboding. The man at the stern of the tug threw a heaving line with a weight on it for the sailors at the bow to catch in the air and haul aboard to bend on it successively thicker ropes leading to the heavy towing hawser they had brought up from storage below decks with scarcely a sound.

Gaudin saw the tug captain at his open steering position midships reach up to the whistle cord to make low-pitched hoots from its steam whistle to draw the attention of other vessels in the Basin to this sailing vessel about to depart under tow. Gaudin knew all eyes on him and his ship. Although departing sailing vessels not an uncommon sight at Blackwall, a hush descended on other vessels in the Basin as the scene took shape. With a sense of reverence men on all sides stopped talking and looked on to witness the event of the vessel setting out. Some vessels, they knew, would not return from the cruelty of the sea.

Gaudin focused on the steering wheel of the *Lady Lampson* to make his 30-foot-wide hull line up behind the tug on a short towline. He wanted to make his ship slip through the centre of the 40-foot wide gate opening without scraping paint off the sides.

The tug led the way out sounding its whistle again to warn vessels outside in the approaches on both sides of Blackwall Entrance to be ready to avoid collision with the apparition of a helpless sailing vessel unable to manoeuvre under tow emerging.

It all happened in moments. Tug and tow moved out into the River in the fog and turned downstream into Blackwall Reach of the Thames. Everyone on the quarterdeck relaxed and looked around with smiles on their faces, basking now in the dim sunlight showing through the fog. Gaudin felt chill, but held back shivers lest it be seen as fright. The tug laboured on ahead through the winding river channel in the midst of other marine traffic running up and down the River. The tug's steam whistle sounded a long blast followed by two short blasts at intervals to warn shipping traffic chock-a-block in the fog she had another vessel in tow as a dumb hulk at the end of a towline and to take care to avoid collision.

Busy shipyards lay to port at the outlet of the River Lea as the tug turned into the next sharp bend to starboard in the winding channel of the London River. Making distance downstream, Gaudin couldn't see the shoreline through the fog, smoke, and murk. The lookout at the *Lady Lampson's* bow kept a close watch to call out aft to describe the tug about to change course. Gaudin stood at the starboard rail to give steering orders to the helmsman who could see nothing of the tug under the high bows of the *Lady Lampson*.

Daylight ended early. The *Macgregor* signalled back the need to stop as they neared Gravesend on the south bank of the River. With the forward movement of the ship slowing, the men at the bow of the *Lady Lampson*, heaving together and singing a shantey, hauled in the rope hawser from the tug to the steady clicking of the ratchet mechanism of the capstan, one of the new patent appliances on deck to lighten the load. The Mate saw to tying up to the buoy in the River off Gravesend and the tug came back to tie up alongside. She kept steam up in her boiler with shovels of coal stoked into the fire through the night. Gaudin ordered the mate to lamp out the ship and for the ship's bell to be sounded at intervals to warn marine traffic the ship lay at anchor at the side of the channel. He sent Captains Herd and Adamson ashore in a small boat that came out for them. All else around lay still and in darkness. The flood tide water in the river slipped past with scarcely a sound.

He gave orders for the crew to muster, and then set the names of the men in each Watch, Port and Starboard, one Watch for the Mate and one for the Second Mate. Not that the men in either Watch do not have the run of both sides of the ship during their watch time on deck, and especially in an All Hands on Deck situation where every man, including the cook and the captain's steward, runs to his station.

The day ended in rain and fog, which continued through the night. Next morning the *Macgregor* took up the tow again downriver against a fresh breeze blowing out of the east. Gaudin pondered for a moment what words to write in the ship's new logbook he keeps to show Captain Herd on returning to London, but decided he'd write only that at 6 a.m. they cast off from the buoy at Gravesend in rain.

On reaching the lightship marking the sandbank named on charts as The Tongue at the mouth of the Thames, Gaudin dismissed the tug and ordered sail set with course to be steered to clear North Foreland on the way south to the Downs.

Mister Irvine left the ship before noon in a pilot boat that came out to pick him up. The *Lady Lampson* cut a swift course under sail through the middle of a pile-up of anchored older sailing vessels in the Downs.

Some fully laden, others empty and sailing in ballast, all awaiting orders to be towed in to the London Docks to load or unload cargo. Hails from her Lookout forward warned of conflicting shipping traffic for the captain to give steering orders. By 8 p.m. that evening they passed South Foreland and set all possible sail. He went to his cabin to make an entry in the logbook to record the beginning of the Channel passage.

Gaudin could do no better than to make the maiden passage to Esquimalt in a time of two weeks short of six months. The long passage to the Pacific Northwest ended at 11:30 p.m. on 31 July 1869. He sailed the *Lady Lampson* into Esquimalt Harbour without a pilot. He had come there twice before in the *Prince of Wales*. He knew the way in. The visibility enabled him to keep the shoreline in sight. The taking of a pilot remained not compulsory. Gaudin gave orders to let the anchors go in six-blessed fathoms of clear water and lamp out.

Here and there on the maiden voyage things had not gone well, but the arrival late on a summer evening made up for any annoyances and irritations. Only night birds and sentries on the shore at the Naval Base who recognized the ship's light signal witnessed the *Lady Lampson* enter the harbour for her first time like a moving shadow on the moonlit waters. A blue heron at the edge of the beach called out her shcrawking annoyance at being disturbed and dogs on the shore began to bark at each other to break the spell.

He hoped no one would ask him the number of days taken from the Downs on this maiden voyage. The crew could count days at sea. They would know their captain's embarrassment at the length of the passage from mid-February through to the end of the month of July. Other captains will classify it as a *very* long voyage and would tend to look down on him for taking 163 days from the Downs to Esquimalt. With this in mind he planned to be ready with an explanation to the Factor, the senior company fur trade officer in charge at Fort Victoria, whom Gaudin had learned he had to respect and take orders from. The Factor greeted him with fresh pipe tobacco and a bottle of rum. He laughed as he poured out two mugs, "What took you so long, Gaudin?"

"Well, sir, a maiden voyage of 163 days from the Downs not too shabby if you take into account a prolonged winter storm in February that made us lose seven days sailing from one side of the Channel to the other before we could be off and running south. The mates had the hands on deck familiar with the drill, the sails, and the rigging before the end of the ten days it took to sail from the Downs to Ushant. And let's not forget the eight days of storm west of the Horn to reach up to 55 South in the Pacific. My little ship was not at fault. The ship's hull design and the low sail plan with no canvas set above her Royals makes her stand up to her sails when making to windward_____."

"I know something about tacking ship, Gaudin. Company brigs on this Northwest coast have often carried me to Fort Simpson on the North Coast. I have seen some bad times at sea on the way to pass outside of the Queen Charlottes as Captain Cook did in 1788. The hands on my vessel were no longer green by the time they rounded the Horn, but even so I have seen confusion reign on deck, even in daylight when every man can see what he is doing."

"Sir, you are correct. The requirement to learn the ropes tells the story: on coming to know the ropes, the hands soon could move on deck with purpose. As for tacking ship, sometimes it does not work out well. I don't blame the hands when it doesn't. The timing for me to give my commands becomes critical. Even you, sir, a landsman, will realize that our handy little sailing vessel can't begin a tack from a standing start. I bear off on the helm to gain speed sailing with the wind before turning into the eye of the wind. That will set the momentum to carry me through the turn. At the right moment the wind will begin to push against sails taken aback at the front end of the ship to add push to the momentum in the turn. I keep an eye open for the sound of the flutter of canvas at the start of the foretopsail luff, which tells me more about the wind's direction than the wind on my cheek. The moment that sail begins to luff tells me the actual wind direction, which otherwise could be hard for me to determine if it be night and no moon to light the seas. It also helps me tell where we are in the turn to put about into the wind on new tack."

The old Factor said he knows the word *luff* and he asked Gaudin to go on to explain more about *tacking ship*. Gaudin could see the old fellow took a genuine interest as he provided a full explanation.

"I must keep up the momentum in the turn to defeat the wind trying to take my foresails full aback, which would stop the ship. Hauling the boom of the spanker on the mizzen amidships helps move the stern in the turn into the wind. The spanker sail luffs until I can see to it being set to draw wind on the completion of the turn. The clews of the foretopsails when no longer drawing wind flap and flutter loose as the bow swings to face into the wind. The lines, blocks, and canvas slat, bang about, and make a fearful cracking noise. The hands know I am content to leave the foremast sails with the wind pushing back on them, but not for too long, lest the ship be taken aback. If I have set the right momentum, those sails by presenting an obstruction to the wind can keep the bow turning across the wind as I intend. I must be thinking about getting the sail or sails set on the mainmast swung around to fill with wind on the new tack. I get the wind to help when, with exquisite timing, I give the command to the hands at the braces to *Mainsail Haul.* I learned the term *exquisite timing* from Captain Adamson, pretty fancy language for me. It may look at first I have given the command too early, but the momentum I have set can carry it through. The hands let the main lee braces go, leaving their yards free for the men hauling on the main braces to swing the yards on the main to regain the wind_____. All hands on deck including the cook and my steward will be ready to work like madmen to do the hauling work to avoid fouling the flaked main brace lines lying underfoot on deck. A hand forward will lead the jib sheets of the luffing jibs across to the other side to harden in the wind on the new tack, but I am getting ahead of myself. The mates see to the hands using the new patent deck winches to get the sails trimmed to fill with wind to best advantage. Even in everyday sailing I cannot abide layabouts on deck. The mate on watch must attend to the constant necessity to trim the sails to keep the ship moving at best speed without a word from me to do it. Having come around in the turn, I get the hands running to the foremast yard braces on the weather side to be ready for my next order, *Fore braces.* The hands spring to do what they need to do there. On the lee braces being eased, the foremast yards swing to fill with the new wind. I rely on the mates to supervise the hands trimming the sails and picking up the slack fore braces from deck to coil and hang in place. They do that as I look on with keen attention, order the spanker set to balance the helm, and attend to steering the ship to stand on the new tack. An orchestra will collapse in noisy confusion absent a conductor: as will the ship be, without me to lead it."

The Factor remarked on the long mainsail yard and the large spanker sail.

"Yes sir, you are correct in saying so, and that yard makes for a large mainsail. I will use the main whenever possible, and especially in light airs, but let me go on to *wearing*____. We wear ship when the wind so strong and the seas run so high I dare not turn into the wind to tack ship. The foresails blasted aback in such a condition can dismast a ship far from any help_____. The violence of the wind that brings on such a sea will force me to turn to steer the ship off the wind with immediate benefit from the wind strength being diminished to make sail and gear handling easier. Wearing ship much like running a gauntlet with *alarums* and dangers at every point in the run around the wide curving course off the wind to emerge back out sailing against the wind and sea on a new tack, slanting into the wind on a much different compass heading than before. To do it, sir, the yards must be moved and the sails trimmed to take on a new slant into the wind, which is more easily said than done."

"Pray tell me what happens when you decide to '*wear*' ship in a bad storm, Gaudin."

"The weather will long have had me bring in the mainsail and upper topsails to ease the ship's motion at sea. Perhaps, I will have set only lower topsails and the fore topmast staysail, which I often name the inner jib. Even though the fewer sails set will ease the work of the handling of sails and gear in wearing ship, the hands must work like men possessed to carry out my orders under the supervision and direction of the mates, the Mate at the fore and the Second at the main. All hands depend on the man at the helm and me to use our skill and attention to prevent the ship being blown over broadside-to with the lee rails under at any point in the wide teardrop-shaped turn off the wind. The initial turn puts the ship running sideways to the wind. Under flying shreds of low dark cloud, fearful ragged walls of foam-flecked water loom high to sweep the deck. Drenched, we fight to maintain footing on deck in water shipped deep aboard from windward. We scoot low past ocean peaks of sea in a dark tumult. No mere jumble of sea, but storm waves in dense ranks moving to crush men foolish to try to sail against them. In a trough between wave tops I can see nothing, but on being boosted up by waves on a steep rise, I can focus to find a spot in the seas to turn off the wind. I aim to steer to get out of this danger as soon as I can. As the ship will pivot on the main I am happy to order down the mizzen spanker to allow sail on the foremast, filled hard with wind, work to push the bow into the turn downwind when I choose."

"Gaudin, I have seen the sails on the mainmast a'flutter when wearing ship."

"Yes sir, you will see that in the early part of the turn on wearing ship when the helmsman puts the ship beam-to the wind. I am content to have the sails on the mainmast luff when they come edgewise to the wind to ease work at the braces. I see to steering the ship and I watch the time passing to gauge how the hands work under the eye of the Second Mate to brace the main yards for the wind that will come from a new angle when the ship completes the turn to a new course. I must be ready for my next command. When wearing ship we change direction by circling off the wind to port or starboard as I choose to put the wind coming on to the other side of the ship."

"I saw Captain Kipling do it in the *Dryad*, Gaudin."

"Yes sir. But let me explain what happens later. Let me draw it on the slate. I am wearing ship to become able to steer in the direction I could have put about to tack into the wind, had sea conditions allowed_____. On turning off the wind, the ship comes beam-to mounting seas on one side of the ship during the first part of the turn off the wind. That happens again on the other side of the wide circle I am sailing in to wear ship. By the time we get to find beam seas again, I will have steered with purpose to put the wind to come on the other beam. In between those times the helmsman and I must be sharp to keep the ship driving straight sailing downwind when mounting seas come on the stern from behind. Inattention can put the ship turning broadside-to and going under. To limit the risk of seas boarding and putting us out of control when beam-to on the first occasion, we turn downwind as soon as we can. The shrill weird moan of the storm wind through the rigging quietens in the initial turn off the wind, but we become much more aware of the noise of the seas in motion. The wind slings us forward downwind into the wear without any apparent regard to our will in the matter until we can stand on, standing up to the wind, and *standing* on, as we say, steering the new course into the wind. While twice in the wearing ship turn I must steer out of the danger of beam seas boarding as soon as I can, the state of the seas can prolong the wearing of ship. Often I must bide my time before I can steer to stand on into the wind again on the new compass heading I have chosen to take up. Watching and waiting for the mates and the crew to work the sails, I rely on the man at the wheel to keep the rudder ready to carry out my steering orders to complete the turn to wear ship in the new direction. But in spite of the trials undertaken, wearing ship easier done and less risky than trying to put-about by turning into and through the wind in a storm. Any ease seen in wearing ship derives from the diminished force of the wind on the sails and gear when turning off the wind."

"That's quite an explanation, Gaudin. You have more to say than most captains I have talked to. But I have seen the FOREsails a'flutter."

"Yes sir, as I meant to explain, the sails on the foremast lose wind and luff after the hands have braced and trimmed the sails on the mainmast to fill with wind again. The ship will have begun to move in the downwind arc of the turn. Sail set on the mainmast will blanket the foresails, which lose wind and luff until the hands brace them to be ready to use the wind in the next part of the turn in concert with my raising the spanker on the mizzen aft."

"Tell me more, Gaudin, about the spanker in wearing ship."

"Well sir, I will haul down the spanker on the mizzen early in the first part of wearing ship and I keep it down until I need it up again in time for the wind to push the stern through the last part of the turn into wind again. And I keep it set to balance the helm as we set a new course. A fore-and-aft sail, the spanker is easy to set or douse from the deck."

After a long pause as the Factor weighed his explanation, Gaudin summed up.

"We will have turned off the wind to change course. As I have said good reasons may exist to wear ship. With the wearing of ship completed, the crew will have turned the yards on the main and the foremast to slant the sails to catch the wind now coming on the ship's other side. The ship sails on a new tack against the wind."

"You hang a large spanker gaff on the mizzen to my eye, Gaudin."

"Yes sir. The 35-foot gaff for the spanker sail makes for a sail that catches wind. The sail plan for this 400-ton barque done by a shipyard genius. You see the foremast set forward on deck to permit the long mainsail yard room to swing without hitting the foremast."

"I have seen captains mighty concerned during a wearing of ship, Gaudin."

"Yes sir, in the North Atlantic and in the Great Southern Ocean, especially, wearing ship can expose the rudder to be pitched up to be damaged by a sea following faster than we can sail. The helmsman must not lose control when steering with the waves pushing from behind. If he does, the ship can broach-to and come broadside to the seas. A complete disaster far from any help when wind and seas blow the ship over, masts, sails, and all, broadside-to the force of the wind. Walls of water will have driven the hands off their stations on deck into the sea in a blink of the eye. The immense weight of the wind and sea can sink the ship, and drown us all_____. The flame of our manhood snuffed out in a moment of bad luck or inattention."

"You paint a sorry picture, Gaudin."

"Yes I do, sir, and it would be a sorry place to be. But let me describe a happier end. If a tack undertaken in safe sea conditions *misses stays*, which is the expression when the ship fails to put about, the ship lies there with sails on the foremast taken aback and the captain looking silly. The bow can fall off without having come through the wind, but the captain can steer to turn off the wind to end up heading in the direction he wanted to sail in the first place. All is not lost. From that position, he can wear ship by turning off wind."

The Factor nodded and went on to speak of matters concerning the cargo Gaudin will be carrying back to London.

8

AGNES MEETS GAUDIN

In the heat of the hot still summer afternoon in mid-August 1869 Agnes' father came rushing up to the house and into the kitchen, near winded. He called out for Agnes, who came running downstairs from her bedroom.

"Gaudin is in Esquimalt to unload cargo _____ before the *Otter* tows her out to Sooke, which is quite extraordinary. In such a rush this time she will not be towed into Victoria, at all _____. I will go to meet him in town when I know he can come_____ I have sent an invitation to him to come to stay over with us."

Agnes cried out for pleasure and disappeared upstairs to her bedroom with her mother to plan. On her own she had found no girl in town called Gaudin her own, but she thought it just as well the ship will not be coming into the Inner Harbour for them to dazzle him with flashing smiles and sweet chat.

A week passed. Her father went into town and came back to report his findings at the dinner table.

"The town has become alive with talk of Gaudin's new barque in Esquimalt. Those who have seen it speak highly of her trim appearance."

Agnes picked up the local newspaper to read with pride the big news of the day in town. The newspaper must have sent a reporter out to get a story from Gaudin: -

The Hudson's Bay Company barque Lady Lampson – 412 tons register and has carrying room for 700 tons of freight. She is a new vessel built at Sunderland and launched on December 23 last. She takes her name from the lady of Sir Curtis Lampson, one of the magnates of Fenchurch Street, an American by birth, but naturalized in England and one of the investors in the Atlantic Cable. The Lady Lampson is provided with all of the late improved appliances, such as patent windlasses, iron frames, wire rigging, etc. The hatches, deck settees for passengers and handrails are all teak. The barque is commanded by Captain Gaudin, well known to many of our readers as first officer of the company's bark the Prince of Wales. The Lady Lampson is a model of neatness, her condition after a long sea voyage reflecting most favourably upon the captain and officers. Surveyed to be classed A1 at Lloyd's.

Agnes now went through torment in her mind as her father learned bits and pieces of information from town. The crew of the *Lady Lampson* took days to unload the heavy mechanical cargo consigned to the Royal Navy at the Esquimalt Naval Base. Word soon followed that Gaudin would stay aboard to supervise unloading the remaining general cargo to the company wharf in Esquimalt. Teamsters will transport it into town by cart, which will enable the Company to dispense with towing the vessel into town. This strategy will enable the ship to be towed to Sooke without delay to load lumber for South America.

A week later Agnes' father came back from town to gather everyone around to hear him report.

"Captain Swanson told me the *Otter* went alongside the empty *Lady Lampson*, riding high in the water exposing her underwater copper sheathing, to put a line aboard to tow her to Sooke. He said Gaudin decided the weather looked favourable, and that he could save time and expense by loading only a minimum of ballast to steady the empty vessel for the 26-mile tow west to Sooke Harbour to load lumber floated out from the sawmill on the shore."

Her father drew a picture on a slate to show her the route along the shoreline through the narrow inner waters inside Race Rocks past Beechey Head, a headland jutting out from the shore of Vancouver Island.

"Beechey Head is not named after Beachy Head in the English Channel as you might think," he said, "but after an esteemed Royal Navy Officer on this Pacific Naval Station, not a misspelling of the name. Remarkably, Gaudin will take the lumber to Chile in South America."

"Oh Papa, how wonderful for the sawmill to find a buyer for its lumber."

"Yes, that will provide employment for the men. Let me go on : the *Otter* towed the *Lady Lampson* through the narrow winding channel, two 90° turns, into Sooke Harbour on the last of the flood tide. Swanson says he regrets the *Otter* put the *Lady Lampson* aground at the edge of the harbour. To the sound of angry shouts and the sight of activity on board to kedge off, Gaudin anchored in deeper waters of the harbour at the end of the day. The Committee in London does not give captains who allow their vessels to become stranded a second chance. His first business will be to unload the ballast to make room for the lumber to be put into the cargo holds. The vessel will be unstable until the weight of cargo comes aboard. Other Sail has come to the harbour to load lumber, which may put a strain on the ability of the sawmill to float out the lumber in the form of rafts to the ship as fast as Gaudin would want."

After a long silence Agnes' father spoke again.

"So Agnes, we must expect some delay before he can come to see us here."

"Papa, now that he is captain why can't he leave the loading to the First Mate? You once told me most captains arrange it that way. Won't he take his ship to sea without coming to see us?"

"I am sure he will come, Agnes."

"You have shown me Sooke much closer to the ocean at Cape Flattery than Victoria, Papa. Why won't he decide to make sail and leave straightaway to Chile?"

"Captain Swanson reports he and Captain Gaudin have become good friends. The young captain looks for a chance to break free from his duty to come. Swanson will keep me informed."

"But Papa, he must sail as soon as all the lumber is on board, won't he?"

"Captain Swanson told me to tell you he thinks Gaudin will be able to take the time to come to see us."

Swanson followed up to say Gaudin had been delayed by the Chief Officer's difficulty understanding how to keep a proper tally of the timbers coming aboard. Her father took time to explain how the crew use ship's tackle consisting of the main yard on the mast with blocks and ropes to lift the heavy deals out of the water and swing them aboard to lower into the hold.

"Agnes, the word is spoken as ship's TAY-CULL, not TACK-CULL," he said, "Swanson says the yards are all *a'cock-bill*, a terrible messy sight for a seaman to look at instead of showing squared up in parallel, like soldiers on a parade ground. Gaudin won't leave until he has things under better control,"

"Oh Papa, I am worried he will not come."

"No, daughter, Captain Swanson will make a trip to get him as soon as Gaudin sends the signal. Don't expect Gaudin to make a ride for miles through the forest into town. The steamer will bring him when he is ready to come. Please do not fret about it, child."

Within the week Captain Swanson ran the stern-wheel steamer *Enterprise* with Sooke-bound freight on board to justify the trip to pick up Gaudin and bring him into town. Her father met him with his horses and carriage to drive him out to North Saanich. They arrived in a clatter of hooves on the path in front of the house.

After Gaudin shown the bedroom to wash up Anderson went to find Agnes in her bedroom.

"He can stay three nights," he said. "The Mates will complete loading the lumber and he is now free to enjoy time with us."

Agnes asked her mother to help her arrange her long auburn hair down the back of her dress.

"Your light blue eyes, blush and fair skin will look good to this young man waiting downstairs to meet you, Agnes," her mother said. "Do stop shaking and get a hold of yourself."

After a moment or two to compose herself, Agnes swept downstairs with steps as light as a cat to be introduced and to hear him speak in his deep voice like no one she had ever heard before.

"I am honoured to make your acquaintance, Miss Agnes."

"And I yours, sir. I do hope you enjoyed the drive out from town past farm, field, and forest."

"Yes, the dry road made for a swift passage. I'm amazed at the large evergreen trees, which grow so tall and do not shed leaves."

"Yes and they provide the lumber to build the houses we need in this new country. Log houses just won't do. Let's all do go outside to sit on the front steps and talk."

Agnes found herself speaking in a voice so soft she did not recognize herself.

"Father has sherry from Portugal for mother and for me already poured in the glasses. I expect he will have whiskey for you men."

In the late afternoon sun they sat down to talk. Agnes, finding herself ill at ease, made a suggestion to Gaudin to go outside.

"Let me show you Papa's English Country Garden. The bank of climbing roses behind it gives the farm its name, *Rosebank*."

Gaudin took her hand and they walked out a distance from her father and mother, passing through a rustic gated net and cedar fence past six-foot high foxgloves and hollyhocks in the garden. Agnes flushed with pleasure to see Gaudin had difficulty keeping his eyes off her as they strolled past the summer flowers in the late afternoon sunlight. Doing her best to stand with her shoulders back and stomach in, never letting her shoulders slump, she thought he should be given time to take a good look at her without the clutter of her looking back at him. For a moment she averted her eyes to look down to allow him time to see her long eyelashes displayed to best advantage. And then she came back to engage him with her eyes flashing bright. That happened more than once as the two of them talked. Susan had shown her how to do this in the company of men she chose to favour. The thought thrilled her, how long before she make eyelash butterfly kisses with him?

Agnes' mother rang the little bell to call everyone to the table. On the way in through the door Agnes caught a glimpse of a pale new crescent moon in the southwest. She drew in her breath and held it for a moment. Susan had told her that the time of a new moon is full of portent. A friendship begun at the time of a new moon will last.

Gaudin joined the family at the long table for dinner by lamp and candlelight in a room that was dark even at midday. The evening meal began with her father saying his favourite two-word Latin Grace *benedictus benedicat*. He then cut into the large roast beef, which he called a joint of beef, and passed portions on the china plates for Agnes to add the new potatoes, green peas, deep red beets with greens, and carrots. She passed a dish of deep yellow farm butter to spread on them.

"These vegetables come from the farm garden," Agnes said. "The fish net, which Papa traded with the local Indians for, keeps the deer from jumping in to the vegetable garden to nibble and flatten everything as if a storm had passed through. The same kind of fence we put up to save the flowers."

Her mother joined in to speak.

"Agnes and her father grow their garden so I have food for the kitchen all summer long. Her brothers keep me supplied with beef, chicken, and venison meat, so we are a well-fed family."

"But all of us prefer farm food to salmon," her father broke in. "We had too much of it salted and smoked in the fur trade. Even a fine fillet of fresh salmon cannot take the taste of it out of our minds. Agnes often goes out in her canoe to catch young green cod before they grow too large. An ugly fish brown on the outside, but its flesh is pale green before cooking. We like it fried with our butter to turn an appetizing white in a pan."

Agnes saw Gaudin's eyebrows shoot up at the mention of *canoe*, but he waited for another to speak first.

"Oh a canoe. Please tell me about it, Miss Agnes."

"I will show you tomorrow, sir. I'll tell you all about it then, a long story."

The dinner began with the ladies being served first, her father saying to eat before the meat gets cold.

"The Anderson family of Scotland has much to be proud of," her father said, "but no silver or any other item of intrinsic value has come across the ocean to me. This china and silver service came from Monterey by way of San Francisco and is Spanish in origin."

The table had been set with china and silver cutlery her father had won at cards in Cathlamet on the Columbia.

"Of course, I think the worst of the persons responsible for the distribution of my grandfather Doctor James Anderson's estate. Not even a book passed on to me from his legendary library, such a pity. He married into one of the old families of Scotland when he married Margaret Seton of Mounie Castle in Forfarshire, west of Aberdeen but she died in poor health after giving birth to many children. As the property was not his to keep on her death, he moved to Edinburgh to write and publish his writings. Not a medical doctor but a man of letters from the University. After the children had grown he lived near Richmond on the Thames with another woman he married. After her death he remained at Isleworth in the late 1700s and early 1800s supported in his endeavours by wealthy patrons who fostered his intellectual activity in the fields of agriculture and animal husbandry. Doctor Anderson received letters from George Washington, the first U.S. President, asking for advice on agriculture. My grandfather was pleased to correspond with him in some detail."

With hardly a pause, her father continued to hold the floor.

"You may not know the local inhabitants at that place name on the Thames near Richmond do pronounce its name as EYE-ZELL-WORTH to make strangers who cannot know the local pronunciation point themselves out."

"Oh Papa, you must be quite incorrect," Agnes interjected. "Strangers who think they know some English might well pronounce the name as isle -worth."

"Yes, Agnes, but you prove my point, don't you see?"

Agnes decided not to say anything more about it and to remain silent while her father went on endlessly on the subject of the Seton family connection, not least his late cousin, Lieutenant-Colonel Alexander Seton. Said to be a gifted mathematician and linguist, but best known for being the commanding officer of the British Soldiers ordered to stand fast in ranks on deck who died heroically to save the women and children put in the few boats on the troop transport vessel the *Birkenhead*, an early iron vessel troop ship with an unreliable compass, which came too close to shore not far past the Cape of Good Hope in a storm on her way to India.

Agnes spoke to get her father off the subject.

"Papa tells us your ship loaded her cargo at one of the London Docks. Please tell us about them, sir."

Agnes' father, hard-of-hearing, kept on talking.

"I may not have made it clear my father Robert Anderson being one of the sons of Margaret Seton, now lives with my mother at a place called Sutton on the south shore of Lake Simcoe in Eastern Canada, but enough of that, please tell us about your ship, the *Lady Lampson*."

"I will tell you about the Docks later, Agnes," said Gaudin. "In answer to your father: my command is not really a ship, but a barque. Some newspapers spell the word as '*bark*' with a **K**, which is common usage. Even though only a barque, we take pride in her and call her a ship as a term of affection, I think. Ships are larger vessels with the square-rigged sails on all of the masts. A barque requires a lesser number of men for crew with square-rigged sails only on the foremast and the main. The third mast, aft, the mizzenmast, we use to set a large fore-and-aft sail called the spanker with a small topsail above it for sailing in light winds. We set sails on all three masts to balance the helm. Here, I will show you on the slate I see on the side-table. From the bowsprit we set a number of jib sails, the rope lines or '*sheets*' we use to set them to harden in the wind must be led from one side of the ship to the other when we turn about on another tack. She sails well, but is no match for any of the famed Ocean Sailing Greyhounds you may have heard about, all of which require more crewmembers to handle the sails. Our ship looks like a rich man's yacht with teak woodwork on deck and gold leaf scrollwork at the stern counter. On my orders the crew painted a white trim line along the ship's side to accentuate the sweep of the vessel's curving sheer, which seamen always love to look at."

Then remembering items he should have included in the letter he wrote to his father last year, Gaudin told the Andersons his barque does not have such a narrow build, nor such a sharp and conspicuously concave bow as the earlier and larger American clipper ship, the *Sea Witch*, which set time records out of New York to and from Canton and San Francisco. As with the *Sea Witch*, the ship's designer called for the builders to make a neater job of the joinery of the ship's timbers and planking at the bow to cut the weight of the customary and ornate covering boards aft from the bowsprit on both sides. Needless weight would slow the vessel. And no figurehead: instead a finely carved depiction of the head of a mystical animal from the Lampson family coat-of-arms set without ornate display at the top of the ship's bow stem under where the bowsprit will extend forward.

"In another tribute to American sailing ship design of the day," he added, "the builder placed a wooden white-painted taff rail around the outside edge of the long raised quarterdeck aft."

Before the evening ended Agnes' father had much to say about the subject of the Pacific Northwest when he arrived in 1832 and more about the remarkable Margaret Seton and his esteemed grandfather Doctor James Anderson of Edinburgh.

Seemingly starved for conversation, her father had Gaudin responding to talk on other subjects, too. Agnes, fascinated by Gaudin's deep voice, hung on his every word. At one point Gaudin spoke to enthuse about travelling close along the shoreline from Sooke to Victoria with Captain Swanson in the stern-wheel steamer *Enterprise*.

"You were in good hands with Swanson," her father said. "From England as you know. On this coast since '42 on Company sailing vessels. By '58 he became the captain of the company steamer *Beaver*, which you may not know sailed out from England in 1836 for use in the fur trade on this coast. Swanson runs the *Otter* in winter when heavy winds and sea can be expected between here and New Westminster. He runs the more lightly built steamer the *Enterprise* between Victoria and New Westminster in the summer season and on local runs such as to Sooke when the weather permits, little more than a river steamer."

Gaudin spoke to end a short silence.

"Going through Race Passage in daylight with Captain Swanson enabled me to gain local knowledge rare for a visiting sailing vessel captain_____. Some would say too much could go wrong, but I look forward to being able sometime to slip through Race Passage with the

Lady Lampson under sail. I mean to say, only at the right tide and in the right weather and in the right circumstances, sir."

Agnes wondered what he meant by the excitement in his voice. She thought that this would be considered a daring move for a sailing vessel captain to make. What an exciting life this man led! Of course, her father asked him to explain the occasion that would permit him to carry out such a manoeuvre.

"Inbound to Esquimalt on a waning flood tide, as an alternative to being set back by the tide current in the Strait of Juan de Fuca turning to ebb too soon to push me back out to Cape Flattery," Gaudin said, "I can now consider taking any usable wind out of the southwest through southeast to turn downwind to nip inside Race Rocks on the last of the flood tide, and sail through Race Passage past William Head and Albert Head to anchor in Royal Roads and wait for the tide to enter Esquimalt Harbour. A handy move I'd be proud to make, sir. If the wind dropped the ebb could edge me back out, and nothing lost."

Even though her father kept Gaudin involved in wide-ranging talk after their early dinner, later in the evening Agnes and her young captain went outside in the dark to walk in the garden under the stars. Breathing in the scent of her father's roses, Agnes felt a sense of comfort being out of sight of the lamplight in the farmhouse. Holding hands, they became involved in the heady steps of a whirlwind romance.

Next morning after an early farm kitchen breakfast, the two went outside to saddle up the horses, and they kissed in the barn, and they kissed lying in the hay. She thought him very forward, but she did not mind any of that. For him to draw near and close made the tips of her breasts flicker and harden under her loose fitting blouse. Not an unpleasant sensation she dared herself to think as she revelled in the feeling and moved her shoulders to make the sensation last. Susan Moir had painted such a cutting word picture of this man, but Agnes liked far better her own vision of him as no tame cat. That he could ride a horse came as a complete surprise. She hadn't imagined a sailor riding a horse. He told her he had never seen a woman ride astride with such ease, nor look so wonderful doing it. She led through the woods and forest trails to take him to Canoe Cove to see her West Coast Indian cedar dugout canoe. On the way she stopped to show him her log cabin in an open grassy clearing in the Anderson forest. Her brothers had built it for her as a birthday present. The scent of sawn cedar lingered still. They tethered the horses and walked in the warm sunshine across a wide patch of green grass filled with sweet little wild strawberries. She picked a handful of the berries, which she held in the palm of one hand for the two of them to savour as they sat on the warm grass.

"Come, Jim, I will show you the cabin."

Inside, Gaudin turned to see the long soft-as-sable full-length cape, which Agnes had told him about, lying in the sunlight streaming through the door from outside. He bent to touch it, saying,

"Please tell me the story about that," he said. "It must be connected with the fur trade. I have never seen such a thing before."

"It's made from glossy fur sea otter pelts. Indian Women from the Northern Tlingit Indians made the cape from prime sea otter pelts selected for their uniform black colour. Grandpapa Birnie traded for it through Tshimshian Indian middlemen 30 years ago when he and his family lived at Fort Simpson on the Nass River. He made a present of it to my Grandmamma. She gave it to me before I came up from Oregon four years ago. I could use it better than she could now, she said."

Agnes, mindful of her thoughts whenever she stretched herself out on it, loved the feeling of the fur when she spread her fingers out at her sides to touch and feel its softness.

He sat down beside her. With their eyes searching each other out they spent the time together.

Agnes called the end of it. "I AM enjoying just looking at you, sir! And hearing your voice speak. You talk so fine. But time is flying. We should go now to see the canoe at the cove to be back in time for lunch at the house. They will be waiting for us."

"We can come back here afterwards for what the Spanish call a siesta," he said.

And they did, each afternoon, that day and the next.

On that first afternoon they talked endlessly, ending up with his proposal for marriage.

"Agnes, dear girl, at my age I have no time to court you. I want to marry you. Will you consider marrying me next time I come to Victoria and sail with me to live in Jersey?"

She answered without any hesitation.

"Yes, I will marry you, Jim, and go with you to Jersey," she said, "but I must tell you I would rather not live on a farm. I do ask that you find a place for us to live in town where our children will have others to play with."

"St. Helier is the town," he said, "I will look when I go there next.

My older sister Marie and her husband live not far away. and will be good friends when I am away at sea. I will go in now to ask your father if he will agree to you marrying."

He gave her a family silver brooch and a locket to wear.

"We cannot set a wedding date," he said, "because I do not know when my ship will return. I am loading lumber to take to Chile in South America. I do not know what ongoing cargo I will find there."

Agnes saw him looking at her lower lip trembling.

"I cannot be back next summer, but I will be back by the next Christmas. In the meantime I should be able to settle where we can live in Jersey."

"Oh, that is such a long time for me not to see you, Jim," she whispered. "Why can't we marry and you take me with you now?"

"If only I could, Agnes, but the ship sails from Sooke under charter terms that make that impossible. For another, how could your father arrange the wedding on such short notice? I am about to sail. Please wait. You will like living in Jersey and meeting new friends when I am away at sea."

Her father and mother were in complete agreement Agnes should marry Captain Gaudin. With the couple in each other's arms her father announced the engagement to the family.

Afterwards with the hour late Agnes and her mother left the room, leaving Gaudin and her father talking, smoking their pipes, and drinking brandy.

As word of the engagement spread neighbours came to call. Agnes felt flights of newfound joy as her father introduced Gaudin to friends and neighbours as her fiancé. What a wonderful sounding word, she thought; and she, his fiancée.

The two did find moments to be alone together before Gaudin returned to his ship. After an early breakfast next day the pair rode their horses all over the Anderson property and had another engagement for tea for two in Agnes' log cabin.

"Jim, Grandmamma Birnie told me about men like you when she told me what I ought to know about men. I know what you were about to do belongs between husband and wife. I am enjoying my time with you, and find happiness in the thought you will take me to live faraway."

The hours of the last afternoon stretched on until 4 p.m.. The farm alarm bell came as a timely intervention to bring them, her hair somewhat dishevelled, riding back from the log cabin to read an urgent message brought to the house by a rider from Fort Victoria for the captain to return to the ship. Agnes knew Gaudin came close to having his way with her. Her gentle protestations were not really to be believed. He had such a sure hand. She felt as though she were a musical instrument and he, the player who touched the keys. Feeling completely within his power, she loved it as she snuggled into him. The Anderson family pecked when they kissed. Now she found her whole body responding to feelings and sensations she had never experienced.

Agnes, 19 going on 20, considered herself ripe for marriage and ready to be taken wherever he willed, a stirring thought in itself she dared to think.

After the departure of the *Lady Lampson* from Sooke, too far out from town for her to get out to see, Agnes waited for a letter; but no letter came. Instead, Gaudin sent a telegram at Christmas from Coquimbo, Chile. It arrived in the dead of a cold North Saanich winter in time for Agnes to read aloud in front of the main room fireplace to the family assembled for the Anderson family's New Year's Eve 1870 Scottish celebration.

Although the telegram merely stated SOON HOMEWARDS STOP MERRY CHRISTMAS AGNES AND FAMILY, Agnes felt relief to know he made the effort to be in touch with her. She knew everyone used the word ' *homewards* ' to mean England, so she realized he would be sailing there before he could return to Victoria.

"Papa, where is Coquimbo?"

After taking a book from the bookshelf to show her the map of South America, he told her the telegram would have been sent across the Andes from Valparaiso to Montevideo; and from there by the undersea cable connections between South America and England; and across by Atlantic Cable to New Westminster; and on by mail to Victoria.

"Here is a map showing the coastline of Peru and Chile," he said. "Gaudin must have sailed north from Valparaiso to Coquimbo."

"He does have such a long way to go back to London doesn't he Papa?"

"Yes, it is a long way but the climate in Chile will be pleasant and sunny at this time of year," he said. "It will be summertime now in Coquimbo: it will still be summer when he arrives in England on the other side of the world with whatever cargo he gets. The hard part will come when he rounds Cape Horn, but, eastbound, the wind and waves will be pushing him along, not opposing him."

9

GAUDIN IN LONDON

On a warm day in May 1870 everyone at the round table at the Tor-
rington Arms public house off West India Dock Road in East London
listened as Gaudin told his brother officers the sorry tale of delay in the
Lady Lampson's extended maiden voyage. One captain began by asking
him in a quiet voice he must have thought none of the others could hear.

"I want to ask you about the rumour your Mate stayed in his bunk
for most of the voyage. Can that be correct?"

A man nearby called for quiet to hear Gaudin's reply.

"That's correct, Captain," Gaudin answered. "I don't know what got
into him. I had to take on the Mate's work. With the onset of heavy
shipping traffic in bad weather to keep a lookout for in the approaches
to the English Channel, I called on our experienced Ship's Carpenter to
stand watch on deck with the Second Mate again. And the day came
when even the Second Mate logged off duty on being hurt in the leg by
a falling yard in heavy seas. The Carpenter came back on deck after that
to spell me off at times to allow me to go to my bunk to get some sleep
with my clothes on. He waked me when he saw trouble coming, and I
came on deck running."

Pointed questions followed. Gaudin put them aside by starting with
an account of the long delay at anchor in Valparaiso Bay before orders came to sail 200-miles north to Coquimbo to deliver the lumber
through the surf to pile on the grass. More pointed questions followed
as Gaudin told the story.

"In the usual course the Chief Officer would have taken charge of
unloading the lumber on arrival at Coquimbo," Gaudin said. "It started
out that way but ended up in a 40-day debâcle."

At that last word ears pricked up. The word chafed, sounding like a
scriber on a slate board. Some knew the word. Others did not. Gaudin

told them he found it difficult to talk about. Urged on by loud murmurs, he nodded to say he would.

"Parts of the story a man's mother would not want to hear told about her son's life at sea," he began. "The trouble began earlier, but I will start with us in a tropical paradise at Coquimbo. I anchored the *Lady Lampson* fore and aft close in to where the gentle surf line begins to break. The crew unloaded lumber from the ship onto rafts that came out from the shore to ferry loads through the surf. Men on the shore heaved the lumber up to pile on the grass. The job under a hot sun took far too many days. I had the same men stay on the job to bring out loads of heavy rock from the shore on their rafts to ballast the empty ship. None of them hurried, which exasperated me. We hauled the rocks up from the rafts in large wicker baskets to lower into the hold to make our empty ship stable enough to weigh anchor and sail out to sea."

Gaudin told the story of how they sailed 700 miles farther north up the west coast of South America to unload the ballast and begin to take on a cargo of bags of nitrate of soda at Iquique. He began by saying,

"As far as I can make out, this is the beginning of a new trade that will keep sailing vessels busy for years, and the larger the vessel the better. We took the *Lady Lampson* even closer in to the shore at Iquique. The wide bay offers good anchorage in most but not all weather."

Another captain interrupted to ask, "I hear Iquique had a terrible earthquake in recent years, Gaudin. Did you see any signs of it?"

"The town did show sign of recent earthquake damage to the buildings," Gaudin said.

Another asked him to tell them the story of the nitrate passage to London.

"I will get that in a moment. The bags of nitrate came out from the shore at Iquique in fits and starts and finally stopped altogether. Orders came by telegraph to leave Iquique and find a full cargo of the same stuff at a cove close by to the north, the name of which I cannot say in Spanish. The English call it Mexillion Bay, but I saw a faded sign on the shore marking it as Mexillon Bay."

The group at the table listened with evident attention, but a senior captain from another company at a nearby table stood.

"I am much more interested to hear about the cargo of lumber your vessel carried from the Pacific Northwest in your little vessel. Tell us about that, Gaudin."

"Not much to tell, captain. A dreary slow job to load the heavy timbers, which go by the name of *deals*, which were floated out to the ship from a sawmill at Sooke and taken aboard using ship's tackle. Buyers in Valparaiso balked at accepting it. I don't know the ground of complaint. The ship's charterer finally found a buyer at Coquimbo, and I received orders to go there."

Another at the table spoke.

"I hear lumber from other places in the Pacific Northwest, Burrard's Inlet and Puget Sound, comes in high quality, Gaudin. Is that right?"

"I don't doubt it, captain. At Sooke the fir trees in the forest stand high and straight. You have to see them to believe what I am telling you. If ship owners want to make money carrying it for half a year at sea they will need to send larger vessels to carry it and they must find a faster way of loading the lumber than we could."

"Well, that will be up to your company," the first captain interrupting said. "If they lost money on it you won't be sent to do that again, I'd wager."

After a long silence Gaudin went on to give his account to them mostly without much further interruption. He told them he had brought his barque into anchor in Carrick Roads at Falmouth England a month ago in the morning of 18 May 1870 after 87 days at sea, loaded with this new kind of cargo of bags of nitrate of soda dug out of the desert in the border coastline country, lying between Northern Chile and Peru.

"Gaudin, are you sure you did not carry seagull shit, _____ I mean that stinky dirty cargo called *guano*?"

"No Captain, I am thankful we were not driven into carrying anything like that. The nitrate of soda comes in bags filled with dry chemical earth dug out from the Atacama Desert on high ground in Northern Chile. The Valparaiso Ship's Agent told me he heard talk every day of Chile and Peru going to war over the disputed territory. The product appears to be in much demand in Europe. Buyers use it to make smokeless gunpowder, the better to hide the positions of guns firing. The stuff can also be used as fertilizer to grow crops."

"With Prussian ambitions fueled by the Seven Years War, nitrate of soda will be much in demand in Europe I'd say."

No one at the table spoke for a long moment before one of the men asked a question.

"I hear you must take precautions to keep the stuff dry to prevent it from catching fire or exploding. Is that correct, Gaudin?"

"Yes, the Agent advised me to take every opportunity to open the hatch covers to let air into the hold to ventilate and keep the powder dry, which can be a dangerous business when waves run high and threaten to come aboard into an open hatch."

The men drank their ale and filled their pipes in silence, then one of them asked Gaudin to go on to tell more about the voyage with the nitrate.

"Well, I will touch on how the passage homewards ended up. Only a month ago I took a room at the Devon Pride Inn at Falmouth to wait for a telegram telling me where to take the nitrate. I expected a pilot boat at the Scilly Islands carrying orders for us. If none, my orders were to proceed to enter the ship at Falmouth and send a telegram to London. On the morning we departed Peru I decided to head the start page of the new part of the logbook *From Mexillion Bay to the Scilly Islands* as a bit of sorely needed humour."

"What nonsense! That shoreline we have been warned against has no harbour for deepsea vessels."

"Disregard that Gaudin. Nobody cares about that. How many days did it take for you to sail on from Falmouth to London?"

"Seven days and nights in light winds, captain. Orders came on 19 May to take the cargo to London. I sailed immediately and arrived in Blackwall Dock under tow on 25 May."

A messenger burst into the Inn where the captains were talking and made a hesitant approach to the table.

"Begging your pardons, kind sirs, but I have an urgent message for Captain Gaudin_____. Captain Herd wants him to come in to see him now, this afternoon. The carriage I came in waits outside."

The carriage took him into London to the company office. An hour later the young captain and the old seadog in charge of all of the company's sailing vessels met again. Captain Herd came out of his office to greet him with evident warmth and pleasure.

"Come Gaudin. Let's sit and talk in my room. We have a big table there to roll out my charts."

First they ate the midday meal of sliced cold roast beef, Herd's favourite chutney from India, and bread rolls with yellow farm fresh butter carried in to the room by his steward on a shining silver tray as before. Later Captain Herd picked up the logbook out of a bag and handed it back to Gaudin.

"Start with the more recent entries, please. I have read them, but I want you to tell me all about the voyage of the *Lady Lampson* in the same way you did when you returned a year and a half ago from Montreal in the *Ocean Nymph*. I want in particular to hear you speak about your passages at sea to get west of Cape Horn. My time at sea took me sailing in the North Atlantic and to Hudson Bay, but I did sail in the Tropics as an able seaman working my way up to command. You cannot always choose the path you walk in life. Employment came to me in colder places. Happily, my path ended here where I can live in comfort. On second thought, begin with telling me about your arrival back in the Channel. I have the last part of the logbook fresher in my mind. We can go back later to the earlier parts of the maiden voyage of the *Lady Lampson*."

Turning the pages Gaudin picked up on the bare bones of one of his entries to remind him.

"On 13 May 1870 the *Lady Lampson* at 47°18' North 21°16' West north of the Azores in the North Atlantic on her return to England."

"Yes Gaudin, a good place to begin."

"At 6 a.m. with little warning we shipped a *very* high beam sea from the west over the bulwarks that broke some of the *t'gallant* bulwarks. As you know, sir, we added a top section on the bulwarks, which we fancy to call the t'gallant bulwarks. I gave orders to bring in the fore t'gallant sail and middle staysails as we continued to ship great quantities of water the length of the ship, an unsettling experience as the ship showed signs of being overpowered by the weight of the water on deck before the scuppers can clear it all overboard. At 9 a.m. we shipped a *very* heavy sea, which broke through the lee bulwarks back to the poop and set all spare spars and everything else loose about the decks, which I took a hand in helping the crew put right. By 16 and 17 May the ship sailed in fine weather with a breeze out of southwards. We steered to keep clear of a large number of other vessels during this time. Finally off the Scilly Islands and not seeing a pilot boat, we made for Falmouth. On the way in to that place Falmouth Pilot Cutter #6 came out to meet the ship and put aboard Charles Chard, licenced pilot. As no orders for us at the signal station we came to anchor in Carrick Roads in five blessed fathoms at 5:30 p.m. and sent off the Pilot. The Chief Officer continued his many days of being laid-up and off duty and would remain so until the end of the voyage."

"Doubtless, you will be pleased to know he sent in a letter asking to leave your vessel. As I have no other ship to send him to, he will look elsewhere for a berth."

"Perhaps I showed my displeasure over the trouble we had loading the lumber in Sooke. I blame myself for leaving him in charge before satisfying myself he understood his responsibility to keep a proper tally to record the lumber taken on board. How to keep a tally, at all, appeared beyond him. I will come to that later in the logbook."

Turning the page of the large logbook to remember, he continued.

"Next morning, 19 May, I set the crew painting our weather-beaten vessel outside where it can be seen. Went ashore in a hired boat on ship's business at the Port Office and to speak to the local agent for the Ship's Charterer William Gibbs & Sons. I asked him to send a telegram for orders."

In a moment of silence Gaudin thought back on how, walking in town, his legs continued to sense the movement of the ship at sea. He recalled the extreme pleasure of having hot water brought up to his hotel room to be put in a large tub. He remembered thinking how wonderful to be a captain and to have this chance to get ashore to wash in hot fresh water after months at sea. The kitchen at the Inn brought up food and drink for him in his room, such food as he had not tasted for months. And then he slept. Wakened from a deep sleep by a loud knock on the door in the late afternoon, he read the cable telegram from London to take the nitrate cargo to Blackwall Dock in the Port of London.

"I welcomed the news we were not to be sent to some other port than London to discharge the nitrate, sir. Who knows what port the Honourable Company might then have sent us on to from there?"

"You seem very anxious to get back to Victoria. Did you meet the young lady there you told me about before you sailed on the maiden voyage?"

"Yes sir. I will be leaving to go to Jersey in a fortnight to settle where we can be living. With your permission I intend to bring her back with me in the *Lady Lampson* after we marry."

"She must be made of stern stuff if that's your plan. Go on with your account from leaving Falmouth."

"I hired a boat on the shore at 5:30 p.m. the same day, 18 May, to take me back out to my ship, which lay anchored in Falmouth Harbour in a state of readiness to sail. Boarding, I remember saying to the Second Mate, now fit after his recent injury, which had him off duty, 'Mister Farrow, if it pleases you, make sail and weigh anchor. Against the night breeze dropping altogether I hired a tug. Be prepared to take his heaving line and bend on our towing hawser for him to take us out.'"

Herd paid close attention to Gaudin's description of the scene of the tug towing the *Lady Lampson* on a short towline, moving out towards the English Channel passing by the Black Rock to starboard and the high headland lying to port at St Anthony's Lighthouse.

"Yes, Gaudin, I can see it now."

"Out a safe distance and a night breeze promising, I ordered the tug to cast off. The wind then dropped to a calm, wouldn't you know! Daylight the next morning 19 May found us drifting offshore with sails set, but limp and flapping in light southerly airs and calms throughout the day. The ship made slow progress up the Channel. Finally, we came abeam Eddystone Rock Lighthouse at noon with only 30 miles since our departure from Falmouth. By midnight the ship sailed on a course of *East by South* following the southern shore of England in a light westerly wind and under the stars of an early summer sky. Fine weather favoured the ship for the first part of the day on 20 May. The wind came up a bit to enable us to set and carry all of our studdingsails as we slipped along in the damp quiet stillness of wispy fog during the last half of the day with the hatches lifted to air the nitrate. By dead reckoning the ship's position at noon lay 18 miles southwest of St. Catherines Point on the Isle of Wight. Noon-to-noon since Eddystone Rock the ship had come a heartening 130 miles with little wind."

Gaudin continued after a pause to pour fresh mugs of hot coffee and rum. "I will go on now if I may, sir. Next morning I looked around to see numerous ships also sailing in the Channel in light wind and fine weather, which lasted through the day. Cross-Channel passenger ferries steamed in and out of Southhampton moving like sprites. From the thin streaks of black smoke streaming from their smoke stacks, no one could doubt they burn coal. I must tell you, sir, small steamers in the Pacific Northwest often burn sawmill wood not usable for lumber, which makes white smoke, but sparks from the stacks can start a fire in the trees and bush on a close shoreline. The larger steamer vessels burn coal from the mines at Nanaimo, 100 miles by sea from Victoria."

Gaudin went on to sum up several pages of the logbook by recounting that the *Lady Lampson* continued to make way up the Channel in frequent calms with all of her sails set to catch the fitful slants of a summer breeze. By noon he logged sighting Beachy Head 15 miles ahead. And in the days following he logged passing Dungeness Point and South Foreland before coming in to anchor in the good holding bottom provided by the sand and mud in the Downs. Backing the main

yard to stop, he waited for the arrival of the paddlewheel steam tug
Captain Herd ordered on receiving the news from a watchtower near
Dover that the *Lady Lampson* had passed flying signal flags showing her
number.

"By now, sir, the sailors were beginning to think what the shore
would mean to them. I myself began to think of going home to Jersey
in July to stay over with my parents."

"Yes Gaudin, you will have some time off now. Tell me more about
the girl. Where does she live?"

"Near Victoria, sir. I met her last August. We plan to marry, live in
Jersey, and have Gaudin children."

"You are now free to go to Jersey after we talk again tomorrow.
When will you leave?"

"I expect to stay a fortnight in London before I leave for Jersey. I
have much to keep me here until then."

"Please go back to where you left off in your account."

Turning the page, Gaudin recounted that the tug appeared out of
the fog to take the *Lady Lampson* in tow. Running in the fog, the tug
tooted the mournful sound of its steam whistle to warn other vessels she
towed his vessel close behind.

"As soon as we came well into the London River I ordered the jib
boom unshipped and brought back in, sir."

"Yes Gaudin, not an easy task. The bowsprit projecting forward and
high as she does on your vessel could cause no end of trouble under tow
when towed swinging around in the Basin at Blackwall to tie up. In any
event, the Dock charges by every foot of overall length alongside, so the
shorter we make the vessel, the better. Now, it's too early for us to stop
this talk. I want you to go back to the beginning of the maiden voyage
from London in February more than a year ago. Take it from when you
dropped the pilot and set sail outwards. There will be time to talk about
the passage homewards from South America later."

Gaudin turned the pages of the logbook back and began again.

"Can it be more than sixteen months since I left London on the
maiden voyage? Yes, it has been that long. A lot of water left behind
since then. On 22 February 1869 we cast off from the tug and set sail
in a fair breeze at 5 p.m. and soon dropped the Pilot Mister Irvine. We
left South Foreland behind with all possible sail set by 8 p.m."

"What a wonderful beginning for you, Gaudin, being able to go as
far as that so soon after leaving London. Instead of an adverse wind and

a long stay at anchor off Folkstone, you were off and away."

"Yes sir, but as the logbook shows the luck did not last. By 10 p.m. off Dungeness Point I ordered the Royals down in wind squalls out of the northeast and the cold winter rain of February. And the wild winter weather became worse when the wind backed to blow against us. That forced us to beat against it to transit the English Channel. Other vessels must have been there to present a danger, but we saw none of them in the dark of the storm. Two nights later on 24 February I sighted the Casquets Light off the north coast of Guernsey. Not wishing to close that dangerous part of the coast with the Casquets name that made me think of funerals, we came about to point the ship back across the Channel to the south coast of England on another long board with freezing spray high in the rigging and the decks constantly awash."

"Seeing a lighthouse coming from near Jersey must have made you think of home. You did not take leave to go home for Christmas '68."

"Actually no time to leave London. I had friends and my new ship to attend to. The ship's registration papers named me as the *Ship's Husband*, which I proved to be when rigging and fitting her out to sail."

Gaudin's account continued. The winter storm did not let up. Four days later found the ship in the widest part of the English Channel beyond sight of land, head-reaching back toward England in confused seas, thunder, lightning and hailstones with the barometer falling fast.

"Never a thought of turning back," he added, "neither could we point into the wind, but we could bear off to head-reach in the rough and tumble of the gusting winter storm wind and sea in the shallow waters of the Channel. We could not see the shore to gauge our position. I was certain it lay too close for comfort in a heaving-to. In any event I did not know how well this new ship would behave in a heaving-to. Later in the voyage I rigged a shorter trysail mast abaft the foremast to set a loose-footed Spenser sail of my own devising from a gaff. Setting it helped keep way on the ship."

"Yes Gaudin, some vessels do not take to heaving-to_____. You wrote in your logbook you finally left the entrance to the Channel off Ushant ten days out from the Downs on 4 March. Then you were off and running in the open ocean to the southwest with a northwest wind on your starboard quarter. Hours later the wind turned to blow from the northeast, strong to push from behind."

"Yes sir, after such a prolonged passage to come clear of steep seas in the English Channel we made good time in the ocean in all weather from our position off Ushant at northwest tip of France, a long large windswept rock with no trees on it. We English have corrupted the name of the light in French Ile-d'Ouessante to *Ushant*."

"I like the sound of our name for it better," said Herd.

"The name Ushant for the most westerly island will stick, sir. Even the French seaman will shorten the name to make it sound like Ushant."

"I have interrupted you, Gaudin. Please continue."

"After three days of fast sailing we came into North East Trades' kind of weather, sun and puffy white clouds and steady wind from behind on our port quarter and with wind squalls and warm rain to keep us on our toes."

"I took keen interest in seeing how you kept way on the ship in the Equatorial zones, Gaudin, more so in the Atlantic than the Pacific."

"Yes sir, we kept moving in light airs coming from all around the compass. Off Africa on 21 March at 04°49' North 22°58' West I saw conditions as light wind and sultry, gloomy, and the sea lit from below with phosphorescence in the calm water reflected back by the yards and rigging. Weather dark and cloudy, and so altogether dark I could not see forward the length of the ship."

Gaudin turned the page and went on again.

"And on 23 March calms and humendously hot at 02°60' North 22°40' West. Then on the 29 March after crossing the Equator with our usual lack of ceremony to mark the occasion, light wind and sultry weather with continuous sheet lightning in clouds banking up high all around the horizon."

"What does that word '*humendously*' mean, Gaudin?"

"I don't know sir, but Captain Adamson used it to describe hot humid weather that makes crew cranky. It sounded right to me."

He turned the page again and carried on. "On 5 April in very hot weather we made way against a strong swell on the ocean. In the darkness of night came vivid flashes of lightning ahead to the south-southwest. All around us showed occasional broad phosphorescent flashes under the water close alongside. Must have been large schools of small fish being chased by bigger fish we expected to see any moment burst out of the smooth unruffled surface of the water."

Gaudin turned pages to pick up on entries made ten days later on 15 April 1869.

"After sailing well in the South East Trade Winds coming at us from South Africa, we have now come much farther south well off the coast of the Argentine. First light presented with a dark threatening appearance, a fresh breeze ruffling the surface, and vivid flashes of lightning all around the horizon. Then the wind dropped off to a light air. We sailed on with it over a jumble of cross swells, which put the ship in a cranky mood and made everyone fitful. But the noon sight showed 37°19' South 49°00' West and us having made 145 miles in the last 24 hours, which didn't seem likely without the help of an ocean current. Ten days later, 62 days out from the Downs, 26 April, a dark morning began with a strong gale out of the southwest and a high sea running at the beginning. I ordered the Royal Yards down. I thought the lessening of their weight aloft might help us westbound in the heavy weather ahead off the Argentine and around the Horn. We are sailing fast without Sail set on them. Upon sign of it moderating some, I ordered up the foresail, the upper foretopsail, and the jib. My plan to divide the topsails into smaller upper and lower topsails proved out well. We crossed upper and lower topsail yards with mast tracks to ease raising them. I could better handle the ship in some wind and sea conditions with only upper topsails set. The wind veering to come from southward allowed us to tack to the west-south-west to steer to make landfall on the coast of Tierra del Fuego and then follow the trend of the coast. We will turn at Cape San Diego to enter the Strait of Le Maire, but I am getting ahead of myself. We are not there yet."

"Gaudin, I must interrupt you. It is getting late. Jump ahead now and tell me about the Horn and show me on the chart I am laying out on the table."

"Well sir, I will get there by saying that by the end of April, we were sailing 100 miles or more off the coast of the Argentine and coming between Patagonia and the Falkland Islands. I am following Captain Adamson's recommended route. On 26 April at 49°40' South 62°02' West we made good weather of it sailing through steep seas coming from a *Pamperos* storm that came down on us from the Andes, blowing from the west across the wide-open plains in the Argentine called the *Pampas*. The clouds foretold its arrival and we were ready to run with it. Under reduced sail, only the foresail, upper topsail, and jib, the strong gale of wind with heavy squalls hit us hard, made us list to port with the main rail under. But our good little ship sailed out of it without any further alarm."

"Gaudin, point out to me on the chart your track from the Strait of Lemaire to the Horn."

"I will do that, sir. As you hear me out you will understand why I stress the transit of the Strait of Le Maire westbound to get past the Horn. I cannot get the picture out of my mind of those turbulent seas and frigid rockbound shores with only rare sun to give warmth. As you can see from the chart, the width of the opening to the Strait compares well with the width of the Strait of Juan de Fuca, but the tide currents can run much faster off Cabo San Diego. The timing to enter the Strait of Le Maire is critical because the flood tide current in the Strait can run against us faster than we can sail against it. We must wait for the tide to turn to ebb before we can begin our a'westering into the Pacific. With the ebb, we make distance under sail through the Strait in the direction of Cape Horn, 120 miles ahead. If too early for the time of high water in the Strait, the westbound captain can keep distance off the northeastern shore of the tip of Tierra del Fuego in the back eddy or dodge about to await the beginning of the ebb tide to enter the Strait. Passing Cape San Diego at the correct time will take us a long way toward the Horn before the tide turns adverse. Given the correct tide, handy vessels like the *Lady Lampson* can go to windward into adverse winds to enter and transit the strait. The tiderips show a bottom of rock shelving shallow off Cabo San Diego. We do not cut too close to it. Before I forget to say it, we have to be careful not to be deceived by Cabo San Vincente when running down in the back eddy past the thick beds of kelp off the shoreline to reach Cabo San Diego. Far too easy in poor visibility to mistake the false cape to the north of the true cape and stand in to the trap of the shallows of Thetis Bay between the two capes. No lighthouses as aids to navigation, which makes for another reason to be in these waters in Southern Hemisphere summertime when we can see the shore in the light sky at midnight and be guided by what we see."

"What's the story about the standing waves in the Strait, Gaudin?"

"We can run into opposing steep ocean waves inside the Strait on rounding Cape San Diego, which make this no place to be out in a boat jigging for cod. On this last voyage, the ebb once established and running against the waves, soon flattened them. At least, that has been my experience. A moderate breeze turned light and then freshened again. The *Lady Lampson* entered the Strait of Le Maire after the ebb had taken hold. We found no standing waves. We sailed through the Strait on a reach in fair winds coming from the northwest often with a touch of north in it to enable the helm to come up to take advantage of it. To starboard we passed 20 miles of high rocky ledges and cliffs, broken by the opening into Good Success Bay before we turned the ship's heading away to the southwest. Looming high beyond to starboard stands 4,000-foot Bell Mountain, which the Spaniards named *Campana* for its bell-shaped form. When we passed Good Success Bay on the southern coast of Tierra del Fuego the lookout hailed the deck to see the ship in the bay. To murmurs of approval of my crew I gave the order to turn in to investigate the sight of a derelict vessel at anchor, sails in tatters on the yards. I put out a boat with men eager to investigate. No clue as to the whereabouts of the crew, who may have perished on the shore from this severe climate or at the hand of hostile naked natives in the trees English sailors have heard about. These thoughts made us more aware of our own situation in this damp and dark part of the World far from help."

"As I recall, Gaudin, Drake entered the Pacific by sailing through the Straits of Magellan and, on leaving it, storms drove him south and east to what he called *the uttermost part of the earth* before the wind changed to allow him to turn to continue westward around the World. The Dutch seamen who came there named it Cape H-O-O-R-N. Please go on."

"Yes sir, what a brave performance by Drake at a time when English sailors knew not the bounds of the earth or how much ocean lay before them as they struck into the Pacific. We sailed on to pass Barnveldt Island on our weather beam. Cape Horn visible in the distance ahead on 30 April. Clear sky at first followed by fast moving lowering gloom of cloud that ended any thought of sunlight breaking through. I could not avoid thinking of the unreality of the light northwest offshore wind under the dark cloud: so unexpected in these parts and so out of proportion to the rapid movement of the curtain of dark cloud moving above us to the east. But the wind did allow us to sail on a reach in drizzling rain, heeled over to port, and punching into ocean swells coming from westward not yet driven by storm. No millpond as we drove to the southwest to lose sight of the Horn, sharpening our course up to starboard whenever possible to gain Westing. By day's end on 2 May, 67 days out from the Downs, we saw ahead the *Islas Diego Ramirez*."

Captain Herd remarked the tales of Drake and the early Spanish navigators had always fascinated him.

"I have often thought that we should consider those islands as a monument for the two brothers, Diego and Ramirez, who discovered those rocky islands in the middle of Drake's Channel."

"Yes sir. My schoolmaster in Jersey taught me their family name, Nodales, sir. I doubt any seamen have ever taken the time to land there, not a tree or bush on them, just two wet windswept mounds of rock more than fifty miles out in the middle of Sir Francis Drake Channel, a good landmark for us that day. To accord with Captain Cook's recommendation to mariners we drove farther southwest, hoping for the wind eventually to back to the southwest to enable us to turn to put the wind on our port beam to make Northing to sail clear into the Pacific. The ship made heavy weather of it for eight long days and nights before that damnable wind would back to enable us to take up the new slant into the Pacific."

"Tell me what happened in those eight days."

"The first day found our little ship beating to the southwest of the Horn beyond sight of any landmark in heavy seas with decks often awash up to our hips. On the weather turning to come on fine, we turned to put about to the northwest. But a turn made too soon: by noon the following day we drew close enough to Cape Horn to sight it again, this time only 12-miles distant to the north. We had gained little distance made good to the west overnight against the weather, the sea, and an adverse Southern Ocean Current. The wind dropped off and a steep ocean swell began rolling in from westward under ominous low dark cloud without wind to disturb the surface."

Running his finger down the page, he continued.

"By 8 p.m. we sailed in driving rain and a freshening westerly storm with Cape Horn not yet behind us. By midnight change of watch the ship under only lower topsails fought a heavy gale of wind with squalls and rain into and through the next day. You know the movements of a sailing vessel at sea in a storm: the ship rolled, yawed, and pitched in the darkness. Crew with their lifelines made their way forward from one handhold to another, decks awash sluicing them clear of anything not tied down and secured. At noon the next day Islas Diego Ramirez bore *West by North* only 20-miles distant. We had not yet passed them. Again, our efforts gained little Westing. The crew exercised the axes to chop away ice from rigging and the top hamper. The damp, the cold, and the misery came at a time when no one suffered seasickness, but the frostbite, the swollen fingers, and saltwater boils on the body afflicted us until we came much farther north. You have seen the log entry where I decided to write that the good little ship is doing well in these heavy seas. I thought those words expressed it well to say how she kept her bow lifting up to shed the floods of water that came when she plunged into towering waves. The iron frames of her new type of construction are doing a good job of keeping the planking from working and opening up to allow water leaks into the cargo holds."

"Yes Gaudin, that's a blessing."

"The ship, behaving well, kept moving in a continuation of a heavy gale out of the west–south–west with violent squalls and a cross-sea in the early morning hours of 4 May. Later, I ordered the mizzen staysail set when it became apparent to me the ship was tending to fall off into the trough of the sea. At mid-morning I sighted another barque in company on the port beam too far away to speak. Dull and heavy looking clouds on the horizon, but I was able to take the noon sight to show 57°40' South Latitude 68°45' West Longitude. So you can see we are not yet clear of the dangers of the Horn and the Outer South Chilean coast. The wind changed in the early afternoon to come out of the west with heavy squalls of snow and hail, which continued into the night watches. In the morning we tacked to southward with first light sky presenting a wild appearance. Handed in the mainsail, and then the foresail, but kept sailing as fast as before. Before noon a strong gale out of the north struck with sleet that came as ice hail coming in like grapeshot fired in a broadside from the low clouds alongside, not possible to evade when standing on deck. Difficult for me to describe the violence of the elements against which our little ship laboured. I could not imagine the sea conditions could become worse. Noon sight showed only 24 miles in the last 24 hours. And the barometer kept falling. In the early afternoon the wind backed to west-north-west with violent squalls. As I do not intend to sail south of 57° for fear of ice in the sea, I had the Mate call All Hands on Deck to wear ship to northward at 3:30 pm. Soon afterwards we brought in the lower fore topsail and the main topsail in terrific squalls that flattened the wave tops and made the rigging lines howl and moan. By nightfall the barometer came down to a low 28.24 inches and we saw lightning in the dark sky to the southwest. Before midnight the wind turned to come from the west. A short time later we witnessed a violent wind change, which came down on us with snow and hail squalls out of the west-south-west. These weather conditions remaining the same through to the dark on the morning of 8 May made our time on deck difficult. Lulls more frequent by 8 a.m. enabled us to set the foresail and the main. The Chief Officer laid up and off duty for the first time. Two barques seen sailing in company but were too far off to speak. I sent the hands aloft at noon in violent squalls. Only 30 miles made good in the last 24 hours. By late that night the wind backed to come out of the south with a rising barometer, which enabled us to set more sail before the new watch came on at midnight. On 9 May with squalls about to afflict us, I gave the order that sent men up to reef the topsails. We sailed on. With another heavy squall threatening to come down hard on us in towering seas, we brought in the mainsail and upper topsails to wear ship to southward carrying only the foresail, upper topsail, and jib. Heavy snow and hail squalls followed. Soon the wind backed to come from the south by early evening. We wore ship again in a strong gale, squalls and towering seas. The wind continued through the next day. Violent squalls, rain, and a head sea began the day of 11 May, but when the gale showed sign of dropping off after breakfast, I ordered the mainsail and upper topsails set and took the opportunity to re-shoe the inner jib stay fitting on deck, which had come adrift in the storm we had come through. I could then set that sail to harden in the wind to balance the helm and ease the steering. Later the wind backed to turn to a strong gale varying from the south and to the west of south. But it dropped off in cold frosty weather by nightfall. At midnight I called the new watch to stand-to in squalls, hard frost and snow. They faced poor footing on the slippery deck and in the rigging on this Great Southern Ocean cruise in the heartless waters lying to the south of the Roaring Forties. The wind dropped to only a light air by morning, but a heavy ocean swell from the west had our vessel rolling and pitching, and the masts describing arcs in sky. By 4 p.m. the wind freshened up from eastward against the swell for a wet and uncomfortable time on deck. The Chief Officer logged himself off duty again, unable to stand the fatigue. By 10 p.m. the wind came on from a new direction, a sudden shift to blow from the southwest. Within the hour the wind backed to come from the southeast in a strong wind and squalls of cold driven rain, which dumped down on us from dark clouds to afflict us. The ship continued to make way through the jumble of towering peaks of cross-seas under low clouds, all of which made me wonder how our little ship survived."

"I think, Gaudin, you have told me your ship took eight days trying to get north of the Horn's latitude fighting sea spray freezing on the rigging before she could fight herself clear of the terrible weather and take up a slant north into the South Pacific?"

"Yes sir, the winter weather in the Great Southern Ocean sunk our chances for a fast passage 50 South in the South Atlantic to 50 South in the Pacific. We could do better if we could arrange to depart London in late summer or by the end of September."

Herd made no comment and Gaudin turned the pages to pick up on another entry some days later to let him remember.

"Daylight began on 18 May with a continuation of strong gales and a tremendous sea on from the west and south of west. Almost stopped as her bows plunged into the waves, I gave the order to bear off, followed by calling all hands to wear ship to stand on to the northwest. By noon I calculated our new position farther north at 54°36' South, but a clearing sky followed by a wicked gale wind with snow squalls made me decide not to try adding more sail. In the afternoon the wind dropped enough to allow setting the mainsail, inner jib, and the main top staysail to make way again. With barometer rising I gave orders to send the men up to let the reefs out of the main topsail in heavy snow squalls, which carried on into the night. Next day weather conditions improved on our way north of 54°26' South 78°00' West, but we ran in and out of snow squalls and occasional hail in air too cold to hold precipitation as rain."

"Gaudin, looking at the 78° West longitude line on the chart, you were then not far from the dangerous rocky coastline of Southern Chile?"

"Yes sir, that's right, but I bank on the Humboldt Current beginning to help keep us well offshore. We used our sails to keep moving north and away from danger. I hoisted the Royal Yards again ready to use when we could. Bringing them down for the heavy weather off the cape helped ease the rolling."

"Soon you reached the South East Trade Winds?"

"Not as quickly as I had hoped, sir. Not until 10 days later, 29 May, that I could sight Isla Mas a Fuera at 34°12' South 81°55' West. By that time we had been running for days in warm and sunny weather. The Trades came in strong by 4 June to help us make distance, day in and day out. But by 23 and 24 June we hit the first of the equatorial calms at 14°07' North 119°4' West, sailing in which we endured weather consisting of light wind, dark clouds, heavy rain in great heat. I think we must find a better way to sail through the Equatorial zone in the Pacific, sir. The American Clippers made great runs to San Francisco from New York. We should find out where they aim to sail when they cross the Line in the Pacific to accomplish such good passage times. We spend too much time trying to sail through calms on our standard route."

"We will look at what that American Matthew Maury has written about that, Gaudin. Go ahead in your logbook."

"By 19 July we had gone beyond the calms and the Equatorial Zone to fall in with the North East Trades, which we used to take a long fast slant to the northwest to reach a noon position at 42°13' North 137°15' West. Falling in with a fine northwest breeze, we steered a compass course of *East-North-East* toward the coast of Northern California making runs of 200 miles or more every day. And by 21 July we continued with the wind out of the north to reach a position at 42°30' North 133°20' West, which is well offshore Cape Mendocino. Here, I will point it out on the chart. Early on 30 July sailing in light wind and fog we made landfall at Destruction Island off the coast of Washington Territory. Captain Adamson taught me not to avoid making landfall in this latitude, far better than finding yourself loitering off the dangerous West Coast of Vancouver Island with storm winds coming up to drive you farther north, if the onshore ocean current doesn't set you on the rocks first. By 7 p.m. we sailed abeam Cape Flattery Lighthouse in a breeze. During the night we turned to sail into the Strait of Juan de Fuca with the incoming flood tide in light airs, which continued until late afternoon next day when the wind roused strong out of the west to take us speeding up the Strait in clearing weather to arrive in Esquimalt Harbour late at night on 31 July 1869. We were pleased to end the voyage anchored in six fathoms of blessed calm water with the cable veered out to 15 fathoms in a quiet, dark, and peaceful place. The rattle of anchor chain set off a shcrawking sound of complaint from the blue heron on the nearby beach and set distant dogs barking at each other. Lamped out, set the anchor watch and prepared for the morrow."

"This time, Gaudin, you did not have your vessel towed to enter Victoria's Inner Harbour in Victoria Town in state for all of the citizenry to see you as the main event of the day?"

"Some early risers on the morning of our departure from Esquimalt to Sooke days later may have seen us creep away under tow, but as you say, sir, the townspeople did not see our vessel placed alongside the company wharf to draw crowds. As you know sir, the company used its other ship bottoms to move fur pelts during this time."

"How many days did you lie there before you departed to go to this place called Sooke?"

"Much longer a time alongside the wharf in Esquimalt than usual to

unload heavy mechanical cargo for the steam warships in Her Majesty's
Naval Squadron. I will tell you the story about our long stay in Sooke,
but first, everyone finds the Native Indian place-name, Sooke, hard to
pronounce. You hear me say it as the locals do. They say it like soot in
a chimney, but end it with a K instead of T. But back to the time we lay
alongside the wharf in Esquimalt. I decided to stay on board for the 11
days it took to unload the heavy machine parts and other cargo for the
Royal Navy. I continued to stay on board during the loading and trimming of ballast to steady the ship for the upcoming 26-mile tow around
into Sooke Harbour. The crew in our boats used their oars to haul us
back out from the wharf to anchor in the Harbour. I sent able seamen
ashore at liberty on 12 August, but I remained aboard. Next morning at 6 a.m. in fine summer weather we weighed anchor for Captain
Swanson to bring the company steamer *Otter* alongside. The *Enterprise*
had broken down and could not run until repaired. The *Otter* towed us
along the shoreline of Vancouver Island and, despite our size, through
the narrow winding entrance to Sooke Harbour. Here I will show you
on the chart where the coastline lies."

Herd asked about the Olympic Mountain Range in Washington
Territory.

"Sir, I find it hard to describe the grandeur of the high mountain
scenery across on the other side in the Strait, like nothing in Eastern
Canada or in the Maritime Provinces."

"Go ahead, Gaudin."

"In swinging to the wind at anchor in Sooke, we grounded aft, so
hove her out at once into deeper water to anchor by head and stern at
the top of the flood tide at 1 p.m."

"How long did you remain in Sooke during the loading operation?"

"Thirty days, sir. We lay in the harbour for an unconscionable
length of time and did not get underway until Saturday 12 September.
We lost many workdays waiting for loading crews to come from shore-
side on some weekdays and most Saturdays. No work at all done from
shoreside on Sundays."

"You had a sorry time of it in Sooke, Gaudin. If I can help it you
will not be called on again to load heavy timber deals out of the water
alongside using your own tackle. Larger sailing vessels, I hear, will be
coming with steam-powered winches to do this kind of work."

"Sir, I can tell you the company ought to consider building its own
steam tugs. The tugs available do a fine business towing larger sailing

vessels than ours to and from Cape Flattery and then to the Burrard's Inlet for lumber and to and from Nanaimo for coal. But to tell you more of my story, I must say I took some time ashore in Victoria when the *Enterprise* came back into service to arrive in Sooke on other freight business, and I managed a ride back into town in her. A fast stern-wheel river steamer, you would think ill fitted for rough-water work anywhere on the coast, but Captain Swanson runs her here in summer, choosing his weather to run or stay in the harbour. I followed up on my new friendship with retired Chief Trader A. C. Anderson, who entertained me at his farm in the countryside 20 miles north of town. His daughter, I intend to marry."

"How do you think she will like living in Jersey?"

"She has grown up on a farm, so I expect she will find it little different from where she now lives. Shipboard life, however, will be a big change, not least, hearing new words on deck like: haul, ease, let go, heave, trim, make fast or secure, overhaul, belay; also serving, flaking, seizing, worming, and parceling of line. I'll explain it all."

"What arrangements did you make to be towed out to sea from Sooke?"

"In a spell of fine weather in September I called on Captain Swanson to come to tow us out of Sooke Harbour. He steamed the *Enterprise* out from Victoria in the evening to lie alongside overnight to wait for the fog to clear in the heat of the next day's late summer sun. He is an Englander long with the Honourable Company on the Pacific Coast and a fine old man who earlier showed me the way through Race Passage inside Race Rocks in case I ever need to be sailing there. The fog cleared. The *Enterprise* began the tow with a breeze out of the east. Instead of towing us out at the end of a line, the steamer in position alongside, pushed us outside to the harbour entrance with a spring line on to take the strain. The tugs in the Pacific Northwest tend to handle placing a vessel alongside a wharf in this way, rather than swinging the tow in at the end of a towline. As they cast off Swanson gave us a toot of his steam whistle and the crew of the *Enterprise* gave us three-cheers and wished us a *bon voyage*. A fair breeze out of the east filled our sails. We sailed down the Strait to the open sea. A wonderful painting this would have been with a bone in our teeth and making nine knots or more, the Olympic Mountains distant behind in the sun, and six other Sail coming in from the ocean and beating up in the Strait, crossing our bows during the few hours we took going out. How grand we all looked with our sails set and drawing! "

"That's a good place for you to stop, Gaudin. Please come again tomorrow to go on to tell me about your passage to Valparaiso."

10

ONWARD FROM SOOKE

The next morning's talk session with Captain Herd began with a remark that took Gaudin aback.

"As I recall, Gaudin, your logbook shows you took 67 days to reach Valparaiso? Others tell me that too long a time for the passage to take."

"Yes sir. I aimed to use the winds to make a faster passage, but we didn't arrive until 19 November 1869. I'd do better another time."

"Tell me about it."

"Sir, early on 12 September the *Enterprise* came alongside to use a spring line to steam us out of Sooke Harbour into the gentle ocean swell running against a fresh easterly breeze outside in the Strait. Sails unfurled and towlines dropped, we immediately set sail to make distance out to sea, turning south off the American coast at Cape Flattery. At 47°18' North 126°55' West we spoke the sharp-hulled American clipper *Shooting Star*, now down to carrying coal to San Francisco. Neither she, nor the smoke from the tug towing her from Nanaimo, had been in sight when we set sail in the Strait off Sooke. After dropping her towline, she began her run under sail to overtake us. With her sails filling and studdingsails set, the *Shooting Star*, longer and faster, came up from behind us with next morning's sunlight from the east shining first on her upper sails. It took all day for her beautiful shape to come over the jagged line of the westerly wind waves on the horizon behind us to pass two cables off and draw ahead. We saw the crew of the clipper working hard trimming sails to make best speed. Such a splendid sight! None of us could take our eyes off her. But I must say we all found great satisfaction in seeing our ship not being passed *too* quickly on our track south."

Gaudin turned a page.

"We navigated south past Cape Flattery well offshore the North

American Coast in fine weather and fresh westerly winds, sailing as fast as we could with the wind more often out of the north, pushing us along from behind. Nothing held us back for days on end. On 23 September, sailing to follow the trend of the Mexico coastline, we came to 23°11' North 121°50' West, which, put us far out from that coast. We fell in with the zest of the brisk North East Trade Winds. We made great speed through the water in constant seaspray and warm saltwater awash on the deck, but as I will explain, I made the mistake of sharpening up on a course too soon to head to Valparaiso, which lay thousands of miles ahead."

"I enjoyed the descriptive entries in your logbook."

"Thank you sir, I tried to write it for you to read. In that same afternoon of 23 September a freshening wind out of the northeast and a large swell made up against us in humid 80° Fahrenheit weather. Hauled down the main t'gallant studding sail and found we did as well without it. At sunset the sun showed an ominous dark red appearance. The wind, an outrider for the North East Trade Wind, rose again fresh out of the northeast. A high bank of clouds stood without any apparent motion on the horizon to the southeast, sea birds stopped flying, and dark little patches of scud cloud flying fast overhead from the northeast scurried low over the masthead."

"I can picture the sight, Gaudin."

"Even though we had the advantage of a wind that favoured, we found ourselves punching into heavy cross-seas that rose against us to put the ship faltering. At midnight in continuing discomfort I took in the Royals, the foretop and lower studdingsails and the upper topsails to make the ship take up an easier motion in the seas. At 20°25' North 120°45' West we carried on in a southerly direction with no reduction in speed and with far less discomfort."

"That can so often happen on reducing sail, Gaudin. Please go on and tell me about your passage."

Turning the pages Gaudin carried on.

"Twelve days out from Sooke, 24 September, the day presented with an unusual yellow misty sunrise. The sun rose on the open ocean above a bank of heavy dark cloud having an apparent slow northerly movement. Low scud cloud again moving fast from eastwards. I brought in the t'gallant sails to make the ship's motion easier in the sea. At noon the sextant sight showed us at 29°95' North 120°45' West. 176 miles made good since the previous noon, but in the afternoon the ship moved with evident hesitation again in heavy cross-seas coming from the southeast and the southwest. Those seas put *Lady Lampson* off her stride as they ran into each other as if taking deliberate steps to oppose our movement southwards. In spite of the difficulty we passed and left behind two other Sail seen distant ahead in the morning. Passing both vessels caused immense enjoyment on board because we carried no more sail than the others."

"Yes Gaudin, such a small matter can do wonders for men at sea. Do go on."

"On the weather improving at 10 a.m. I set the main t'gallant sail, outer jib and middle staysails. We observed a strong glare throughout and weather unusually close and sultry. By afternoon the ship made scarce headway against alternating head and cross-seas. I observed strange weather conditions, the sky overhead clear one hour, followed with only light cirrus clouds on high and torn and ragged clouds banked high on the horizon around us. By nightfall the sky became less foreboding than last night. I ordered the fore t'gallant sails set above the rest to make speed again. At midnight the cloud condition in the sky appeared worse with ragged clouds aloft passing overhead from the southeast at a great rate out of proportion to the wind on the water."

Turning a page Gaudin went on again.

"During the next night the wind turned to come in rude blasts out of the south and then from the east, which headed us and forced us to steer off to keep way on the ship. On the wind dropping off altogether the ship quit sailing. The sky presented a wild appearance at first light, but a patch of blue sky seen overhead provided some encouragement. No sign on the horizon of the two vessels seen yesterday. We must have left them behind during the night. By mid-afternoon the air became close in a sultry temperature of 87° Fahrenheit. Our bows plunged into a ponderous head sea. The ship's hold remained tight, making no water despite working of ship's timbers with the constant plunging of the bow into the head sea. Motionless heavy clouds lay all around the horizon. The sails hammered against the masts in most helpless manner. I kept the ship sailing in one direction or another as the wind backed and veered. We were not making distance in these conditions, which kept the crew's teeth on edge, and mine also. For the remaining daylight we could do nothing to make way, just knocking about in a cross-sea with waves running against another in short peaks of agitation. By nightfall a heavy bank of dark cloud came up in the southwest. It rose high toward us before receding back in magical fashion without imparting to us any clear meaning. At nine p.m. I felt a light air out of the northeast on my left cheek, but nothing came of it. Next morning the wind came on strong enough to make distance to the southeast on a port tack with all sail set, but the wind did not last. Soon we were left dipping our bows in a pitching movement into a strong swell making up from southwards. Clouds rose up high from that direction to give me a warning of wind coming, but little came of it as we slogged along in a most unhappy state."

Gaudin opened another page.

"On 26 September, 14-days out from Sooke, with the wind now out of the north to favour us, at 9 a.m. we passed and spoke the British barque *Wood Hall*. We steered to pass upwind a cable off. '*Eleven days out from Frisco for Liverpool*' came their captain's megaphone call across the water sounding weird and strange as from deep in a Well. Great excitement showed on both vessels, but more on ours because we, the faster, even though we loaded high with the deck load of lumber. By sunset, after divine services on deck this Sunday, we could see her astern, lower topsails-down, and showing only t'gallants and Royals above the horizon."

"Gaudin, you conducted Divine Services according to regulation?"

"Yes sir, but I have made it clear I do not insist on them attending the service I as master am required to hold. I am interested to see the many who do come. The more come, I might add, after a show of the blue flickering light of *St. Elmo's Fire* in the masts and rigging during an electrical storm."

"Yes Gaudin_____, always a spooking sight. Please go on."

"The wind left us on 28 September. A dead calm followed in 92 degrees Fahrenheit heat at 14°57' North 118°55' West. Two large sharks and dolphins swam alongside, the sharks lazy and the dolphins full of life and movement. On the last day of September I had the ship running in heavy rain and wind squalls, which made for great activity on the deck. Some of the crew caught rainwater in canvas sacks, the helmsman adjusted his steering to bear off in the wind squall to help those tending the sails. Lightning in the clouds banked up to the east created the impression distant eyes on us: we were not alone on the ocean."

"Please skip ahead to where you crossed the Equator, Gaudin."

"Sir, we crossed the Line at 120° West Longitude, which will tell you how much of the South Pacific Ocean remained between us and

Valparaiso, which lies in much the same longitude as New York City. Sailing in light airs at the Equator we saw tiderips in the water, strong enough to affect steering. I calculated a current setting to the northwest against us, an extraordinary phenomenon, perhaps an upwelling of the Humboldt Current. I have no idea how deep the bottom lies beyond soundings."

Gaudin explained they ran through more calms and squalls of wind and downbursts of rain to reach the cheerful air of the South East Trade Wind, which filled the sails but prevented them from steering a course direct to Valparaiso.

And he went on with his account.

"I had thought the farther down the eastern side of the Pacific off Mexico we could penetrate, the less distance we would have to sail to arrive in Chilean waters. But after crossing the Equator and falling in with the South East Trade Winds, they barred me from taking up a heading direct to Valparaiso, and instead sent us slanting southwest toward the South Pacific Islands. Of course, that made me realize I should have sailed our usual route south from Cape Flattery and not wasted precious time trying to take a short cut."

"Yes Gaudin, I understand. Once over the Equator, you couldn't do any better than use the South East Trades to take up a slant to the southwest in a wide part of the Pacific Ocean, passing to the east of the Marquesas and the Tahitian Archipelago."

"Yes sir, and after we sailed clear of the Marquesas, we sailed as far south as Pitcairn Island before we could turn to find winds to take us eastward to Valparaiso."

Gaudin turned the pages.

"On the morning of 22 October, a thousand miles beyond Tahiti and 40 days out from Sooke, we passed eight miles off Isla Henderson, low and unremarkable. Knowing the island's latitude and longitude, I checked the ship's two chronometers to be certain I could rely on them to calculate longitude for navigation onwards. In the afternoon with a rising barometer, the wind out of the east-south-east increased to such a strength that I ordered the Royals down to ease the motion of the ship."

Herd drank from his mug and re-lit his pipe.

"Gaudin, how are you going to explain the use of the Royals to the woman you say you intend to marry?"

"I will tell her I set them at the uppermost level of the *Lady Lampson's* sails to give speed to the vessel, but we do not cross skysail yards above them. Sailing vessels with larger crews do that. I don't know why master mariners write the word Royal in the logbook with a capital R, but they do; and they never use capital first letters to write the names of the other sails."

Gaudin went on to say that in this instance he brought down the Royals because the ship could sail on as fast as before in the rising wind without them, heeling less and with an improved ship's motion felt on deck.

"Had you decided not to push on farther south from Pitcairn to reach the westerly winds in the Great Southern Ocean?"

"Yes sir. Before the end of the passage I wished I had, but I had taken up far too much time to get down this far. Going a longer way around to Valparaiso might have been a better choice than the route I chose. I used up almost 30 days to sail two thousand miles from Pitcairn to Chile in alternating wind and calm, which necessitated much sail handling to cope with the wind systems encountered in the region of changing temperate weather south of the Tropics. In contrast, and as you know, sir, the wind direction and the barometer readings remain nearly constant in the Tropics."

Herd asked about the landfall on the Chilean coast.

"Sir, the high lighthouse at Angeles Point helped us make the approach into the bay at Valparaiso by night. I followed Captain Adamson's teaching to approach Valparaiso from a long way offshore to intercept a compass bearing of northeast to the unmistakable shape of the snow-covered peak of the 23,000-foot volcano named Mount Aconcagua. At the end of day we all could see the peak standing low in the sky as a beacon lit up in rosy tints by the setting sun in the west. We were miles out from shore, so I could turn the ship towards the coast and sail on without any fear of getting in too close, too soon. On the mountain peak bearing *Northeast* by compass I could turn the ship to take up a heading to steer in that direction with assurance of clearing reef hazards closer in north and south of Angeles Point. Expecting to soon sight the lighthouse light at Angeles Point in that day's early morning darkness, I sent the lookout up to the masthead and waited for him to hail the deck, *'Deck ahoy! Light ho! Dead ahead'*."

Gaudin told Herd he climbed to check the identity of the light flashes and that the light came from Angeles Point, and not from some other light on the coast.

"Sailing in on a southerly night summer breeze we kept offshore of

Angeles Point to clear outlying reefs, sir. With the anchors and cable ready at the bows, all hands on deck, and under reduced sail, the *Lady Lampson* slipped along through the water in silence. At 2 o'clock in a beautiful summer morning on Friday 19 November 1869 we entered the two-mile wide opening of the bay. Numerous anchored vessels lay ahead, all lamped out to show us their positions. Not much light showed beyond in the town, which remained quiet. The water on the bay lay still with no gusts of wind coming down from the heights to harry us on deck or make the rigging sing an unsettling song. We anchored far out to await a pilot."

"Please draw me on this slate where you anchored."

"We anchored far out in 30 fathoms. In the morning I hired two whaleboats with a rough looking crew of Jack Tars on the oars to pull us to an anchorage closer in. The pilot never did show up."

"By daylight what could you see of the town?"

"Well sir, I could see how the harbour lies open to storm winds out of the north that come in the Southern Hemisphere winter months of July and August. The buildings in town cluster on narrow low ground in the eastern corner of the harbour with steep high crests of hills to the east and southeast with gullies called *arroyos*, which cut the habitations into separate clusters not far across from each other."

Herd said he had heard seamen in port can find drinking establishments high on the shore.

"Yes sir, that's correct; but as events turned out, I spent no time in them. At daylight I could also make out a few fine private houses called *villas* elevated above the shore overlooking the harbour."

"I recall reading your logbook entry that you could not report your arrival to the British Consul on account of his premises having burned down during the night."

"Yes sir, the fire must have happened before we arrived. I saw no flames on the shore coming in as late as we did."

"When did you begin to know you'd be delayed?"

"I found out about it the morning I landed in town, but not why the delay. I jumped at the opportunity to take a ride from a gig that came alongside to offer rides to shore. I did not want to take my seaman off their work on deck to row me in the ship's boat. The boatman agreed to stand by to bring me back. A Mister Jenkins came up to introduce himself. He told me of some delay to be expected and that he represented the ship's charterers, Messrs William Gibbs & Co. of London, in Valparaiso."

"Yes I know them well. As the Factor in Victoria may have told you, the charter reads, ' *Sooke to Valparaiso and further and back to London.*'"

Gaudin nodded, and picked up again with his account.

"Jenkins told me the tale of the fire and that I must come back tomorrow to the Consul's Office, but in the meantime he took me to the office of the Harbourmaster, named the *Commandante*, to enter the arrival of the ship, naming Gibbs & Co as ship's agent. On reading what I had written, the man at the desk smiled and nodded and wished me a good day in Spanish. I came back to the ship to waste a whole day with no word coming. I kept the crew busy cleaning up and painting to make the ship fit to be seen. The day ended with a fresh breeze from the south in fine weather. The large Dutch barque the *Cape Horn* arrived in port late in the day to move to an unloading berth. Answering my hail, her captain called out his time as *70 days from casting off the tug at Cape Flattery.* With pride I called back to him that we came in 69 days from casting off the towline from the steamer *Enterprise* off Sooke, half a day's sail to get to the Cape. So, sir, our little ship did well. The Dutch barque carried a load of lumber from a sawmill on Burrard Inlet. I wanted to land my lumber ashore before he did, but sadly I did not. Jenkins told me the Spanish naval bombardment of the town several years ago stimulated the market for lumber. Also frequent earthquakes afflict the entire coast with widespread damage to land and buildings, which might make you expect a lively demand for lumber. I asked myself, do the charterers seek to find a better price for the lumber, keeping us here under the charter, twiddling our thumbs?"

Gaudin paused to light his pipe before going on again to talk about his logbook entries.

"On 20 November I decided to move to a berth in the harbour to be ready to discharge the lumber on the shore. I roused up the crew at 3 a.m. and hove up the anchor cable short. At 6 a.m. the pilot and the little steam tug I hired came alongside to put lines aboard. They towed us close in to shore where I could moor with both cables out full length to secure the ship. In the event of a fire on land or other emergency we could be ready to haul them in and move back out into the harbour."

Gaudin explained he went ashore to meet the British Consul at his temporary premises. Jenkins met him on the street with profuse apologies to say his principals want the ship to stay at anchor because they have no place on the shore to unload.

"To my astonishment Jenkins said no one has yet bought the cargo.

'Come with me to the Exchange Hotel,' he said. 'I have instructions to put you up there at our expense for as long as you are here.'"

"I'm sure he said you'd enjoy the cantina and the food."

"Yes. Jenkins took me to the hotel to be shown my room. I returned to be rowed back to my ship. I saw no means of forcing the issue. Jenkins explained the terms of the charter contract called for a specified number of lay days grace to complete unloading, and after that they obligated themselves to pay extra day charter rate."

"Please go on Gaudin. I know all about that."

"A fresh sea breeze came up at the end of the day, sir, which lightened my dark mood as I walked back to my hotel room, but I did wonder how this delay would end."

"Gaudin, your log entries do not show it," Herd said, "but I take it that during the weeks you stayed on the shore, you went back on board every day to make log entries to show the crew variously employed to make the ship glisten and shine like the new vessel she is; and to show that you, the captain, knew how to attend to your business. That is what I would have done. I am putting words in your mouth, but am I about right?"

"Yes sir, that's about right. I became philosophical about the ship's delay. I run the ship until the end of the charter and take orders from Messrs Gibbs & Co. whose instructions will be coming to me from Jenkins. Until then I might as well settle down and enjoy the splendid Mediterranean-like summer climate. Every day Jenkins hired a boat to take me to the ship to see that the members of the crew worked to good purpose."

Herd listened as Gaudin continued.

"Jenkins reported again to say no buyer yet. One day he brought aboard a man I had never seen before, and whose name I did not catch, someone to inspect the lumber, but after a short inspection he rejected it as not to be suitable for his purposes."

"Your logbook entries show you kept divine services aboard every Sabbath and sent the men ashore on one occasion to church service in Valparaiso when they made the request," Herd said. "This will enable me to make that report to the Committee. I know one member on the Committee who thinks it important."

"As to the Sunday they went ashore, I am not entirely sure they went to church, but all came back with smiles on their faces, sir."

"From all accounts you had a happy crew, Gaudin."

"Not entirely, sir. Bass, an apprentice, jumped ship early in December, taking all of his clothing with him. I notified the Port authorities, but nothing came of it. He may have seen a better opportunity ashore, perhaps a pretty señorita to marry."

"Oh is it a place like that?"

"Not in the streets, sir. An air of modesty lies about this churchy place, but a man will see lively eyes holding much promise. Jenkins sent a message on the morning of 9 December to say the lumber has been sold to a buyer who wants the cargo delivered upcoast to a place named Tongoy. He followed with a note to say that the buyer has changed his mind, take the ship to Coquimbo. I went flying to my bookshelf to find my coast pilot book and to roll out the charts to show its location. I asked Jenkins where we go after Coquimbo, but he wouldn't know until later."

"Tell me about the passage to Coquimbo and why you came to be so long delayed there."

"I roused the people up at 5 a.m. on the clear still morning of 10 December to pull us out with our boats to make fast to the buoy farther out in Valparaiso harbour. I found the standard procedure here calls for departing sailing vessels to make out to those buoys to await the coming up of the afternoon breeze from the south. With no further word from Jenkins as to a destination after the lumber comes off the ship at Coquimbo, we cast off from the buoy and made sail with a light breeze out of the south at 5 p.m."

"Tell me more of your navigation northward."

"The passage to Coquimbo required me to stand well offshore to avoid running the risk of tide currents stranding us on the rocks on the wind dropping off at night."

"Please go on."

"By midnight in hazy weather the ship chased north through the water making speed with a push from a freshening southerly wind of gale strength. I set the inner jib, foresail and reefed the upper topsail. Nothing more needed to make best speed through the water in brisk sailing conditions. By 7 a.m. a heavy sea is on. I order all plain sail set in a freshening wind. At noon the ship sailed 18 miles off the Rio Limari River, the outfall of which disturbed and changed the colour of the seawater. By 4 p.m. the ship passed clear of Punta Lengua de Vaca and left it behind in the distance. We failed to reach Coquimbo before dark_____. In these latitudes, as you know sir, the dark comes sharp with no twilight. As no lighthouse at the entrance to the harbour to guide us, I gave orders to stand out to sea on a port tack under only reefed lower topsails and mizzen and foretop staysails. The wind blowing a heavy gale from southwards all night and during the next day churned up what ocean mariners can only describe as *a tremendous sea on*. The ship made bad weather of it as we continued to stand out to sea to put a safe distance behind us from the hazards of the continental shore. The time came to turn about to head back towards shore, but the wind too strong and the seas running too high to even attempt to put about by turning into and through the wind, so we wore ship off the wind to take up a new slant back towards the shore. I set the mainsail again later when the wind lessened."

"Wearing ship an uncomfortable operation with the high seas running, to say the least."

"Yes sir, but in this instance with warm air about and lots of sea room, we completed the wearing ship maneuver with ease. The three weeks ashore had cheered the men. On coming closer in, I turned to sail the *Lady Lampson* in an easterly direction with reef'd topsails on a reach back towards the coast. We sailed on all day and into the night in haze with the wind out of the south now coming onto the starboard side of the ship. Next morning I kept the reefs in the topsails as the wind continued strong. By noon the wind dropped off to baffle us in disturbed seas. Coquimbo Bay not yet discernible in the haze. By early afternoon on 13 December, sailing in a light wind to come in closer to shore, I could identify our old friend of two days ago, the landmark of Punta de Lengua de Vaca. The wind dropped off, but enough of it remained out of the south for us to sail well outside of the hazards off Pajaros Ninos Islets to enter Coquimbo Bay late in the afternoon. As no lighthouse yet built, caution requires daylight to enter."

"I know a little Spanish, Gaudin. The point reminded the mapmaker of the tongue of a cow, but what tragedy does the naming of the islands tell of?"

"No sir, not a tragedy involving little children as you might think, but a name to tell of the multitudes of Jackass Penguins, which have a call or cry that sounds like a child in distress. The Chileans call the penguins *child birds = pajaros niños*. The pilot came out from the shore to lead us to anchor close to shore in eight fathoms of water where a low and lazy ocean swell coming in from the southwest felt the least. We veered out 30 fathoms of cable and swung the stern inshore, the bow rising and falling in the gentle swell breaking on the sand beach with a slow chanting-like sound that could have put us all to sleep. Cleared up the decks and stowed the sails."

"Gaudin, you lay at anchor for forty days, from 13 December 1869 to 22 January 1870. An incredible length of time to unload a cargo of sawn lumber, forty days to unload timber! What explanation can you give?"

"I will tell you the sorry story, sir. At daylight on 14 December I let the wind carry the ship closer in to the beach before re-anchoring with 30 fathoms of cable out seawards and 45 fathoms of chain streamed aft to hold the vessel steady. As long as it stayed daylight, the light-ers, called *balsas*, could come out from the shore to take on the loads of lumber we lowered to them by the ship's tackle. We sent the deck load of lumber over the side first; then the crew opened the hold to begin pulling out the lumber. Slow work despite the effort and no more than three loads made it in through the surf to the beach each day. This went on each working day in sunshine and fair weather up to the day before Christmas when only one load went to the shore. The crew spent the remainder of that day clearing up the decks and cleaning ship."

"Your log records repairs to leaking decks in the heat?"

"Yes sir. Every day the Ship's Carpenter Alex Chapman re-caulked the deck and the tops of the foc's'le and saloon deck houses to fill the seams, which opened in the heat from the sun."

"Good thing you had no paying passengers to complain of water leaking onto their bunks."

"Yes sir, and thank you for having such an experienced ship's carpenter on board for the maiden voyage. I will be telling you in my account of the voyage we needed him also for his experience on deck at times in bad weather."

"I will be interested to hear you tell me of what he did then, Gaudin, but tell me, did Church holidays on shore interfere with the unloading?"

"Well, yes sir, the church holidays did interfere. No work ever done on Sundays and no work done on Christmas Day, or the day after, or on New Year's Day. I sent sections of the crew ashore in succession on leave. The hands became quite adept in launching the boat back into the surf to return on board happy and laughing, dripping wet from the adventure. On the day after Christmas the crew washed down the decks to keep the planks from shrinking in the heat. Two days after Christmas I hired men to come out from the shore in boats to add their strength to complete the unloading by 29 December 1869. The next morning's peace broke upon a complaint from shore the ship made *short delivery*."

Herd said he knew all about that.

"I know you sent a letter to the Secretary of the Honourable Company in London to tell of it, but tell me more about it from where you stood, Gaudin."

"The Chief Officer could not find his tally sheets from Sooke. For two whole days I took him and four of our men ashore to re-count and measure the lumber piled on the shore. None of the new tally on the shore proved anything other than shortfall in delivery. I found the tally result unsatisfactory. The Chief Officer crumbled under the stress of his own criticism for his mishandling of the loading at Sooke. Of course, I told him I was ultimately responsible for his job of work being done in a proper fashion, which didn't make it any easier for him."

"I am amazed by your later logbook entries, Gaudin, which show him laid-up in his cabin and logged as *off-duty* for almost all of the remainder of the voyage back to London."

"Yes sir. He also left me to see the ship provisioned on leaving Valparaiso. I found none ordered. Fortunately, I asked the right question in time to avoid sailing with no provisions, but his default delayed our departure by a day."

"Yes. Gaudin, a ship's mate has a distinct role to play in the management of a sailing vessel at sea. In addition to doing his duty to your satisfaction, he is under a special obligation to the ship's owner. How did you handle the watches at sea from then on?"

"To murmurs and looks of approval from the crew, I had taken on the Mate's Watch. I asked the old experienced Ship's carpenter Alex Chapman to stand watch with Second Mate Mister Farrow. I told him to listen with close attention to any suggestions the Carpenter made, but to use his own judgment. I relaxed and went below from the main deck after watching Farrow manage the sails for part of his watch."

Herd asked a question about the effect of the tropical heat coming down onto the deck, and Gaudin replied,

"Yes sir, the first opportunity came on New Year's Day, a feast day on shore with no lighters coming out, so I had the crew wash down the decks again to keep the deck planks cool and to prevent them from shrinking in the heat. They holystoned the decks on the next two days during the time I took the Chief Officer ashore again to take a second look at our previous count, but no better result this time. Jenkins would have to deal with the complaint from the man buying the lumber."

"Your logbook shows you were offered a cargo of hay, Gaudin. How did that come up?"

"Someone came out from the shore to ask me to take on a load of hay destined for Iquique but nothing came of it. I did not warm to the idea of taking a cargo of hay into the hold, which could cause a fire at sea by combustion. I went ashore by boat rowed in through the surf on 5 January to send a telegram to Jenkins to report readiness to sail and to ask what would be the future employment of the vessel under the charter. I followed up with another telegram the next day to ask if my coming to Valparaiso would be of any use in arranging that matter."

"I don't suppose your crew suffered at all in this delay in such a temperate climate?"

"No sir, not in the least. I arranged for fresh food and provisions to come from the pretty little Spanish town of La Serena where I went to send the telegrams from the railroad station to Jenkins. A stream runs past the town to flow into Coquimbo Bay. Lush farms cluster nearby and farmers bring their produce and meat into the farmers' market in town. The inhabitants must find pleasant living there. I must remark upon the bird life in the bay and on the shore at the mouth of the stream. We caught many brightly coloured fish from lines out from our boats to bring back to the cook to prepare for us."

"What a wonderful break from shipboard fare of hard biscuits and salt meat for your cook."

"Yes sir, Charlie Rugg turned out some good food from the galley stove, and he showed us he could bake loaves of bread, which Farrow and I had as toast to spread Dundee Marmalade on for breakfast. On the 7 January the people busied themselves clearing up the holds of debris from the lumber cargo and tossing it overboard."

"I find people here in London do not understand me, Gaudin, when I use the word *people* as you just now did."

"Yes sir, I suppose some would not know what I mean: you know I refer to the members of the crew. Shall I continue with my account?"

Herd nodded and told him to continue.

"A letter from Jenkins came delivered from the shore out to the ship. He wrote to tell me to stay at Coquimbo and that my presence in Valparaiso would be of no use until he can read the report he expects by the next steamer from the north. He wrote the date for her arrival in

Valparaiso remained to be notified."

"Oh Gaudin! Such a delay and you missing a good time of the year to be rounding Cape Horn homewards."

"Yes sir, four more days passed in fine weather with the vessel at anchor in Coquimbo Bay while I waited for further word by telegram from Jenkins. I had the crew variously employed doing needed work. On the fifth day I ordered the sails to be set loosed in the warm wind to dry the dampness in them. Three more days passed with no further word. During that time I wrote my first letter to the Secretary in London. I planned to give it to Jenkins to send in the next mail. My letter confirmed the short delivery: in fact, out of the supposed 333,945 feet of lumber, only 306,561 feet came to be delivered. I could not account for the shortage. None lost overboard in the loading at Sooke or during the voyage. The buyers also complain of the poor quality of 255,590 feet of rough lumber, but I suggested that the buyer, not having stipulated the quality of the shipment, should have no remedy against the ship or the Company in respect of the cargo. My letter to London ended by saying that Messrs Gibbs had requested me to come to Valparaiso by steamer to consult with them about the future employment of the vessel and that I hoped soon to be able to send word the vessel can be put to good use. The steamer came earlier than I expected so I had to scramble to make a quick exit from the *Lady Lampson* to get on board."

"Gaudin, you must have worried that Gibbs would find a *guano* cargo?"

"Yes sir, such a dirty cargo. Indeed, I hoped Jenkins might find a copper ore cargo from copper mines nearby. I could not entertain the idea during that time of taking on ballast I would only throw off before loading the ore from the shore nearby."

"Gaudin, you have told me you left the ship to travel by steamer to Valparaiso. How did that excursion come about?"

"Jenkins put the trip in motion. Pacific Steam Navigation Company operates the steamer *San Carlos* up the coast from Valparaiso. I boarded her southbound on 15 January at 8 a.m. Jenkins arranged passage and the best cabin on board for me. The captain, an Irishman name McGuinty, invited me to come up to the pilothouse. We yarned together for much of the voyage. He had served in Sail before he came to work in South America to learn this interesting coastline. He predicted I would end my days in Steam, and I said I hoped not."

"You made a fast turnaround at Valparaiso, Gaudin."

"Yes sir, as the logbook states I arrived to be put up at the Exchange Hotel at noon on 16 January 1870, did my business with Mister Jenkins, waited for word back from him, then departed Valparaiso at 8.30 p.m. the next day in the steamer the *Payta*, which is another coastal steamer. She took me north to bring me alongside the *Lady Lampson* at anchor in Coquimbo Bay at 2 p.m. on 18 January. I swung myself back on board and immediately gave orders to ballast the ship from the beach. This proved to be hard work in the heat to load sufficient rock ballast into the hold to keep the ship stable for a passage up the Chilean Coast to Iquique. Mister Farrow and I had the people take it into the holds on 18 through 21 January. The next day we spent getting the vessel ready for sea in all respects and unmooring to move offshore_____."

"Let me interrupt, Gaudin. I am getting on in years, and I am tired after a long day. Please come to my office tomorrow and we can go on from there."

11

THE CHILEAN COURTESAN

Warming thoughts fill my mind as the cab carried me through the streets back to my lodging on West India Dock Road. Later I found sleep long in coming. The talk that evening about the maiden voyage of the *Lady Lampson* ended with Herd saying I had made a fast turnaround in January at Valparaiso and that he'd call me in again in the morning to carry on with my account.

But I had not told Captain Herd the whole story about my unexpected junket to Valparaiso and the quick return I made to the *Lady Lampson* at anchor in Coquimbo Bay on the coastal steamer S.S. *Payta*.

Of course, Herd had no call on me to tell him of the thirteen hours and forty minutes I contrived to be back with Consuelo Cochrane a second time. Magical moments sprung loose for that woman to lift me up into more of the same caper we'd had forty days earlier.

The events leading to meeting Consuelo came rushing back in my mind. Orders to take the lumber cargo north to Coquimbo Bay in Chile tore me away from her in mid-December 1869 at the end of a fortnight together. For the next 38 days I thought of little else than imagining impossible ways to be with her again.

Jenkins knew what to say to have me come running after I unloaded the lumber to the shore at Coquimbo. He gave me the opening I ached for when he sent the telegram to ask me to come down the coast to Valparaiso by the coastal steamer the S.S. *San Carlos* to talk about a cargo and a destination under the charter.

I lost no time to send a telegram to ask Jenkins to notify the lady of my arrival. Jenkins knew the connection between us. Likely he'd give her the message in person so he could take a good peek at how she dressed to show off her feminine endowments. I do not know the man but my guess he'd enjoy a curious excitement to see her face light up on receiving word of my return 38 days after she'd last seen me. I knew that look.

When we did meet again she referred to the foul-up in our plans to wave to each other when the *Lady Lampson* sailed in December. My explanation accepted and put behind us, she and I made up for lost time in the precious few hours we had together again before I took the next steamer back to Coquimbo, spent.

Now in London five months later I thought back to the sheer joy she'd brought me in a two-week sojourn followed later by that overnight reprise in Chilean Southern Hemisphere summertime. In the midst of difficulty, Consuelo appeared like a rainbow after rain. My spirit fit hers like fingers in glove, a phrase that stirs me now.

The ship could not accept the delay I told Jenkins, but I found I could do nothing about it. He explained his employer Wm. Gibbs & Co of London acted as agent for Señor Alejandro and others in a syndicate of Chilean businessmen to charter the *Lady Lampson* to bring the lumber cargo from Sooke to Valparaiso, further, and back to London. The terms of the contract of charter contemplated delays.

Jenkins took me from his office to meet the portly Señor Alejandro, who put me up at the Exchange Hotel where I could sign chits, do any business I had, and live in luxury. Neither of them said anything specific to confirm it, but Jenkins told me enough to suspect the Señor's syndicate needed my ship to be available to them and the delay only a pretext to keep the *Lady Lampson* in port under the terms of the charterparty contract. They hope to use the time to conclude arrangements with several levels of Peruvian and Chilean authorities to obtain a permit to ship a nitrate cargo from an area 900 miles north, the borders of which lie in dispute between the two countries.

The Señor complimented me on my *impulse*, he said, to move into shore, but he has no buyer for the cargo in Valparaiso. Be so good, he said, as to take your ship from the berth in the harbour to anchor farther out in the Bay. This would save the Syndicate added expense. Jenkins will speak to the Commandante of the Port to arrange the necessary permissions and for an anchorage to be allocated not too far out in the Bay. Before taking leave of me he intimated I would be sailing up-coast to unload the lumber at some other port, and he asked me to remain patient.

The vessel's movement out into the harbour from the berth accomplished by early afternoon, I came back to the shore for Jenkins to walk me on on cobblestone-paved streets up steep steps to what I took to be Señor Alejandro's Villa.

Early summertime comes to Valparaiso in the month of November, which made for a pleasant stay in port for the two weeks my duty required to keep the ship lying at anchor. Señor Alejandro had invited me to bring my overnight bag and stay at his *Isla Villa*, which overlooked the Bay from a high vantage point where he said I could look down to keep my ship in sight.

Valparaiso lies in the same South Latitude as Southern California lies in North Latitude. The weather can be warm and pleasant like parts of the Mediterranean in season. The gardens and pools of Isla Villa abounded with singing birds and tropical flowers. The scent at night from the flowers of pale yellow jasmine climbing vines flared my nostrils.

A slim elderly manservant, Miguel, ushered me into the cool inside foyer, which had a fountain flowing in it. He had been told to expect me. Señor Alejandro appeared coming down from the sweep of a wide stairway, beckoning to a tall slim younger woman at the top level. At first she appeared to pause, but then I saw her walk down the staircase into the foyer like she owns the place. As she came closer I could see her sandals jeweled with turquoise pieces. A third generation Chilean of mixed blood, part dark Spanish and part European-Celtic perhaps, or German_____ the black hair and the dark blue eyes. Abundant shining long black hair tumbled and fell in waves on her tanned bare shoulders. She wore her hair to show her ears, which, from the front view, presented a fair width of head, which I noticed and thought significant for some reason I did not understand. I sensed this woman had a mind of her own, and not a servant accustomed to taking orders from anyone. But some instinct told me her eyes showed she would not keep me at a distance.

My glance focused on her eyes, which sparkled in the light; then, I focused on her nose, such as I fancy Cleopatra must have had, not retroussé, tilted-up only at the nosetip to add a twinkle to the smile on her face.

As she stepped down the stairs I shot a glance at her long slim legs, the colour of coffee and cream high in the slits on both sides of her long white dress. I know I caught my breath when she took her right arm away from the railing and stepped off the last step to move with purpose toward me, her eyes fixed on mine.

She stood beside Señor Alejándro for the introduction, as tall as I am, perhaps a tad taller. I noticed she does not wear a wedding ring. She could have been his daughter, but in an instant I knew not so, much closer in age to him, Señor Alejándro, and perhaps a bit older than I am.

"Señorita, this is Jaimé Gaudin - Capitán Gaudin, Señorita Conn-SWAY-Lo."

He got my family name sounding right, but he spoke my first name as HY-MEE. Consuelo sensed I didn't know. She explained how she speaks my name James in Spanish. With evident pride she spelled out her last name, C-O-C-H-R-A-N-E, a good Scottish name she said.

Without holding it back until later to leave me wondering, Señor Alejándro speaks unambiguous words that set my heart pounding: Señorita Consuelo will care for me while he is away. I knew by this time he would be in northern parts of the country for a month or more.

At first struck breathless by the vision of this woman I had not expected to be in the house, I summoned up words to express my pleasure at meeting her in a Spanish sentence I knew. I asked how she spells her name, saying it as I heard it, CONN-SWAY-LO. I said it sounded like a pretty name to me. She said her mother gave her the name of Consuelo so she would be known as a woman of helpful suggestions. She spelled the name out for me in the same way as she had spelled out her surname Cochrane. Of course, now I understand. My French word *conseil* comes from the same word root.

I basked in the warmth of her smile when she spoke to compliment me on my pronunciation in Spanish, and I became aware of the pleasing scent of her hair wafting close as she reached out to take my hand in hers as we mounted the wide curving steps to the upper level and out onto the lamped tiled terrace to see the setting sun and a pale slice of a new crescent moon low in the sky.

Leaving me standing to take in the view, Señor Alejandro led her to a sofa on the terrace facing me, but, despite the panorama, I looked at little else than her lissome movements as she slid onto the sofa with easy grace.

Now that I knew I did not trespass on another man's wife, my senses told me to put myself forward without fear of rejection. I did not hesitate to move toward her as I returned her gaze. I found I liked getting a closer look into her sparkling eyes. She had eyes that light up and shine when she smiles. Some women possess that quality. I was quite enchanted by how her mouth and lips can move even when she is not speaking to take on an impish, even mischievous appearance as if she is about to say something quite funny. Her chin dimple held me looking and wanting to discover more about this woman. Not a pretty face but one that gave promise of fire and a willing response to set a man's heart pounding.

Caught at the waist and cut to leave her back and shoulders bare, her long white dress drew my eye to her slim waistline and hips and the rising lines of her bosom to see more than a mere hint of her feminity. The bright white of her dress formed a pleasing contrast to the texture of her smooth tanned skin, which glowed with a light of its own, and overall, the pleasing scent of flowers. In a memorable moment she stood to move close to me.

I had not noticed until that moment she wears silver earrings on her ear lobes and bracelets up her bare arms and a white scented flower in her hair. I couldn't tell you now on which side of her head she wore it. I know a custom in that respect exists but I have never paid it much heed. In some situations I have found myself to be more forward than I would be prepared to admit.

In this idyllic setting I heard her speak to me in a clear voice,

"Tonight the new moon in Sagittarius touches the Sun. The time of any new moon favours plans a-foot."

"Oh, that's good news, Consuelo," Señor Alejandro said. "I do have plans a-foot, as you have learned to say the word."

"So do I," she said without any hesitation, but the moment passed without me or the Señor saying anything. I drew in my breath and averted my eyes away when I heard her speak again.

"The Moon is the woman and the Sun is the man," she said, "and they are in conjunction at the time of a new moon."

I had an inkling of where she was heading, but I remained tongue-tied and unable to return her steady gaze. I did not press what I should have seen as my advantage. Señor Alejandro remained silent, but only for a moment. He broke the silence to talk about the political situation developing between Peru and Bolivia and the possibility of war that could embroil Chile. Even when the chat moved to political and trade matters, Señor Alejandro encouraged Consuelo to speak her mind. Her questions and remarks showed intelligence and wit.

Although the red wine, which Consuelo called *veeno teento* made my mouth pucker, I found the taste of it improving the more of it I drank, and the more often they brought me into the conversation to talk about myself and the life I had been leading. Yes, I was not a married man. I have no home to go back to.

Help in the kitchen carried up hot food to place on the table late into the evening, and we came inside to eat after much talking and drinking on the terrace under the stars in the high northern sky. Restful guitar music from indoors filled the air during most the evening. Señor Alejandro explained his position in life, a native son of Santiago Chile, a widower with no children, and a man of business. He will leave at dawn tomorrow for distant meetings to permit him and his partners to develop nitrate of soda deposits in the desert a thousand miles north in southern parts of Peru near the coastline. The nearest town, Iquique, will grow in size and the trade coming from that region will bring profit to his syndicate. A large fleet of sailing ships, he said, will come in time to carry nitrate to Europe for fertilizer or as an ingredient of the best gunpowder for ship's guns and artillery. Eventually Consuelo excused herself and in Spanish bade both of us a good night's sleep. Her leaving came too soon for me. The terrace fell silent, but Señor Alejandro got up to pour glasses of cognac for the two of us, and he produced cigars to smoke on the terrace while we talked. Later he led me to an upper level of the house to my bedroom, a large airy room with windowed doors overlooking the harbour where the *Lady Lampson* lay lamped out. He told me he hoped I would feel free to move back and forth into town, to my hotel, and out to my vessel whenever I wish. In any event, orders for the ship will be delivered to me here unless I tell Jenkins otherwise. Tomorrow morning Pablo will pick up my laundry, he said.

The night passed.

Morning came with a kaleidoscope of images in succession: a maid padded in to open the curtains over the windowed doors leading to an upper terrace to awaken me. She carried in a pot of hot coffee and fresh fruit. Another servant came to pour hot water into the tiled bath causing steam to rise to the windows. He gathered up my clothes for washing. I got myself up to look out to see my ship still there. I quaffed the coffee and nibbled on the fruit. I know I must take a boat out to check the state of the crew but I am in no rush to do that. I throb to see Consuelo again and I ache to learn the unspoken message she had been putting out to me last night. I put on a bathrobe left for me and walk into the bathroom to wash. A long soak in the tub came to be interrupted by a soft knock on the door and Consuelo came in with her hair

piled high on her head. She stood tall over me for a moment with her
long white bathrobe tied tight at the waist to make me notice her trim
waistline, and then she slipped off her sandals.

Around her neck a wide black throat band with a pearl at the front
of it caught my gaze. Gold necklaces gathered deep and heavy, disap-
pearing down, drawing my eye to the swelling of her breasts showing at
the top of her bathrobe. I gauged their fullness as she swung her der-
rière onto a wicker chair. She rearranged just how the bathrobe hung,
and crossed one slim tan leg bare on top of the other and looked at me
with her remarkable nose and chin uplifted.

"Did you sleep well, El Capitán Jaimé Go-Dan?"

I told her I had taken a long time to doze off, but afterwards fell
off into a deep sleep. She said she hadn't noticed last night I had black
eyes. That's why they looked so large in the candlelight. I want to look
in them again, she said.

As she said that she turned and moved to get the light from outside
into my eyes and she came close. My heart beat faster. A pleasing scent
filled the air_____. After a pause, she spoke again.

"You like the agua caliénte?" I knew she meant the hot water but I
couldn't speak above a low murmur.

"I have strong hands," she said in a low throaty voice. "I will pound
your back and shoulders to bring you comfort. Please come out of the
water. I will help dry you off, and I will lead you into the next room for
you to lie prone. I think that is the word the English use, for me to use
my hands on your back."

In coming out, I slipped, and sent a huge splash onto the tile. She
shrieked, but drew close with a large bath towel in front of her. I quickly
took the towel in my hands. She grabbed one end of it and swung
around me to dry my back and shoulders.

"Your bathrobe lies where you left it," she said in a soft quiet voice,
this time. She took my hand and led me to the padded table stand
where she said she would *min-ist-er* to my aching body. I asked her how
did she know my body was aching. She said she could tell from the way
I held my head.

In time she told me in a firm tone of voice to please turn over and
close my eyes. This turn of events came not as a complete surprise to
me. I have known women in the East Indies, London, and Montreal.
They do not talk much but know every step to take to bring pleasure to
a man. This woman is different. She spoke like she had some schooling

and must be a well-placed courtesan of some means and standing in town at the call of Señor Alejandro.

Lying in the morning light streaming through the shuttered windows, and taking deep breaths to fill my lungs, I closed my eyes to imagine what would she do next. Keep your eyes closed she said as she kissed my eyelids. I did what she told me. I returned her kiss on my lips with feeling and held up my arms to hold her, but she made me keep them down to my sides and told me to keep my eyes closed. Not yet Jaimé, let me *rise* myself for the two of us together, she said. I felt her hands stroke my forehead, then my ear lobes, first one and then the other, and then both, bringing on in me a sense of vague longing and surging restlessness.

She told me she never hesitated to use her hands and fingers to make her presence felt, and I believe it. It went on and on for a long time. She moved my arms to turn the palms of my hands up, then I felt the tip of one of her long fingernails scribe a tiny circle on them, slow at first but ever mounting, like a veiled Arabian dancer moving her body in dance. She brought me back to the world with a firm squeeze on my forearm. I opened my eyes to find her bringing her face down to put her lips and tongue to the nipples on my chest, kissing first one then the other and flicking her tongue on them before using her fingers to shape them to kindle a fire as I closed my eyes again. She kissed my lips again and held her cheek on mine as she put a warm hand in between my legs above my knees. I did nothing more for a moment of silence broken only by the birds singing outside the windows. I opened my eyes and reached out to drop off her bathrobe, which I saw now no longer tightly closed. I decided to slip off the table and come up all standing to become an actor in this play. As I did this she made a deft move to let her hair come cascading down in an instant onto her shoulders, releasing an indescribable scent of cut sweet fruit with a touch of lemon to flare my nostrils. We stood face to face. Oh! How she moved in close to drag her hardened nipples in slow movements across my chest in a most provocative manner.

Hold me tight, Jaimé! she whispered.

I said she had met my good friend Gunnar. She drew back a bit to look and ask how did I spell that name? I told her and she said it back as GOON-Air. I asked her what kind of name is that? She knew it as an old Viking name. I said something silly like perhaps men from Jersey have Viking blood in them as a result of their raids to find young women 900 years ago. At that she moved in to hold me tight.

Standing close together she did not stop me using my mouth and tongue to open her lips to play with my tongue on her tongue as a woman in Montreal taught me to increase her desire for the encounter to continue. We kissed like that for a long time. I moved my arms behind her to hold and pull the sides of her hips to me to keep the pressure of her warm naked body on mine. Both of my hands down onto each of her buttocks outlined the shape of how her body felt to me. She told me she loved her body being touched and moved away to reach over to a shelf to bring back a purple glass bottle containing an aromatic oil of some kind.

"Put some of that on your rough hands and fingers to soften them, Jaimé. Let me lie down on that table with my eyes closed for you to touch me."

I did what she asked with her stretched out full length showing me her back and her long legs and the soles of her feet for me to touch. I touched my fingertip nails to her skin and then down her bare backside, scratching lightly to leave tip marks, but only lightly to tease.

She whispered, "Oh! Please keep doing that!" And I did.

But the moment came for something else: "Watch out," I said. "I'm going to turn you over."

I had her enthusiastic help, and she closed her eyes again. I did to her what she had done to me, forehead, ear lobes and lips, and then moved both hands to shape her proud breasts standing up for me to touch. Soft sounds of pleasure came from her lips as my senses filled to the sight of her moving her hips and legs on the table in a most provocative manner.

In a moment she spoke in soft voice, no longer a whisper. I am going to stand up. Let me clamp my earrings onto your ears, she said.

Speechless at the prospect, I did nothing to stop her. She lifted up her shoulders to make a waving motion to present her upper body assembly of breasts and nipples in rampant display to make me reach out to touch them. Standing with her warm bare skin touching me, she kissed my hands, and wiped the perspiration from my brow. Our eyes engaged and my heart pounding, I watched her take off her earrings, one after the other, in slow deliberate movements. She clamped them on my ear lobes, first the left, then the right, and she laughed and murmured; now you are mine_____. I have caught you Jaimé!

I thought back for an instant to a moment in time with Agnes when

she moved her fingers to touch my ear lobes: she told me her Grandmother Birnie had spoken about the Pend Oreille Indian men whose
name shows they hang earrings from their ears because they like the
feeling.

With the fingers of her one hand grasping my left nipple, she
reached down to take a firm hold on Gunnar, which fairly bristled at
the touch. I felt a fresh surge of stir and tingle and a sense of warmth
below in my loins. Still standing, and closing my eyes, I drew in one
deep breath, then another, to keep the moment.

My thought of Agnes ended on Consuelo moving to hold Gunnar
in one hand and using her other hand to hold my right thumb, tight.
Without a sound to break the silence she held it tight, moving her hand
to make clear to me she knew where this play would end. She whispered
in my ear, "I think you understand, Jaimé."

In a fluid movement, Consuelo lay herself back down on the table,
asking me to come to her body with my hands.

I had other plans in mind. I told her to turn over *prone* as she told
me the word the English use. I made a playful move to spank a buttock.
She cried out not to. I let a drop of her oil in a bottle fall into the cleft
between her buttocks to make it run down when I used my hands about
her hips to lift and hasten its descent.

She did not object, and told me she loves the feeling of my hands
moving to follow the shape of her body from behind; it makes her feel
warm and wanted, she said.

On her backside I made my hands, fingers, and thumbs felt.

As if in sympathy with the thought, at one point she lifted one
shoulder after another to swing her breasts across the silken sheet on
her table. To end this show of her delight, she turned her head to glance
back to tell me in a whisper she would now stand. In a contented daze
I let her lead. Slim in her golden skin and wearing nothing on her body
except her black throat neckband, the one with a pearl at the front, she
held her arms up, hands together, palms toward me, swaying her hips
like a dancer I'd once seen. Wagging her shoulders in engagement, she
closed her eyes and drew in a breath as she took my hand away from its
hold on gathered hardened nipples on her breasts. She asked me to put
my first two fingers into her mouth for her to wet them. Please, she
whispered, put them where she pointed when she lay herself back down
on her table. She made that movement in a contagious flash. I did what
she asked when she opened out her legs. As my fingers moved in to

find a warm, wet, and slippery place, she closed her legs on my arm and murmured a soft sound. She cupped her breasts with her hands and her body loosened and moved about in a voluptuous manner in response to the movements I made with my fingers to please her. Never had I seen a woman make such body movements, except in my sailor's dreams. She ended it by sitting up at the edge with her legs together and turning to face me and flaunt her breasts at me, which led to an inevitable urge to put out my hot hand to hold them again. With her arms down at her side in acceptance, she turned her eyes down to see the span of my right hand bring them together in captive display, tilted up. The gentle squeeze did not displease. She reached out with her closer hand to hold Gunnar with a firm grip in time to settle him. She did not want to let him go, she said. Let's go to your bed, she said. And we did, neither of us realizing the passage of time. We lay together for a long time of calm before I said, when are we going to have something to eat? She said something in Spanish, which I took to be meaning, Oh! You terrible man, Jaimé!

And that night we did it all over again. I awoke in the morning, spent. She awoke every morning full of life and energy. This woman never had a blank look or a frown on her face. So much energy! She never looked passive or put upon or taken advantage of like some women I have known.

During a warm rain on the roof one afternoon I asked her to put on a fashion show in her bedroom for me. I spoke these play words of nonsense: Why don't you dress up by putting on all of your underclothes and dresses for me? No, not all at once, but put on a show for me. I will stand beside you helping with the laces, tying up, doing up, and taking down. I am good with knots and laces and will tighten them to make your waistline look even smaller, I said.

I stood to face her. With help from me she put herself into and out of her lacy, silken things. She laughed and giggled like a schoolgirl, finding delight in frolicking about. She built up a slow cadence tease of snuggling and backing into me with predictable results. This black corset came from Paris she said, turning to flaunt her breasts at me, which put me in a complete distraction. Please help me put it on, Jaimé, she said. My cheeks flushed with excitement. I could see another wild afternoon coming with a woman sailors imagine and do not often find. She could have been dissembling, of course, but I believe I did not disappoint her. Responding with as much spirit, energy, and initiative as I could summon up, I rejoiced in my own stamina.

For more than two weeks we lived together in joy and laughter at the villa on the hill with a view of the harbour. Maids and servants did our bidding to keep the place and to run the kitchen. I forgot Agnes during days of abandon in the midst of tropical birds singing in the trees amid the scent and colour of tropical flowers of all kinds, hibiscus, especially the scented yellow jasmine vines. Nightgowns got short shrift as we slept bare skin to each other, she snuggling up to me whichever way I turned. Some mornings I awoke to the fantasy occasioned by her hardened frisky nipples boring little holes on the skin of my bare back. Any movement I made in response led to another, and another.

I remember the day I asked her to make a short skirt with a wide hem she could whirl to make the hem swing out and twirl high to show off the shape of her long legs. She did make a little black dress to hang loosely from her shoulders over a slip of silk that fitted more closely to bind her bosom. Started as a chemise, she said, she ended up making a dress shorter than I had imagined, barely half way to her knees. And no stockings to cover the length of her legs' bare skin showing.

She would not dare wear it on the street or at someone else's house, she said. The women would hate her for it and the men would not feel comfortable staring at her with eyes giving away their thoughts. She paraded back and forth in little more than her little black dress on more than one of the afternoons, saying she wanted to look into my eyes to guess what Jaimé is thinking.

I enjoyed seeing her swing her shoulders and hips to walk the distance before casting off the little black dress over her head in a heap on the floor and come back to me. Even though seabirds flying and ships on the blue sea beyond lay in view through the open door onto the terrace, I looked at little else than the shimmering of reflections of light from the pool playing on her face and the lifting of her unfettered breasts winking at me in marvelous tremor from within as they gave gentle trembles from her movement on foot. The shape and movement of her breasts in front of my eyes prompted me to catch them on the swing as I helped her put me on my back, looking up at her inimitable smile. Nay, not just to touch, but for me to gather in my hands as she mounted my firm slim waist and kneeled over me to let me respond to the inevitable urge in me to take her nipples to my lips and tongue. In later days, she had her ways to get me to shave off my beard, then, cleanshaven, softly doing it. With her inner thighs and knees pressing close on each side of my waist as if she were a jockey riding a horse, she perched there, full weight in her bare skin to keep me down. Reaching behind her to touch Gunnar and tell him to wait, she gave a slow wiggle to her hips, and bore down to press her flesh closer to mine to foretell the ending she looked for in this turn. Time and time again on these warm days, we led each other on, often ending up on her thick Persian rug, fitting into each other like fingers in a glove in a union we each yearned for. If not on the floor, and if she beckoned to the padded table I first lay out on, I took her hand to lead her body into position on it for me to press on into a new turn.

She had told me that I could call her by her pet name, Kitty. I asked her about her family and where she grew up, but she put her finger on her lips and said, I will tell you nothing more than my name Kitty; and she didn't.

In a moment of calm she told me the moon in Sagittarius at the time of my birth made the new moon in Sagittarius on the evening we met, *serendipitous*. I had not known of that last word, but Consuelo knew. Laughing, she had told me she had Gypsy blood in her and that she is a kind of a Witch. She had asked me earlier my date of birth: I told her I was born on 23 January 1838 in the morning, just before sunrise. Later she came back to talk about my horoscope, telling me Venus opposed Jupiter at the time of my birth, which meant money will flow too easily through my hands. Also Jupiter's position at the time of my birth made me the powerful man she said I am in bed with her. You will not want to speak to others about our friendship, she said. Saturn in the sky at the time of birth meant trouble in my career, but I would recover from it because the Sun did not conflict with Saturn in the sky at the time of birth. The gathering of four planets and the Sun at the time of my birth told her others enjoy being with me. I did not know what she was talking about. Living in a daze over this woman, my mind thought of little else than her eyes, and her lips, and her precious body. She filled my mind with images of the way she chose to wear her jewels and clothes with nothing else in mind than to draw my attention to her face and body. Among the many long dresses and gowns, I especially liked the long black dress the hem of which she swept out to one side when she danced a slow Spanish dance for me, wearing shining black leather high-heel boots. If not using her orange fan to open and close as she danced, she made sharp clicking sounds with black castanets in both hands to add sparkle to the song she sang.

Daily, I went to the ship in mid-morning to make logbook entries concerning ship's business, notably the remarks passed on to me by Jenkins to justify the ship remaining in the harbour before returning every afternoon for *Siesta*.

I went aboard to conduct divine service on Sunday, 28 November 1869, and again on 5 December 1869 for those crewmembers not on shore leave.

I sensed how happy I would have appeared to my crew. I think I could detect from the looks on the faces of some, they were taking shared satisfaction concerning what they imagined I did with my time ashore. No one said anything about that to me, but I made sure every one of them who wished had leave ashore.

The night before I left her in December found us on the warm tiled floor. I don't know what I did to make her ready for this, and I question how I would get her to do it again. Sitting on my lap wearing nothing but her bracelets, earrings, and her wide black throatband with a pearl at the front of it, she pulled gently on an ear lobe of mine as we caressed and whispered to each other in the warm summer air coming in from the window. I sat in a silly daze of enchantment. The two of us stopped speaking to munch on fresh fruit and drink chilled wine mixed with fruit juice. Glass chimes sounded quietly in the breeze outside. Then she clapped her hands, and stood for a moment to summon up Gunnar with her thumb and two right hand forefingers before putting her face down to use her lips and tongue to set him glistening wet with a flow of saliva from her mouth. I piped up faint protest, but she did not stop. She whispered in my ear, *Let's do it like the animals do*. Without another word she put down her head and shoulders to the tiles, sending her long black hair cascading out onto the floor like a fan opening. She put one shoulder down, and reached between her legs to find me in position and a willing player in this turn. I let her guide Gunnar inward a prolonged completion of the act. Leading up to when we ended it together in wondrous response of body, some wanton instinct had my hands reaching down to place my thumbs and forefingers at the nipples of her breasts pendant for me to haul down on, but not so as to hurt.

Oh Jaimé! she said. Why hadn't we done it this way before?

We came together like two bent spoons in a spent tangled heap of bodies on the floor. I don't know why I say *bent*, but that's the way it felt_____, but not bent so much that I did not know the flesh and bones of a woman's body lay close to me. I pulled the quilt over to cover the two of us. We slept until the sun came in through a window to wake us. Laughing, we stood to embrace in the warm sunlight.

On 9 December morning Jenkins told me he had sold the lumber to a buyer who wants it delivered up the coast to Tongoy. The message came delivered as we were seated on the terrace for a sunlit breakfast in the afterglow of the night before. Her eyes lost their sparkle, bringing me back to reality. I sensed she wanted to talk, but I didn't know where to begin. All I could think of saying: I have never been able to hide my feelings. Other people can see right through me. I asked her if she found it easy to dissemble her feelings. She told me that she did not find it easy, but she could make herself appear happy when not. She thinks many women can make themselves look happy when they are not. Men, she said, cannot hide their feelings, but she told me she does not hide her feelings about me. Her eyes welled up as she said in a husky whisper I would leave her and never return. I knew this to be so and I wept as I answered her plea to take her with me: I could not do that I said; the food and living quarters for her aboard ship would be a bore and a disappointment compared to the life she had ashore. For us to marry and live in Valparaiso would not be possible I said, and she nodded, but she said I could take her to live in San Francisco, No? I told her I would not do that because I could not give up the command of the *Lady Lampson* and the job with good pay I now had. I put in years of service to be given command of that vessel and I did not want to give it up. She said I could take her back to Jersey, but I told her she would hate the place after living the life she has lived in Valparaiso. She would find it difficult to get to know my family. She would find the weather dull in comparison.

I had told her I would be taking the ship up the coast 300 miles to unload the lumber. She asked me to take her with me at least that far, but I dismissed the question with a wave of my hand. I had three thoughts at the back of my mind to bring back the reality facing me:

One: this sleek animal of a woman needs no encouragement to be attentive to anything a man could desire, but how could she possibly live with me on or off the ship; and if not on board ship, how could I possibly live with her when I must be away from her for a year or more? And what would I find when I returned?

Two: What had become of my life plan to raise a family: Consuelo told me she could not have a child, which I took as encouragement to continue having at her. I am sure a better way of saying that exists, but

I am a seaman and can think of no other way to say it.

Three: Has my Chief Officer loaded provisions for the next leg of the voyage? My mind had not focused on shipboard matters for some days.

I told her in a matter of fact way that I had much to do to ensure the *Lady Lampson* ready for sea as I hurried my breakfast and got up to leave. She beseeched me to come back by steamer to be with her again if a loading delay comes at the northern port. I told her I'd put the idea in my pipe and smoke it, or words to the same effect. I sensed my mistake and instantly regretted it. Consuelo, offended, surely took my words as not called for and unemotional, but she smiled back her inimitable smile, dissembling.

At that first ending of it between Consuelo and me on 9 December last year, I fought an impulse to turn to look back at her face. I knew that would have been my undoing. I resolved to keep going down the steep cobblestone steps to fetch a boat ride out to the *Lady Lampson*.

I had taught her how to distinguish the *Lady Lampson* from other sailing vessels: she could look to see me standing on my quarterdeck when I sailed out of the harbour. Intending to speak words to denote the certainty of it, I told her that the *Lady Lampson* would move out to a mooring buoy to await the afternoon breeze to go to sea. You can look for me with your telescope, I said. I will look for you as the ship begins to move under sail, I told her. But I missed the afternoon breeze and the ship did not sail until the next day. She would have watched to see no ship's movement in the afternoon and would not understand. I remember my sense of unhappiness that Consuelo will feel disappointment and think ill of me for making a promise, and not keeping it. On the *Lady Lampson* sailing out to sea in December, a day late, I had turned to look with my telescope to see her, but saw no one on the terrace, looking.

The same wrenching departure at the door came again in January as I left to catch the steamer taking me north from Valparaiso to the *Lady Lampson* at anchor in Coquimbo Bay, but on this second time of leaving her I saw no point in turning to wave: I would not be back again to say I had.

12

HOMEWARDS LADEN DEEP

The next day Captain Herd called Gaudin to come in to talk again about the maiden voyage that had ended back in London in May 1870.

"Sir, I ended up last night telling you I arrived at the Exchange Hotel in Valparaiso before noon on 16 January 1870, did my business with Mister Jenkins straightaway, and came away with orders to sail to Iquique in ballast. My steamer departed Valparaiso at 8:30 pm 17 January. I arrived back in Coquimbo Bay at 2 p.m. the next day."

"Yes Gaudin I remember. Please go ahead."

"The *Lady Lampson* rode high and empty at anchor in the gentle swell with my crew lining the deck. The steamer circled around her stern to come alongside to drop me off with my bag. I swung myself back on board and stepped up to the quarterdeck for Mister Farrow to welcome me back. On finding the mate remained off duty I gave Mister Farrow orders to load ballast. I told him we sail to Iquique to load bags of nitrate of soda to take to *God Knows Where*. Farrow looked puzzled. I explained we wouldn't know the destination until later. The people took the ballast aboard from lighters on 19 through 21 January. Hard hot slow work in the Tropics until we could cast off our moorings. The rollers now came in from the ocean to make the surf break on the sand with an unsettling rapid-pounding sound. I gave the order for men in our boats to pull us out into the Bay. Out a safe distance we waited in the morning calm for a wind to fill the sails. On deck at noon I felt a light wind coming from offshore out of the northeast, enough now to weigh anchor and move straight out to sea with all possible sail set. We do not want to tarry close in, but the lack of a good wind prevented us from clearing Pajaros Ninos Islets and their hazards until 8 p.m. At the end of the day we sighted the last of the sun lighting the distant tops of the Andes low on the eastern horizon."

"And the darkness fell without twilight?"

"Yes sir, as I mentioned yesterday, no twilight in the Tropics and darkness comes all of a sudden at the end of day. In the early morning hours next day on 24 January, a light wind came up from the south for me to order studdingsails set from t'gallant and upper and lower topsail yardarms on both sides of the foremast and the main. The additional sail area opened out like the petals of a flower under the stars to keep the ship moving north in clear weather. I marveled at the Humboldt Current colouring the rough sea an astonishing shade of deep blue in daylight. The water in Coquimbo Bay had been more green than blue. In the ocean far from shore seabirds fly aloft in clusters to follow the ship, but at Coquimbo Bay pelicans and other seabirds gathered on the beach and flocked on the water's surface."

"I have heard stories of the multitudes of fish on the surface of the water in the Humboldt Current. Did you see any?"

"Yes sir. The *Lady Lampson* ran chasing through schools of fish swarming, darting, and exploding off in all directions. White-sided dolphins kept pace and played in the water at the bow as if calling the ship to follow them. The south wind freshened by early afternoon to drive us on with the help of the Humboldt Current. Sensing the helm out of balance, I had the people move ballast aft in the hold that day and the next to bring the bows higher out of the water. The *Lady Lampson* could then slip along, cutting through the water as the designer meant her to."

"In the daylight could you see the tops of the *Andes*?"

"No sir, we could not see the mountains. They stood hidden from us in haze lying over the water. For four days and three nights the *Lady Lampson* sailed north in the refreshment of breezy winds out the south to put the distance behind us in a summertime-south-of-the-equator-pleasure cruise at sea. On the morning of 28 January we sailed in silence through fog on a slightly ruffled sea toward where I knew the harbour at Iquique lay. The fog did not lift. I could not be sure how close in we had come to the shore, so I hove the mainsail yard to the mast to stop the light wind filling the sail. Soon the fog lifted. We eased sheets to allow the sail to fill again. The lifting curtain of fog revealed a sight of buildings in the distance lit by sunlight on the shoreline. Murmurs of approval from the hands on deck followed."

"What was that about, Gaudin? Pleased your navigation on target?"

"The reaction of the hands on deck would have been different, I suppose, had I struck a landfall on an empty barren coast. I supposed they anticipated leave in town, sir, but none of them said anything, of course. We came to anchor at 10 a.m. on Friday 28 January 1870 in 15 fathoms, veering out cable to 45 fathoms. I took a boat ashore at noon to find the little Spanish town in siesta. I roused up a grumpy British Consul to report our arrival. No sign of activity on the shore. Unable to assume the shore will send out a full load for us, I gave orders for the people to discharge only part of the ballast overboard. I sent off just enough ballast to keep the people busy all afternoon. The German barque *Carolina* slipped in before dark to anchor behind us. This day ended at midnight local time, noon the previous day at Greenwich, to begin the logging of harbour work."

"What did Jenkins tell you about the nature of the nitrate cargo?"

"He told me the bags will be the first to be carried as cargo for Señor Alejandro and his syndicate. The cargo must be kept dry and the holds opened up often at sea to ventilate the hold in the interest of preventing fire and explosion."

"Tell me how you handled it."

"I stopped work discharging rock ballast until I could find out how much nitrate cargo awaited us. Taking out too much too soon could capsize the ship in the gentle swell coming onshore. I went ashore to speak to the British Consul again and found no instructions or orders had come for us there or at the office of the local agent for Gibbs & Co. Chilean railroads afford telegraph connections on the long coastline, but I didn't see they provided much in the way for passenger traffic. I came back to the ship to spend three days at anchor not knowing what would be done to provide us with nitrate. Thinking that Gibbs' Agent Hilliger would crack the whip to get things moving, I decided to clear out more of the ballast in the hope bags of nitrate would appear on the shore for us."

"What did the port at Iquique look like, Gaudin?"

"The *Lady Lampson* lay in a safe anchorage in the northeast corner of a large bay open to the sea and to the north of a small island close off the town formerly covered in layers of seabird excrement, guano, but now bare and used as a graveyard for English and other foreigners_____. *Yes, a graveyard on a foreign soil.*"

"The word 'soil' takes on new meaning doesn't it," Herd said. "I mean to say, the centuries of seabirds nesting there and fouling their nests."

"Yes sir, that expression does take on a new meaning in Iquique. A steep high slope rises immediately behind the town on the shore to bar sight of anything lying to the east. I understand beyond the slope lies the Atacama Desert and a rocky barren where the native workers dig up the nitrate in primitive working conditions. Wreckage of ruined buildings in town lies on all sides from the last earthquake two years ago, but I could see some re-construction work had begun."

Herd asked what loading facilities stood on the shore for Gaudin to use.

"None sir. Some bags of nitrate in piles on shore ready for loading, but no port official had given clearance to move any of it. As I thought it likely Gibbs & Co would act to move mountains for the bags to come clear for us, I decided to have more ballast removed the next day. We hove out as much additional ballast as I decided left the ship safe, and I hired a stevedore to come aboard to lay dunnage in the form of matts and battens in the bottom and at the sides in the hold to protect a full cargo of nitrate bags against breakage. Another official holiday on the shore presented on 2 February with all offices closed. I could see two longboats on the shore to all appearances ready to bring cargo bags out to us, but for three days none of them would come out from the shore to bring the bags of nitrate to us. Even though the Chileans claim jurisdiction over the port, the *lancheros* stood by their boats on the beach and refused to lift a finger to move a load out in their boats until clearance papers came from Peru. Can you imagine, sir, another whole day lost? On 5 February the wind and a ground swell got up with heavy surf on the beach, but that did not stop the lancheros who now rushed to launch their boats into the surf to come out. We took in three longboat loads of bags, using our own tackle to haul up the bags from the boats and lower them to the local stevedore and his helper in the hold. The bags were too heavy for any one of us to lift ourselves. One local balsas raft pressed into service, far less handy than a longboat, turned over in the surf with five large bags lost in the waves. The anchorage lay open to any sea developing."

"And on Sunday no work done?"

"Yes sir. Said to be the Lord's Day on account of it being Sunday, but they could not have come out in the heavier surf breaking on the beach the whole time. On 7 February I hired one long boat and three men from the shore to take five boatloads aboard. Next day someone cut the buoy rope to the kedge anchor to hold longboats for the unloading.

We dragged for it all day without success. The Chief Officer again logged as laid up with some illness keeping him in his bunk. Mister Farrow and I took charge of getting in four more longboat loads, the last available to us at Iquique."

"So, you could not get a full load from Iquique?"

"That's right sir. I went ashore two days later on Wednesday 9 February to ask agent Hilliger send a telegram to Jenkins to report. The reply came in a matter of minutes. Hilliger ran to catch me short of the boat to hand me the telegram, with our orders to complete the cargo at Mexillion Cove. Hilliger took me back to see the map on the wall of his office. He warned me not to confuse the place with another with similar name, Bahia de Mejillones de Sur, which lies some distance south of Iquique and north of the Chilean port of Antafogasta. Back on board ship I raced to my pilot book and charts to find the cove named Mexillon, a short sail to the north from Iquique. I decided to write the name of this place in the ship's logbook as Mexillones Bay because that spelling comes closer to the Spanish word Mejillones for the long dark shell of the mussels shellfish that grow underwater on the rocks."

"Did you eat any of the shellfish?"

"None of us would try them. The experience of Captain Vancouver at Poison Cove on the British Columbia coast with the shellfish poisoning death of some of his sailors in 1793 continues to linger even today in the minds of British seamen."

Herd asked Gaudin to tell him about the ship's departure from Iquique.

"With the ship light in the water with little ballast, we sailed straight out to sea with an offshore evening breeze at 5 p.m. 9 February. I sent nine of the crew down in the hold to manhandle the nitrate bags to lie flat and even across the bottom of the hold. The Iquique stevedores had left it in a low wedge pyramid amidships. After four hours I backed the main yard to stop the ship from moving any farther out to sea. As I expected, the breeze dropped to a calm overnight. We drifted in the dark under the stars a long way out from the shore. At daylight I set all possible sail to use the morning breeze to sail north to a dry rocky shoreline. We came to anchor in the bay off Mexillones Cove at 1 p.m. the same day. No other vessel sighted in this isolated bay on a desolate stretch of coastline or in the offing. A Gibbs & Co local agent came out in a small boat. He pointed out the place for dumping our remaining ballast and then directed me to the loading berth, which lay in a narrow confined cove several miles to the north. We weighed anchor and without making sail let the wind and tide drive the ship across the bay to the place where the Peruvian Government permits vessels to discharge ballast overboard."

"Gaudin, you said you let the wind and tide drive the ship: sailing ship captains do often use the word '*drive*' to explain the ship drifted with the force of a tide current or drifted with the wind with no sail set, that is, under bare poles."

"Yes sir. My schoolteacher taught me the word *drift* comes from the verb to *drive*. In the same way as the word *thrift* comes from the verb to *thrive*, but I am not sure you can take it too far, because the word *drive* in relation to a ship drifting may be an old-time meaning of the word. Nowadays we say the coachman *drives* a horse and carriage, and a ship's master who continues to carry sail when others reduce it may be said to have been *driving* his ship too hard."

"Yes Gaudin, and then the word means whatever the speaker intends. But get on with it, please."

"We commenced heaving out the remainder of the ballast at 3:30 p.m., then moved the ship to an anchorage closer to the loading berth. I gave notice to the local agent for Gibbs & Co that the ship lay ready to receive cargo. I must say, a great improvement here over facilities at Iquique. The organization and *savoir faire* of Gibbs & Co really showed up. They answered my call to send a stevedore from the shore to place the bags of nitrate in the hold. That dynamo of a man came on board with his mate to help. I warped the ship in to a loading berth in the cove, mooring ship head and stern with 30 fathoms of cable each way to ride the gentle swell coming in from southward. Not long to wait. Soon the first of the longboats from the shore came alongside loaded with bags of nitrate of soda by the half-dozen from warehouses, which stand behind a nearby point of land at this lonely place. The sunlight, quite blinding, made us squint to see the ocean in the distance, the bluest of blue. Whales surfaced and huge stingrays burst up out of the water in the distance, flying. And overall, the sunlight, a fine breeze, and the high pitched keening calls of seabirds flying fit the gay mood of everyone on deck, befitting the thought the ship would now be homeward bound after a year away."

"Yes, Gaudin, failing to find a full load and creeping away from Iquique in the night to find the cargo at Mexillones must have been a disappointment, but now joy and laughing out loud made life easier.

You have not mentioned seeing sharks."

"Yes sir, we could see them, their menacing fins slicing the water at the surface, and also, lurking deep under the ship when we looked down in the green clear water overside. We spread out the studdingsails as awnings in hot dry weather to stem the deck's showing signs of leaking. The ship lay here for ten days during which longboats from the shore brought out 15 boatloads of nitrate bags every day. To set this pace the strongest men in our crew worked with a will to man the oars of the longboats, adding their strength to the men hired from the shore. Fine weather, as I have said, but with a swell coming in to the loading berth on the shore, which caused the ship to lift and bridle against the anchor chain and the restraining rope lines. The Chief Officer laid-up throughout. Second Mate Farrow and I spelled each other off supervising the picking up of the bags from the longboats with our ship's own tackle and lowering them to the stevedore and his mate, who placed them in the hold."

"You are really saying that you and Second Officer Farrow were running the ship?"

"Yes sir, that's correct. A village lay inland of the bay, but I had no need to go ashore to ask for permits. I had no formalities to attend to even though Mexillones Cove in Peru. The Gibbs & Co agent handled everything. He told me to expect orders for the nitrate destination delivered by the pilot boat at the Scilly Islands off Land's End. If no orders with the pilot boat, proceed to Falmouth."

"Yes, Gaudin, Falmouth for Orders is a common disposition made for cargoes homewards these days in vessels not on regular runs, but the *Scilly Islands* for orders is new to me. No wonder you had such fun heading the pages of the logbook onwards as that of a voyage from *Mexillones Bay to the Scilly Islands.*"

"I worried you might send the *Lady Lampson* to Liverpool or to a port in Europe, sir. And that on the turnaround you might send us orders to go to some destination other than Vancouver Island."

"I know all about your desire to return to Victoria, Gaudin. Tell me more about the loading operation. You must have more to tell me about it."

"Fine weather throughout, but as I said a heavy swell began to set in to the cove to make it an uncomfortable berth. On the last day we took in another ten longboat loads. I calculated we had a cargo of 13,609 quintals net of nitrate of soda in 4,625 bags. I could now send the South

American stevedore and his mate ashore. Strong cheerful men, they did their heavy work laughing and singing even when I kept them at it to fill the hold full to the sides. The look on their faces showed me they didn't like that, but they couldn't speak English to tell me why."

"Gaudin, we now know the loading of the nitrate proved to be a learning experience. Marine insurance underwriters require ship captains to insist on the local stevedores placing the heavy nitrate bags in the hold in the shape of an elongated rectangular pyramid-like form flat at the top with a width half the ship's beam to permit ventilation. The people at Iquique knew about that, but the issue did not arise because they had so few bags of nitrate for you to take on. You went north to Mexillones to find your full load. The stevedore at Mexillones knew the requirements, but you didn't. He bowed to your insistence they keep loading to pack the hold full to the sides and corners. More's the wonder fire or explosion did not destroy the *Lady Lampson* at sea beyond help on your way homewards. Please go on to tell me about your departure."

"A chancy life we have at sea, sir. I didn't know. I loaded the *Lady Lampson* a foot deeper than usual at Mexillones, 16 feet forward and 16 foot six inches aft, but her sailing qualities did not suffer, which says something about her good design. I took in our longboat and cleared up the decks. Next day 19 February presented calm at the beginning of the day. I sent a boat out with men to pick up the stern moorings at daylight and went about getting the ship ready for sea. Took in the starboard anchor and unbent the cable. By 4 p.m. I could see the beginning of the wind out of the south on my telltale thread hanging in the mizzen rigging. I have had enough of this reliance on my cheek to tell the wind."

"Yes Gaudin, but the captain must never demean himself to hold a wetted finger to the wind. He must be above doing that even in the dark, lest someone see him, and show himself less than the all-knowing being he is supposed to be."

Thinking on it, Gaudin paused a moment before going on.

"I took sextant sights at noon to check our position in relation to our known latitude and longitude of the place and found the chronometers # 1502 and #2030 correct. With hands singing the *Hurrah Boys! We're Homeward Bound* shantey, we took in the port anchor and unbent the cable and saw everything secure about the decks. You could cut the air with a knife in such an emotional moment. Men had tears in their eyes to know their ship will now return to England's Shore."

"Your logbook states no other vessels in the offing waiting to follow you to load at Mexillones. I think this passage an experiment by the Chileans."

"Yes sir, you are likely correct. You may be interested when I tell you I heard some talk at the Inn that ship's masters will soon resume the custom taken from the Portuguese of hoisting the Sign of the Cross to the maintop on departure, but being Protestants we will name the occasion *Hoisting the Southern Cross*. Some ceremony will be made of it with ringing of ship's bells to send the loaded vessel on her way. At Mexillones we made a solitary and lonely departure as we crept off from the cove to make distance offshore before the day breeze ended. But in truth, the stevedore and his mate cheered us away with a farewell good-bye, and that meant a lot to us on leaving this lonely shore. The cheers from those men counted."

"Did you feel unease about setting out on such a long passage from the other side of the World so alone? I know Jersey sailormen place stock in superstition."

Gaudin took a moment to answer.

"Yes sir, I had a passing thought about leaving port without a send-off in the form of a benediction from other seamen, but soon dismissed it. With the sun low in the west lighting the hills and mountains inland, we made sail straight out to sea before darkness fell on 19 February 1870. I took bearings to establish our position 15-miles out, and marked an X on the chart to show the place at sea from which I made my departure, 900 miles north of Valparaiso."

After a long silence Herd said, "Let's talk later. Please return at four o'clock."

****

"Gaudin, I read your logbook to be saying you set your course to avoid the opposing stream of the Humboldt Current flowing at sea from the south."

"Yes sir, we sailed out from Southern Peru on a port tack with a freshening wind out of the south, which stayed fresh the night through. I aimed to make a good distance out away from land to avoid becoming stranded on the shoreline in the dark by tidal currents flowing in an unwanted calm."

"I have the picture, Gaudin. You sailed southwestwards across the Humboldt Current flowing north?"

"Yes sir, the set to the north soon became evident with the stimulating effect of the cold water current on seabirds and the fish. I will use the logbook again to remember and tell you more. We sailed through that night and the next day into a rising wind and sea, although the wind freed a little in direction to allow the port tack to be described as more of a close reach steered to the south of southwest. But the ship pitched as she punched her bows into the seas and shipped much of it aboard to wash the main deck clear of anything not secured. I brought down the Royals, main t'gallant and mizzen topmast staysails, and the gaff-topsail. Doing so had little effect on easing the ship's unhappy motion. Wind and rainsqualls harried us through the next night as we struck out into the ocean on a compass heading of *Southwest by South ½ South* to sail across the northerly set of the Humboldt Current, which we wanted to get out from as soon as we could. Couldn't turn to southward yet, of course, because we needed to run clear to the north of the Juan Fernandez Islands, 500 miles and more to go on that heading before we could turn south. Next day at 20°26' South 72°28' West I set all possible sail in light and unsteady winds; we carried on for days under dark cloud in squalls of rain in the sudden changes of wind force and direction coming with the onset of a squall. In daylight, of course, we can keep a lookout to see the slanting cloud and rain in the squall dropping down hard. Squalls on a dark night without moonlight hit with no warning and we can do little but react."

"Please let me interrupt you again, Gaudin. I recall entries in your logbooks about *Isla Mas a Fuera*. I have learned that name in Spanish means simply the Outer Island of the Juan Fernandez Group of Islands."

"Outer Island doesn't sound very original, does it, sir? Perhaps the Chileans will find a better name."

"The Juan Fernandez Islands have so much early history involving that Englishman, the man with the French-sounding name, Dampier. But please go on, Gaudin."

"Yes sir, I could have the ship hold a sharper course to southwards whenever the wind allowed the helmsman to steer a course closer into the wind. In this way we continued sailing towards the southwest, but edged south whenever the wind backed to allow. We made good speed through the water most days. I wanted soon to turn toward Cape Horn."

"Yes Gaudin, I can understand why you held course to the southwest rather than put about to stay closer to the South American Coast, only to run back into the Humboldt Current, which would have held you back. When could you ventilate the cargo holds?"

"We did that for the first time two-days out, sir. When the wind went light we opened the hatch covers to let it siphon the air out from below and allow in fresh air. In some sea conditions you do not dare open the hatch covers. The bags of nitrate must not get wet. Every day I also checked the cargo holds for water leaks more than once and pumped out any small amount that had come aboard."

"When could you begin to steer towards Cape Horn?"

"Not until ten-days out on the first day of March at 30°49' South 90°15' West, and a thousand miles west of the central Chilean coast. In the days preceding we endured light and baffling southerly airs over a lazy ocean swell that made up from the south on an empty ocean. In unexpected fine clear weather we made only 60 miles in 24 hours. The next morning opened with a clap of wind coming on the starboard side out of the west for the first time since leaving Mexillones. Jubilation on deck followed on my order to turn the ship for the first time to the southeast. The experienced hands knew we could now steer to make best speed on compass headings to the southeast where Cape Horn stood ready to test us."

"What steps did you take to check the rigging to be fit for the Horn?"

"We took the opportunity to set up the main rigging and backstays to be fit for the run past the Horn, and we unbent the best sails to be ready to use again. I thought I might order the weight of the Royal Yards down when we come farther south to lessen the violence of the rolling when we begin to run downwind in heavy seas. The wind and seas then will be sending us sailing as fast as we can without the Royals being set, but until that time I will have need of them. The wind did not last. Midnight came with the wind having lulled away to a calm. Morning came with a gentle breeze, fine weather, and a strong swell from the southwest. I ordered the hatches opened for ventilation. Clear weather came on the second day of March. In the afternoon a gentle breeze came up from the southwest. I set the starboard foretop and lower studdingsails and sent up the main t'gallant studdingsails to take advantage of the wind by such a blossoming out of light canvas. But nothing stays the same for long. The barometer moved down gradually in the evening.

Squalls came down hard on us again after dark as if the Gods thought us worthy of a beating."

Gaudin turned the pages of the logbook and paused before speaking again with a thought that had occurred to him.

"We will take two weeks more to get down to the approaches to Cape Horn. The next morning followed a night of increasing wind from the west-south-west. Strong ocean swells coming on from the southwest all through the night had our bows punching into them to create instant sheets of spray and walls of solid water shipped from forward to flow knee-deep on the decks until sent overside. The next day a heavy cross-sea made for uneasy going as we punched through them. At noon on 3 March I calculated our position to be at 34°58' South and 89°21' West, which placed us well out in the Eastern South Pacific. We had passed beyond the South East Trade Winds into the area of equinoctial storms south of the Tropic of Capricorn in the month of March to harry us on our way southwards."

"You aim to make your way through this part of the South Pacific to reach as far south as the Roaring Forties? And then nip even farther south into the Fifties to get around the Horn, which sticks down south to 56 degrees of South Latitude?"

"Yes sir. You have all of that correct. The Horn projects that far south. In the meantime we would have normal equinoctial storm weather to pass through. To get back to the third day of March: from noon to midnight a fresh breeze out of the west to southwest came up to push us with a fall in barometer from 30.25 down to 29.90 inches of Mercury. A strong ocean swell built up sent the ship lurching to the southeast into great humps of swell, not an easy motion for the ship to take up carrying sail. Great waterfalls of cold seawater come over the bulwarks to sluice knee-deep on the deck. At 4 p.m. four squalls hit in quick succession. I gave the orders to take in the studdingsails, the Royals, the t'gallant sails and the light fore and aft staysails. We ran through squally weather all night. I observed the sea as *very* luminous in the dark, not phosphorescence, but something else I couldn't explain."

"No sleep for you that night, Gaudin."

"Young Farrow doing a fine job as Second Mate, but I missed the eyes and help of the Chief Officer who remained laid up in his berth. During the night of 4 March we ran on to the southeast toward the Horn in a continuation of squally weather thrashing down on the tops of ragged rolling peaks of a *tremendous*, and I mean a tremendous ocean swell, pushed by the wind out of the southwest, moving past us, fast. Our little barque shipped great quantities of seawater as I drove her on under low torn-apart fast moving dark clouds. An unhappy condition for the ship as she slowed in the water for one long moment on the upwind side of the wave, sails and rigging digging in their heels, chafing at being held back. And in the next few moments we surged on in a wild ride when the crest of the next wave picked us up to sling the ship forward, only to pause as the wave slid under, forward, to be lost in the haze ahead. Our vessel fought to keep her head up. Rolling and pitching on the rises showed me chilling glimpses of an expanse of breaking seas to windward as far as the eye could see. And down in the troughs of these ocean waves I could only take time to shift my weight to keep my footing and catch a glimpse of tumbling walls of dark grey-green foam-flecked water by day, dead black by night. Regularly manning the pumps kept the ship *perfectly tight* as you prescribed the standard for me to attain. On the wind turning to come more from the west and moderating I steered to head to the south of southeast to reach higher latitudes to the south, and I ordered Mister Farrow to send his men up into the rigging to set the t'gallant sails above the upper and lower topsails. My noon sight at 37°37' South 88°20' West showed 190 miles made good on a track of *Southeast by South* since previous noon. We have edged into *Roaring Forties* wind and weather. No little amount of haze, spume, spindrift, and spray in the air being thrown off from wavetops by the frantic wind, making for poor visibility. The ship doesn't drift through the waves, but sails of her own motion forward into them as I force her slow to make Southing every time the wind allows. In the afternoon the wind increased in strength and the waves mounted higher. The ship laboured, faltered, rolled, and lurched with wind coming on the starboard quarter. But, at times she ran freely in surges, pushed by wind and sea together. The helmsmen take short spells at the wheel to cope with the following seas kicking hard against the rudder when the stern pitches up. They steer to average out the swings from the compass heading I have given to one of them, the other man at the wheel acting in unison. The averaging out of the quarter points of the compass can befuddle a tired man's mind. If they lose control, we are all lost. In the afternoon the wind from behind increased and filled the air with spray blown off the cresting wavetops to drench the deck. I decided to order the t'gallant sails down. Farrow sees that done as the evening ends in squalls and cold rain. At 11 p.m. I order the outer jib taken down and the staysails set between the main and the foremast to ease the ship's motion."

"The man at the helm who has an eye for the compass and the sails at the same time has his job cut out for him in these conditions."

"Yes sir, especially at night when the lamp for the compass flickers and dims and the helmsman cannot see how the wind flutters sails to give him clues how to move the spokes of the steering wheel best. And a job for the rest of us on deck for a sharp lookout for hazards as we come farther south, icebergs, drift ice; and not least, congested sailing vessel traffic coming from the other direction the closer we get to the southern tip of South America."

"I imagine that all the while you were looking for a lull to open the hatches to ventilate the nitrate."

"Yes sir, that's right. Three weeks out from Mexillones on 5 March more of the same boisterous weather conditions during another week of sailing with the wind in following seas. In the afternoon the wind lessened, but the seas continued to run high. I set the middle staysails and the flying jib again to keep up the ship's speed to the east and southeast, but we're making no more than 120 miles noon to noon_____ no clipper ship passage."

"Gaudin, you cannot expect clipper ship passages. Only a longer sharper vessel can maintain speed through seas. Think about it: the wind you feel in your face on deck feels like a gale when you sail against it in a fresh breeze. Not to take away from your little ship or to lessen the dangers you face, I'd say the *very* size and speed of the clippers makes it worse for them and for the men in them. The rider of the faster horse will feel the wind the most. If you handle the sails to stay afloat through the worst of the brutal force of the wind your little ship will come out, whole. But let me ask, you are now well south of the latitude of Valparaiso: does not the nearness of the Southern Chilean coast pose a peril?"

"Yes sir, but we sail too far from the coastline to see it. I am aware of the peril but I intend to keep far enough out from the coast to remain safe. To your other point: yes, our smaller and slower vessel has an easier time of it, but as you say, we cannot drive our way to windward as well as a heavier sharp-hulled clippership can. Witness, the horrid week we endured when westbound and trying to reach 50° South in the Pacific on the maiden voyage, eight whole days in the Pacific, west of the Horn, fighting just to get north of the latitude of Cape Horn. I'll never forget it, but I should get back to this passage with the bags of Nitrate of Soda: on 7 March more of the same wind and weather with a strong swell in squalls of wind and rain. The noon sight showed us at 45°42' South and 83°31' West, which meant we made 159 miles since previous noon. The Chief Officer remained laid up and off duty. I ordered our Ship's Carpenter Chapman, an experienced seaman, to stand watch with the Second Mate. I told Farrow to feel free to consult him if he sees fit before calling me on deck. Farrow didn't resent it. Some mates would. Next day, 8 March, daylight came with less wind, but with squalls and occasional slight showers of rain. We set all possible sail to make distance. None of us wants to stay in this part of the ocean. By afternoon the wind fell off to light with occasional showers of rain to beat down on the dark surface of the ocean swell with a force we could see and hear on deck as a sizzling sound. By midnight the wind fell off to no more than a light air from the southwest. The barometer rose to indicate fair weather on the way."

"About time, I'd say, Gaudin."

"Under an overcast sky in the early morning darkness of 9 March, a light wind now blew from behind to favour us. Outboard of all plain sail, I set flying all of the starboard studdingsails in a heartening display of canvas to move the ship downwind at best speed on courses steered varying from to the south and southeast to take best advantage of wind shifts. During the day low clouds from the southwest passed occasionally over the ship dumping showers of cold misty rain. By noon my navigation showed the ship's position within 150 miles of the southwestern rockbound Coast of Chile at 50° South Latitude. On the wind making up its mind to blow from northwest by early afternoon I ordered a complete set of studdingsails to be set on the port side to replace those to starboard. The watch made fast work of it. The men jumped to it and showed great pleasure and pride in making the ship go faster on a compass heading closer to the shoreline lying ahead but not yet in sight."

"That must have taken some nerve, Gaudin."

"Well sir, I am not so sure of that. I had to change tactics by dark when a heavy cross swell made up from the southwest to give hint of an ill wind behind. On a course of *South East by South* the ship rolled in a heavy swell making up from the wind behind us. The waves came aboard to sweep the deck to keep us wide-awake. I hauled in the port studdingsails. By midnight a cheerful fresh breeze came out of west-north-west to enable us to sail on the same compass heading of *South East by South* at the same speed as previous. The barometer remained steady, which I found encouraging. A sudden wind shift came at 3 a.m. on 10 March to blow from the south with the skies clearing up. I set all of the light canvas sails and turned the ship to head in the direction of Cape Horn on a compass course of *East-South-East*. A barque flying German colours, likely bound for Chile, passed to windward too far off for us to speak. A far larger vessel I am sure than the distance made her appear. She soon disappeared in the haze aft. My noon calculation of 51°40' South and 79°10' West showed our ship made 185 miles to the southeast in the last 24 hours. The afternoon came in with fair light winds and another strong swell behind us from the southwest, giving hint of distant storms having produced them. The southern autumn fair wind continued in clear weather. The ship made distance, rolling with the swell. I set outboard of all regular sail the fore t'gallant and lower studdingsails to port and starboard, followed by the main t'gallant studdingsails to keep up ship's speed on the winds turning light. The pumps attended to and we found the ship *perfectly tight* against leaks. The late evening sent us cloudy weather and increasing winds from the southwest to keep us on our toes, considering the nearness of land. Next noon 11 March showed us at 55°24' South 77°39' West and having made 175 miles on a track of *East by South* in last 24."

"You are coming closer to the Horn?"

"Closer, yes, but not quite yet, sir. I know I am sailing safely to clear the *Islas Ildefonso*, which stand in the sea far ahead to port. After I pass abeam of them I will pass to the north of *Islas Diego Ramirez*, which we hope to see soon to starboard 56 miles southwest of Cape Horn in Sir Francis Drake Channel. I must not forget to mention that when eastbound around the Horn in poor visibility we must not mistake the headland standing far ahead to port at *False Cape Horn* as the real Cape."

"Yes Gaudin, I know some eastbound unfortunates, thinking they had passed the real Cape, have sailed to their destruction on the rocks lying 50 miles to the northwest of the true Cape Horn. I have heard it said some lucky ship someday will blunder on past the *False Cape Horn*, but succeed in passing through the uncharted rocks and islands lying north of the Horn and come out safe on the other side."

"Yes sir. Luck has a lot to do with it. I am painfully aware all aboard rely on me not to wreck the ship, sir. I am gratified, but say nothing when the experienced hands spy landmarks they know, such as the Cape itself, and spread the word among the crew they have confidence in me."

"Yes Gaudin, pity the shipmaster who does not have the confidence of his crew. I must check to see what soundings Captain Cook made in his explorations in these waters in the late 1700s. Please go on with your account."

"From my own observations, sir, the depth of water offshore the southern end of South America must shallow steep in a short distance from immense ocean depths in the Pacific. That would account for the steep pitch of storm seas off Cape Horn in Sir Francis Drake Channel. South from there, I mean, south of Diego Ramirez, takes the ship into deeper water, but in that direction *There be Dragons!* I mean to say, icebergs and packs of drift ice low in the water, which are not so easily seen. Icebergs can gleam in the dark, but drift ice floats low in the water, invisible. All of which provides another reason to round the Horn westbound in the daylight of southern summertime, the better to see and steer to avoid the hazard. Also in the prolonged twilight and daylight hours we can run closer to the shorelines we know and use as landmarks."

"I understand, Gaudin. Captain Adamson must have warned you to be on guard for alarm on deck when the lookout cries *ice ahead* and the crushing necessity as I recall him telling me, to reduce sail in the dark when all instinct cries out to make speed to sail away from this terrible part of the ocean."

"Yes sir, he did teach me about that, but let me go on. By 11 a.m. on 12 March the wind came up to a strong breeze with a heavy sea out of the southwest. I ordered the studdingsails down, followed soon by the Royals, but the ship maintained her speed. I calculated our noon position at 55°50' South 73°02' West, which enabled me to calculate we had made 186 miles on a track of *East by South* since previous noon. We ran on in a fresh breeze from the west-south-west in the afternoon of 12 March in hazy weather with a heavy jumble of sea on. The barometer is steady at 30.02 inches, which I took to be a good sign. At 5 a.m. we caught a glimpse of the Islas Diego Ramirez abeam bearing due south in poor visibility but far enough away to be of no concern. At 8 a.m. the wind dropped off and the ship complained to me I had her trapped under low black cloud. She rose and fell, pitching and rolling in seas that can best be described as a jumble of dark hollows amid tops of ragged roller waves that towered up masthead height, which shoved us about as driftwood. But we are not stopped. The ship rolled about making little headway until moments came for the upper sails to catch wind to send us lurching along to put distance behind. The Chief Officer remained laid up and off duty. In improving conditions at noon we had Cape Horn in sight bearing northeast of us on the port bow, a rocky island over 1,000 feet high. Jubilation reigned on deck as we came abeam of the Horn six miles off. We saw her beset by the seas breaking on the headland and on rocks close in at the foot of Drake's *Uttermost End of the Earth*. Some of the more experienced hands on deck knew the shape of Cape Horn by sight and they chortled like contented ducks."

"Your two passages in the *Prince of Wales* with Captain Adamson must have given you some good experience around the Horn, Gaudin?"

"Yes sir, in particular, I recall 3 October 1867 when I made a sketch to help me remember. The *Prince of Wales* passed Cape Horn homewards to London from Victoria in the season of spring in southern waters. We were passing abeam of the Cape under high overcast cloud in clear visibility. Captain Adamson sent me up the main to catch a plain view of the Horn and the adjacent islands, Hermite, Herschel, Woolaston, Barneveldt, and the whole southern end of the high snow-covered southern foothills of the Fuegan Alps standing in the distance behind. I prized the opportunity to imprint the landscape panorama on my mind's eye to use the next time passing."

"Yes, Captain Adamson like Captain Cook himself would close with the shore to fix ship's position, but do go on."

"Yes, but this time the *Lady Lampson* passed as close in as I would want. The noon position at 56°08' South and 67°32' West showed us having made good 197 miles in the last 24 hours. By afternoon the wind dropped to light under a clear sky. I ordered in the studdingsails, which were doing no good in a jumble of leftover seas. At nightfall the rigging sang with a new wind from offshore, out of the north. I set all possible sail to make best speed. By 11 p.m. I added the port studding-sails in a light northwest wind, but the wind did not last. We drifted in a restless sea. A rising barometer cheered me, but then began to drop, which I took as a bad sign. We did not want to linger here in a position of danger not yet far enough away from the Cape. By the noon sight next day I calculated we'd made only 60 miles in 24 hours."

"Do go on, Gaudin."

"For the next two days, 14 and 15 March 1870, I sailed my ship eastward in fog, which an increasing cold wind out of the north-north-east did nothing to disperse. By noon the next day the noon sextant sight showed we had made good 182 miles homewards since previous noon. Staten Island lay out of sight, distant to the north in low cloud and rain. Dark grey seas in the form of silent high roller waves sent by a distant storm from the west rode in formation high and steep, marching eastward, to intimidate and make me feel our vessel far too small to be sailing here. With no wind on the sails to stiffen the ship the *Lady Lampson* reacted as a naughty child, rocking back and forth from side to side, putting her lee rails under and causing discomfort on deck. On the wind rising in strength we moved off at speed in thick haze and misty rain, but I soon ordered the Royals brought down to ease the ship's motion through the water. After 4 p.m. the barometer began a marked drop from the earlier high reading of 30.08 inches at noon. At 6 p.m. we tacked to the north and then to the east in decreasing wind to keep the ship moving to make distance. The fog in the cold temperatures became so thick in the 9 p.m. darkness we were unable to see farther than a ship's length ahead. Fearing the ship would fall in with drift ice, I gave the order to take down the t'gallants and all light fore and aft sails to slow the passage of the ship through the water, and I ordered a sharp lookout. By midnight the barometer falling fast to 29.58 inches led to expectation of a usable wind, but none of any help came. All that night the wind kept coming from the north-north-east, which headed us and left us no option but to turn to starboard, southeastwards. But in the early morning hours of 17 March we could turn to carry sail eastward through a sullen grey rolling sea in fog and frequent showers of misty rain. We sailed our ship alone on a wide expanse of ocean with no other vessel in sight. At the same time other sailing vessels far to the northwest would be striving to enter the Strait of Le Maire to pass Cape Horn on their way into the Pacific. This brings me to explain why we sail to avoid meeting them. Everyone eastbound wants to get past this terrible part of the ocean. The waters lying between Cape Horn and Staten Island provide no place for eastbound vessels to dodge about to wait for a favouring flood tide current to push them through the Strait of Le Maire into the South Atlantic. In any event, fog and low cloud often obscure sight of that Island. Prudent navigation calls on us to set a course to pass outside the island before turning north to sail into the South Atlantic. On 17 March the sextant sight calculations show the ship's position remained far south at 56°14' South and 54°11' West, but nevertheless I enjoyed the comforting thought we had taken gradual steps northeastwards away from the possibility of ice."

"The ship's cook the only man on board with fire to keep him warm?"

"Yes sir, perhaps, but my steward kept a fire lit for me and Farrow at our table off our cabins below; and the men in the fo'c'sle cabin on deck forward stored fuel to light a fire in their stove, but only for so long as I could contrive to set a course that did not lay smoke down on my quarterdeck. At noon a favourable fresh breeze came from the west-north-west, but by 6 p.m. I ordered the t'gallant sails brought down to ease the ship's motion in squally weather from the southwest. At 10 p.m. on the wind changing to come from the south-south-east I ordered the t'gallants set flying again to keep the ship driving hard into the darkness to make distance homewards. No man can find peace or contentment in this pitiless part of the ocean."

Gaudin turned the page.

"The early morning hours of 18 March found the ship sailing fast in squalls of wind and rain with all possible sail set. We make distance to the northeast. The wind dropped off by mid-morning as we ran into yet another heavy jumble of a steep cross-sea to set our little ship moving with hesitation. At noon I calculated our position at 53°17' South and 49°40' West of Greenwich, which meant we'd made 250 miles to the northeast in the last 24 hours. This put us 500 miles off the coast of the Southern Argentine where we do not see any other shipping traffic. Westbound sailing vessels keep closer in to the Argentine shore lest they miss the Strait of Le Maire in dark weather and blunder into the maw of the Westerlies. Some unfortunate westbound vessels have been driven back to sailing south of Africa to reach the Pacific. By early afternoon the wind turned to blow from the east-north-east as we went to windward on a starboard tack in clear weather. But soon the wind dropped leaving only a strong ocean swell from the southwest. As daylight ended we sailed through large numbers of small white birds flying about the vessel, not sea birds, but of a species I knew not. A strange sight so far from shore: none lit on the rigging or on deck. By nightfall a wind from the north headed us, so I turned to steer to the east, using the wind to sail on a reach. But overnight I turned the *Lady Lampson* to steer north into the South Atlantic. Next morning the men on deck chortled at the better turn shown by the sun's position and they smiled at how fast we now moved through the water."

Gaudin paused to fill his pipe with fresh tobacco and to light it.

"On 19 March with all possible sail set we sailed northeastwards in dense fog not dispersed by the strong breeze out of the north-northwest. At noon I calculated 168 miles since previous noon and the ship's position at 50°16' South and 46°57' West. No one counts the time it takes to sail with the prevailing westerlies from 50° South in the Pacific to 50° South in the Atlantic. The wind freshened and the skies cleared. But by 1 p.m. a brisk wind out of the north headed us. We bore off to eastward only to be headed again by the wind veering to the northeast. But that ill wind allowed us to put about and turn to tack to the north-west making distance. By 6 p.m. we saw lightning in the cloud building behind us. I brought in all light sails and the t'gallant sails. The weather turned squally at midnight with a falling barometer. At 1 a.m. on 21 March the ship made way in long lulls of little wind marked by heavy downpours of rain, vivid flashes of lightning and sharp peals of thunder, which made such a racket I judged they boomed and rolled close at masthead level. Within minutes we faced a wind out of the north-north-west from the direction of the Argentine and a heavy ocean swell, which may have originated from a *Pamperos* stormwind churning up the waters closer to the Argentine shore. No wind yet, but at daybreak I set the upper topsails and the staysails to take advantage of a light air. On the wind's direction changing to come more from behind, I ordered the t'gallant sails set above the lower sails to sail with it."

"An autumn wind at sea off the Argentine can make for a busy time, Gaudin."

"Yes sir, that's right, but it's no longer cold as we work our way north into the South Atlantic. At noon I calculated we made good 151 miles on a track of *North by East ¾ East*. The ship's position at 49°13' South 43°27' West put us well out into the South Atlantic Ocean and 800 miles to the east of the Falkland Islands. With no other westbound Sail expected in this part of the ocean, we sailed alone on a wide expanse of sea. By early afternoon we were sailing fast under all plain sail. Late in the afternoon squalls from the northwest blasted down out of the building clouds, forcing me to bring down the Royals and upper staysails. Sailing on into the night on 22 March, we found wind coming from the northwest with a touch of north in it. By 1 a.m. the ship sailed close to the wind on a port tack, steering on a course of *North East ½ North*. We put the miles behind us with all possible sail set, heeled to starboard. A fine breeze blew all day with a rising barometer. The wind did not disperse the haze and mist, which held throughout. At noon I calculated the ship had made good 228 miles on the same track as the compass course we had been sailing. In the afternoon the wind turning to favour, we ran with the bloom of studdingsails set for the rest of the day in another heartening display of canvas to catch the wind. By 1 a.m. on 23 March I sailed the *Lady Lampson* on a compass heading of *North East by North* in a fine breeze continuing out of the northwest, but soon, on the wind dropping, we were limping along with little wind in the dark cloud with light showers of misty rain. On the wind making up in squalls at three in the morning, I had Mister Farrow take down the light sails. Within the hour, the wind settled down to allow me to give the order to set all plain sail. By 5 a.m. we added the fore t'gallant studdingsails_____ and the Chief Officer returned to duty for the first time since Iquique without shedding any information on his past disability. At 9 a.m. I called out for the Watch to look at the colour of the seawater, which had changed from a dark blue to a green colour. Under normal conditions this would warn of shoaling waters, but considering our location, far away from land, not likely. I had no idea of the cause, perhaps an undersea volcanic eruption. Soon we were back in the deep blue sea and breathing easy. The weather cleared with the wind steady from the northwest on our port side for the remainder of the day. The moderate breeze and clear weather took us 198 miles on track of *North East by North*. Not bad for this little barque loaded with bags of nitrate of soda to draw a foot deeper than her usual sailing trim. By 9 p.m. the wind now came more out of the west, which favoured us, but the weather became cloudy with misty rain. On April Fool's Day I steered the *Lady Lampson* to the northeast in more wind than sea from a position 700 miles south and east of Cap Frio on the coast of Southern Brazil, but an early wind out of the southeast came up to have us sailing on a fast reach on a compass course of *North by East ½ East*. The *Lady Lampson* sliced through the water in a most heartening manner. At noon I calculated a track made good of 230 miles since yesterday as we favoured the western side of the South Atlantic Ocean. With her short waterline length of 121 feet, the good little ship cannot ever do much better than that. The sextant sight showed the ship's position at 27°14' South and 30°00' West. The 23° plus or minus South latitude of the Tropic of Capricorn, depending on the slant of the earth at the time, lies ahead, as does the distant rocky island of *Isla Trinadade*, which lies in the ocean 700 miles northeast of Rio de Janeiro. Next day, northbound up the South Atlantic at 1 a.m. on the second day of April the helmsman steered on a compass course of *North by East ¼ East*, taking advantage of a fresh easterly breeze. The clouds favoured us with occasional tropical dumps of rain in squalls to wash ourselves and clean the deck. By 8 a.m. I gave the order to set all starboard studdingsails to take advantage of the wind having turned to come more out of the south in clear weather. The actual track made good depended on the man at the wheel steering to keep the sails full as the wind direction varied and hands keeping the sails in trim. At the noon sight I calculated the ship's position at 23°30' South and 29°56' West of Greenwich Longitude, northeast of Rio de Janeiro and 700 miles off the coast of Brazil. The day followed into night with pleasant breezes and fine weather, but a strong ocean swell from the southeast caused the ship to roll and the tops of the masts to make slow arcs in the heavens. By nightfall we ran into wind squalls, dark cloud, and passing rain-showers, which the men caught in canvas bags to drink better tasting water than they could find in the casks filled at Coquimbo. On the morning of the third day of April the weather remained cloudy with a strong rolling ocean swell from the direction of South Africa, thousands of miles away to the southeast. Since sunrise the wind had been unsteady and at times almost a calm. The Chief Officer logged off duty to stay in his cabin again, this time for the remainder of the passage. Again more watch-keeping time came for me, the Second Mate and Chapman, who came back to stand watch with Mister Farrow. After making the noon sight to show 21°14' South and 29°52' West and calculating the ship made good 124 miles since noon yesterday, I sent a nimble seaman up into the rigging to tell me what he could see by looking around the horizon. I did not show surprise when he called out, *Land ho! Close off the port bow.* Cheer and jubilation came expressed on deck. My crew viewed the sighting as just another example of my good navigation, but to my dismay I knew different. My calculation of the ship's position in the ocean would have put Isla Trinidade out of sight. On checking my navigation sights and calculations, I wrote a note in the ship's logbook that a significant set westward over the last several days can be accounted for only by an ocean current in this locality."

"Gaudin, I have read your explanation in the logbook and I have gone over your navigation calculations from the Horn onwards. I am satisfied you were set to westward by an unexpected current in the ocean, so please go on with your account."

Gaudin breathed a sigh of relief.

"Thank you sir," he said. "As we drew ahead we all could see the tip of one of the peaks on the *Isla Trinidade* in plain view ahead close off the port bow. The island lies northwest to southeast so it appeared as a single peak from this angle. From a broadside angle the island would be seen to consist of four steep peaks arranged on high rocky ground, each not much more than 1,000 feet and unadorned by any cloud above to mark its location any time I have seen it_____, an unlikely apparition to find at sea in the Tropics."

After a pause Gaudin picked up again to go on.

"Trinidade could easily be passed from a greater distance off without seeing it. No more than a speck in the ocean, but seeing it did give me the ship's position. I knew my exact position in the World when I departed Mexillones Bay, and I knew it again when off Cape Horn. In between times my estimate as to the ship's position on the globe depended on the accuracy of my sextant sights and my best reckoning each noon of the ship's track through the sea."

"Yes Gaudin, and when you found Trinidade and estimated your distance and bearing from it, you fixed a new point of departure for the last part of the voyage to the English Channel. This would lessen the chances of an error in steering the ship when sailing in fog and rain in the approaches to the English Channel."

A long moment passed with neither speaking.

"But to go on, if I may sir, that afternoon produced light and variable winds out of the east and northeast and frequent calms with occasional showers of rain and a strong ocean swell rolling in from the southeast. At the same time, contrary to what we might expect, low dark clouds scudded fast toward the direction the swell came from, but nothing untoward resulted. Daylight ended with light airs from the east and northeast. A blast of wind to help me drive the ship north would not come tonight."

"As best as I can see, Gaudin, you sailed up the South Atlantic on a track shaped to lie in a northeasterly direction towards the bulge of Africa, but you turned north before you reach sight of that continent?"

"Yes sir, that's right. The ship made way in hot, humid, and often windless weather. We changed sails and turned the ship again and again to use fitful squalls and blasts of wind and rain to keep moving. Tempers flared in a trying time of irritation and physical discomfort. We will not find the North East Trade Winds to take us slanting to the northwest in the Atlantic Ocean until after we cross the Equator and sail through the troublesome calms and thunder and lightning storms in the Horse Latitudes. We champ at the bit to reach the westerly winds in the North Atlantic, which will enable us to turn the ship east to the English Channel. On Wednesday morning 11 May 1870 our day at sea began with strong wind and squally weather out of the north-north-west blowing to stir up a strong cross-sea to knock down yesterday's previous sea. The curtain went up on a new scene as we sailed into another part of the ocean and into a changed sea and sky. At 11 a.m. I set a new compass course of *East by North ½ North* with the wind square out of the northwest in gale strength to send us home. Word spreads of this to bring jubilation in the crew, even though we began to roll in a ponderous manner and take seas aboard washing the decks at the end of each roll. I ordered sail set, the t'gallant sails, the middle staysails, the spare inner jib, and the flying jib set out forward to act as a wind vane to help keep the ship steering straight in the following seas. Satisfied that no sail drawing wind blanketed another, we drove on. The noon sight found the ship at 43°30' North and 22°25' West of Greenwich, which showed we had come well north of the Azores and heading for the English Channel."

"In my day," Herd said, "we called those islands the Western Isles. They have been Portuguese for as long as sailors can remember. Englishmen never found a reason to take them away from them. But please go on."

"By early afternoon on 11 May, even though the force of the wind had lessened, we sailed with a tremendous sea on, pushing us from behind. We had made 230 miles noon-to-noon the previous 24 hours. This sea condition makes the ship roll her main rails under. Despite her high freeboard above the waterline, we ship great quantities of water to fill the decks deep until the scuppers release it overside. I hear talk of large steel German Cape Horn four-masted barques with a raised mid-deck coming to be built, which seems like a clever idea to prevent too much water coming on board to weigh down the ship."

"Yes Gaudin. You're right on that. Please go on."

"Haze all quadrants in the afternoon. We could not see far in any direction. By nightfall we slowed our pace as the wind strength lessened and backed to the south of west. Squalls and rain showers battered the ship. The noon sight shows 45°00' North and 27°47' West. I calculated a run of 140 miles made good. When the rain stopped I took another opportunity to open the hatches to ventilate the cargo. The wind increased in strength in the afternoon. I saw the clouds giving the appearance of even more wind, so I ordered the Royals and all light fore and aft sails brought down in anticipation of higher seas ahead. Daylight ended with more rain and wind squalls coming down to harry us. From midnight through the early hours of 12 May the ship drove on to eastward with decks awash as she rolled from one side to the other. With the accompanying ship movements you'd expect, the seas overtook and ran under us to rage on into the darkness ahead. I took station on my deck. The helmsman strove to keep the ship heading on the compass course I had given. The lookout standing on the foc'sle housework hung on to a stay to scan the seas ahead for other vessels in the murk, but the wind blew the tops off the high waves behind, destroying visibility forward. We could see nothing. In the first part of the morning watch the wind fell to light in rain as we ran on in boisterous seas. I saw my barometer needle falling. The wind increased in strength and the ship ran under all plain sail in quartering dark grey seas, the tops of which we found ourselves looking up at. In the afternoon we encountered even worse weather conditions in haze and poor visibility. The air turned cold, but by now we dressed for it. I gave orders to bring down the fore t'gallant sail and the middle staysails. Mister Farrow ordered his watch jump to get it done. After midnight we continued to ship great quantities of water on board to run off through the scuppers. In the early hours of 13 May the ship continued to run in strong winds, squally weather, and seas now even higher than yesterday. At 9 a.m. a great sea came aboard to smash down the lee bulwarks the distance from the gangway to the break of the quarterdeck, breaking loose the spare spars and everything else not well secured about the decks. To add to the turmoil, the leach rope of the main t'gallant sail broke. Nothing else to be done than to send men up to fist the sail furled. The seas did not subside. The noon sight showed the ship's position at 47°18' North and 21°16' West of Greenwich, which meant we had made good 212 miles since previous noon. We were left to plow onward into the receding backsides of ocean waves moving past us faster than we could sail. The next wave following surged the ship forward again."

Gaudin paused to drink from his mug then went on.

"In the afternoon, even though the wind lessened, the ship faced into a high cross-sea from the northwest and from the southwest. Wind and rainsqualls slanted down from low dark clouds to make conditions worse in lumpy going. I gave the order to reduce sail. But at 3 p.m. the conditions improved and the rain stopped. I ordered all plain sail set. By nightfall the wind came on again in force, this time square out of the west. On the wind and sea moderating, I set all studdingsails to run with the wind. The westerly wind carried us along in conditions that gave another opportunity to open the hatches to ventilate the nitrate. By midnight on 15 May the ship sailed on in fine weather. I ordered all available sail set to take advantage of it. At daylight a large number of sailing vessels and steamers appeared on the horizon with us, some outbound and others inbound as we are. I lost sleep in crowded and dangerous waters. My Chief Officer has long been off duty AND now my Second Mate suffered leg injuries and off-duty. I am running this ship with the help of the Ship's Carpenter, who spelled me off and came running to call me when he needed help. The noon sight showed 49°19' North and 9°44' West of Greenwich, which meant we made 126 miles in the last 24 hours. We sailed now in about the same latitude as Victoria, British Columbia. A pleasant breeze and fine weather in the afternoon gave the opportunity to open hatches for a final session to ventilate the bags of nitrate cargo. At the end of daylight I gave orders to bring the anchors over the bows and the cables up from below decks to bend to them, and had Mister Farrow on deck again to make ready to let go. On 17 May the ship sailed abeam the Scilly Isles in a fine breeze from the southwards. As no pilot boat showed up I set a course for Falmouth. Came abeam the Lizard Lighthouse to starboard at noon bearing due north. At 4 p.m. I signaled the shore for orders for the vessel to be notified to us. On no reply, I sailed my ship in to anchor in five blessed fathoms of water in Carrick Roads at 5: 30 p.m. I would catch up on sleep as soon as I satisfied the Quarantine Officer who appeared with his boat alongside to ask his questions."

"From then on you have already told me about, Gaudin. Before we break I want to ask you whether you have found that Dutchman's theory about great storms at sea and which way to steer to avoid the worst of it, to be of any help to you."

"Yes sir, I have put this theory to good effect to keep the ship safe in a severe storm. His unusual name was *Buys-Ballot*, or something like that. I learned about his theory in London before sailing with Captain Adamson. In the Northern Hemisphere, standing on deck with your back to where you decide the actual wind direction lies, the centre of the storm will lie in the direction of your left hand held straight out to the side. For that instance we steer to starboard to sail away from it. In the Southern Hemisphere the converse applies. So you can see it depends on locality. In any event, in the low latitudes, or south of the Fifties and the possibility of ice, or the proximity of a lee shore, other considerations apply to make you decide to steer where you will, regardless."

"Well, Gaudin, at my age, I am happy not to be thinking of such things and to have a shore berth. After supper let's get to talk about your second passage to Victoria, which is now the capital of the larger new Crown Colony named British Columbia."

"Yes sir, and I am hoping you can tell me more of the rumours I hear about the Star of India Medal to be awarded to the man De Lesseps who built the canal between the Red Sea and the Mediterranean."

"The rumour getting about is correct, Gaudin, except I cannot confirm that Queen Victoria has been moved to act. Instead, the medal may be cast on orders from the Directors of the new Crystal Palace in London who see some good coming to that enterprise from news of the ceremony to award it to Ferdinand de Lesseps. The canal has been completed and many in London fear that none of the increasing steamer traffic to and from India will come to London."

"Yes sir, a port too far. Liverpool and Southampton will benefit from it."

"I see it plain, Gaudin, that the heavy sailing vessel traffic to and from Calcutta will cease, and Bombay and Karachi will emerge as the main ports in India nearest to the new canal. The investor members of the Committee of the Honourable Company with funds of their own to lay out will see opportunity to back extensions of rail and harbour in India and at Liverpool and Southampton. But let us go back to talk about the Crown Colonies in the Pacific Northwest, which you must now know something about."

"Sir, with the Royal Navy Squadron and British Army Garrisons in both Victoria and New Westminster, the Americans south of the Forty Ninth Parallel will see this place as an outpost of the British Empire."

"Yes Gaudin, I hear not only the Colonists but also the local Indians need protection against raids by Northern Indians coming south in their large cedar canoes to capture slaves. Perhaps the tales are exaggerated. Chief Factor Douglas explained in a Report to the Committee in London that some of the trouble came from a group of Cape Fox Indians from the southern end of the Alaskan Coast lying north of the Queen Charlotte Islands. They had paddled their long canoes south to Puget Sound to work to earn money. Some found work at Fort Nisqually, but other bands were less fortunate. One American Settler on the shores of Puget Sound hired a group to clear land in 1854. On presenting to be paid for their work, the settler refused to pay them and shot and killed their chief for no less than *impudence*. The aggrieved group on their way back north in their canoes landed at Cadboro Bay near Victoria, stole a sheep for food from the company farm and assaulted the farmkeeper who tried to stop them. But that incident occurred more than ten years ago.[5]"

"Mister Anderson may have heard something about that, sir. I will ask him when I take the *Lady Lampson* to Victoria next time. He did mention the raids to capture slaves as the rough and ready way they have to avoid inbreeding. I know he has mentioned the headland named Cape Fox from his early passage in the company brig *Dryad* from the mouth of the Columbia River to Fort Simpson on the Nass River in 1833. He regards the southern native population to be a peaceable people, but he considers the Colonists rely on the Imperial Power to protect them from a lingering fear of incitement to an Indian Uprising, which afflicts the American West. The Indians from the northern waters are taller and stronger, so the Colonists see them in their canoe passages south in strength as all the more menacing."

13

GAUDIN BRINGS RING

He navigated his way from London past Cape Horn into the Pacific to bring the *Lady Lampson* back to Victoria sixteen months later in early January 1871, but for many days nobody at the farm knew he had arrived. Agnes' father met him in town to enjoy a hot meal together before they drove the horse and carriage to the farm on roads covered in a light fall of winter snow.

Agnes, upstairs in her room, heard the sound of them arriving. An attentive audience gathered to greet him in the room off the kitchen when he and her father came through the door.

Gaudin began to talk about his departure from the London Docks early in August last year, but he stopped in mid-sentence.

"Where is Agnes?"

Her father lost no time in speaking.

"I am sure she will be down in a minute, Gaudin. Please go on to the story you told me on the way here."

Upstairs in her room, Agnes heard all of the talking downstairs. She decided she would wait no longer. As Gaudin began to speak again she rushed down the steps to scurry over to take a seat with her mother on the other side of the room facing him.

She spoke in a rough tone of voice.

"I would have thought, sir, you might have first told us why we have not heard from you for such a long time."

"Don't take her amiss, Gaudin," her father butted in to say, "Agnes is in a bit of a snit over what she has seen as your neglect of her, out of character, I must say."

"I do apologize Miss Agnes," Gaudin said. "I wanted to get back to see you again as soon as I could."

"Sir, I know you sailed from Peru almost a year ago. You could have sent me a letter from Chile, but no you didn't."

"Agnes, the ship ran into fearful difficulties getting cargo homewards. I did send letters to London on company business, which Gibbs & Co sent over the Andes to Montevideo, and on further by mail packet to the Caribbean and on from there to England, but it never occurred to me I'd be able to send you a letter you'd receive before I could be certain where the company would send me next. I do apologize."

"That doesn't make any sense, sir. So much time has passed."

The younger children clustered around Agnes' mother, and the room fell deathly quiet.

"You met my father four years ago," Agnes said, "and you came to the farm to meet me almost two years later. You promised to marry me, and I have been waiting for you. I counted on seeing you sooner. How can you expect me to be full of good cheer today?"

"Miss Agnes, I am sorry. I have been living a mariner's life. I wrote a letter to your father from London telling him about the *Ocean Nymph* and the passage I would make in her to Montreal. Did he get that letter?"

"I will answer him Papa. Yes he did. Papa also heard about the *Ocean Nymph* from the company office in town. I knew you'd be gone a long time. All the more reason for you to have sent me a letter, I'd say. You cannot know how slowly time passes here."

"I sent you a telegram from Coquimbo two Christmases ago. Didn't you get it?"

"Yes, it did come in time for our New Year's Day dinner more than a year ago. Thank you, sir. I don't know what I would have thought if you had not sent the cable."

"And I sent you a letter after I landed in London with the nitrate in June last year, telling you of the prolonged maiden voyage after I left Sooke in September. I wrote the good news I would be bringing the *Lady Lampson* on her second passage to Victoria. Didn't you receive that letter?"

"No sir, I did not," said Agnes.

"In that letter I wrote I had an engagement ring for you, and planned to give it to you in a quiet moment. I'd better do it now to take the chill out of the air. Here, I have it in my jacket pocket."

Agnes stood open-mouthed as she took the ring in her hand.

"Oh, it IS beautiful_____. I don't really know what to say, Jim."

"We can talk about it in the morning, Agnes. Put it under your pillow tonight."

"Yes, we can talk tomorrow morning. I won't wear it until you put it on my finger."

"Yes, Agnes, let's talk about it then."

"It's late now and a room full of listening ears not the best place for you two to talk," her father said. "Gaudin please tell us about your voyage and why you could not be here in time to celebrate Christmas with us."

Resolving to say nothing more, Agnes sat to listen. Had she already said too much? Perhaps not, and to use an expression her father taught her, perhaps she should press her advantage? She wiped the frown off her face to show her interest and smiled to dissemble, another word her father taught her.

Gaudin told the story of having set one of the best times yet recorded for the passage from London to Esquimalt Harbour by a company vessel.

"One hundred and forty days and 20 hours from dropping the pilot," he said. "I aimed to arrive by Christmas but the winds conspired against me to prevent arriving until three days after Christmas."

Agnes almost bit her tongue when she interrupted him before he could continue.

"Can that be a record, sir? From August to the end of December, wasn't that an uncommonly long passage?"

"No, not at all. A particularly good passage time if you start counting the time from the hour and date of letting off the pilot. Let me tell you of the good luck that let me postpone letting off the pilot. The wind and tide outside the mouth of the Thames warranted making sail and going on without the tug as soon as we came clear of the Thames Estuary at North Foreland. I dismissed the tug, but I did not drop the pilot. He asked to stay on with us until later. A fair wind carried us down through vessels anchored in the Downs awaiting orders for a dock to clear for them to come into."

"Now this was in summertime weather, wasn't it?" her father interjected.

"Yes sir. The wind having dropped off and the tide turning to flood against us as we came up on Dungeness Point, I gave orders to dodge about under sail in the back eddies behind the Point until the tide slackened off. Our fine sail-handling crew regained old form to impress

Mister Irvine, the Pilot. We braced the yards and sailed to put on a show for him. On the turn of the tide we sailed on past the Point. The wind out of the east kept fair to take us farther along the south coast of England to see the shape of the Isle of Wight ahead in morning haze. Despite the fair wind freshening, I had to give an order to back the main yard to lie in the water off Ower's Lightship, which lies stationed in a position close east of the Isle of Wight. Waiting for a sailing cutter to come out to take Mister Irvine ashore, he told me he'd enjoyed seeing the crew sail this *handy gem of a barque,* his words, which had moved so well for him to see in light winds we'd experienced. He had come with us to visit a daughter living near here. I did not count time for the voyage to begin until we sent him ashore and set sail again."

Agnes knew the map of the English Channel from earlier conversations with her father, and she knew captains reckoned their records from the time they drop their pilots and that they usually drop the pilot back at the Downs. She asked herself if Gaudin did not take unfair advantage of other captains by pushing his starting point 150 miles farther west at the Isle of Wight, but she kept the thought to herself.

Agnes' mother spoke to warm up the room with cheerful talk.

"Captain, did you get to spend some time at home with your father and mother last summer?"

"Yes Ma'am, I had a wonderful summer with them in Jersey and with friends in London before sailing. I had almost two-months' leave but came back to the ship early to take charge of the work being done to make ready for sea."

"Did you get to see your brothers who go to sea as you do?"

"No Ma'am, I didn't see any of them again this time, other than my oldest brother Thomas, of course, who runs the farm, but I was happy to see my older sister Marie, now married with two children and living with her husband on his property."

None of this talk did anything to raise Agnes' spirits. She fought back a vision of lying in the summer hay in a barn on the Gaudin farm, which Susan Moir warned against. Did she really want to go to live there with people she did not know? But she kept the smile on her face.

Agnes' father spoke up again to keep the talk going.

"Tell us how close you came to making it here in time for Christmas."

"Storms in both oceans off South America delayed our making landfall at Cape Flattery until the afternoon of the day before Christmas. The morning light on Christmas Day showed us with five other barques in the Strait beating to windward in a light easterly wind. To the evident pleasure of the crew *Lady Lampson* left them all to leeward in jig time. Abeam Race Rocks at nightfall with the dim lights of Victoria reflecting off low cloud a dozen miles away, the wind died. The ebb began to push us back out to sea at ten o'clock that night. Tiderips gripped the ship, turning her like a piece of driftwood in the current, which in three hours drove the ship 15 miles back toward the entrance of the Strait. Such a miserable turn of events for the end of a fine passage! We drifted most of that day and the next in the Strait off Sooke in cold flat-calm weather. A brisk wind came up out of the east at 4 p.m. to fill the sails. With the flood tide assisting we tacked to make distance across the Strait, leaving our old friend Pillar Point abeam on the American side before turning about to take another tack. We rounded Race Rocks at 10 p.m. to anchor in Royal Roads to wait for tide and daylight to enter Esquimalt Harbour, where we fetched up at anchor at 7 a.m. next day, 28 December last year."

"Tell us what happened to prevent you being in touch with me when you arrived in Esquimalt a month ago," her father asked. "This, I think, you should tell Agnes."

"Yes, a terrible wind storm came up and parted the lines to the ring bolts holding the *Lady Lampson* to her moorings at the Navy Dockyard wharf in Esquimalt," Gaudin said. "I had a difficult time securing the vessel. My duty kept me from attending your Anderson family Scottish New Year celebration, which was my loss."

Aware she must be putting everyone else's teeth on edge, Agnes spoke to bring a hush in the room, again.

"Captain Gaudin, we know the *Enterprise* towed your vessel into Victoria's Inner Harbour to lie alongside the company wharf a few days later, but a fortnight passed before you were in touch with Papa. Didn't you have a Chief Officer Mate to do the harbour work?"

"Oh Agnes, it is not as if I could walk down the street to knock on your door. I decided I could not leave the ship. I took the responsibility of watching over unloading the cargo and stowing homeward bound cargo. A poor job done there could come home to roost on the return passage. Before the *Enterprise* steamed off about her business elsewhere, I took the opportunity offered by her being in town at the time to tow us back to Esquimalt, where I could complete the loading of the homeward cargo from the wharf there. I stayed on board the *Lady Lampson* to check that the additional rock ballast I ordered for the passage to London had been sufficient to make the ship stable for sea. I loaded the ballast to see the result. I mean to say, how the ship lay in the water. This required me to stay on board to oversee the work done in harbour in biting cold winter weather. That took until 24 January."

Agnes' father spoke to break a long silence that followed.

"The month's weather has alternated between windstorms, heavy rain, and times of brief clearing so you would have had difficulty coming out on the roads to see us any earlier. It is getting late. I will show Gaudin to his bedroom. We will all look forward to a warm, cheery breakfast in the morning."

Next day after breakfast Agnes bundled up with warm clothing and a cloak before taking Gaudin out for a walk.

"The length of time we have been apart is so evident," he said. "You no longer put out your hands to touch me as lovers do, Agnes."

"Oh Jim, help me. I know I have been holding back to show my hurt."

With his embrace and kiss she felt the old magic again, and she did her best to make up with him. She asked him to put the ring on her ring finger, and he did. Agnes now felt secure, but unprepared for the next disappointing turn of events.

"Agnes, even with my family's help I have been unable to find a house for us in Jersey. Our wedding cannot take place until I bring the *Lady Lampson* back to Victoria in January next year."

Agnes stopped walking and turned to look at him.

"Oh, Jim that will be in 1872," she whispered. "I will ask you a second time, why can't you change your mind about taking me back to live in Jersey? Why can't we marry and live here?"

"We did talk about that before, Agnes. I do not want to live here away from the home I have always known. I am sure you will be happy living among my friends and family in Jersey. I will go back and continue looking for a place for us to live. I do not want to marry until I can provide a good home for you as a ship's captain should."

Despite the look she was giving him to show she was not happy about it, he would not consider a change in plans to make a home in Victoria. Agnes said nothing more about it.

Gaudin went back to the ship with plans to return the next week for their engagement party at the farm.

Her father said, "Agnes, you are a stoic."

"No Papa, I am not indifferent to pleasure or pain. I know what stoic means. I recognize I can do nothing to change the course of events."

"I cannot understand the difficulty about finding a place for you to live."

"Oh Papa, I sense perhaps some Gaudin family problems have arisen or his own lack of money may lie at the root of the uncertainty about where we will live. Those are questions I thought I shouldn't ask him."

"Perhaps I should talk to him about it, Agnes."

"No, Papa, please don't!" Agnes almost shouted. "I don't want to drive him away. I have not changed my mind about him, but I must admit he does not seem to be his usual buoyant self. I am sure he will change."

Agnes helped her mother and young sister Rose with her father's plans for a lunch party to announce her engagement to the tall young sea captain to friends and the family. Gaudin came out to North Saanich at the end of the month to charm everyone. With rain only a memory, the weather turned clear and cold to allow the guests to drive their carriage rigs out the 20 miles to Rosebank on dry roads. Her two aunts came from town with their husbands to take part in the happy gathering with much food and drink.

A week later Agnes, proudly wearing her new diamond ring, rose at the crack of dawn to ride with her father to Esquimalt Harbour to see her Jim take his ship out of the harbour at noon. The two of them on the beach did not have long to wait. Her father packed a lunch for them to eat while standing by a crackling driftwood fire. He produced a flask of whiskey. Agnes asked for a sip, gasped and blinked her eyes, then asked for another. Soon the smoke from the *Otter* appeared off Saxe Point steaming toward them. They watched her enter Esquimalt Harbour and steam alongside the *Lady Lampson* to take on a towing hawser to begin the tow out of the harbour in calm seas. Gaudin knew she would be there. She saw him wave when the tug and tow passed close off the western shore of the harbour entrance. She waved and called out his name even though she knew the sound would not carry their distance apart.

"Papa, Jim told me the ship will cast off the towline on reaching Race Rocks with the beginning of the ebb tide to help them on their way to Cape Flattery. The wind would soon get up against them, he said, as they sail out of the Strait, but they will have the ship flying in a series of tacks in fine windy weather out to the Ocean."

"Agnes, I have no doubt that this will be so."

In her mind's eye Agnes could see the lonely little ship standing out to sea in next morning's sunrise, which she thought would be exciting for him. But, as she found out a year later, the wind became light and the ship made slow progress. Twelve hours sailing to make only 50 miles before the ship reached the open sea. She then dipped her bows into the ocean swells and turned to run with a strong wind out of the north to put the miles behind her, southbound for Cape Horn.

Agnes and her father returned to North Saanich. Two days later on a day Agnes would long remember, she took her father aside in the garden to talk about a subject she had kept to herself without telling anyone other than Susan Moir.

"Papa, I have not told Jim yet of the Indian blood that runs in the family. I am afraid some of the townsfolk and busybodies may have told him already. I don't look it, but some in town classify me as a half-breed even though I am far more Scot and French than Indian. You know people do speak the term *half-breed* as a slur."

Her father said he would talk to Gaudin, but she responded in an instant,

"NO! No! You must not. I must look into his eyes when I tell him to see what he really thinks. You're a man and men cannot tell as well as a woman."

Agnes saw her father looking quite dismayed, but speaking as if to end discussion of the matter, he made a statement.

"The union of a Metis and a White can produce remarkable children and some of them very beautiful, witness your sister Eliza."

"No, Papa, that does not help. I must tell him before we get married. I want to believe you Papa, but I will be bringing to the marriage what other eyes in town may look down upon. I surely cannot hide it from him as I have been. I will worry how I will say it to him for yet another year."

****

One year later in January 1872 Gaudin sailed the *Lady Lampson* back into Esquimalt Harbour from London. Agnes met him at the front door.

"Don't take off your coat, Jim," she said. "Before you say anything

I must tell you something I have been meaning to say for a long time. Here, help me on with my coat so I can walk outside with you."

Gaudin, looking puzzled, helped her on with her coat and took her arm to go down the steps to walk outside in the lightly falling snow.

"What do you want to tell me?"

She stopped walking to look into his eyes.

"I meant to tell you before, but I feared to. I am fair-skinned and have blue eyes and auburn hair, but you don't know I have Indian blood."

"I doubt that, Inez."

After a moment of silence, Agnes said, "Jim, why do you call me EEN-NESS?"

"That's a Spanish name for *Agnes.*"

Agnes turned to continue to walk with her arms crossed in front of her chest.

"I like the sound of it, Jim," she said, "and the way you say it."

She stopped and turned to look at him again.

"Please don't distract me. It's true," she said. "Most people here speak the words *half-breed* as a term of contempt to denote a person having any amount of Indian blood."

"Don't worry your pretty head about it," he said.

"Let me go on, and tell it to you, please. I am proud of where I came from, but I want to be sure you won't blame me for not telling you. A Frenchman voyageur in the fur trade named Beaulieu, a *half-breed* some people will say, took a Cree Indian woman to be his wife 75 years ago."

Gaudin heard her say the name as *Bewley*. He said nothing and a moment passed as Agnes took in a deep breath and sighed before she spoke again.

"We never did know her name. Their daughter Charlotte, born at Red River in 1805 came with them as a two year old across the Rockies with David Thompson. She grew up to become my grandmother Birnie in Oregon. Long before the English defeated the French in Quebec the original Beaulieu pushed west from New France and the Great Lakes into the headwaters of the Mackenzie River close to the Arctic Circle to trap the best furs in the north."

"Your father told me the English could not stop the French from trapping or trading on land with rivers and streams that did not flow into Hudson Bay."

Agnes carried on, ignoring his interjection.

"I have no idea what women that man Beaulieu and his generation of sons had their children by," she said. "I only know Grandmamma Birnie told me my great-grandmother Beaulieu was a Cree Indian."

"Many of the Company Officers in the West have Cree wives," Gaudin bantered. "Anyway you are talking about something no one can blame you for. Do you expect me to tell you I won't marry you now, Inez?"

"Oh Jim, I WANT you to marry me but I cannot assume it would make no difference to you. Even with me fair-skinned, we could face prejudice from those in the community who know this about me. I am sure it led to my family moving out of town from Victoria to North Saanich before I came up from Oregon in 1865."

"Agnes, please stop. Your father told me he chose to move close to where the native population lived in North Saanich to show his disdain for those in town who became alarmed about the Indian Wars 20 years ago on the American side spreading north to Canada. The fear reached such an extent that the Hudson's Bay Company cancelled an advertised sale of prime Sidney Island real estate by auction. Your father also told me he couldn't refuse the offer Mister Pritchard made on the Victoria house."

"Jim, that has nothing to do with it. I need you to go into marriage with your eyes wide open. You must never be able to say I didn't tell you."

"Inez, it makes no difference to me you do not have pure English or Scotch blood or whatever. Even if you are right, all more the reason to come with me to live in Jersey where your looks will be proof against what you fear here. Nobody there'd know."

"Yes, but someday we might return to live in Victoria and face wild distortions of what I have told you."

"Let's not worry about the future, Inez. I myself I have something to tell you. I have had trouble finding a house to be proud of. I have really tried hard to find a place in little St. Helier town. We must delay the wedding until I return next year. By then I shall have a house."

"Oh Jim, I AM so disappointed. Can't you change your mind about living in Victoria?"

Gaudin remained dead set against Agnes' wish to marry and make a home in Victoria, but neither of them broke off the engagement. He sailed away again.

To her dismay and sorrow during the time Agnes waited more than a year for him to return, her mother died. After the funeral her father wrote with pen and ink in the family Bible: -

On 17 March 1872, Sunday, about 10 o'clock a.m. it pleased God to summon to himself my dear wife. She was buried at the St. Stephen's Church Cemetery on 19 March, the Very Rev. Dean Cridge officiating.

When she looked at the entry later a second time she saw that her father fastened to the page a clip of her mother's dark red Birnie hair.

Later Agnes spoke to her father to say she had read what he had written. His eyes welled up when he said her mother had not been a public figure. The newspapers would not write a report about her death. He seemed not able to speak at all. Agnes gave him a hug and whispered in his ear, "We both miss her, Papa."

She turned to devote herself to comforting her grief-stricken father and siblings and caring for the family. Grandmother Birnie lived on for another six years. Agnes wrote a letter to inform her of the death and told her of the funeral, saying her father, stricken with grief, could not write. Aware she dashed cold water on her own thoughts of marriage to Gaudin, she added a note she had her hands full with her father and the farm to look after. How could she leave her father now, she asked herself?

Agnes' father sent Gaudin a telegram to the Hudson's Bay Company at its cable address *Beaver London* informing him of his wife's death.

Her father now went through a sad time. The Birnie family sisters in Victoria, Amelia Wark and Mary Charles, grieved over the untimely death of their older sister Eliza, born at Spokane House on 10 August 1822; not yet 50 when she died. They and their husbands attended the lonely funeral and interment at St. Stephen's Church of England country churchyard in Saanich.

No letter from Gaudin came on ships arriving in Victoria. Truly despondent she spoke to her father.

"Papa, I do really wonder if I will ever see Jim again."

He must have seen other women she dared herself to say to her father.

"Papa, will he really come back? I am torn by doubts he may have changed his mind about marrying me. If he does come, will it still be the same between us? I keep asking myself, will he tell me he is breaking off our engagement?"

Other moments did come when instead of panic and fear, she found herself all a-buzz with joy and excitement about the future. "Oh, The agony of it all, Papa!"

14

CAPTAIN AND MRS. GAUDIN

Early in January 1873 Gaudin brought the *Lady Lampson* back from London on her third passage westbound around the Horn. Agnes met him in the early afternoon cold rain at the front gate. They embraced.

"Inez, we can now marry. I have a place for you to live and the company has given me permission to carry you back to London in the *Lady Lampson* as a passenger with your own cabin. That doesn't happen often."

Agnes drew in a breath.

She had wondered how the two of them would manage sleeping crammed into his small bunk berth.

"Oh my own cabin! How wonderful, Jim, but I do hope the rules aboard ship will allow me to talk to you on the way."

"Yes, I am in charge of things like that, dear girl, and you will likely get invitations to spend time with me in my cabin."

"Oh that's pleasing," she said. "I am excited about seeing London with you, Jim. I have thought about that for years."

"The crowds in the streets of London Town will be a new experience for you," he said. "And the fast steam train to Southampton and the speed of the new cross-channel ferry steamers to Jersey will astonish you."

Agnes brimmed with hope and expectation. He had come back to her and their wedding would take place in days. The man she adored had not drawn away as she feared.

She spoke after a moment that seemed awkward to her.

"I am worried, Jim, about how your father and mother and the rest of your family will take to me."

"I am sorry to say you will see much more of them than I had thought. For the present I will be taking you to live on the family farm.

I have seen the well-furnished apartment they have made for us in one end of the farmhouse. I am sure you will like it."

"Where is the house on Jersey, Jim?".

"Not on the coast but towards the middle of the eastern half of the island in an ancient old stone farmhouse by the name of La Maitrerie."

"Where does that name come from?"

"I don't really know," he said, "but I think it may be a play on words stemming from the original owner's family name LeMaitre of long ago. But I must tell you my father and mother have moved from their old home named Croix au Maître to live with my older brother Thomas and his wife the former Jane de Gruchy, the daughter of an old established family in Jersey."

Agnes paused for a moment before she asked,

"How will they like me moving in with them, Jim?"

"They have agreed," he said.

Agnes thought that seemed a strange answer to make. What kind of life lay ahead for her there? How would the Jersey family receive her into their midst during the 300 days her husband would be away at sea and never home for Christmas?

"Jim, what will I do during the time when you will be away at sea?"

Agnes thought he looked blank for a moment, taken aback by the question.

"My older sister Marie Renouf and her husband live on property nearby," he said. "They have two children, Hannah, called *Nan*, and Clement Edwin. Marie supports my plan to have you live in Jersey and shows great excitement and delight about you coming. I am sure you and she will become good friends and find a lot to do together."

"I hope so, Jim," she said.

"You have lived on a farm in North Saanich, Inez. The farm in Jersey will be little different except the early people on the island cut down most of the forest long ago. The climate in Jersey can be warmer than here in Victoria even though both lie close to the same Forty-Ninth Parallel of Latitude, so you will enjoy living there. You can take the horse carriage into town at St. Helier, which has cobblestone streets with interesting shops and good schools for children."

Agnes remembered she had told him she would like to live in the town with the pretty-sounding name.

"But you will be away from me every Christmas."

She then heard him give a convincing argument.

"I would not have been with you for Christmas this year had we been living in Victoria. The winter weather in the Pacific off Oregon and Washington often makes for a late arrival in Esquimalt when we sail from London at the end of summer or later. Late September departures make for me arriving here at the end of January. I say again, for us to be living in Victoria would not have me home for Christmas. When you are living in Jersey I will always be home and with you for much of every summer between voyages. That you can think of as the other side of the coin."

The romp and frolic in the hay Susan Moir foretold crossed Agnes' mind...

"Agnes, you show great pluck. I know you always wished for a summer wedding with your father's flowers in the garden and a display of flowers in the church. Here I am asking you to marry me in the dead of winter."

"Oh Jim, don't worry about it. Leave the decorations to me. I know what to find. I know you will give me a chance to adjust, and I will make it up to you for waiting for me for such a long time."

"Well Agnes, I think you have been the one left to wait."

They embraced and she kissed him back before going into the house to join the others gathering in the front hall to greet the sea captain from Jersey.

Later at supper Agnes sat listening to her father and Gaudin talk. Her father had much to say, starting with an item he had not spoken to Agnes about before:

"A '*Thomas Gaudin*' shows up in books as the Grand Master of the Order of the Knights Templar in Paris immediately preceding the lamented Simon de Molay, who ended up burned at the stake. It may be that the name Le Maitrerie for the farmhouse you and Agnes will call home may have a connection with Templars who dispersed in the 1300s when the Pope issued a Papal Ban against the Order. As indeed may the name of your father's former family home in St. Martin's Parish Jersey, the name of which you told me was *Croix au Maître*."

"I have never heard that, sir, but the Gaudin family in Jersey does trace itself back to the 1300s. My father married a daughter in the Payn family."

"A medieval knight by that name Payn with no E at the end is connected with the founding of the Templar Order. Your mother could have descended from that line."

"Amazing sir. Some of my uncles and cousins owned early commercial sailing vessels flying a house flag with the Masonic square and compasses design sewn on it."

"How interesting, Gaudin, I daresay the isolation of the Channel Islands made them a place of refuge or sanctuary for the influx of immigrants going back as far as the Celts. And then the Waldensians and the Vaudois folk fleeing from religious problems in Europe in the Middle Ages came to settle in the Channel Islands. Some say the Vaudois were driven out from the eastern parts of the Balkan Peninsula centuries ago. The memory of man runneth not back to the place where they came from in more ancient times. More recently, English families opposing Oliver Cromwell found haven in Jersey."

Agnes gasped.

"Papa," she said, "Jim will think you talk as if you have studied in Europe to be able to speak of such things! "

"Agnes, my parents sent me to school in London before I came across the Atlantic to Montreal, and I have been reading ever since then, so please, shush."

Gaudin saw a chance to speak in the silence that followed.

"I can spell *Vaudois* as you say it, sir, and I can be quick to acknowledge that the blood of Jersey people came to be mixed with that of other folk coming there to find refuge over a span of a thousand years."

"I expect so, Gaudin, I daresay the admixture not badly serving the generations that followed. The Celts, Angles, Saxons, and Vikings, a rum lot, some of them. The high and mighty of England and Europe would do well to admit the mixtures of blood made them what they are today. But let me go on to add this little tidbit of information I remember: the Vaudois people stemming from eastern Europe ran into opposition from the Church in Rome for the ritual swearing of the oaths, *By God's Blood* and *By God's Teeth*, which Rome considered blasphemous."

"Well sir, all that DOES interest me. Some early Gaudin family in Jersey 500 years ago spelled their name with a V as Vaudin. I grew up hearing the common oath, *God's Teeth*, which I have found myself using in trying times at sea."

"I never heard that oath until I sailed in the company brig *Dryad* on this coast in 1834. I have told you much about that time but I didn't tell you I heard seamen on deck mutter, God's Teeth under their breath to express their exasperation about how things were going for them and their ship at the particular time," said her father.

Gaudin took up the conversation again after a pause.

"I find it a fascinating thought I may have had Vaudois ancestors. They may have had black eyes such as I have. Black eyes are not uncommon in Jersey."

No one said anything in response, but Anderson ended the silence with a question of Gaudin.

"Let's talk about the wedding. Gribbell, the Rector of St. Paul's Garrison Church in Esquimalt can come on the of sixth of February at two o'clock. Will that fit in for you?"

Gaudin agreed, and next morning he hastened back to the ship.

****

A week later he made a quick trip back to stay overnight at Rosebank. He and Anderson sat bundled up in warm clothing in armchairs on the front verandah, smoking their pipes and basking in the low winter afternoon sun to talk and drink whiskey before dinner. Agnes overheard some of it through an open window. She heard her father speak first.

"Hearing of the wedding date some people have expressed surprise that your wedding banns were not read at the local church, St. Stephen's. You have not been there yet, Gaudin. It's off on a side road half way into town from Rosebank. Some say I am having another argument with the Vicar on some matter of church doctrine, but they don't know the church dispensed with banns in the circumstance of you not being a local person and your set early departure to sea."

"I have met Gribbell and admire the man," said Gaudin. "I don't have time to spend getting to know the Vicar of St. Stephens and listen to him lecturing me on the obligation of marriage and social customs."

"Don't worry about that," Anderson said. "In my respectful opinion the Vicar of St. Stephen's Church busies himself far too much in setting himself up as arbiter of acceptable dress and conduct for the young daughters of Saanich. He told me I should rein in Agnes riding her horse about in less than what he considers womanly attire, and I told him to mind his own business. In any event I would not have chosen the Vicar to perform the ceremony. I know Agnes has never taken to him."

On the wedding day Agnes' brother Alex rode south on the West Saanich Road to meet the Rector on his horse and lead him to the farm. Gribbell handed Anderson a note from the Vicar to show that he has been authorized to perform the wedding ceremony. This departure from the arrangements made directly with Gribbell displeased Anderson, who wanted happier things to think about than to remonstrate with Gribbell, who had had the wit to clear coming out to Saanich with the Vicar. Anderson dropped the issue as something over which he had no control.

Later that afternoon the wedding guests assembled in the house.

Anderson met Agnes at the foot of the stairs to give her his arm to lead her into the drawing room where Gribbell stood to perform the ceremony. The fireplace crackled in the hearth. Lamps and candles lit sprays of Oregon grape leaves, red holly on glossy green leaves, salal, grey pussy willows, white snowberries, and off-red wild rose hips gathered in the woods. A light skiff of snow lay on the ground. The northeast wind dropped off in strength and no longer waved tree branches about.

Alexander Caulfield Anderson, he liked the name out full, sat in a chair at the side of room to listen to the buzz of conversation going on in the crowded room. He sensed an air of peace and calm reigning, which gave him leave to ruminate on the memories flashing through his mind like the images he saw produced at the kaleidoscope demonstration seen in London a year before sailing to Montreal in 1831. He fought down his feeling of inferiority for putting on such a small wedding and reception. Nothing like the spread he put on for Eliza's wedding more than a dozen years ago when he had money to do it; now this the best he could do. Gaudin's Second Mate will stand as best man. No bridesmaids. No flower girl. But Agnes stands tall, smiling, and looking radiant in a white wedding gown she made for herself. How happy his wife would be to know this day had come.

Anderson knew that his own charismatic presence annoyed some men or caused them to envy him. Now only 59 years of age, his hard life in the fur trade in the Interior made him look older. His air of seniority, trim white head of hair, and polished manner of speech made him appear to be a man of letters and set him apart as a man to be reckoned with. Of these things he had no doubt whatever. But his thoughts on this occasion focused on his own wedding at Fort Alexandria more than thirty years ago, and on the joy that came to him on becoming Eliza Birnie's husband.

In a moment of awkward silence he became aware that all eyes were on him, expecting him to be saying something. By then all knew he would make the toast to the bride. Words whispered in his ear brought him standing again. Even though he should have left the toast to an old friend of the family, he had things to say he would not leave to another, and he didn't care what some might think. From the bursts of applause, sotto voce calls of *hear, hear* and the after-buzz of conversation in the room, he felt certain the toast to the bride he made met everyone's expectation for fine words well said, and he sat back content, knowing all eyes were on the bride and groom.

The wedding guests cheered the bride and her groom as young Alex drove them away in a horse and carriage on the trail to take them to Agnes' log cabin with darkness soon to fall. The guests dispersed to get home or to lodgings before dark. The winter weather in Victoria in the month of February can be cold and wet, broken with outbreaks of Arctic air that stream out the Mainland Inlets to bring dry colder air and often sunshine to the Coast. Clearing skies this night and bitter cold, but all so beautiful with bright stars. The northeast wind blew dry and cold through the trees. Tendrils of wood smoke rose from the chimney in the clear night's sky. Icicles hung from the edge of the roof. The two entered to find a warm and cozy room with a fire, which Alex had set earlier, aglow in the stove.

Their life together began here at Agnes' log cabin. She had filled the cabin with utensils, china plates, mugs, and cutlery. Brother Alex set the fire in the cabin stove in the morning of the wedding, leaving a good firewood supply. A large pot of water for making coffee in the morning sat at the side of the stove.

The soft black cape made from many sea otter pelts sewn together lay on the cabin floor like a blanket as before. Agnes knew Jim liked looking at her lying out on it. This time she felt much more at ease. She took the initiative to stand and lift it up to put around her, and she began to whisper to him as they embraced.

And so the wedding night began in the forest in the cedar cabin her brothers made her for a birthday present. Late the next afternoon they returned to Rosebank for a warm greeting and a night's sleep in Agnes' upstairs bedroom.

Packed and ready to go to town next morning, Agnes made a tearful farewell to her family at the front gate. Her father drove the newly-weds by horse and carriage to stay in town for a round of parties her husband arranged to show off his bride to the shipping fraternity.

Finally, Gaudin took Agnes aboard the *Lady Lampson* with her baggage, which he stowed in her passenger cabin in the saloon on the main deck aft at the break of the poop deck, a name she would not say, preferring the word quarterdeck.

On deck she asked her husband about the Royal Navy Squadron vessels lying at anchor in the Harbour.

"Why are they flying all of the flags?"

"They are dressed with their lockers full of signal flags, my dear, in our honour. The flags on top spell out the word: W-E-D-D-I-N-G."

Agnes heard her husband order no sounding of the ship's watch bells until morning, so as not to disturb them. To guard the valuable cargo against theft the crew took turns standing three-hour harbour watches. She and her husband talked the night out in his cabin under the quarterdeck to the sound of quiet footsteps of the watch pacing the deck.

Next day the new Chief Officer Campbell supervised the loading of the last of the cargo. Earlier he attended to topping off with tons of rock ballast from scows brought alongside and placed in the hold to keep the ship steady. In England, Samuel Plimsoll M.P. had not yet been able to see the legislation passed to confer stringent ship inspection requirements to enable the Board of Trade to prevent overloading of merchant vessels. This year, 1873, however, did mark the year when Parliament created a Royal Commission on his motion in the House of Commons. A Plimsoll Line Mark at the side of the hull to govern loading of cargo on commercial vessels would become mandatory: in the meantime the ship's master would continue to decide how much to load.

In the early morning rain of 18 February 1873 came a light air out of the east to promise a fair wind for the *Lady Lampson* to depart from Esquimalt Harbour at midday before high tide. The ship began to stir at the side of the company wharf in Esquimalt. After a hot breakfast Agnes walked the deck in the morning light with her husband to witness the scene of increasing shipboard activity.

The crew in the two boats pulled the ship away from the wharf to anchor in mid-harbour to await the arrival of the Hudson's Bay Company's steamer the S.S. *Otter* taken off her freight run. No small tug, but a bulky steamer about as long as this relatively dainty sailing vessel being towed. She steamed in alongside to throw a heaving line aboard at the bow. The *Lady Lampson's* crew bent on a succession of heavier ropes leading to the towing hawser to be lowered to the steamer to wind on her towing bitts to tow with.

Agnes stood enthralled at the sight and sound of the sea shanteys sung by the crew as they pushed on the capstan hickory bar spokes around and around to pull the port anchor up from the mud at the bottom of the bay, dripping wet seaweed. After they worked with a will to bring the heavy anchor over the bow rail, she peered to see them wash off the mud and seaweed with deck tools before lowering it onto its stocks, not quite underfoot for seamen to stub their toes on when running on the forward deck.

"Now, my dear, the passage to London will begin with the *Otter* taking the strain on the towline. We depart this harbour an hour and a half before high tide."

"Why before high tide?"

"Two reasons: one, in case the tug runs us ashore on the way out_____."

"Why would it do that?"

"It wouldn't intend to, my dear, but if it did, the tide would be continuing to come in and help to lift the ship off and permit the hapless tug to continue towing."

"That does sounds like a good idea."

"I will continue: and a second reason to leave well before high tide_____, after we pass Race Rocks we will be running under sail for the full six-hours or so of the ebb tide current, which will take us all of the way to the ocean off Cape Flattery."

With tears in her eyes, Agnes waved at her father standing on the shore with his horse near Fisgard Lighthouse and he waved back. Like her sister Eliza in New Zealand, she might never see him again.

On the way out to Race Rocks the crew climbed the masts to set the sails on the yards ready to be unfurled off Race Rocks. The steamer tooted its mournful whistle to the cheers of her crew who lined the deck to call out *bon voyage* as it turned to steam ten miles back to Victoria. The light air rose to a steadily increasing breeze out of the east to fill the sails. The *Lady Lampson* came to life, moving under sail for the rudder to take hold. The Mate sailed the ship out the Strait of Juan de Fuca in fine sea conditions. Keeping to her cabin or standing at the bulwarks at the main deck, Agnes and her husband found time to talk about their plans and the voyage that lay ahead. He had told her why they would not stand at the taff rail on the quarterdeck lest the Mate mistake it: taking charge of the conduct of the ship from the Mate at this point not in her husband's plan. The mate would see the captain coming on the quarterdeck as a signal he has taken charge without a word being spoken. A freshening wind out of the east in the afternoon filled the sails to push them out to Cape Flattery by evening.

On deck the offwatch Second Mate spoke in his Scottish accent to Agnes.

"Such a bonny beginning for the passage to London, Ma'am," he said.

All that changed at midnight when the ship began to roll in an oily ocean swell unruffled by wind, which had dropped off. Agnes felt the deck move under her feet, which made her feel queasy, then ill to her stomach. She had not expected to be seasick. She had often paddled her small West Coast dugout canoe when it rolled in rough water. Even on the steamer crossing the rough water in the Strait from Olympia to come to Eliza's wedding in 1860, she wasn't.

Tatoosh Island and Cape Flattery showed themselves abeam six miles off under an overcast sky as the ocean swell began to lift and roll the ship in an otherwise smooth calm in the water. Agnes had taken her eyes off the arcing mast tops when she heard Mister Campbell speak.

"Going nowhere fast. It will take a long time to sink Cape Flattery aft below the horizon."

Those words, sink Cape Flattery aft were enough to bring on a fresh spasm of her stomach's revolt.

The wind switched to come out of the south, which sent the *Lady Lampson* on a lively port tack straight out to sea in the gathering darkness. By morning the wind veered to come strong out of the northwest, varying from the north in gusts. By nightfall a freshening winter gale of wind chased the ship south through mountainous seas on the fastest way to travel from Victoria to London England in 1873.

Morning found Agnes feeling no better and the ship running fast under clearing skies. For three days the *Lady Lampson* loaded 15 feet deep into the water continued on her wild dash south.

Although sailing downwind not her best point of sailing in the estimation of those who knew her, the ship gave every impression that she enjoyed being a ship, playing about in the waves in a rambunctious manner. The tops of her masts described deliberate arcs in the air as she rolled her gunwales under to wash the decks clear of anything not tied down.

The lone passenger in her cabin on deck, the captain's seasick bride lived out the first few days at sea in misery. Word that Cape Mendocino and the coast of Northern California lay miles off to port in the sun through the daytime haze did not interest her. Nor did the teeming clusters of graceful seabirds in the air keening their calls as they followed the ship looking for fish moving on the tumbling surface of the sea. The flocks burst into excited activity when they swooped down to snatch and fight over scraps of fat and bacon rind the cook threw over the side for them.

On the first day out Gaudin ordered the ultimate tool in a sea captain's chest to be set, studdingsails. The mates ordered the men to rig these sails outboard from the foremast t'gallant and topsail yardarm ends to catch more of the wind to make the ship move faster. As the long high bowsprit sank to split the wave top ahead, the plunging bows sent sheets of spray to be caught by the wind. For an agonizing moment of unease, the ship held before her bow pitched up again as the sea-wave that had come from behind slid under to lift the bow and disappear ahead. The ship never would catch up to that wave, which disappeared from sight as the bow pitched down to plunge in again. At the same time, as if to show that she could not be easily bridled, the whole of the ship yawed and rolled as the helmsman at the wheel on the open deck at the stern strove against the kick back of the wheel in his gnarled hands. He kept the wheel turning to keep the ship driving straight with her sails filled out hard with wind.

Her husband had told her a sailing vessel at sea will become the embodiment of a living spirit that is best seen when she fights to hold up her head against the sea. And she found out later to avoid becoming seasick, a seaman learns to make his eye imagine a horizon lying beyond the now raised-up and then tumbling-down jumble of waves trying to find their own level. But Agnes now could only sense that the ship came up and rolled one way the very moment the deck dropped and yawed to the other. Variations of these wild movements followed each other without any warning to drive her to her only refuge, the berth in her cabin, made more spacious by the unneeded second berth secured out of the way against the bulkhead, which sailors call the wall in the cabin.

At midnight eight hours ago, at the turning of the sand in the hourglass and the ringing of the ship's bell to mark the change of the watch, she burst out on deck from her cabin to scramble to the leeward rail with a mournful cry. She knew puking to windward would not do: she did not make that mistake.

Even though her instinct told her she could go overboard into the water when her side of the ship reached the end of the roll, she closed her eyes and held the rail with a fierce two-handed grip.

She opened her eyes at the top of the roll to see the water in the sea streaming past aft at the side of the ship. This told her the die had been cast. She could not now turn back, but must make the best of it. In her mind she felt a sudden twinge of deep sorrow: I am no longer Agnes Anderson; I am Agnes Gaudin wife of the captain of this appalling little ship.

Not having kept down any food, the retching came and continued to come again and again without vomit. She realized her husband had seen the whole embarrassment when he rushed down to her from the quarterdeck with a robe to put over her nightdress and to hold one hand on her forehead and the other on her back.

"I could not ask your Steward to clean up the mess I would have made in the cabin," she groaned.

"Don't worry, Inez, you will be all right soon. Let me put you in my cabin bunk now to get some sleep."

Under the covers and shivering she could not get the picture of the dark heaving ocean surface out her mind, but she did drop off to sleep.

By the next morning she began to feel better. The Captain's Steward Sam Powder came with a bone of cold meat and salt in a saucer.

"Ma'am, the Doctor has sent this and a dry biscuit. He says chewing on it will make you better."

Starting with a small nibble, she began to gnaw on the meat, dipping it into the saucer to salt it before chewing on it again. She began to keep food down.

Agnes knew her husband had noticed her need to season food with so much salt. She told him she developed her taste for salty food growing up in the fur trade, which used salt as a meat and fish preservative.

Agnes began to worry someone might have overheard last night when she called out about *this appalling little ship*. She really did not think any such thing. She shared the admiration felt by everyone concerning the ship and wanted everyone on board to know it.

Dressed with warm clothing, she soon went on deck. At mealtime below she enlivened the conversation at the table with her husband and the mates Mister James Campbell and Mister James Fall. Later she took the opportunity to speak to John Reeves, the ship's carpenter, and to Manuel Antoine, the *Doctor*, and to thank him for his special help to end her seasickness.

The waves behind continued to mount up high and steep, but Agnes now knew they would slip beneath the stern counter and disappear under to lead the ship on. She could now dare to look back at them looming. Worse seas she knew will lie ahead when rounding Cape Horn. Her husband discounted them to her, but she knew better from what she had heard. He must be trying not to alarm her about their danger.

"If breaking wave crests threaten I will ask Sailmaker Jeune for a canvas bag to leak whale oil slowly out aft. The contraption streamed astern works to flatten the tops of the waves to save the ship from being overwhelmed."

"Why, Jim, can't you stop the ship from rolling so?"

"The ship's wild motion these last three days and nights can't be helped," he told her. "When a loaded sailing vessel drawing 15 feet of water turns to run downwind in a heavy following sea, I cannot do anything to prevent it except to change course to sail where we are not going. Of course I can't do that."

"Jim, the poor man at the steering wheel struggles so hard to do his job."

"Yes Agnes, steering a sailing ship with the wind and waves coming from behind does not come easy for any man at the wheel. He must plant his feet on deck and fight to hold the ship on course. The ship's design makes the ship want to turn back into the wind."

Gaudin set his course to fall in with the North East Trade Winds far out at sea off Northern Mexico. The westerly winds carried the *Lady Lampson* down to a position 200 miles off the coast of Southern California where the wind out of the northeast off the mountains inland blow strongest. The new wind will sling the ship onward in a continuation of speed to put the miles behind. All aboard will find joy in fresh drinking water gathered from rainsqualls and sailing in the warm air of the North East Trades. Soon her husband will show her the stars in the Constellation of the Southern Cross for the first time.

The newly-weds talked on deck each evening. Later in the passage when south of the Equator and sailing in southern waters, Agnes asked where he and his vessel were sailing three years ago in March 1870. He took her below to his cabin to consult his collection of personal logbooks, which he did not hand in to Captain Herd.

"Well, Inez, we sailed from near Iquique late in February of 1870 with a full cargo of bags of nitrate of soda packed heavy in her holds with the ship drawing sixteen feet forward and sixteen and a half aft instead of our usual fifteen forward and fifteen and a half aft."

With this start he went on to tell the story of that passage, a shortened version of the account he gave to Captain Herd two years ago on returning to London.

"To avoid the Humboldt Current, which I told you about, I sailed hundreds of miles out into the Pacific before turning on a course to take us a thousand miles and more to leave Cape Horn behind on the port side. And from there, two hundred miles or more out into the South Atlantic; then another five thousand miles to reach the English Channel in a little less than three months. By then the Chilean charterers of the ship would know where to send me to unload their cargo. It turned out to be London. Otherwise, the ship could have been sent on other voyages before ever returning to Victoria."

"How awful," Agnes gasped and cried out, "You might never have come back for me. Did you know that?"

"Yes Inez, I knew that possibility when I started the nitrate voyage, but I did come back to you, didn't I?"

"You did come back for me, but you took such a long time, Jim. For a time I wondered whether you would come back, at all."

A long silence followed.

"Jim, you are very quiet. Your eyes make you look miles away. Please tell me what is bothering you?"

He didn't say anything. Mistaking his reaction as one related to the time at sea and not wishing to talk about it, she spoke again.

"Instead of three years ago, please tell me where you were two years ago in March 1871? But wait, we can talk about that tomorrow. I can feel the ship heeling over and I hear the Mate shouting. You'd better go back on deck. I should go to my cabin."

They embraced and kissed before she left to go on deck and then down the steps to her cabin on the main deck.

She went to sleep that night with visions of tropical islands with palm-trees blowing in the South East Trade Winds. He had told her those winds blowing across the Eastern South Pacific would help him sail the ship South to clear the Marquesas, the Tahitian Archipelago, and countless atolls marked on his charts. Thanks to the Royal Navy, mariners knew the latitude and longitude of the islands they were passing. To sight and identify them would enable him to fix the position of his ship and to check the accuracy of his chronometers, which told time by Greenwich, giving peace of mind for his navigation onwards.

Days later on deck one morning Gaudin spoke to call out the sight of Pitcairn Island.

"There lies Pitcairn Island to starboard," he said, "lurking in fading colours in the far distance to the southwest."

"Jim, have we reached the Great Southern Ocean yet?"

"We are coming soon to the northern edge of it. You can now see the large ocean swells under the waves beginning to come from the southwest. Soon the wind will change to come from that direction, too. On that happening we will turn to sail toward Cape Horn."

From this position at sea, he explained, they would proceed farther on to the south to come to the Great Southern Ocean. The storm winds would come in endless succession, the winds varying from the northwest, the west and the southwest. The wind coming from behind would push the ship 1,700 miles or more towards Cape Horn in mountainous seas.

"This will not be dainty sailing, Inez. You will see the ship fighting to keep her head up, spindrift coming up from the scuppers to flit across the deck like tumbleweed in the desert and a hundred other sights you have not seen before. We will all be glad when we get into the South Atlantic. You will be surprised when you awake and come on deck soon one morning to see a remarkable large white bird floating in the air close to the side of the ship. It will not be alone; others fill the air nearby in silent company. Crew regard them with respect, if not awe, as an apparition of the presence of guardian angels for their protection against the perils of the sea. Albatross do not flap their wings or soar as eagles; they float in the air with no apparent effort as they slip in the wind with a mind to watch over us for days on end, so different from the lesser birds that squabble and make high-pitched sounds as they wheel about to fight for some morsel to eat before slipping out of sight in the ship's wake."

"I have already become familiar with the sound of wind on the ship, but won't it become more of a worry?"

"The wind will take on a shrill whistling sound over a steady moan as the decks roll and pitch, but it will not become a worry. We get accustomed to it."

"Living on the wet west coast of British Columbia as I have, I have become accustomed to short days and dark wet winters, so I won't be too upset by the wet and the darkness, Jim."

"You may find comfort in knowing we will be arriving in England in the summer season there. Farther south in the next few weeks, you will see dark skies and short hours of daylight. Often foretelling a storm, you will see little ragged dark clouds scud past, low, to disappear in the haze ahead. Blowing spray torn from the wave tops will become haze and 'sea smoke'. The colour of grey will show in swatches of black and darker grey on sea and in the clouds, relieved only by the white of the spray and foam that will be all around us."

"What about the rain? I have heard it is worse than at home, and that the rain rains steady and cold, Jim."

"Yes, a cold steady rain and salty spray will come to those on deck. You will want to stay dry and warm below in my cabin. The rain will hit into the eyes and seep into the sleeves of jackets and run on down into men's socks. Those on deck will find it difficult to keep warm and dry even in the Southern Hemisphere summer months."

"I have heard terrible stories of ice and ice bergs, Jim."

"The range of the ice varies with outer limits marked on charts. By the time we sail south of 46 degrees South, I take special care to keep watch for drift ice jostling low in the waves ahead. In the Prince of Wales I remember one dark night we reduced sail rather than accept the risk of going under after a collision with the ice that lay on all quadrants and made the air cold. In calmer times I have learned to smell ice, a scent distinct from ordinary smells at sea. Particularly in those waters, which concentrate flows of shipping traffic going east and west, we keep watch for ships crossing our bow coming from the opposite direction. We rely on the sharp eyes of the lookout on watch to give warning to steer clear of both ice and other shipping."

"The waves mounted high behind us when we sailed south past Oregon and California: will they be worse when we sail towards Cape Horn?"

"In the worst of it, Inez, the waves gather more strength and become enormous. They will mount high behind to look like overhanging cliffs. Then they will pass under the ship, which ends up lifting the bow. Some waves loom higher than others. The ship will fight to keep her head up, and we all will be proud of her."

Agnes now began to put her thoughts together as if she were going to write a story about herself. Perhaps she could tell parts of it to their children when they grew up in Jersey and asked her for stories about herself when she had been young. She had embarked on this voyage with joy in her heart and anticipation she would find happiness. She wanted to make it a happy story.

15

SECOND THOUGHTS

Agnes and two-year-old Marie came back from Jersey to Victoria on the *Lady Lampson's* sixth annual passage from London. Gaudin landed them in town in a snowstorm at the end of January 1875. Agnes stayed in a hotel to wait for a break in the weather for her father to come into town to take them to live on the Anderson farm. One year later Gaudin brought the *Lady Lampson* back to Victoria on the wings of the winds of winter to catch a ride out to the farm to see Agnes and plead she return to live in Jersey again. He came with a story too awful not to be true. His older sister Marie, already widowed by her husband's unexpected death, had been killed in a horse buggy accident. Her young son of some promise, Clement Edwin, had come out of it unscathed, but daughter Nan, suffered serious injuries. Gaudin asked Agnes to return to look after the Renouf children and caretake their property.

With Agnes packing to be ready to sail tomorrow, her father and Gaudin talked while they sat outside on the veranda with Hudson Bay Blankets over their shoulders to keep warm in the winter air, drinking whiskey, and smoking Gaudin's cigars.

Each with cigars now well lit, her father began the conversation.

"Agnes wouldn't let me smoke in the house, Gaudin."

"Yes sir, that's the way it was for me when I had her in Jersey, but I was always there in summer, so it didn't matter much. May I call you Alex, sir?"

"Yes, please do. I hope you do not mind me calling you *Gaudin*. I mean no disrespect. No one in the fur trade spoke first names. It comes more easily to me than trying to say *Jim or James*_____. Agnes tells me she has agreed you take her back."

"Yes Alex, I finally gave up my plan to live out the end of my days in a house on the green fields of Jersey. She agreed to go back to care for my sister Marie's children. Marie and she were as sisters in the year Agnes lived in Jersey. My news of her untimely death upset Agnes. She will do all she can to help, but I had to promise to bring her back to settle in Victoria when the Renouf property can be sold in five years."

"I will look forward to that happening, Gaudin. But I worry how she and the little ones will take to the rough ocean passage and I spend a lot of time thinking about the life she will lead in Jersey away from kith and kin, and you away at sea so much of the time. Tomorrow you take them away from me. I suppose I will manage. Did the prospect of living in a new house in Jersey make it possible for her to agree to go back?"

"Perhaps so, Alex. I am not sure what tipped the scale, the new house, or my promise to bring her back to Victoria in five years, perhaps both. Some might view Marie's death as a divine intervention. We Jerseymen are a superstitious lot."

"As to the superstition that prevails in Jersey I leave that for you to judge, Gaudin. Nothing in my experience has led me to place any faith in a conceit of divine intervention."

"I find some comfort, Alex, in knowing she took to the sea on her first passage to London as my bride; and the same when she came back with me little more than a year later. With that experience behind, I'm sure Agnes will enjoy the sea voyage this time."

"Well, Gaudin, I do remember when you arrived back to Victoria to drop Agnes and Marie off with me at the end of January last year. In truth, I did need her to stay here to look after the house and family during my long illness after the election campaigning. I thought I might become a Member of Parliament in Ottawa, but that was not to be."

"Agnes' return must have enlivened everyone in the farmhouse, Alex."

"Yes Gaudin, and much celebration when Agnes gave birth to wee Mabel at the farm in June 1875. I am sure I have said that to you before."

"I certainly remember my happiness to know all was well with her when I picked up the cable telegram in London announcing Mabel's birth on 21 June. On that date I had the *Lady Lampson* in the North Atlantic south of Ireland about to set a record 113-day return passage."

After a long pause Anderson spoke again.

"Please tell me what you have heard about me in town."

"Well, Alex, if you insist, I have heard some consider you to be a difficult man."

"Of that, I have no doubt, Gaudin. It goes back a long way. I have long faced opposition and conflict, not least from British Columbia's first Attorney-General Carey who took a scunner to me back in the early days when we first moved up from Oregon to live in town. In self-fulfilling prophecy, he mistook me as having no regard for him."

Gaudin felt moved to be frank.

"Much of that may have proceeded from the way you carry yourself in public," he said. "You DO have an air of superiority. Men of lesser birth see you as putting on airs, and they feel offended. Won't you admit they envy you?"

"You go much too far on that, Gaudin, but I will admit I will not change my ways to please others. I have worried our children might find life difficult for having inherited my faults. God knows my wife had none; they might turn out well, after all."

Gaudin spoke again after a long moment when neither spoke.

"One man in town who will remain nameless told me he thought you to be a bitter man, Alex, bitterness on account of the notable Sir George Simpson's ill-treatment of you in the Company Service. How correct can that be, Alex?"

"In truth, I did not allow that man to bend me to become a singer in a chorus of praise of him, Gaudin, but a sense of propriety has kept me from uttering statements others would take as unseemly for a gentleman to speak. I have kept my thoughts about him to myself. I have never spoken my mind to others about him. I can be accused of many faults, but none can say I have spoken ill of another man."

Anderson stood up and went inside to the bookshelf to bring back his copy of John McLean's early publication of a narrative of his years of service to the Hudson's Bay Company to show to Gaudin and speak again on taking his chair.[6]

"I hope a future reader of this book will think well of me for having penned my own critique on a page in the book. Here, lift the lamp to read the words I wrote on the page to the effect that McLean's criticism of Simpson would have been better left unwritten."

Gaudin looked at Anderson's writing on the page.

"I knew from the first day I met Simpson he did not like me," Anderson said. "I cannot forget the look of disregard on his face

6 John McLean's Notes of a twenty-five years' service in the Hudson's Bay territory Publisher: London, Richard Bentley, c 1849 Description: 2 v.,21 cm. Call Number(s): Library NW 971H M163 Royal BC Museum

whenever he saw me in the hurly-burly and rapid movement of men in the canoe brigades departing west from Lachine in March 1832. Looking back on it now, I think he mistook me as relying on my Seton family connection to obtain advancement when all I looked for was his approval at the outset of the movement westwards. I found it a relief to be left behind from the express canoes to labour in the freight canoe brigade to Sault Ste. Marie and across the top of Lake Superior to Fort William and beyond."

"Perhaps, Alex, it would be well for you to speak to me of your grievances and get it off your chest. We have time and I am a good listener. Tell me."

Anderson filled his glass again, sat down, and began to speak.

"Yes, Gaudin, my wife's death left me without anyone I could confide in without feeling I added a burden on their shoulders. Please do not tell Agnes about any of what I am going to tell you."

Gaudin said he would keep it all to himself, and Anderson continued to speak.

"Indeed, it may help me to gather my thoughts together to tell you of them instead of letting them fester in my mind. Let me start with the year 1851 when I elected to retire as a partner of the company. That year should have been a high point in my life: in truth, it marked the beginning of the end of my career at only age 38 after twenty years' service with the Honourable Company. Here I am today at 62 with so much water and wreckage left behind in the wake, as you might describe it. Over long winter nights at Fort Alexandria in my early thirties I wrote out a manuscript in pen and ink entitled *A Narrative of Thirteen Years' Service with the Hudson's Bay Company Between Montreal and the Pacific*, which I thought would be of general interest to many in England and the United States. But even my brother Chief Factor James Anderson could not get it published when he took it to England in 1857 on a furlough I could never have hoped to take. He wrote a letter to me to say he showed it to our Uncle Alex Seton, well connected with the Committee of the Honourable Company in London. I take it as probable he and others may have stifled its publication because the time inopportune: the renewal of Royal Charter granted in 1670 to the *Gentlemen Adventurers* trading into Hudson Bay faced debate in the House of Commons and opposition from many quarters in Parliament at that time. The men my brother consulted may have seen my remarks concerning relations with the Indigenous Peoples to be troublesome.

You can understand I suffered terrible disappointment after spending so much time writing it all out, and labouring to make copies, to see it not published. Somehow the copy I sent to a notable in Oregon, Mister Tappan, has not been returned, but I hope it may turn up someday. But to get on with what I intend to tell you: I may not give you a chronological account, but will touch on matters as my memory thinks of them. Will you bear with me?"

"Yes Alex, please go ahead."

"From 1849 to 1851 I held the posting as senior company officer at Fort Colvile at Kettle Falls on the Upper Columbia River, lying just south of the Forty-Ninth Parallel where your wife was born. With the rank of a Chief Trader, one rank above the junior officer rank of Clerk, I provided my family with better living quarters in a far better climate than at Fort Alexandria on the Upper Fraser River. I will get to tell you more about Alexandria before this night is out. The Committee named Fort Colvile after a personage in London held in favour by those who have influence. The last part of his name is spelled with one L. From Colvile every summer I enjoyed leading the horse brigade carrying fur pelts cross-country west over the mountains to the Okanagan River, and on farther to the Similkameen River Valley to cross the mountains on the Hope Trail, heading for Fort Langley. You may not know Simpson established Fort Langley in 1828 to better serve the British Columbia Coast with the prospect of falling back on it if required to vacate Oregon by an adverse settlement of the International Boundary. I enjoyed seeing the country I passed through in conducting the summer brigades for three years, but I found no pleasure in my dealings with some of the fellow officers. I could not abide Manson and some others from New Caledonia joining forces on the Hope Trail. Rather than endure the *tomfoolery* when the Colvile Brigade and the New Caledonia Brigade came together at Langley, I chose to sleep on the ground outside the walls of the fort. Nor do I treasure the memories of the labour of lining or tracking the loaded boats against the current of the Fraser River back to Hope each year_____; and of the labour remaining to load the trading goods and supplies from the boats onto the backs of the packhorses of the Brigades to take over the Hope Trail to Colvile. Our hands had to be good at handling horses."

"As I remember it, Alex, you had early experience with horses bringing fur pelts down from New Caledonia to Fort Vancouver on the Columbia in the mid-1830s?"

"Yes, Gaudin, I began to do that every year by brigade packhorse from New Caledonia to Fort Okanogan on the Columbia, awakening from sleep with the noise of bird calls in the dark before sunrise and learning never to let your horses suffer from pasturing on a kind of wild vetch that flourished in places during brigade season. The unwary could judge the pleasing green leaves sprinkled with tiny clusters of attractive red-purple to blue flowers to be succulent forage. The likelihood of being forced to vacate Fort Vancouver by a new International Boundary led me to put myself forward to suggest new brigade routes to take our furs to the littoral and to bring our trading goods and supplies back into the Interior. I traced out the routes of my annual explorations west and south from Alexandria on the map the Province paid me to make in 1867. Come inside to lamplight for me to show you on my copy of the Map."

Back seated on the veranda Anderson carried on after explaining his use of the word *littoral.*

"Blessedly, the name of Fort Alexandria on the Upper Fraser River," he said, "does bring back one joyful memory, that of my wedding, which came a year after my first posting as the junior officer in charge of the trading posts at Fort Fraser and Fort St. James during the years 1835 to 1838. James Birnie and his wife Charlotte came with their 14-year-old daughter Eliza north from what I choose to call Fort George-on-the-Ocean up three rivers and overland to Fort Alexandria for the wedding. You should not confuse Fort George on the Fraser River with the Fort George on the Columbia. The former lies downstream from Fort St. James in the north. Chief Trader, later promoted to Chief Factor, Peter Skene Ogden, the senior company officer in New Caledonia, conducted the ceremony and signed the marriage contract. He showed me his parchment of authority from the Governor-in-Council of Lower Canada and the Indian Territories to the West as the most Western Justice of the Peace in the country. I idolized that man. No church bells, but ringing cheers from the fort and from the local Indians assembled for the celebration. I had first seen Eliza Birnie when she and her family joined the vessel from their camp on the shore of Baker's Bay behind Cape Disappointment, and I sent from the ship to help with their luggage. They had come from Fort George by small boat to live in tents on the shore during weeks of wind that kept the *Dryad* at anchor, unable to cross the Columbia Bar. On the shore in the wind and rain during this time Mrs. Birnie gave birth to another child, a daughter Charlotte, who, ever in ill health, died twenty-years later. Finally, the weather let up, and we all gathered on board for Hudson's Bay Company brig the *Dryad* to depart over the Columbia Bar in April 1833 en route to northern waters in the opening shot of the company's campaign against the competition offered by the sailing vessels of the Maritime Fur Trade on the North Pacific Coast.[7] Eliza was then almost 12 years of age and I eight years older at 19. I daresay I noticed her and began to start thinking of her as a prospect for marriage in time. I talked about her in those terms in confidence with Doctor Tolmie when he and I spent most of 1833 and 1834 together at Fort McLoughlin, which I will come to in a moment. I showed you its location on my map of the upper coast. Neither Tolmie nor I had the money to ever think of making a trip back to England to find a wife. He and I were in this part of the World for life. But to get back to my story: I sailed in the *Dryad* with Birnie and his wife and their children more than 40 years ago, now. Birnie went with orders to take charge of Fort Simpson-on-the Nass River in a land of cloud and heavy rain, close to 55° North Latitude. Crews of three company sailing vessels assisted to carry out his orders to close the fort, which was located some distance up from the mouth of the Nass River. Only the small company schooner *Cadboro* could reach it using sweeps on a rising tide to anchor in a river pool. Birnie's orders required him to use the men of the expedition to re-establish the fort at a place closer to the ocean."

"Was it named after the governor?"

"No, after Captain Aemelius Simpson, who came west over the Rockies in late 1826 to support the company's marine service on the coast.[8] The new site would be closer to Indian settlements at the south end of the Alaskan Panhandle, notably at Kaigani, which everyone called Kigarney, at Clemmincitti and at Tongass in sheltered waters in behind Cape Fox. The Honourable Company purchased Captain McNeill's brig the *Llama* (with two L's), but I refer to her now as the *Lama* (with one L as her name came to be recorded by the Honourable Company). I know no one cares about this sort of thing today, but you hear me pronounce the two names differently. The headman in the Columbia, Doctor McLoughlin, hired McNeill for his local knowledge of the trade in furs in the region. Captain McNeill showed me pages at the back of his logbook with sailing directions to enter the harbours of the places I named a moment ago. I remember going upriver the Nass to be a member of the parties put ashore to burn all that couldn't be carried away in

<hr/>

[7] Log of the Dryad HBCA 1833 1/281 Reels 2M18-1M19
[8] http.geonames.nrcan.gc.ca/native_e.php; HBCA A.12/1, fol.65

a funeral pyre. This took place to the whooping and hollering of the Indians, who were showing their annoyance at the fort being moved away from them. The new fort established and the Birnies left behind at their new home, Doctor Tolmie and I sailed south in the company brigs. Tolmie went in the *Lama* and I went in the *Dryad* to establish a new trading fort on an island 200 miles or more down on the central coast. For the first part of that passage, I have the vivid memory of the landmark for the navigation in and out from the sea, high and steep Dundas Island, named by Captain Vancouver 80 years ago. At the end of a summer day and with most of us holding our breath, we slipped out south through a narrow pass on the east side of it. A good breeze from the north assisted the passage at low water slack tide. I overheard Captain McNeill's remark predicting they will likely name this channel leading in and out of these Narrows, *Hudson Bay Company Passage*, in commemoration of the work the Company Sail on this coast will now be doing with him to guide Captain Kipling in the *Dryad*, or words to the same effect. He did insist on saying *Hudson Bay*, not Hudson's Bay. When asked if he knew where the rocks and reefs were located he remarked with some cheek, I thought, he didn't know where they were, but he knew where they were not, which caused a big laugh. In truth, he knew the way to sail through these waters. We prized his skill as we headed south through open water sprinkled, he said, with islets, rocks and reefs to find Banks Island and Principe *Canal* discovered by the Spaniard Perez in 1774. Not a canal, of course, but a long narrow channel. McNeill reminded us that the Maritime Fur Trade captains had been sailing these inner waters ever since Captain Duncan came in his sloop the *Princess Royal* to circumnavigate and name Princess Royal Island on the central coast a decade later. He told us we were not to think we were the first people sailing in here. As I said, Gaudin, the Honourable Company recorded the name of McNeill's former American Brig *Llama* as the *Lama*. I say it again because I remember Doctor Tolmie and I noticed the real name painted on a plank in fading letters, but no one ever undertook to correct the name in the company records. As the brigs sailed south through narrow channels, wind and tide separated them, each anchoring every night in dry weather, it being unsafe to sail through narrow channels in the dark. Word spread on deck the captains logged one bay at anchor as Cook's Harbour, which set me thinking they knew Cook had struck into these waters by way of Dixon Entrance to explore in secret from the Spanish after leaving Nootka in 1778 and before sailing north to Alaska and the Bering Sea.[9] Surprising, Gaudin, because Captain Cook's book published after his death in Hawaii, glosses over his passage north from Nootka. We stopped in several places to wait for fog to lift or for a favouring wind and tide. But to go on with the story, the summer 1834 became great fun for me at age 20. The company sent a brig to take us, Tolmie and me, from Fort McLoughlin to form part of the expedition sailing north to Alaska under Ogden's command. Doctor McLoughlin sent him with orders to set up a trading post inland from the mouth of the Stikine River. The Russians from Sitka objected to us being there and threatened warfare against us. We withdrew on Ogden agreeing to focus on trade inland on the rivers, leaving the coastal trade to the Russians, the agreement subject to ratification in London and in Russia. Our triumphant little fleet sailed away south through Clarence Strait on the wings of a northwesterly summer gale of wind past Cape Fox back into waters long familiar to our captains, and now familiar to my inquisitive mind_____. Gaudin, you talk about your studdingsails: Captain Kipling in the *Dryad* set them to great effect on our boisterous romp south from the northern waters."

"I shall have to see the charts for that part of the coast to understand your account, sir. I have never been there."

"The Company sent Tolmie and me back to spend the winter at Fort McLoughlin to trade with the Indians, but soon the *Cadboro* called in again with orders to take me back south to Fort Vancouver. That changed my life. Ogden took me north with him in the spring when he took charge of his new command in the Interior long-named New Caledonia. I had not talked with Mister Birnie about marrying his daughter Eliza. Now settled in my new posting at Fraser Lake and the Birnies and I being so far apart, I sent a letter to Mister Birnie asking to marry their daughter Eliza. Here comes Agnes calling us in supper. Let's carry on with this afterwards."

Later that night the talk continued as Agnes packed to go on board the *Lady Lampson* the next day.

"In truth, Gaudin, I spent my happiest years at Fort St. James, which I soon chose as my headquarters. Ogden sent me to take charge of the small northern posts at Fraser Lake and Fort St. James, from which I provided a tributary stream of fur pelts to Fort Alexandria for the annual brigade south to Fort Vancouver through a wondrous dry grassy

9 HBCA log of Dryad 1/281-282 Reels 2M18-1M19 PABC A/B/20.5/L16J McNeill, William H fonds Lama logbook 1833

country behind the mountains on the coast. In these brigades we followed in the steps of The North West Company, which had pioneered
the fur trade westwards over the top of the Northern Rockies into New
Caledonia and on to the mouth of the Columbia. No shack in the
woods for us at Fraser Lake: it even had a bastion."

Gaudin interrupted to ask about the winter weather in New Caledonia.

"I remember my first winter being subjected to risk of death from
exposure when ordered east to travel up the Fraser River and cross over
the Yellowhead Pass to Jasper's House in the heart of the Northern
Rockies to pick up a shipment of buffalo leather hides. We departed in
good season with canoes for the headwaters of the Fraser. Planning to
return before winter, we placed the canoes en cache near the headwaters.
From there we marched overland to Jasper's House, but we had to wait
for the packhorses coming with a brigade, running late. My party took
the hides overland back to the canoes in winter weather. We fell in with
an early freeze-up of ice on the river, which rendered the canoes use-
less. I could only leave everything behind to lead my party in snow and
freezing temperature back to safety at Jasper's House. Safe arrival with
the sight of the snow-covered mountains all around under the light of a
full moon makes for a vivid memory of the event. Jasper House on short
rations could not allow us to stay. With a compass to maintain direction
I led my group of men and women on a journey for days without proper
winter clothing overland across an empty wild landscape to Edmonton
House to save our lives. We arrived half dead to be revived by Chief
Trader Rowand's pemmican and hospitality. On recruiting our health
and being re-clothed and re-provisioned, we made it back in December
to Jasper House to press on with snowshoes over the New Caledonia
Portage to Tête Jaune Cache to pick up the cached hides and pull them
over the snow to Fort George on contrived sleds. I had some good
strong Frenchmen with me. I made it back to the warm fires at Fort St.
James. My wife, pregnant with our first child, thought I'd died. She had
a sad Christmas waiting for John McLean's search party sent out to find
us or bury our bodies."

After a long silence Gaudin asked what use were the hides.

"Oh, we had a good use for them, Gaudin. We put them on the
backs of horses the better to carry loads on Columbia Brigade south to
Fort Okanogan, and for the return to New Caledonia."

"Why to that place, which I do know lies far inland up the Columbia from Fort Vancouver?"

"Fort Okanogan had a large *parc* to pasture the horses waiting for the brigade men to return by boat from Fort Vancouver with loads to carry back on the brigade trail north on the west side of Lake Okanagan_____. Enough of that, and to go back to our wedding later in the summer of 1836, which pleases me to talk about: my bride and I made our departure to the sounding cheers I have told you about. The sight of the leaves on the trees already turning yellow under a clear sky as we set out on horseback cross-country to take up my station at the foot of Stuart Lake at Fort St. James lives on in my memory. I considered it a boon to live in a beautiful lake country full of trout, game to be shot for food, and salmon to be caught and smoked for eating. A good stream flowing south provided easy access by canoe to all points. The birth of our daughter Eliza the next year gave life to our little community: Indians from miles around gathered at the fort to see the white child_____. Our winter in the north had us living in a small log cabin for me to go out on snowshoes to make contact with the local Indians. I aimed to induce them to come to the fort to trade their capture in fur pelts for trading goods I had in the storeroom. The men, boats, and horses of last summer's brigade from Fort Vancouver carried all of this, some of it heavy, up to New Caledonia. I kept books to account for every item_____. Now, the Honourable Company's Sail around Cape Horn carried the trading goods from London to the Columbia River and to Fort Vancouver because terrain and the distance overland made supply to the Pacific from Montreal impracticable. My fur trade training at Lachine on the western outskirts of Montreal during the winter of 1831-32 taught me the local Indians would be quick to adapt to a narrow slot of time open for trapping activity predicated on the necessity for conservation, which taught that no man should trap furs during the mating season even though pelts then might be all the thicker. Timing is everything. Prime pelts taken in the winter cold will have begun to thicken after a summer of their purposeful activity in search of food. As the Indians knew pelts they took in the summer period would be thin and without value for trade at the fort, they didn't bother to trap at that time. The respite from trapping left the posts free to attend to brigading out the *Returns* during a time when rivers not in freshet and the road to the south becoming dry for travel."

"What a learning experience for you, Alex."

"Yes Gaudin, it was that. These were the years I found favour in the eyes of everyone: well, almost everyone, but not the troublemaking preacher who descended on Fort Vancouver preaching hellfire and damnation. I had a fearful argument with the Church of England Preacher Herbert Beaver who arrived in Fort Vancouver from England obsessed to perform marriage ceremonies for fur trade couples who had become husband and wife without benefit of clergy. The Birnies accepted the direction to marry again in church, but I got my back up, refusing to accept the criticism. Above all, I rejected Beaver's assertion that Birnie had taken his daughter up into the Interior to live with me in Sin. I sent him an angry letter stating my argument and held him up to ridicule. I claimed legal precedent in the Courts of Lower Canada upholding the fur trade ceremony as an enforceable contract of marriage between a man and a woman. But all that brings back the memory of Fort Alexandria and how I came to be sent to York Factory in 1842. How shall I say it? I have never told anyone, not even my wife, but I will tell you the sorry tale."

After a long silence and pouring out more whiskey from the bottle, Anderson continued.

"Gaudin, I have decided to speak to you about several matters concerning that man Simpson. I have never said a word of it before to anyone. The earliest instance of Simpson's machinations affected myself at Fort Nisqually when Simpson touched there on his Round-the-World Tour in 1841-1842. I do not doubt that Governor Simpson contrived to have Doctor McLoughlin, the officer in charge of the Columbia Department at Fort Vancouver, send orders for me to ride on an errand over the Cascade Mountains to Yakima Indian country, which I could not accomplish in time to return to Nisqually to meet Simpson, who would be passing through to board the steamer *Beaver*, anchored offshore to take him to Sitka to meet the Russian Governor. I had heard stories about Simpson. I carried out my orders to the letter and then rode hell-for-leather on a 75-mile short cut back high over the mountains at Naches Pass on the northern flank of Mount Rainier in time to greet Simpson with my nineteen-year-old wife Eliza at my side. He said no more to me than, *That was a smart aleck thing to do, Anderson.* I found myself given no opportunity to follow up to talk to Governor Simpson before he came through Nisqually on the next stage of his Tour to take the company barque *Cowlitz* to Siberia."

Gaudin asked what would he have said to him.

"At this late date I am not sure what I intended to say to him, undoubtedly something to display my suitability for promotion. I had thought I had laid foundation for such a discussion in my letter to Doctor McLoughlin stating my unhappiness in the Service of the Honourable Company and my desire to leave the Company to move to live and work in Hawaii unless I could obtain a promotion. I received no reply. Years later I came to realize both Simpson and McLoughlin would have seen my letter as no more than a pathetic gesture to gain attention and favour. How had I come to be in such a state? I barely remember 1839. I came down from New Caledonia to Fort Vancouver at that time in poor health. Doctor McLoughlin sent me with my wife and children to the small company farm at nearby Cowlitz River to recuperate, close enough for him to tell me how to run the farm. Respite from his close oversight came when he sent me to run the larger farm at Fort Nisqually, but its more distant location did not stop him from sending detailed letters telling me what to do. I say Simpson came on his Tour in 1841 expecting me not to be present for his arrival. We did meet as I have said, but no chance to talk came. On his final departure from the fort he put a young man in his *entourage* into residence at Nisqually with a view to obtaining a report on my stewardship of the farm, which annoyed me no end. Next spring 1842 with my health recovered, I rejoiced in orders sending me in charge of the York Factory Express from Fort Vancouver to present the Accounts of the Columbia Department. At first I took my orders as a sign of favour, but the signal honour I expected ended in my downfall. Let's go in now, Gaudin. Agnes has the children in the kitchen. We can say goodnight to them and come back outside to talk."

Later, Gaudin and Anderson carried on their talk out on the veranda with blankets over their shoulders to keep warm. Gaudin lit a lamp to light their faces as they spoke in the darkness.

"I go on to tell you more, Gaudin: my orders required me to take my wife and family to Colvile and leave them there to await my return and go on by fast canoe to York Factory. Simpson's *private* letter to me in 1836 absolving me of the allegation of mismanagement inquired into over the Leather Party complaint I faced at that time emboldened me to think I could count on him for the kind of favour I detected in my new assignment. I mistook it. I cannot avoid telling you of the feelings of remorse I carried on my return from York Factory in late fall 1842. To this day I nurse the suspicion Simpson asked Doctor McLoughlin send me to present the Accounts of the Columbia Department to the Annual Meeting of the Wintering Partners at York without warning I'd be called in for questioning on items in the Accounts. I showed the partners assembled I had little grasp of the operations of the Columbia Department. Few around the table at York Factory would now voice support for me in terms of promotion. I found myself grinding my teeth in snatches of sleep on the route back, and I agonized what I could say when I rejoined my family at Colvile. Even though my orders sent me back as senior officer in charge of the headquarters of the New Caledonia Department at Fort Alexandria, I received no promotion and returned west in anguish."

Gaudin asked to see another map to show the route taken. Back in the house by lamplight to show the route, Anderson continued.

"My orders attached me to the westbound Columbia Brigade combined with other brigades for a 60-day journey across the Prairies in the heat of summer in loaded York Boats to Edmonton House. As an officer I rode the short-cut trail from Carlton House. The main group laboured up the North Saskatchewan River against the prevailing wind and the current with the boats. The brigades separated at Edmonton. A month to make the Rocky Mountain Portage over Athabasca Pass with early snow beginning to fall. On returning to Colvile, the lateness of season permitting no delay, I set out with my young family on horseback cross-country in November weather bound to take charge of Fort Alexandria in the heart of the Cariboo. Five days riding west from Kettle Falls over the mountains to intercept the brigade trail from Fort Okanogan leading north on the west side of Lake Okanagan. We reached Kamloops to pick out fresh horses in the *parc*. I found them huddled in the trees to catch and saddle. No one at the fort lifted a hand to help as precious hours passed in a time of violent wind and weather out of the south bringing rain, milder air and mud on the ground for the valley. I can remember it all, even now, thirty years later. The senior officer in charge at Kamloops and I never did get along well. Offered no help, I did no more than sign for the horses and supplies I drew from the fort establishment. From Kamloops we headed west to gain access to the high ground of the Cariboo up through the draw at Deadman's Creek to follow the brigade trail north up on the route used in summer to and from New Caledonia. I knew the way without a guide. The Cariboo winter winds whistled, now finding only bare ground without any sign of vegetation or greenery for the wind to surge and billow through. Our horses suffered without enough feed, and I could detect little sign of cheer in my lonely family group. Before reaching Alexandria I played across my mind what I could do to recover and make my mark. Six years at Alexandria would bring me a chance for notice."

"Alex, what do you mean by *notice*?"

"Well, Gaudin, although Fort Alexandria might be thought remote, I remained determined to have the Honourable Company give me my due. My reports of farming to reduce the need for Fort Vancouver to ship up foodstuffs and my explorations to find a new brigade route, I hoped, would set me apart for advancement. Indeed, promotion did come in 1848 with my orders to take the charge of Fort Colvile with its large agricultural and flour-milling component. The new posting, however, came without promotion in rank. Men junior to me were promoted to chief factor, which grated. My health and that of my wife began to suffer. My superior in charge at Fort Vancouver, my friend Chief Factor Ballenden, later told me he could do nothing to help me despite his appeal to Simpson phrased in terms that I was one of the most *intelligent* officers in the Columbia Department. Birnie confirmed my worst suspicions over drinks of hot rum at Cathlamet why Simpson withheld promotion for each of us."

"Agnes did tell me that Simpson withheld promotion for her grandfather Birnie but not why."

"Yes Gaudin, Birnie despaired of any hope for further promotion. He never rose above his Clerk's officer rank and took retirement in 1846. I understood Birnie to be telling me he knew for a certainty Simpson's ill treatment of us came in retribution for our respective robust young wives having denied him access when husbands absent on errands. Evidence of the punishment for Birnie came soon after Simpson's first visit of inspection of the Columbia Department over the winter from November 1824-April 1825. Simpson departed on his return east, having left behind orders for Birnie to leave Colvile to travel north to work for the Slave Lake Brigade. That required him to make a journey far up the Columbia River to cross over the Rockies at Athabasca Pass before proceeding overland to the banks of the Athabasca River at Fort Assiniboine. From that point Birnie's orders forced him to proceed by boat north down that river to Lesser Slave Lake and work the remainder of the year before coming back out south in April 1826 with the Slave Lake Brigade carrying furs to York Factory on the shore of Hudson Bay itself. Can you imagine being sent on such an errand after such an idyllic beginning for their lives, the Birnies, in charge at Fort Okanogan, which is where the river flowing south from Lake Okanagan joins the

Columbia River?"

"Yes Alex, I remember the spellings you told me about. Would he have taken his wife and family with him or was he sent out to go without them?"

"Birnie absolutely refused to tell me anything about that time; and his wife Charlotte likewise. I can say it would have been in keeping with the custom of the fur trade that she would have accompanied him with their child. The officer in charge of the party would be expected to cope with them coming."

"And to have the benefit of their extra hands for work needful to be done?"

"Yes Gaudin, that's the way it might have happened, but it's too late now to know. It must have been a trying time for both of them in either event. Birnie inferred Simpson aimed to make her sorry she had denied him, he in hope of finding a change of heart for his next official inspection of the Columbia Department."

Anderson remarked he knew little of Simpson's next visit in 1828.

"I cannot say that any importuning later took place," he said, "but I doubt that Simpson would have deigned to have had any further contact with either of them."

After a long silence Anderson continued with his tale.

"A certain Captain Aemilius Simpson, Royal Navy, late of the company's Marine Service (not to be confused with the Simpson I have been talking about) came west from Montreal with the same brigade that Birnie traveled with. Simpson came overland to captain company brigs on the Pacific Coast. During the brigade travel west he came to know and like Birnie. Simpson's travel west originated in Montreal; and from there by fast canoe to join the Columbia Brigade at York Factory. I have his account of the travel to the west on third-hand hearsay. That brigade combined with the Slave Lake Brigade and the New Caledonia Brigade set out from York in mid-July in five loaded boats carrying 60 men, destined for Edmonton House, there to divide. I recall my own later experience in 1832 and 1842 covering the same route coming west and using the North Saskatchewan River. From Edmonton House the Brigade took a week with loaded horses on an abominable road through swamp and strewn fallen burnt trees to reach Fort Assiniboine on the banks of the Athabasca River. On gaining the river, the combined Columbia and New Caledonia Brigade transferred the loads into boats to line up against the current for a week to reach a point where a man from Jasper's House met the boats with packhorses. The two brigades split at Jasper, the one headed west over the Yellowhead Pass to New Caledonia. The other, the Columbia Brigade, a party of two-dozen men leading more than a dozen loaded packhorses took the best part of two weeks to cross over the Rockies at Athabasca Pass. Having left the pack horses to pasture in a meadow on the eastern side in mid-September, they marched on with the loads on their backs to descend the steep face of the *Le Grand Côte* to reach the River at Boat Encampment to find Mister Dease, the officer in charge of Fort Colvile and his men, who had come up the Columbia River in three boats, waiting for them under the trees in the cold rain. Some of the men in Dease's party were returning east: they took their loads from the boats to pack up over the Pass to find the horses in pasture in a meadow beside the trees on the northeastern side of the Pass. Rather than go on foot, they caught them to carry themselves and their baggage to Jasper's House on the next step of their journey east."

Anderson remarked his 1867 Map, which Gaudin had seen, marked out the route of Athabasca Pass and the journey down the Upper Columbia River through the Arrow Lakes, which he sprinkled with French-Canadian fur trade names, like *le trou* for an opening from narrow places in the path.

"At Boat Encampment, which is shown on the map, with the winter approaching," Anderson said, "Birnie likely would have been called on to help repair the cedar-planked boats to make them usable. Once afloat, they got underway downstream to make the dangerous passage past the rocks in one set of rapids after another going down the madness of the Upper Columbia River into the Arrow Lakes and beyond to Colvile in only five days of travel. Not a bad time to travel the River, except continuing low water in the river made for picking a route through and between great standing rocks and boulders that diverted the flows. Birnie went down the River to Fort Vancouver for further orders. He stayed on the coast until he retired at far too young an age in 1846_____. The thought occurred to torment me, Gaudin, that Agnes on Jersey with you absent at sea could be in no less danger of being put upon by a predatory man such as I saw Simpson to be."

"Coming from Jersey, and thinking I know the people there, Alex, you will be glad to know such a thought never will cross my mind."

"That may well be so, Gaudin. I hope so. I thank you for taking my young son Arthur with you to go to school in Jersey. If that doesn't please, I ask you and Agnes to send him on to a school I know about in England. I cannot keep him in school here to pick up bad habits of speech. I am sure he will give his older sister Agnes no trouble."

"I expect to bring the *Lady Lampson* back to Victoria again in January next year. I will bring the young Renouf son with me for you to take under your wing. I intend to continue making my annual passages to Esquimalt each year, but by the end of '79 the *Lady Lampson* will have been ten years on the Ships' Register: Lloyd's of London will charge a higher premium to keep her sailing insured. Railroads across the continent may end the company's sailing vessel traffic to the Pacific Northwest. The Committee may decide to sell her and I may be forced to look elsewhere for another vessel to command in days of uncertainty."

"We have been fortunate to have seen you every year."

"God willing and opportunities offering, I can promise to be with Agnes and the children in Jersey every summer."

"That event, Gaudin, could put you in a vessel sailing to other parts of the World. For you to get so involved would put it beyond your power to carry out your promise to my daughter to bring her to settle in Victoria after Edwin's coming of age permits the administrator to sell the Renouf property, wouldn't it?"

"I don't know what I can say, sir, except to say that Gaudins keep their promises."

16

CALLED ON THE CARPET

Chief Factor Charles sent a message yesterday he would see Gaudin at the office at 10 a.m. today, All Fool's Day April 1878. A fresh south-west wind swept the Inner Harbour. Two days of rain had ended. His boots will stay dry when he goes out onto the street. The hotel room had no stove and the night had been cold. Gaudin looked out through a clear patch he scratched off the inside of the glass of the frosty window-pane to see the wind marking out spreading cats-paws on the water. The Sooke Hills and Mount Finlayson stood in the distance, lit by the sun, white from a fresh fall of snow overnight. The cold outside cheered Gaudin to know the mud on the road will crunch under his boots into shreds of brown and white crystal breaking under his step.

Gaudin dressed, put on a face of false good cheer, and ambled in loose steps downstairs from his hotel room to show any who might be interested he felt no fear of the outcome of this morning's talk with Charles. But he did not have the stomach to eat breakfast. The bad taste in his mouth persisted.

From the time of his first arrival in port twelve years ago as Mate in the Company barque the *Prince of Wales*, the local press lionized Gaudin for his willingness to talk and yarn to give them *copy* to write a report of his recent passage from London in their newspaper. He became accustomed to being greeted in the street by strangers with warm words of welcome, but now he found a daunting reception. Few spoke to him. Those who did averted their eyes and walked by in quick time, evading his efforts to engage them.

The newspaper reporter whispered about the scuttlebutt he'd heard noised-about among townspeople: Gaudin had been down in his cabin on the night of the stranding intent on shaving off his beard when he should have been on deck attending to his duty. His wife in Jersey, who would he have been rushing to see on shore?

Deep down, Gaudin relied on Birnie-Anderson family ties to save him. He counted on Chief Factor Charles feeling called on to treat him with extra care on account of his marriage to a daughter of Alexander Caulfield Anderson, now 64, who had become active behind the scenes as an *éminence grise* in Canadian Federal politics. Although no one could say he had any constituency of local support, some knew he could count on men in Ottawa seeking his advice on questions concerning Fisheries and Indian Affairs. Anderson could be a figure for the Honourable Company to heed.

Gaudin arrived early at the office he had often attended on ship's business and sat in a chair in the anteroom to wait. Comforted by warm memories of his past meetings with Charles, Gaudin felt more relaxed than he expected. He relished the thought his recent letter to Mister Armit, the Secretary of the Honourable Company at 1 Lime Street in London had well explained the recent 'rescue' of his ship. Two days ago Charles had asked him to write and hand in the letter for him to send. The Committee would see him as no nincompoop, he thought. His concise neat handwriting would show him to advantage to the men in London: -

Victoria, March 29 1878 to William Armit Esq, Hudson's Bay Company, 1 Lime Street, London. Sir, I have just received a communication from Mr. Finlayson, Lloyds Agent in this port, sent to him by Mr. Thomas Pamphlett, who contracted for the unloading of the Lady Lampson, in which he imputed to me motives of the basest nature, not only to myself, but also to my officers, and the management at this place, as you may see by the copy he forwarded to you by this post_____. The contractor had the assistance of the whole of the crew while he was discharging the cargo whether by day or night just as he required. On January 29 it blew a strong gale from the S.E., during which the ship strained heavily and sustained much damage, so that it was deemed unsafe for the crew to live onboard. So I lodged them at Esquimalt where they were always ready to go off to the ship when the weather permitted. The vessel was never left without one of the officers and some of the crew whilst the contractor was onboard, excepting the night of 10 and 11 February when he went onboard after having told me his pumps would not be ready that night therefore he could do no good by going out. Previously on 2 February my first attempt to take the vessel off the beach the starboard bilge was firmly on the ground all the time. The ship was lying on

*her beam ends and the covering board nearly awash. With the heavy swell
that was rolling into the beach, it would have been utter recklessness to try to
move her. The ship would have been perfectly unmanageable with more than
three-fourths of the remaining cargo in the starboard side and eight feet of
water on the lee side and would have gone down in deep water. After engag-
ing a diver to stop the leak, I made a second attempt to float the vessel on the
nights of 7 and 8 February, but again unsuccessful. I determined not to go
to any further expense in floating the ship until some of the cargo had been
taken out of the starboard side, which decision I apprised Mr. Pamphlett. I
have discharged the crew with the exception of the officers, cook, and steward,
and I will send postage bill run up as soon as the ship is sold. I am sir, your
obedient and humble servant, Jas. Gaudin.[10]*

Gaudin stiffened when Charles came out to meet him in the outer
office with a tidy young Englishman holding a sheaf of writing paper
in his hand. Would he be taking notes of the meeting? Gaudin relaxed
when he heard Charles tell the young man to come back at 2 o'clock.
Charles beckoned Gaudin into the office and shut the door behind
them. He bid the captain be seated.

"This is a sorry business, isn't it, Captain?"

"I am sorry to say it IS that, but thank you, sir, for calling on me to
help you deal with the rigamorole of complaints made by Pamphlett to
Mister Finlayson. Thank you also for sending on the letter you invited
me to write to Secretary Armit in London to explain how Pamphlett
had no grounds for his complaint against me."

"Yes, Gaudin, I sent your letter out in the Company mail pouch on
29 March with a letter to him explaining I asked you to write. Outside normal channels for you to write directly to him, of course. I have
never seen such a litany of disordered complaint from Pamphlett. He
must have wanted to jack more money out of the Honourable Company
than his contract allowed. You and he seem not to have struck it off
well from the beginning when you refused to use him as a pilot, and he
wanted to show you up, I suppose. But let's cut to the matter at hand.
How did you run the *Lady Lampson* on Scrogg Rock in the first place is
the question London has been asking."

"It IS difficult for me to explain to you, sir."

Gaudin went on at some length to make a frank explanation he had
not been on deck at the time. He had been mistaken in thinking it safe
to leave the Chief Officer in charge of the navigation of the ship. He
knew he had no excuse for the stranding, but he clung to the hope the

Chief Factor would accept his recommendation to minimize expense and authorize him to make temporary local repairs to enable him to sail the ship back to London. With the record of another successful voyage behind him he hoped to be able to explain the stranding to Captain David Herd, the Company Marine Superintendent. He had always been favourably disposed towards him. He had given him his first ship's command in 1868, the renowned old Company barque the *Ocean Nymph* on a voyage from London to Quebec City and on to Montreal. Captain Herd sponsored him for the command of the new barque *Lady Lampson* over other company ship's masters who would have felt themselves more entitled to command this fine addition to the fleet.

Charles did not interrupt the long account, which Gaudin had taken some time to prepare in his mind. Nor did he show any impatience when Gaudin went on with the wind in his sails.

"With a successful voyage to the Gulf of St. Lawrence completed to everyone's satisfaction," he said, "I sailed the *Ocean Nymph* back into the London Docks two days before Christmas 1868. I missed getting home to Jersey in the excitement of taking over the charge of the demanding work of commissioning the *Lady Lampson* into service with wire rigging to be spliced and set up. I set sail in my new command from London for Victoria on 16 February nine years ago. I know I will have a chance if I get back to London to face Captain Herd. Nine times I sailed the *Lady Lampson* around Cape Flattery into Esquimalt Harbour with ship, crew, passengers, and cargo safe."

Putting forth a wan smile, Gaudin ended by saying again his redemption could come if the Chief Factor would only enable him to repair the ship and sail her back to London as Captain Weynton had been permitted to sail the *Cowlitz* back to London with casks of whale oil cargo almost twenty years ago.

Charles shot back, "That was a different situation. Your vessel suffered more damage. The *Cowlitz*, although hogged, could sail without repairs. Now, the matter at hand: we have transmitted your report that the ship could be well repaired, but I am sorry to say it will be quite impossible for me to authorize those steps to be taken."

His head spinning, Gaudin listened as Charles went on to say he was sorry it had taken such a long time to bring him in to the Office. In the meantime he'd been required to focus on many matters of interest to the Committee in London.

"Not least," he said, "the matter of marine insurance and communicating with the Committee in London by cable telegraph to obtain instructions. I sent a report to London three weeks ago to inform them the *Lady Lampson* had been lightened of her cargo; she has gone back to her original lines and shape; and it did not look like there is much the matter with her. In addition to your recommendation I had the advantage of the survey conducted when the barque came up on the ways in the Harbour. I could not avoid reporting a shipyard in England could repair her at less cost than we could here in Victoria, which supported your request to make your own temporary repairs here and sail again. Against that, as you may know, next year she will be 10 years old. Finlayson tells me Lloyd's will reclassify her to be more expensive to insure. In consequence I must be unwilling to incur too much in expense without authority from London."

After an awkward pause Charles continued.

"London threw the decision on me by their telegram two weeks ago, which asked me if temporary repairs place vessel in same condition as before? No one here could say that, Gaudin, but I went out on a limb to wire back to say she would be seaworthy with temporary repairs for $5,000.00; and I asked them for instructions to send her home with the cargo of casks of whale oil, which I thought they might authorize. Next day London wired back to sell the ship for benefit of everyone concerned."

The last words having sunk in, Gaudin, his heart pounding, focused on what Charles proceeded to say next.

"As you may know, Gaudin, the Committee in London, historically, does not undertake to spend money to repair vessels that have stranded far from home. This policy may stem from the lack of adequate shipyard repair facilities close at hand. Also, as I see it, the policy deters captains from hazarding their vessels for fear of losing their commands. The best example of that policy led to old Captain Brotchie's offer to come back to employment in the Marine Service being turned down on the ground he had lost the last of the company vessels he had charge of in 1848."

Smarting under the implication that he had hazarded his vessel, Gaudin started to say something, but Charles stopped him.

"Let me say that the underwriters have agreed to pay the Company for the whole of the insured value of the *Lady Lampson*. As you know, the ship's cargo has been recovered and sold. I am required to order the ship, herself, and all of her equipment put up for sale by public auction

AS IS, WHERE IS in the first week of April. I have authorized the auctioneers to proceed."

Gaudin, crushed, felt his cheeks flush red as Charles kept on speaking.

"Captain, the truth is that the Company does not need you or your ship. We have the economical use of several barques, and all of the captains we need, Captain Alexander Main in the *Prince Rupert*, pre-eminent among them, even though he did take 157 days to get back to London not long ago. I know you did it in 113 days in 1875; but now what about you? What are your intentions? Likely no sailing vessel lies here for you to command. You have money coming to you from your salary and expenses account. I can advance you 250 pounds today on condition you must repay the money if the Committee does not authorize payment for your passage homewards. How will you travel?"

Gaudin took time to answer and finally stammered out his reply.

"I will travel back to England to meet Captain Spring. He sent me a telegram a week ago asking me to help him inspect sailing vessels for sale in Scotland. Good may come from that. I will take a steamer to San Francisco and consider the railroad to the Atlantic Seaboard and a steamer onward. That may be faster now than steamers homewards from Panama."

"You may find other options when you get to San Francisco."

"Yes sir, that's true. A good command of sailing vessel may be open to me at San Francisco with cargo for England, which would give me a chance to go to my family in Jersey, which will be my first aim. I will have money due to me also from insurance on the value of cargo of my own being carried in the ship. The insurance adjusters for cargo have sold most of it by now. In the meanwhile I must use the time to see how my crew has been making out finding new employment."

Gaudin rose to shake hands and take his leave.

"Thank you for your consideration, sir. I cannot stay on here to see what happens to my pretty little ship at the hands of men who do not love her as I do."

Gaudin refrained from attending the auction. In the interval he visited Agnes' father in North Saanich to tell him what had happened and to speak of his intentions.

"I am hopeful that the telegram I received from Captain Spring asking me to meet him in London will help me find a ship to sail. As to travel expenses I inquired and found 250 pounds insufficient. I went back to Charles and he advanced 300 pounds, which will cut it fine."

San Francisco by 1878 ranked as the largest city on the West Coast of North and South America with transcontinental rail connections for Gaudin to take to New York. No rail across Canada yet. On the other side of the Atlantic, will he find a new vessel? And what will he be saying to Agnes when he gets back to her?

Anderson saw him off on 18 April as a passenger in the steamer *City of Panama* departing for San Francisco. He handed him a letter for Agnes.

17

THE ROVER OF THE SEAS

Back in Jersey on a warm summer's day Agnes opened her front door on Gaudin's knock. He had been away from her for over a year on the Ninth Annual Passage of the *Lady Lampson* to the Pacific Northwest, which London notified her had ended in shipwreck off Esquimalt in January.

"How's my girl?"

She rushed to put her arms around him.

"Oh Jim, welcome home! I will call the children in from the back garden to greet you, but after that please let's sit down to talk, and I will pour us a drink."

Nan Renouf came rushing into the room with young Arthur Anderson. The Gaudin girls followed with Marie leading two-year old Jimmy by the hand. Gaudin made a point of picking them all up and giving each a big hug before Nan led them outside again to play.

"Jim, please tell me about your trip."

"I'll tell you more about it after I tell you Steam in one form or another brought me back to London in an elapsed time that my senses cry out as impossible. I left Victoria on 18 April, and I arrived in London within the month on 14 May. When I returned from Scotland I found London knew of my leaving Victoria from a routine report arriving before I landed but no further detail. The Northern Pacific Railroad east from Seattle has not been completed. No alternative than to take the steamer *City of Panama* to San Francisco in three days on the wings of the northwest wind. I traveled to New York by railroad connections across the United States in eight days. What an adventure! I saw herds of buffalo and cowboys and cattle west of Chicago. The Cunard Line steamer took me across the North Atlantic Ocean in only ten days. In

London I found the opportunity to link up with Captain Spring, who took me by steam train to inspect sailing vessels for sale as far away as Glasgow and Edinburgh. A photographer took our portraits, but I didn't buy a copy because I didn't like the way I looked. Too tired and face flushed. You'd not recognize me."

"Jim, your letter from Glasgow told me about your new barque, so please tell me, WHAT are we going to do now?"

"I will get to that, Inez. Please give me a moment."

"Oh Jim. I never had any doubt you would land on your feet again."

"It's all settled now," he said. "As Spring put up half the money, we share ownership of the barque *Rover of the Seas* registered out of the Port of Sunderland, much the same as the *Lampson*, but not as fancy."

"I am so excited for you, Jim, but is she as good a ship as the *Lady Lampson?*"

"We will have to see about her ability to carry sail. In all other respects she is a twin of the *Lady Lampson*, built from the same plans and drawings by shipyards across the bay from each other and put into service by different owners at much the same time. The *Rover* has had a successful ten-year run of voyages in the South Pacific, which is where I expect to see the *Lady Lampson* sailing under new ownership and flying the Stars and Stripes. If superstitious, the new owner who buys her at auction in San Francisco will not change her name."

"Oh, is there such a superstition?"

"Yes Inez, the superstition persists despite the precedent set by Sir Francis Drake, who changed the name of his *Pelican* to the *Golden Hinde* to no bad effect part way through his epic voyage around the World 300 years ago."

"When will we see the new barque?"

"I don't know. If the weather stays good on our departure, I may be able to swing south to show off my new ship to those who knew me if I can pass close to Gorey to back the main yard to stop to say hello. But of course, you, being so far inland, would have no way of knowing when to ride down the road to the coast to catch sight of us. Perhaps I can find a way to tell you when to watch for us. What fun it would be for me to send a boat in to pick you all up to go out to see the ship before I go on with the voyage."

"Where is the money coming from to pay for the refit, Jim?"

"Captain Spring's money goes to that, Inez. Investing in some of the Lampson's cargo and insuring it put money in my pocket. The insurers' loss, not mine. The insurance and Edwin Renouf's advances have kept my head above water and paved the way to my salvation."

"What will the future hold for you, I mean to say, what cargo will you carry now, and where, Jim?"

"We will never know what the future holds, Inez. But what are you doing for enough money to get by with? I have not been able to send you much the last while."

"Jim, the Renouf property has rental income coming in, part of which the trustee of the estate pays me to preserve the property and care for Nan. Edwin has done well and has told the trustee to send no money to him. We have chickens and a vegetable garden."

Gaudin and Agnes remained silent for a time.

"Inez, in truth I am not facing the best of times, but I must tell you more about my petition to the Governor and Committee of the Honourable Company. I sent in the petition outside normal channels on 14 June. Already this led to me being called to an important business meeting in London last week. I told them about my *Rover* in the shipyard for loading, and I put on my best face to charm them. I told them I stood ready to carry any cargo they or their friends in the business community might see fit to entrust to me. So far, no bites and no promises have been made. They may keep me dangling to see me ready to take a cargo for less money than I should charge, but I cannot wait for them. I have lines out to catch cargoes from anyone who will hire my vessel."

"I would be interested to see the petition. Have you a copy of it?"

"I have in my pocket a copy of my letter to the Secretary of the Honourable Company in London, which I won't read out to you: you will not understand the submissive form of language in it. You will understand I must put on the humble touch of the forelock attitude these lordly men who run the affairs of the Company in London demand. I petitioned the Committee to order I need not pay back the advance made to me by Chief Factor Charles in Victoria for travel expenses homewards. Happily, the Company has allowed me that advance of 300 pounds to get me back to London. That is good news, Inez. Otherwise I would have had to pay it back."

Agnes spoke again, after a long pause.

"If they don't give you cargoes at the present time, perhaps they will have need for you later?"

"Perhaps, but perhaps not. I must tell you I may be away for a long time on my first voyage in the *Rover*. I don't know what ports we will be touching at. The *Rover* may be a tramp looking for cargoes to bring back to Liverpool or London. Steam has taken over the Trans-Atlantic trade to Canada. Not the way I'd like it, but that's the way it is, unfortunately, my dear wife."

"How long can you stay, Jim?"

"I have much to do when I return to London in three days. The *Rover* lies there now undergoing the last of refit and hauling-out for renewal of copper sheathing on the hull. She will be ready for loading by the end of July. I expect to be in the Channel outbound not later than the end of September, but I may not be back to see you for a year and a half or more."

"Oh, that's such a long time for you to be away from us, Jim."

"Yes, but with luck, I will be back sooner: this whole business of shipowner comes with stress and conflict. Just one item for me to mention: I could not leave the barque moored in a London Dock waiting for cargo to arrive alongside for fear of the cost for wharfage. I can now understand the problems that faced Captain Herd in dealing with conflicting demands at least expense. And if I am late getting the ship into dock the Dock Master charges demurrage on freight taking up warehouse space in the meantime. As you can imagine I did some fancy juggling to get the hauling-out work done and finished for the tug to come to tow us into the Dock for loading at just the right time."

"This IS going to be a new kind of life for you, Jim, and for me, too. As you say, your first voyage and return may take you to parts of the World you do not know yet. How exciting for you!"

"The foreign-going part of it I will enjoy, Inez."

"You may be away from us for a long time, but it won't make any difference to our plans to move to live in Victoria when Edwin can sell the Renouf property, will it Jim?"

"Do you remain set on the move, Inez?"

"Yes, Jim, as soon as you can arrange it. The trustee will sell this property to pay Edwin on him reaching 21. We would have to move somewhere else when a new owner comes."

"You can rely on my promise to take you back in 1881 or as soon after that as I can, my dear."

"Until then, you have me living on high dry ground in a fine climate. A good little village lies nearby at Maufant. The winters are mild. I have a good growing season for vegetables in the garden. Dairy food comes to the door from neighbours for sale at good prices. The island economy recovers well from difficult times in the early Seventies. The children and I do well. I still love to bake bread and other good things to eat. The neighbours are good to us. Don't worry about us, dear man. Do go out with the children while I find something for supper tonight."

Later that evening Jim whispered he had put her in a difficult position by bringing her to live in Jersey. He had not known until too late of his parents' plan to move out of Croix au Maître to become part of the old stone household at La Maîtrerie.

"I suppose," he said, "they thought they would be helping out."

"Yes, and for that I should not be too critical, Jim, but it did put me on tenterhooks to keep in Jane's good graces. After all, it was her house."

"Of course, you have hit the nail on the head: I put you in sister-in-law Jane's house and she might have felt she was no longer head of her own house with two other women, one her mother-in-law, in the kitchen."

"When I decided to pack up and sail away with you after little more than a year in Jersey, Jim," she said, "I am sure they were rocked. I might have put up with your sister Marie's cheering me on, but I found my fur trade French embarrassing in comparison to everyone else's ease in the language. They must have thought it rude of me, but I could not help it. I did what I thought was best."

"Don't be too ready to take the blame, Agnes."

"Although the island's size should make us feel like neighbours, Jim, I have been living far enough away from them that I cannot walk over to see them; but, remember, they do not come to see me."

After a long silence Jim said he felt much to blame for the whole unhappiness, and that he looked to a better life in Victoria when they arrived back in Canada.

"I am so sorry I did not make it work, Jim, but won't you take the children with you when you say goodbye to your father and mother? You will have to get a ride to go there. If you want, I will go with you to show we two have a life together. They are getting on in years, and you and they might not see each other again."

"Yes, Agnes, we will go together with the children tomorrow morning before you go away for another long time."

18

THE SINKING 1885

First news of the sinking came from a sailing vessel arriving in Valparaiso from Europe on 31 December 1885. The master of that vessel informed the Lloyd's Agent in Valparaiso, who, in turn, sent a telegram immediately to Lloyd's London by the cable connection from South America to Europe. The mystery remained how news of the sinking on 5 December off the Falklands with no other vessel in sight could have passed across the waters as if by jungle drums.

Agnes, now 36, with four girls and a boy at home in Victoria, had long dreaded a knock on the door with word her husband's ship had sunk at sea. The first she heard of the sinking came in a handwritten note from the Manager of Welch, Rithet's office the day after New Year's Day 1886: the *Rover of the Seas* had foundered, but all aboard reached safety in the Falkland Islands.

She picked up a copy of the local Victoria Colonist newspaper next day to read aloud to the family gathered around her.

A cablegram from Liverpool received yesterday by Welch, Rithet announces the total loss of the barque Rover of the Seas in the South Atlantic; but states the master and crew were saved and had put in to the Falkland Islands. These meagre details are all that at present have been obtained. The Rover of the Seas left this port in September bound for Liverpool. She was chartered by Welch, Rithet & Co and had 16,696 cases of salmon aboard. The cargo was fully insured as was the vessel, which was owned by her master Captain Gaudin, whose home is in this city. The cablegram suggests the date of the news of the sinking as January 1st but this must be in error as no telegraphic communication between the Falklands and Montevideo, and it takes fast sailing packets about 14 days to cover the distance between the two points. The loss of the vessel therefore probably occurred in the sec-

ond week of December. For the past five or six years the Rover of the Seas has been plying between Victoria and London, and she was in perfectly sea-worthy condition when she started on her passage to Liverpool. Observers suppose that meeting with heavy weather off Cape Horn, she sprang several leaks from severe straining and had to be abandoned; and that the officers and crew were either picked up by a passing vessel or reached the Islands in their own boats.

For months before the commencement of the voyage Gaudin anchored out his vessel in the deeper water fronting on the James Bay portion of Victoria's Inner Harbour to save wharfage expense. The vessel maintained a deck watch and lamped out at night to warn vessels steaming in the harbour. Gaudin did Piloting work, keeping the *Rover of the Seas* ready to sail. Finally, Welch, Rithet chartered the vessel in September to take a cargo of canned salmon to Liverpool.

Laden and ready to go, but lacking a second mate and short on crew, the *Rover* sailed out to sea from Victoria on 28 September bound for Liverpool with the cargo, topped up with 12 tons of heavy canvas bags of bones destined for a glue factory.

Her husband bade his wife and family farewell on what turned out to be the final voyage of the *Rover of the Seas*. Agnes knew sailing at the end of September would take the barque out into the Pacific at a time of stormy weather off the rugged coasts of Washington, Oregon, and California. He did not tell her sailing in September would run the risk of encountering an early onset of the hurricane season in the South Pacific.

Over yet another Christmas with him away at sea Agnes agonized what might be happening to him. Her brother James Anderson called by often to see to her comfort and to bring good cheer. Agnes at the piano sang hymns for the family about the Eternal Father who was Strong to Save Those in Peril on the Sea, which put everybody into a sombre mood. They all joined in walking the distance to regular services at nearby St. Saviour's Anglican Church in the locality becoming known as Victoria West.

****

On rounding the last point of land in the ship's boats, Gaudin looked up when one of the men gave a shout, *Ahoy! There's the Royal Navy!* The sight of the warship in the harbour at Port Stanley reminded him of the show of hostility toward him by the Senior Officer of the Naval Base at Esquimalt in 1878. The memory left a sour taste in Gaudin's mouth and did little to soothe his mind.

Coming closer, they rowed the boats to avoid passing too close to the sloop-of-war H.M.S. *Ruby* at anchor in the harbour. The sight of the white ensign at the stern made Gaudin realize that the Navy would busy itself to initiate a formal inquiry into the sinking before he could leave to return home. The Laws of England required the nearest Senior Royal Navy officer to arrange for the conduct of an Inquiry into the circumstances of any sinking of a British Registered Vessel for report to the Board of Trade in England. Ship owners cannot be allowed to sink their ships and claim against their marine insurance underwriters for a contrived loss by committing the criminal offence of Barratry. The Inquiry Report could lead to arrest and prosecution in London's Old Bailey.

He settled the crew into a Church of England Hall at Port Stanley for their first night's board and lodging before he and the Mate followed directions to find their way across the grass to Stanley House to report their arrival. He found the news spread quickly by word of mouth on the Falkland Islands. Next day everyone in town knew Captain Gaudin and his crew had arrived in town, and that they had come in the ship's boats up the eastern outer coastline of the Falklands to Port Stanley over three days and nights of sailing and rowing.

Before crawling into a cot to sleep Gaudin asked for a cable to be sent to Agnes at home in Victoria, but found he could not: the Falkland Islands had no cable connection. The next mail boat schooner sailing regularly between Port Stanley and Montevideo Uruguay, some 800 nautical miles distant to the north, would not arrive in Port Stanley for another two weeks at the earliest, which meant he must wait until Montevideo before he could send a cable home. Gaudin's nerves jangled as he tried to sort out the fix he was in. And would he arrive home in Victoria before any letter? And what will happen to him when the Board of Inquiry sits? And what expense will he incur in the meantime? These thoughts kept going through his mind as he tossed and turned trying to sleep that night. Despite the slow-moving appearance of the place, he felt sure the Royal Navy would move to convene a hearing where he would be required to testify.

At breakfast next morning in Stanley House the Colonial Manager and Lloyd's Agent, Mister Bull by name, spoke to confirm that the Official Inquiry would be held before the end of the month. He went on to report news of his crew.

"Gaudin, I am happy to tell you that members of your crew have already been offered employment here on sheep ranches. The ranchers will be clamouring for them. Some have already gone to spend Christmas at a ranch to see how they like it. Word has come back of their appetite for the fresh roasted lamb meat put before them, which they devoured with a will. The people in the Patagonian Mission vessel have taken the others for Christmas in the mission vessel at anchor in the harbour. Without a doubt they will be asked to work in the activities of the Mission Station, which is located in the islands north of Cape Horn. Being boatmen, their services will be highly valued."

"Mister Bull, please tell me, what will you do to see that those with families in the Old Country can be repatriated, sir?"

"Well, if they communicate that desire to me, be assured they will then become my responsibility, but we may encounter delay in arranging their return to England."

"I will rely on you for that, but please tell me about the steamer passenger service from Montevideo northwards. Mister Ferey and I will wish to travel back to Victoria where we each have family."

"I may not be entirely up to date on this, Gaudin: the British Consul in Montevideo will know what to say to you when you arrive there," Bull said. "A steam packet runs from there to Rio and then another steam packet runs direct to New York_____ You will find hurricane season over. Once the Packet gets past Cape Hatteras you will be free of any difficulty. But how will you go on to the West Coast of North America from there?"

"By railroad to Portland then to Seattle, unless the railroad over the Stampede Pass has been completed to enable direct to Seattle. If I can reach Seattle I can find my way 75 miles home to Victoria, British Columbia in Canada. I crossed the Continent from California west to east in 1878. Travel by railroads coast-to-coast can be done in a week of travel when all goes well."

"I will hand you a letter addressed to the British Consul in Montevideo to explain the circumstances. Please ask him to help you make hotel and travel arrangements. The schooner mail packet from Montevideo won't sail until after Christmas or arrive here until some time in mid-January. You and Mister Ferey can obtain passage in the schooner to Uruguay. In the meantime you both will have time to assist the Inquiry to make a report on the circumstances of the sinking of your ship."

****

On spying his Captain sitting on a rock and looking out to sea, George R. Ferey walked down to the beach to join him. Ferey asked if he might speak.

"Good morning, sir. I have been thinking such luck for us after the sinking, the weather holding as it did. We followed your commands to come coasting up the shoreline in strong tidal currents over a hundred miles from the sinking. The sails you had us rig for the boats before the sinking and the wind and the tide current every night helped us."

"Yes, Ferey, but all that, and the good fortune of the sinking in good weather close to a place of safety make it look like I intended to sink the ship where we did. I fear the Lloyd's Agent may suspect I had a plan to sink close to habitation with a personal escape route back to Victoria in my hip pocket."

"What do you mean, sir?"

"Just look back to the fire on the *Rover* tied up alongside the wharf in Victoria at 6 a.m. on 7 January last."

"What's that got to do with it, sir?"

"Plain as the nose on my face if you think about it, Ferey. The fire could have destroyed the *Rover* had you not put it out. Some people in town bantered I set the fire to collect the insurance. Her useful life had ended. People in town knew she had come back from a long profitless voyage under the captain I hired to sail coal from Nanaimo to San Francisco and onwards with a general cargo to Queenstown, Ireland."

"But sir, you and your friends know you sent the *Rover* in for shipyard work at Nelson Dock before returning. No one doubts that you had the best interests of the ship at heart."

"Yes, and that work cost a pretty penny. On her return to Victoria the *Rover* lay at anchor in the harbour for nine months without a cargo to carry in a time of a bustling economy in British Columbia. What more does a prosecution need to establish a motive to sink the ship and claim on the insurance?"

"But sir, by September you lined up the cargo of cattle bones and cans of salmon for this last voyage: doesn't that show you had confidence in your ship?"

"It's what people think, Ferey. I had not lined up a cargo in England for the return passage. What would I have done had the ship not sunk? Old wooden sailing vessels like the *Rover* are now a glut on the market and face sales forced on shipowners to pay mounting ship's bills."

Gaudin went on again after a long silence.

"Bear with me, Ferey: I can add another motive. Everybody knows the arrival of the railroad across Canada next year will drive the last nail into the coffin. People will say I had every motive to sink the ship and collect on the insurance. I say again, the useful life of the *Rover* had ended. Neither I, nor the ship made money on that voyage to Ireland."

"But sir, you worked as Pilot bringing deep-sea vessels in and out of Victoria in Pilotage."

"Yes, Ferey, two years with little income to me."

"But sir, let me go back to the fire in January. You would not have set fire to the vessel because the insurance applied only to perils of the sea on the voyage that had ended with Captain Dolbell's arrival in Esquimalt Harbour. The fire broke out after the tug towed her around to moor into Victoria."

"Yes Ferey, that's right, but who on the street knows that? We have now lost the ship from a thoroughgoing *Peril of the Sea*, for which there IS insurance; not just a fire for which there was no insurance coverage. The knives are going to be out for me when I make my claim to be paid the insurance money."

"You are too hard on yourself sir."

"Ferey, even if the Inquiry absolves me, I will remain with the task of convincing the insurance underwriters. They can decide to deny their liability to pay the claim and sit back for me to put a claim through the courts. My reputation and the payment of my insurance claim may lie unresolved for years. I have no idea how it will turn out. A dozen years ago I was the toast of the town in Victoria, a town now grown to such an extent with newcomers, I no longer recognize it. I doubt I have public support any longer."

"Sir, you mistake it."

"And I will tell you this Ferey, I could not escape the feeling that our vessel slipping out of the harbour in silence and unseen in the dead of night last September will make it seem to others the ship didn't want to be seen. The newspaper reporter does not seek story copy from me nowadays. Our departure from harbour last September would have gone unremarked upon in the newspaper_____.""

"Don't keep thinking of the worst, sir. Things will get better if you put a smile on your face. People will think you ARE guilty if you don't."

A uniformed Royal Marine came up to Gaudin in the street the day before Christmas and handed him what he said was a subpoena. Gaudin opened the folder it came in and read the enclosure: -

To Captain James Thomas Gaudin: Your attendance is required to give evidence at the Inquiry into the causes of the sinking of the British–registered barque the Rover of the Seas in accordance with law by a Board of Inquiry consisting of E.P. Brooks Esq. P.M.; Lieut. Thring, R.N.; and Capt. J. N. C. Seemans, Nautical Assessor. The hearing will open at 10 o'clock in the forenoon on 27 December 1885 at Stanley House in Port Stanley, F.I. and will continue until all of the evidence may be heard.

That evening at dinner with Lloyd's Agent Bull, Gaudin put on his smiling face to engage him in conversation.

"We have always sailed by with the Falklands in the distance, never landing," he said. "Please tell me something about them."

"Captain, the Falkland Islands comprise sparsely populated sheep farming settlements of 1,800 persons not yet connected by telegraph cable to the rest of the British Empire. We rely on the sailing mail schooner to bring mail from Montevideo. Did you know the colony has a Church of England Bishop whose charge extends to the entire Roman Catholic Continent of South America?"

"No, I didn't, but I daresay he has little constituency or presence over there."

"Yes, precious little. We have a Governor appointed from London, a detachment of Royal Marines, a Government Dockyard and marine ways, a Chief of Police with a force of constables who came seconded from the Royal Irish Constabulary, a Magistrate, a Gaol, a Church, and a Government in London that keeps ignoring a diplomatic note from the Argentine Republic claiming ownership of the Islands it insists on naming the Malvinas."

"Oh, the Malvinas, such a history to the place?"

"Yes Captain, I can spend another evening with you on that subject."

"I will look forward to that, sir."

"Gaudin, please tell me something of the weather wisdom you gained in your sailing days."

"The way you say that sir, makes it sound ominous, as if to say my sailing days are over."

"Think nothing of it, Gaudin. I just supposed you would now

consider going into Steam, but please go on. I do want to hear what you say about the weather."

"I will not go into Steam unless I must. I have sailed past the Horn going and coming a dozen and more times. My plucky wife sailed with me four times around the Horn. Experience led me to make summertime passages for the longer hours of daylight to sail through the Strait of Le Maire, also because it will mean winter arrivals in Victoria. I mean to say winter storm winds at the higher latitudes in both hemispheres tend to disperse the fogs and enable me to keep my vessel moving under sail when making landfall."

"Our mail schooner captain from Montevideo tells us of seasonal storms on the way to and from the Falklands."

"That does not surprise me, sir. In passages both ways past Cape Horn in Southern Hemisphere spring and fall, we encounter big storms in the latitudes south of the Tropic of Capricorn in both oceans."

"Is that phenomenon confined to the Southern Hemisphere?"

"No sir. Similarly, in the Northern Hemisphere often we can run into heavy storm weather off the Oregon and California coasts in the spring and fall, more or less coinciding with the equinox dates."

"I heard you speak to Mister Ferey of the *higher latitudes*. Some have trouble understanding the significance of the expression."

"Yes sir. The Equator is zero° latitude and the South Pole is 90° South. Likewise the North Pole is 90° North. The passage to ice in the sea off the Horn will take us south to the higher latitude of 57° South latitude. 'Lower' latitude would seem more apt, but no one ever says that."

"Yes Gaudin, 57° South latitude tells us how much ice and cold lies between the Horn and '90 South' at the Pole, but let us talk of other things: you will be here over Christmas. Are you a Churchman, Gaudin? Will you attend the Church of England services over Christmas with me?"

"As a mariner I have little occasion to attend church, and I am more often at sea on Christmas Day. At sea, I note the occasion of Sundays and Christmas Day for the crew at the mandatory divine service on board. But yes, of course, I will go to the services with you."

"Am I correct to say the crew is not called on Sundays to work on board ship?"

"Yes, that's correct, except all men understand the need to answer the call to be on deck in the ship's interest."

****

Two days after Christmas, Gaudin, Ferey, and all of his crew filed into the entrance hall at Stanley House. Two uniformed Royal Marines stood guard at and within the door. A cold wind outside stirred up whitecaps on the angry grey water. The fire in the fireplace in the large entrance hall burned bright to warm the backsides of the members of the Board of Inquiry seated behind the long table. Mister Brooks called the proceedings to order at 10 o'clock sharp. Packed in with others, standing room only, the members of the *Rover's* crew assembled to watch. The Clerk handed Gaudin the Bible and called on him to testify under oath.

"James Thomas Gaudin, the evidence you shall give this Inquiry shall be the truth, the whole truth, and nothing but the truth, so help you God. Do you so swear?"

"I do."

Mister Brooks began by saying each of the members of the Board may be asking questions but first Gaudin could make a statement if he wished.

"Please speak slowly," he said, "so we can write down what you say."

"Yes, I will make a statement, sir. My Mate Mister Ferey is here also to make a statement after you have finished with me. I was the master and sole owner of the barque *Rover of the Seas*. I hold an Ordinary Master's certificate No 22,329; it was lost with the ship. I brought off my personal journal and the official logbook, but all the ship's papers went down with the ship. We had no time to gather them in the dark. At the time of the loss I was bound on a passage from Victoria, British Columbia to Liverpool with a cargo of 16,696 cases of canned salmon and 12 tons of bones, in all about 636 tons deadweight. At the date of sailing on 28 September this year, the *Rover of the Seas* had been staunch, tight and well found in every respect. I had every expectation I could find a cargo at a price to take back to Victoria from London as I had on previous voyages."

Lieutenant Thring, the Captain of H. M. S. *Ruby*, asked the first question.

"Captain, please state the events of the day of the sinking."

"On nearing shelter in the Falklands on 5 December 1885 with water rising in the hold, the pumps ceased to function at two o'clock in the morning and the ship began to fill fast. The seas washed over the deck ankle-deep. The ship moved in a sluggish manner and without any of her usual lightness of foot. I gave the Mate orders to secure the wheel, let the halyards loose, and divide the crew into the ship's two boats to be put over the side. The Mate had already broken into a case of salmon cans and gathered some bags of bread from the galley stores for survival on shore. I did not tarry to go below to get my sextant, which I had used for twenty years. I knew the ship's position because we were heading for Port Stanley to repair the pumps. The ship's papers and most of our clothing went down with the ship."

"Please state the ship's position when she went down and the weather and sea conditions prevailing."

"Our position lay in the open ocean 12-miles due south of the Sea Lion Islands off the southeast coast of the East Falkland Islands. The weather and the state of the swell on the open ocean you would term as unexceptional, it being mid-summer in the Southern Hemisphere with only a light breeze out of the northwest. We took to the boats in the middle of the night, but nightlight in these latitudes not dark at this time of year. We could see high points of low-lying land to the north beyond Sea Lion Island. As we drew off in the boats I heard the loud sighing sound and the roar, yes, a roar; then a shrieking sound coming from behind us. We all looked back through tears and saw our beautiful little ship go right down by the head and disappear under in moments."

After a long pause with silence in the room, Mister Brooks asked a question.

"For the record please state the number of men in the boats when you abandoned the vessel."

"Twelve of us in the boats. The Mate and I ran the ship with a crew three men short."

And he gave this answer to another question.

"Being this far south, the visibility remained good all night as we sailed or rowed north in light winds out of the southwest. Next mid-afternoon we made it to land on Bleaker Island to spend the night shivering on a beach of smooth pebbles the size of rocks. Not a pleasant lie for us on a beach littered with shattered ship's timbers and planking driftwood from vessels sunk or wrecked on shores of the Great Southern Ocean. We often catch sight of that kind of drift on the water, especially in the Great Southern Ocean where few opportunities for flotsam to fetch ashore. I will carry on. Resenting our intrusion on the beach, sea lions bellowed and barked and kept us awake. We reached agreement to put to the boats again in the dark. Whenever the tide current or a back eddy favoured we sailed, but more often we rowed the boats up the eastern coastline with not a soul in sight on the low rocky barrens, relieved only by the rocky little peaks inland, which poked up here and there. After another long day in the boats we took to the shore where we saw a stream coming out on the beach. We rushed in to drink the water from it. We found geese and goslings for the taking, made a fire with a flintlock using dry driftwood from high on the shore, and we ate canned salmon and cooked goose meat by the fire to keep warm and dry. Our cook used his thumbs to pluck off the feathers for roasting. We washed by the stream and dried ourselves off from the heat of the fire and made ourselves ready to be seen at Port Stanley. Then we sailed in the night wind. Next day we drew abeam of the cape at the harbour entrance and turned our boats into the harbour. On 19 December we hauled the boats up on the beach, and I reported the sinking and our arrival to the Colonial Manager and Lloyd's Agent at Stanley House. We all were a weary lot, suffering from the feed we'd made ourselves by the fire the night previous."

Lieutenant Thring asked Gaudin a question concerning when the leak became noticed.

"On departing Cape Flattery at the end of September, we encountered strong headwinds and high seas as we drove south," Gaudin began, "but the vessel made little water into the hold despite the plunging of the bows into the seas. The ship pumped every four hours, taking only 20 minutes to half an hour to finish pumping her empty. On coming into the Tropics the ship's planking took up again to stanch the flow coming in, and we only had to pump her out twice a day, morning and evening, taking 10 to 15 minutes to pump dry. All went well until the beginning of December when we fell in with a strong southeast gale. We were well down the coast of Chile in latitude 50° South 95° West. The storm lasted for four days to oppose us from heading in the direction of Cape Horn. Notwithstanding the leak, I was not tempted to turn back to steer for Valparaiso. Despite the American experience in Port Stanley for extortionate ship repair costs, I intended to proceed there to make repairs to the pumps by our own resources."

Mister Brooks interrupted Gaudin.

"I don't think you are being fair to the people in the harbour, Captain. The American experience to which you refer stemmed from the California 1849 Gold Rush when in one 12-month period, 777 sailing vessels put in to Port Stanley for repairs and provisioning, overwhelming the facilities at the port. The demand far exceeded the supply with predictable results not likely to be repeated."

"Doubtless you are correct, sir, but news of the experience of others who needed repair and re-provisioning made me wary and desirous of doing the work ourselves."

"Please go on Captain Gaudin."

"I am aware that some might criticize me for not putting back to Valparaiso, but I did not want to take the time. Captains know that some vessels having done so, never get to put to sea again for one reason or another. The wind and weather turned to favour our continuing on around the Horn to put in to Port Stanley, and we almost made it. We could not determine the number of inches of water being made below in the sounding well because the vessel rolled badly most of the time with the wind coming from behind. We pumped every two hours, and now it was taking 20 to 25 minutes to suck dry. I noticed pieces of cement coming up with the water to choke the pumps. It came up in pieces like pebbles, some an inch in diameter. Fine weather, light winds and smooth seas followed. The ship took up again and made little water, but we kept sounding the wells every two hours as we rounded the Horn. Sometimes she would make two or three inches every four hours. Many days passed with the ship making hardly any water at all. On the day before the sinking we pumped her dry at 8 p.m. and at midnight the Mate coming on watch reported seven inches in the well. As the pumps were sucking dry at 6 ¾ inches, I decided not to pump her when so little to be gained. I did not want to take a man off lookout for land I expected to see in the morning. At 2 a.m. on 16 December the Mate turned out the hands and roused me to report two fathoms of water in the well. I gave the order to let the halyards fly and get the boats out. Everyone knew what to do to move with speed to abandon ship. Yes, we'd had drills to deal with such an event."

Captain Seemans spoke again.

"Please go on to tell us who owned the ship and what insurance you had."

"Yes Captain, I have been the sole owner of the ship for the last two years. Before that, Captain Spring and I registered as joint owners to save the fees of a solicitor for a ship's mortgage. I became sole owner as soon as I paid off his advances by way of loan to buy and refit the vessel. I have been Master on all of her voyages except the voyage to Liverpool, London, and back to Victoria through 1884-1885, but please understand I exercised an owner's close oversight on that voyage."

After a moment of silence in the room, Captain Seemans spoke again.

"That last answer requires me to ask a question about recent shipyard work on the vessel. Please tell us of any such work done in some detail, Captain Gaudin."

"Yes, I ordered the vessel brought out at Nelson Dock in early summer of 1884. The Master Captain Dolbell reported the pumps encountered difficulty in keeping up with water leaking into the hold during the last part of the passage from San Francisco to Queenstown Ireland. I ordered her sent in ballast to London to load cargo for Victoria, but not until I had the planking recaulked and the copper sheathing renewed at Nelson Dock."

"Was the vessel insured against perils of the sea, and have you any explanation for the sudden leak that caused her to founder within the hour?"

"The ship is insured in San Francisco for $15,000," Gaudin answered. "I am not aware of insurance on the cases of canned salmon cargo. I carried the bones without any insurance. I cannot account for the ship springing such a sudden leak."

The Chairman of the Board of Inquiry asked Gaudin to stand down and called on Mister Ferey to testify.

"I was the Chief Officer on the late barque the *Rover of the Seas*. I joined the vessel in London in mid-March 1880 and have been in her ever since. On leaving Victoria last September the ship was in good condition. She made little water. We had rough weather for a week on departure. Nine inches of water in the well in twelve hours in rough weather and seven in fine weather. After crossing the Line we had strong South East Trades until the end of November, when came the bad weather, southeast gales for most of a week, the well showing two inches of water an hour. Afterwards we had fine weather with the ship making seven to nine inches of water every 12 hours; the water being pumped out rusty and with cement."

And in answer to another question,

"On this vessel Captain Gaudin had me take the Watch from midnight to 6 a.m. and he took the earlier watch to midnight. The two of us ran the vessel without a second mate. Water coming up from below through the scuppers ended any pleasant thoughts I may have had that night. I moved forward to back the main yard to stop the vessel dead in the water. I sounded the well and found two fathoms of water in the hold. I called all hands on deck and called the Captain to tell him. He gave orders to let the halyards fly and get the boats out as the ship was sinking. We just had time enough to get the boats out. The water rushed knee-deep over the decks before we finished doing that. We took to the boats. I saw the ship go down. I saved some of my effects, but I lost my certificate and personal logbook."

Lieutenant Thring asked Ferey how the cargo had been stowed.

"Stevedores stowed the hold at Victoria before I could get to the vessel to take charge of the loading. We could not get down to the bottom of the hold where the pumps took suction after they stowed the cargo. Looking back on it, we may have been unable to reach the bottom of the hold when we pumped the ship during the passage."

Captain Seemans asked Ferey whether the ship had watertight compartments.

"The cargo hold has no watertight compartments," Ferey testified. "The pumps were in good working order, but were the old-fashioned type with wooden handles, not the newer China pumps with square shaped pallets."

Another question followed for Ferey to answer.

"It was fine weather at the time of the sinking. In the boats we landed at two places, Bleaker Island and at another place closer to Stanley with a creek coming down to the beach."

That ended the questioning.

"Does anyone else in the room wish to testify?" Mister Brooks called out in a loud voice. "No other man speaking out, I bring the hearing to a close. I will confer with the other members of the Board of Inquiry. Please remain silent while we go into the next room to confer before making a decision."

Mister Brooks came back in ten minutes to call the Inquiry to order again and to read aloud from a piece of writing paper.

"After investigating all of the evidence, we have decided that the leak necessitated deserting the ship for the preservation of life and no blame is to be attached to the Master or the Chief Officer and crew, all having done their duty under the circumstances prevailing. We will send in our Report accordingly."

The members of the Board, attended by the two Marines, stood and strode out of the room. The Navy Officer board member, Lieutenant Thring stopped on his way out to speak to Gaudin.

"Please accept my invitation to dine tonight, Captain. I will send my gig to pick you up at five this afternoon."

A night of good food, drink, and jovial talk followed aboard the warship. The ship's officers, all younger than Gaudin, joined in the talk, showing him a deference he had not expected.

Lieutenant Thring started it off by asking Gaudin to speak of his voyaging in the *Rover* in years since 1878.

"Please tell us more about the Pacific Northwest and while you are at it, tell us something about where you sailed the *Rover of the Seas* during the years you had her. Please give us a good idea of what the master of a merchantman vessel has been facing when sailing to that part of the World."

"I will be pleased to tell you about the passages I made. My ship and I have had a happy time together with a willing crew, but be forewarned, some of this account will involve talk of my family. They are all close to my mind at this time. They will be wondering how my ship is fairing on the voyage. My wife Agnes will not even now have heard our ship has sunk. I may arrive home before my letter."

"Tell us something about your sailing into the Straits of Juan de Fuca. I will unroll an Admiralty Chart for you to point to if you wish."

As Lieutenant Thring had trouble pronouncing the name of the Strait, Gaudin pointed to the opening of the Strait on the chart.

"The locals pronounce the name as the Strait of WAW-N – De'FEW-KAH. The opening to the Strait is comparable to the width of the opening of the Strait of le Maire, which leads on to Cape Horn. The tidal currents in Juan de Fuca are strong, but not as strong as in the Strait of Le Maire. The best way of telling you about the *Rover's* first passage to Victoria under my command comes from the newspaper clipping of the *copy* I provided to the Colonist newspaper reporter on our arrival in early March 1879: I can read it out to you from my notebook."

"Please go on, Captain."

" 'The barque *Rover of the Seas* left the West India Docks on 28 September 1878 and passed through the Downs on 2 October_____. She had favourable winds out of the English Channel, but met with severe gales out from the southwest off the Bay of Biscay and the coast of Portugal. Crossed the Line on 2 November_____. To the southward of the River Plate, the ship encountered strong gales and high seas for 12 days, which impeded progress and washed away t'gallant bulwarks, headgear and all movables on deck. Passed through the Strait of Le Maire on 21 December and Cape Horn four days after; off the Cape with fair weather generally; used up only 17 days from 50 degrees south latitude in the Atlantic to 50 south in the Pacific, where the barque met fine summer weather throughout; crossed the Line on 2 February and made the Strait of Juan de Fuca 18-days later. Entering on the flood tide the ship working its way up the Strait as far as Pillar Point with a 148-day passage almost in grasp, the wind fell calm. In the dark, the ebb current drove the ship back to Neah Bay, which is close to Cape Flattery. A wind sprang up against the ship from the east and increased to a hard gale. At 3 a.m. the wind shifted suddenly to southward in a violent squall attended by vivid flashes of lightning and peals of thunder, the yards and mastheads illuminated by corposants during the whole time. The wind turning to southwest at 5 a.m., the ship ran swiftly with the wind behind to a position near abeam Race Rocks in three hours.'"

"At that time," Gaudin said, "the wind backed to head us, making it impossible for the ship to weather Race Rocks Lighthouse."

A pause followed as the men passed the marine chart between them.

"I took my option to turn downwind to nip into and through Race Passage, which lies between Bentinck Island and Race Rocks, and sail with the last of the flood tide. Here I will show you on the chart. I took the ship in to anchor in Esquimalt Harbour at 11.30 a.m. on Sunday 2 March 1879_____. Corposants, of course, are St Elmo's Fire. I don't know where that word came from, but that's what Captain Adamson called them."

Thring spoke to give an answer to the question Gaudin left hanging: –

"It comes from the Latin for *holy body*, or corporo sancto or something like that, a long history that goes back to ancient days of sailing in the Mediterranean. E-L-M-O is short for Anselmo, an Italian man's name."

"Not a smart passage, 151 days from the Downs," Gaudin said.

"Now that I owned my own vessel and had no rival company captains to show up, the burning desire to set sailing records ceased, just as long as I kept the ship moving with an aggressive spirit alive in my crew to fight the sea. I wanted no layabouts on deck."

"What excitement for you and your crew to come into port in Victoria," Thring remarked. "You must have been a popular man in town then."

"Well, yes, perhaps, except for the Pilot, Captain Pamphlett, whose services I spurned. Pilotage is not compulsory yet at Victoria. But I am sure the report in the newspaper excited the townspeople who knew me from my successful arrivals in town going back for over 10 years. Almost to a man they now welcomed me back as an old friend."

"Please tell us about your other voyages, Captain."

"The first voyage of the *Rover* under my command, which I referred to a moment ago, extended over 16 months from 28 September 1878 to 6 February 1880. Someone whose name I never came to know arranged for the Hudson's Bay Company Office in London to provide me with a goodly part of the cargo for the *Rover's* first passage to Victoria. But I could not find cargoes in Victoria to take back to London. I turned to carry coal on voyages to maintain a crew. The better weather and shore-side attractions in California kept the crew happy, and I found they did enjoy the climate."

Thring filled Gaudin's glass and asked him to keep going with the story.

Gaudin spoke again after a pause.

"I'd left the Company's employment seven years before and did not expect to get any business from them," he said. "After all, they had other sailing barques in their service, the newer *Prince Rupert* for one. For several years, my unknown benefactor kept me with cargoes from London to enable the *Rover* to continue operating in difficult times for Sail. Although my connection with the Company long severed, Lewis & Dryden, the editors of the new book on Shipping in the Pacific Northwest, tell me they classified the *Rover* as *the Hudson's Bay Trader, the Rover of the Seas*. I didn't mind the reputation as such, but it didn't pay as many bills as I would have liked. Of course, I carried some of my own cargo in addition whenever possible. I had a standing order from one of the storekeepers in Victoria to bring him as much new wholesale woolen clothing as I could find. Digging up chances like that to make money filled my pockets each time I came to Victoria from London, but I should go back to telling you about where we went. With a crew to keep in Victoria and to pay expenses, as I said, I turned to carry two cargoes of Wellington coal from Departure Bay to Wilmington, the seaport for a town inland called Los Angeles in Southern California, the first of these within a month of the *Rover's* first arrival in Victoria in early April 1879. I ordered a tug to come into the Victoria's Inner Harbour to put a line on the *Rover* and tow her to Departure Bay near

Nanaimo via the Strait of Georgia to take on the first of two shipments of 700 tons. We contrived to arrive off Race Rocks Lighthouse in time for the ebb tide and a wind to fill the sails after dropping the towline to take us out to the ocean. To do so cuts the expense for a tow all the way out to Cape Flattery. The larger sailing vessels cannot sail about as we can in the Strait. They need to be towed all the way in from the Cape, and out again, but we don't. Give me some paper, and I will draw a sketch of the route through the islands to and from Departure Bay. The steam paddlewheel tug towed us in sheltered waters to and from that place, tall evergreen trees on little islands with white shell beaches and snow-capped mountain scenery on all sides. We made that voyage to Wilmington twice over the period from April to September largely in summer fogs or haze persisting for miles offshore the American coast-line."

"We hear stories of the remarkable California climate, Captain. You must have enjoyed running down the coast with a westerly wind?"

"It's a downhill run from Cape Flattery to Wilmington when the northwesterly winds blow hard. Dana's *Four Years Before the Mast* tells of fighting that wind off the coast on a passage to San Francisco. In Wilmington I found time to go ashore to enjoy the sunny climate with shade under palm trees. At sea off the coast the northwest wind blowing did not disperse the fog, which persisted all along the coast for days. Other shipping traffic crossing our track kept us on our toes. Coming back in ballast, it's a different story. Above all, whatever be the wind on departure, it's vital to make distance well offshore the California coast before turning north to come back to make landfall to enter the Straits of Juan de Fuca. At the end of our second passage to Wilmington we took on a evil-smelling load of cattle hides destined for London. We proceeded straight out to sea to find the North East Trade Winds. Two months of sailing found us eastbound past the Horn on our way to London Docks, arriving on 6 February 1880. My Chief Officer Ferey joined the ship. Wives and families accepted yet another Christmas at sea for their men. After I arrived in London I made a fast wintertime visit by cross-channel steamer to my wife and family in Jersey. Two years had passed since I had last seen them. For the return to Victoria, the Hudson's Bay Company Office provided some cargo again, and I drummed up more to make up the full load. I sailed from London on 16 April 1880, arriving in Victoria in September, rounding the Horn in southern wintertime storms. My brother-in-law James Anderson met me in Esquimalt with a bottle of spirits and stayed aboard when the handsome new steam tug *Alexander* came to tow our ship around into Victoria's Inner Harbour under blue skies and sunshine. No mere harbour tug, this vessel has impressive seagoing lines, which her transit of the waters off Cape Flattery requires. I will draw you a sketch of her with her two raked smoke stacks. Although we sail in and out of the Strait of Juan de Fuca, we do need a tow from one harbour to another, as I have said. I conducted the passage back to England by 22 March 1881. I had been away from my wife and family in Jersey for another year and over Christmas again. I hastened from London to Jersey in time to find that the Renouf property sold and my wife and children now able to sail with me to settle in Victoria. I sailed the *Rover* from London Docks on 13 June '81 to pick them up in Jersey. If you know those waters_____?"

"Yes, Captain, I do. Go ahead."

"Perhaps you can picture us coming to anchor in Grouville Bay at the Port of Gorey on the east coast. My wife and children, my niece Nan Renouf, and young Arthur Anderson came out in boats from the shore under the walls of ancient Mont Orgueil Castle. Arthur's father sent him with me in 1876 from Victoria in the *Lady Lampson* to go to school in Jersey or in England as I could arrange for him. The boy's mother died in '72. Now I was to bring him back to talk to his father about his future. I took all of them on with their kit and baggage for a westbound passage of the Horn to Victoria. Friends waving from the shore bidding us farewell made it a momentous and exciting time, especially for the children. We arrived in Esquimalt on 15 November 1881 to unload our cargo for the Navy before being towed to the Inner Harbour. Again my wife's older brother met the ship at Esquimalt. He stayed on board during the tow around into Victoria for Agnes to enjoy a festive family homecoming occasion. Arthur's father soon called by to pick up his son, and I settled my family and Nan Renouf in a small house on View Street in town. Now a shipowner anxious to carry cargo, I left my family to miss out on Christmas again when I departed Victoria on 13 December '81 and arrived in London on 26 May 1882. These dates I hold in my mind because not a swift passage. My brother-in-law sent a telegram telling me the sad news my wife lost a son in childbirth on 10 June 1882. Again the Hudson's Bay Company Office provided me with cargo in time to sail home, departing London 1 August 1882. I began to think of taking another load of coal to California on my return to give my wife a chance to recoup her health on a voyage in the sun and sea-spray, which could strengthen her for the coming winter, but I could not get the ship back until mid-December, which ended any thought of taking her to sea at that time. But, at least I was back to my wife and children to be home with them for Christmas, our first together for many years, and our first in the Pacific Northwest. The New Year began with me sending an order for a tug to tow the *Rover* to Departure Bay in extreme winter weather to take on 700 tons of Wellington coal for me to sail to San Francisco and back to Victoria by 15 March 1883. Six weeks later the Colonist newspaper reported my *'fine little barque'* had been chartered to load Wellington coal from Departure Bay for Hong Kong and to return to Victoria with a general cargo in three months, paying passengers both ways welcome. None came forward to pay the fare, which I found not surprising in light of the alarm that developed over the news of the change in worldwide weather patterns after the eruption from Javan Krakatoa Volcano. The lack of passengers cancelled my passage to Hong Kong."

"Yes Gaudin, I served in the Royal Navy Far East Squadron at Hong Kong at the time, so I remember the red sunsets and cooler daytime temperatures. It's a good thing you didn't go. Mariners reported they believed the North East Trade Winds and the Monsoon not to be reliable."

"I had hoped to get a good sail there in the Trades and the North East Monsoon and back in the reverse Monsoon and Westerlies in the North Pacific. Shipping lay distressed at this time. I could not get another cargo in Victoria until late August 1883. By this time we had moved into our new house on Craigflower Road, and I had paid off Captain Spring to become the sole owner of the *Rover*. I found a cargo for San Francisco. My wife went with me for this trip. The tug towed us in ballast to Nanaimo to load coal in the hold to take there. Captain Dolbell shipped out as Mate to show me he could run the ship. A tug then towed us up the Fraser River to New Westminster in warm summer weather to put on a cargo of blocks of cedar for roofing shakes to carry as deck load. On the way home to Victoria from San Francisco in ballast I took the time to turn the ship's course out to sea to give my wife an exhilarating sail in the sun to show her those warmer waters before bringing her home with the *Rover* as our own private yacht. Then the ship lay in Victoria until a cargo presented. I began to work out of the port as a Pilot for deep-sea ships and hired Captain Dolbell to keep watch in the harbour and be ready to sail. With Captain Dolbell in charge, the *very* long voyage of the *Rover of the Seas* over the fall, winter and spring of 1884-85 followed after he took another cargo of coal to San Francisco. There, he loaded hides and California Redwood lumber destined to Queenstown, Ireland, arriving there on 8 March 1884. From there she proceeded for shipyard work at Nelson Dock, which I told you about at the Inquiry. She found general cargo to carry to Victoria, arriving back on 7 January 1885 after a six-month passage. No report of her being sighted left me believing she had been lost. Except for a worrisome time awaiting a report from my vessel, my wife and I had been enjoying a year of life in Victoria, picnics with the children, canoe trips on Selkirk Water and up the Gorge waterway, and climbing expeditions. I remember one to the top of scenic Mount Finlayson on a perfect day in May, returning home by nightfall with our horse and carriage."

"What happened next?"

"I continued to work as a Pilot for deep-sea ships. This brings me into the later months of the year, 1885. I had given up any hope of finding a cargo for the *Rover* when I got a line on taking canned salmon to Liverpool. And you know the story of the cargo that sent my idle vessel to sea again."

"What are your plans now, Captain?"

"With the help of the British Consul in Montevideo I will obtain passage by fast steam packet to New York. Then back to the Pacific Northwest by railroad. I will continue to find work out of Victoria as a Pilot for deep-sea traffic. The days of Sail are over, I am sorry to say."

The evening ended late with the junior officers carrying Gaudin back in the gig to the shore amid loud song and good cheer.

Sleep ended far too soon that night as he awoke in the dark with an upset stomach and troubling dreams. The account of the voyages of the *Rover of the Seas* he had given the Naval Officers that evening filled him with memories of the embrace of that remarkable woman Consuelo Cochrane.

Two years ago in January 1883 they had met again in San Francisco. He remembered their time together, and asking her, 'How did you know I was in San Francisco? And what brought you here?'

And her reply, 'Earthquake damage in Valparaiso made it impossible to carry on as I had, so I came north to this city. Months ago the newspaper reported on the sailings of an American-registered barque named the *Lady Lampson* to Honolulu and on to Australia. They did not name the captain. I thought it must be you, Jaimé, and that we could have a future together.'

After a long silence he told her, 'Kitty, so much has happened to continue to keep us apart.'

She said nothing for a long moment, but then it all came out in a torrent.

'A big man in business here told me the whole story about you; that you had lost your command, but managed to buy another ship, the *Rover of the Seas*. Ever since I have been on the lookout for that vessel to arrive in port. Finally you did come, and I sent the letter by messenger out to the ship in the harbour. But, Jaimé, I had not changed my name: why didn't you search me out after you lost the *Lady Lampson*? You and I had talked about San Francisco as a place to live, and a place for you to find a ship to sail. I sent you a letter to say I planned to come to Victoria to meet you. Why didn't you look for me after that?'

He had answered, 'Kitty, it did occur to me to look for you when I made my way through here to New York in the spring of 1878. I learned what you were doing here and could have knocked on your door, but please remember you did not come to Victoria to see me as you had written. I couldn't accept another rebuff after all I had gone through in Victoria.'

'Oh Jaimé, I would not have rejected you. I had no way to know you had received the letter I sent to you in London. I remembered you saying you wanted to make winter arrivals in Victoria. I didn't think at the time of sending you another letter. I am sorry you think me unreliable. I had been persuaded not to make a winter steamer passage up the coast to the Pacific Northwest.'

After a long silence she said, 'Besides, I had business to attend to here.'

After another long pause, he said, 'I heard about you again in Wilmington.'

She said she didn't know a place called *Wilmington* and that she had never been in such a town.

And he had answered, 'It's in Southern California, close to Los Angeles. I made two passages from Nanaimo with coal for that place. I didn't get a cargo for San Francisco until now.'

And she asked, 'Why then didn't you look for me THIS time, Jaimé? Why did I have to be the one to call you?'

He took a long moment to put words together before speaking.

'Perhaps, Kitty, the situation far too complicated for me to explain, but I will try. I sailed my wife and children from Jersey two years ago to carry out my promise to return them to settle in Victoria. Cargo for the ship required me to drop them off in Victoria and sail away before Christmas on a return passage to England. By the time I arrived in London, a cable notified me my wife lost a son in childbirth. With assistance of a good friend named Edwin Renouf, we will move to a fine new property on Craigflower Road later this year. I am obliged not to throw her over the side, now.'

'That is a terrible way of saying it, Jaimé.'

'It would seem that way to her, Kitty. I would not want to do it to her. She has always treated me with loving-kindness. I could not live with the thought of what my children and others would think of me.'

'You don't mean to tell me it did not please you for me to call you to come?'

'No, Kitty, I don't mean that at all. I remember our time in Valparaiso as if it were yesterday. You taught me the word *serendipity*. Your note to me out at the ship came like a bolt out the blue. I have been in high spirits ever since.'

'Yes, I can tell that by looking at your eyes. I know you must go back to her, Jaimé. Please tell me about your *Rover of the Seas* and what you have been doing to keep sailing in these changing times.'

'Kitty, the look on your face and in your eyes gives me a great boost in these difficult times. I now own my barque, but men today don't envy me for that. But enough of that; my crew and I made a near clipper-ship passage down the coast to arrive here last week. I made my departure from a position off Cape Flattery under clearing skies, 400 nautical miles in cold winter gales of wind out of the north and then from the northwest. With the fresh wind behind us we coasted by the dry coastline in from Point Arena. We backed the main yard after passing Point Reyes to take on the Pilot. He took us through the Golden Gate Strait in a grand sail to anchor in San Francisco Bay. I would love to see a photograph of the *Rover* passing close by under sail from any point on that remarkable outer shoreline. Mister Ferey attended to the unloading of the coal on arriving here in port. He will attend to the loading of cargo for the return to Victoria, and I have time to be with you, if you will permit.'

'Yes, Jaimé, I will permit. For now you are here with me. Let me take you to bathe and shave off your beard to see your handsome face. Then you can sample my wine from Monterey. Later, we can dine.'

Gaudin lived in the warmth of California Sunshine on the rooftop garden of Consuelo's House in town for four nights. Oblivious of any care, they took unbridled pleasure in each other in their few days of a minglement of mind and body in the sun. The word *divertissement* in French had occurred to him as he had climbed into the horse-drawn cab she sent for him, but he thought the word far too tame to describe the sense of rampant excitement and adventure that filled his veins from the time he dressed to go to her. The passage of years had not ended it between them, but their time of bliss had no other ending than before, with each of them in tears.

19

THE VALENCIA INQUIRY

Darkness fell by four o'clock. Gaudin called Agnes on the telephone from his Office on Wharf Street to say he'd be late. He had a letter to finish before he could put it in the pouch being sent to Ottawa on the night boat to Vancouver for next morning's train east. She asked Wing to delay the evening meal until eight o'clock. Gaudin came home late in the wind and rain. Agnes came running to the front door to meet him but Wing, with his ear cocked to catch the sound of the Craigflower electric tram, got to the door first to take his hat, umbrella, and coat. Agnes followed with his slippers and cardigan.

"You have such a severe look on your face, Jim. What has happened?"

He remained silent. Agnes put out her arm to lead him into the front room. She knew the pressure he had been working under at the office, and now she wanted him to be thinking only about them and their Thirty-Third Wedding Anniversary. He said nothing as he took off his jacket and his buttoned waistcoat and pulled on his loose-fitting cardigan as a pullover. He handed her the telegram and poured drinks from a bottle of Scotch Whiskey on the desk while she read it. In the silence that followed he stood to fill his pipe from a can of tobacco before he sat down in his armchair to take the drink in his hand.

"The Prime Minister of Canada and his Cabinet Ministers in Ottawa have appointed me to head the Inquiry into the wreck of the *Valencia*."

News of the disastrous shipwreck on the West Coast of Vancouver Island on January 22 1906 swept the town in the continued grip of Pacific Northwest winter wind and rain. The sun had not shone for days. The telegram today from Ottawa told him of the Order-in-Council appointing him to head an Inquiry to make recommendations for improved rescue procedures in light of the experience of the shipwreck of the crack American passenger steamer *Valencia*.

For weeks the townspeople talked of little else than the *Valencia*. Her brother-in-law Arthur Wilby called by with his wife Marie only two days ago to talk about the wreck. Now, this evening Agnes and her husband sat at home recalling the conversation.

"I told him, Agnes, I had been out there in similar weather in my barques and that I know about the ocean current that will tend to drive an unwary vessel into the rocks off the West Coast of Vancouver Island. The storm drove the *Valencia* in too close before the captain realized the danger_____ and by then too late to turn away."

"You and Arthur had some discussion about the vessel being built of riveted iron, didn't you?"

"Yes Inez, I did mention that the compass may have been affected by the iron construction and contributed to steering the wrong course, but that may have had little to do with it."

Agnes said Arthur agreed the captain must have felt himself to blame.

"Yes Inez, the poor soul of a captain would not have been able to see anything in the storm that night. I can visualize the moment when he realized it too late to reverse the ship's grinding halt in the midst of rocks and storm-driven surf with no possibility of getting anyone off. The steamer stood caught in the rocks too far out from the shoreline for anyone to jump off to reach safety on the shore. According to reliable witnesses, even if the officers could have launched the ship's boats to take any passengers off, the boats would have turned over in the surf. All would have been tossed into the water and washed up on the shore, drowned."

After a long silence Agnes picked up to refer to more of the conversation with the Wilbys.

"Arthur said no one could go out from shore to rescue them."

"Yes Inez, the people on board would have despaired of any help coming. More than a hundred died after they had climbed up to cling on the masts and rigging to prevent being washed off the deck by surf_____."

Agnes interjected, "_____only to die by drowning or to be killed by waves throwing them against the rocks. How horrible, Jim. But the public is surely more concerned about the loss of the lives than with how the captain lost his way and ran on the rocks."

"Yes, you are right about that, Inez, but I will have no jurisdiction to deal with events leading up to a wreck of an American steamer. The public will expect me to get to the eventual reason why so many people died. I can hardly be heard to blame my employer for the lack of funding from Ottawa that keeps the Canadian Government Vessel, the steamer *Quadra*, tied up and out of commission from November through March every year, just the very time she could be called upon for rescue purposes."

"Arthur praised you for hiring out the Dunsmuir steam tug the *Czar*."

"Yes he did, but I had no trouble getting Captain Troup to go out with Captain Christensen. With them in the wheelhouse to report, I could be sure of getting an opinion I could rely on. I value the judgment and experience of both men. I am sure they will be called as witnesses at the Inquiry. Both say they took the tug as close in to the rocks as they dared to assess the sea conditions at the wreck. The sight of the tiny figures of people clustered in the rigging as high as they could climb shocked them and everyone on board the *Czar*. The tug, which is not an ocean-going tug, used her steam power in slow reverse to keep from being pushed in too close. Christensen took his tug in as close to the wreck as he dared."

"Oh Jim! I could not hold back tears when you told me they heard thin barely-audible cries for help from the wreck."

"Yes Inez, I can picture the scene of those two men standing at their open wheelhouse windows aghast at what they were seeing."

Agnes recalled Arthur saying Captain Christensen would not put out either of the tug's two small boats to take anyone off as he judged the sea and wind conditions too extreme. In any event their contribution no match to the requirement of taking off a hundred survivors.

"Yes Inez, he did say that. And I said again a storm on the West Coast can be made especially dangerous by tidal currents, which, with a push from a storm wave could have swept the *Czar* into the jumble of rocks that held the *Valencia*. Captain Christensen kept a sharp lookout with his engine-room on standby."

Agnes said everyone there must have seen that help could only come from the shore.

"But Inez," he said, "men from Port San Juan fought their way for miles over trees fallen on the trail along the coastline and through the tangled bush at the wrecksite only to find they could not reach out to the wreck from the shoreline when daylight came. They could only watch in horror."

After a long silence Agnes spoke again.

"Jim, your Inquiry will hear witnesses testify to all of what you and Arthur talked about, but how unfair to get you to come along now to preside over the Inquiry. Ottawa must know you wrote that long six-page report in your own handwriting to the Department's Chief Engineer in Ottawa in April 1894. Your recommendations could have prevented the tragedy."

"Yes Inez, on the eve of taking the charge of the new vessel, the *Quadra* more than ten years ago now, I did send in a list of items they should spend money on to save lives on this part of the coast, but I am not so sure all I recommended would have made any difference."

"Jim, you know they have ignored you completely. How are you going to be able to bring the content of that letter into evidence at the Inquiry if you are not going to be a witness called to testify?"

Gaudin re-lit his pipe and took a long time to answer.

"I imagine the men in Ottawa know that. I doubt the terms of reference when they come from the Federal Government will permit any criticism of what they did or did not do."

"Surely, Jim, it will be your job to criticize Ottawa for its failure to follow your recommendations made 11 years ago?"

"No Inez, that's not the way they will allow it to happen. In presiding over the hearing I will be required to limit the questioning of witnesses by the lawyers representing interested parties. Many will try to pin the blame on Ottawa for neglecting the West Coast. The lawyers may quarrel with my rulings, but I doubt they can get any court to force me to go outside the terms of reference Ottawa lays down for me to follow."

Agnes got up and went over to the desk to pull out of the drawer the copy of the six-page handwritten letter on long paper her husband sent to the Chief Engineer of the Department in Ottawa in April 1894. She said she would read it aloud to him.

"No, don't do that. I know what I wrote, and I know Ottawa received the letter. I sent it in the pouch for express train delivery."

"But Jim, do you mean to say the Inquiry will not be told you sent this letter?"

"Yes Inez, the Inquiry will not be told. I cannot be called to testify at the Inquiry. I won't be able to produce a copy of it. If I were a witness I could do that, but I won't be a witness. In our report at the end of the hearing, neither I, nor the other commissioners can refer to anything not led in evidence."

"Oh Jim, you will get your stomach in knots if you let it go not referred to!"

"I suppose so, Inez, but I have been long required to keep my tongue and my temper in check in this lighthouse keepers' job. My struggle to get Ottawa to help the deserving people in the Lightkeeper Service has given me little peace of mind."

Agnes spoke to break the long silence that followed.

"I know you found joy in being able to come home to potter in your flower garden and grow vegetables for Wing to cook, Jim."

"Yes I'm sure you are right about that, Inez. The sacks of nitrate of soda I had Dolbell carry from London produced an abundant growth in the garden. Perhaps I should cherrypick some of the highlights and read them out to you to find some satisfaction in saying I was right. Here goes: '*Sir, I have the honour to acknowledge your letter,* blah blah blah *and I beg to report on the subject.*

1. The increasing commerce of British Columbia and Puget Sound makes it desirable that life saving stations be established on the Southwest Coast of Vancouver Island, more especially in the region between Port San Juan and Cape Beale_____ The enclosed list of wrecks, which were attended with loss of life, were wrecked between Bonilla Point and Butchart's Point, which forms the eastern point at the entrance to Pachena Bay.' This is pretty much where the *Valencia* went aground. I will read on."

Agnes interrupted, "I hadn't heard that Mister Butchart has a point of land named after him. Why would they do that for him?"

"I don't think the place name is official: it's a local name to recognize he invested large sums of money to log the big timber growing on parts of the West Coast. He meets a large payroll. I will read on from the copy of the letter_____. '2._____Owing to difficulties of communicating news of shipping disasters to the different light stations, we must establish life saving stations within easy communication to a lighthouse, even though this may not always prove satisfactory. As a first step in the way of establishing life saving stations, places of shelter should be established at easy distances from each other, say 5 or 6 miles, in which could be found printed instructions in different languages. 3._____ I have no doubt a crew of Indians could be trained to do good service, but it will be* necessary to compensate them to remain near their station. *Many of them earn high wages in sealing and fishing. 4._____Life saving boats will need a tug'*_____. The motor power life saving boat at Bamfield, for instance, would have taken hours to reach half-way to Port San Juan in a storm. It would have been of no help to the *Valencia*. _____. I will go on to read out from my report: _____ '*I think a boat should be modeled on a New Bedford whaleboat fitted with airtight compartments best suited for the coast, being lighter and more easily handled than the usual self-righting life boat. I believe it a mistake to think Indian canoes would be serviceable in case of a shipwreck in bad weather. Indians are expert in handling their canoes, but they have the good sense not to set out in bad weather. If caught out, they make the best of it. Their canoes can split in two in rough weather. Every tribe has a record of relations lost through such an incident. 5. The services of the C.G.S. Quadra could always be available for this humane purpose'*_____, But Inez, as we both know, Ottawa does not keep the *Quadra* in commission over the winter months. Ottawa kept me from taking her out until March to keep down expense. November through March, that's when the storms come, and the need to save shipwrecked lives greatest, but I will continue reading: -'*A scratch crew could be found in an emergency, but it would take 24 hours before the steamer could start. Under such circumstances hiring a tug would be better if immediate assistance required.* _____ 6._____ -and 7._____*When the weather clears up after a fog sailing vessels are often seen dangerously close to the entrance to Barkeley Sound, drifting up the Sound.*' What I meant to say at that point in the letter, more and better lights and fog alarms to westwards of Cape Beale will have little effect on preventing shipwrecks on the coast from Port San Juan to Cape Beale, which, as I have said, is where the careful navigator will shape his course to; '8._____ and 9._____ and 10._____ *No settlement has been established on this portion of the coast since your last visit in 1892*_____*Since (then) the conditions during the winter months have not changed.*' I was referring to 1892 as the time I took the Chief Engineer from Ottawa there before the *Quadra* arrived from England. I had taken him up the coast in my earlier command, the *Sir James Douglas*. The poor man, a retired Army officer, became incapacitated by seasickness. And I was referring to the same stretch from Cape Beale to Port San Juan. I would have better made a clear statement in the letter that the lack of settlement on that part of the coastline lessened the number of men available for life saving purposes, which I had meant

to convey. I should have written that although the telegraph line put
there some time ago for stranded mariners continues to exist, it is of no
use whatever to persons who cannot reach shore from a wreck to use it.
Also the line is prone to failure caused by windfall trees. A section of
only 10 miles of telegraph line has a lineman Baird, by name, paid to
attend to and keep clear."

"Please stop reading, Jim. You are just making yourself upset."

"I ended the report in the time-honoured manner '*I am sir, your
obedient servant.*' So much of my life in port has been subject to Masters
on the shore to whom I owed obedience. At sea no one could tell me how
to sail my ship. I have happy memories of those times because of that."

"Kate is home from work now and Wing has a special anniversary dinner ready for us in the dining-room. Nan and young Torchy
will come down to the table to join us_____.
Let's go in now for dinner and talk over the good times with them. We
can get to bed early tonight, dear husband."

20

1911

Captain James Troup, the headman at the Canadian Pacific B.C. Coast Steamships, left his office on the south shore of the Inner Harbour on a cold sunny day in January to go for lunch with the usual group of Victoria businessmen at the big round table at the Union Club. Before setting a brisk pace he thought for a moment on the grand job he had, reporting only to the accountants and railroad men in the Canadian Pacific head office who were headquartered over 2000 miles away in Montreal. From his stern-wheeler time in Oregon catering to the interests of the Union Pacific Railroad he knew how to talk to railroad money and convince them on the answers to most questions. The town of Victoria enjoyed a prosperity that came with a rise in land prices and a boom in the economy. The railroads across Canada to the Pacific had brought a growing population to the Western Provinces. The 1911 Census of Canada will show British Columbia as the choice of many people coming from Eastern Canada and the British Isles. The logging and fishing industries boomed with immigrants from many other parts of the world arriving in large numbers to build prosperity for all. He imagined the sight of the steam yacht he will buy to fit in nicely when moored at the east end of the company wharf.

After lunch he corralled some of the men to go upstairs with him through the silent Reading Room to the empty Library. With them paying him close attention he could begin to talk.

"Everyone in town knows the Jim Gaudins are facing difficult times." he said. "The local newspapers have carried news of Gaudin's long siege of ill health."

One of the men interrupted.

"Yes Troup, Ottawa required him to resign his position as District

Marine Agent in Victoria because of that."

Another said, "Yes, he held that position ever since handing over command of the *Quadra* to Captain Walbran over a dozen years ago. He is now 73."

And another spoke to add his remark. "But, Troup, Ottawa made the announcement he retained his appointments as Examiner of Masters and Mates and Receiver of Wrecks."

And another added, "Yes, Troup, what's the difficulty."

Mister Gray lost no time to speak.

"Yes, but few people know those appointments pay nothing. No more than a tip of the hat to the old man who did yeoman service for the Marine Community on this Coast for over 20 years. He leaves his wife no pension."

Troup began again after a long moment when no one spoke.

"We've all seen the advertisements for the sale of their rose-garden house on Craigflower Road. I have learned that the Gaudins subdivided the outer edges of their large acreage on the waterfront over time to sell and pay down the mortgage, but the house with the splendid garden at the top of the rise beside the road has remained theirs."

"Yes, named *Isla Villa*. A fine house with a view over Selkirk Water."

"That's right," said Troup. "The Gaudins have enjoyed living there for over 25 years. But his work as District Marine Agent for Ottawa with jurisdiction over the welfare of his lighthouse keepers and their families has landed on him nothing but anxiety and worry over his inability to get adequate funding from Ottawa for them."

Another spoke.

"I know the Jim Gaudins well. They have found some contentment in their personal lives. Their daughters Marie, Mabel, and Beatrice each married at the turn of the 1900s with summer lawn wedding receptions in the flower gardens, but daughter Kate, hard-of-hearing, poor girl, works in Gaudin's office on Wharf Street. She has continued to live at home."

Mister Gray of Albion Iron Works spoke again.

"I know their son Jimmy. He worked long and hard to qualify at V. M. D. as a machinist and engineer. He is now Chief Engineer on the River Division of the White Pass & Yukon Railway in charge of the personnel and engineering departments of the British Yukon Navigation Company, which operates the new stern-wheel steamers on the Yukon River."

"Gentlemen, this brings me to my proposal: I want all of us to send Gaudin up to the Yukon to see his son Jimmy and his stern-wheel fleet," said Troup. "I am sure he will be well enough to travel. If not, I will send back your money."

Agnes called as many of the family who could come to the house that evening to gather around Gaudin to hear the announcement. Standing, he began to speak,

"Two weeks ago on news of my retirement getting about I had lunch with Captain Troup, who, as you all know, is the head of Canadian Pacific's B.C. Coast Steamships. You may not know he made his early reputation as a captain on stern-wheel river steamers running the rapids on the Columbia and Snake Rivers in Oregon. During lunch he asked me to tell him about the stern-wheeler steamers our Jimmy runs on the Yukon River, which I did. I should make a trip up to Whitehorse to see him, he said. I suppose I just shrugged my shoulders at that. Today he spoke to me again to say he'd raised a subscription from the people in Commerce and Shipping to pay my passage to Skagway to see Jimmy and Nell. Troup told me I'd be arriving in time for the celebration of Spring Ice Break-up at Dawson City. I will go to Seattle first to make a call on Nell's people to pay my respects and tell them of my trip north if I have time."

With her usual bright show of enthusiasm to generate the same response in others, Agnes did not waste a moment to speak up.

"How wonderful, Jim! When will you go?"

"In two days' time. I sent a telegram to Jimmy to say I am coming to Skagway by Alaska Steamship Company's steamer *Victoria*. He wired back to say he'd be at the wharf to meet me and take me on his train over the White Pass to Whitehorse."

No one else in the room spoke. He waited for a moment, and then added an explanation he thought necessary.

"Troup's Canadian Pacific vessels could have taken me to Skagway, of course: they DO run that far up the coast. Troup laughed out loud as he told me those who paid insisted their money NOT go to pay for a ticket on his C. P. R. vessels. So he has me ticketed north on Alaska Steamships, first to Seattle and then north. They wouldn't pay for a C. P. R. ticket saying it would offend a Club rule not to use the club for business."

Daughter Mabel, now 36 and in town to shop, piped up.

"Papa, everyone has been raving about the new Grand Trunk Pacific steamers: why don't you ask to go all the way by Grand Trunk to Skagway?"

"Good question Mabel. The Grand Trunk Pacific does not go that far yet. The new company goes only as far north as the mine at Stewart at the head of Portland Canal, but I expect they will be quick to add a run farther north to Skagway. Grand Trunk has only one aim in life, and that is to compete with Canadian Pacific."

"Papa, do you really have to go to see *Nell's people*."

"Mabel, I could wait in Victoria for the Alaska Steamer to stop on her way north from Seattle, but I do want to see Nell's people. Troup knew about Nell and her family from his time in Oregon. He thought I might like to see them to *pay my respects*, as he put it. I hope I don't get too chilly a reception after all the trouble we caused."

Agnes heard her husband's voice break and falter. Then he straightened his shoulders to speak in strong clear voice.

"I want you all to hear me out. All Hell broke loose in this family after Jimmy wrote to tell us he will marry Nell Cummins from Michigan and to say they would be coming down from *The North*, as he put it, to Vancouver on furlough. Instead of giving them a royal welcome, you, Mabel, wrote back that fearful letter to him. You girls had such grand ideas about Jimmy becoming a lawyer and marrying into Victoria High Society. He had the good sense to live the life he wanted."

Agnes decided to say nothing in the pause that followed. Her husband carried on with the wind in his sails.

"I kick myself I did not insist on him bringing her over to Victoria with him. Nell reacted as you might have expected: To Hell with the Gaudin family. Jimmy came all by himself to tell us of his promotion and to make it clear to us he had so much to look forward to in the Yukon. You girls put up such a ruckus about him marrying that young American woman he met in the Yukon. I can't imagine how any of you could think you had any say in the matter. Jimmy at his age did not have to please any of you."

"Yes, Papa," said one of the daughters.

Gaudin continued to speak.

"The back row of our family camera photograph taken at that time tells the story: the girls standing on the far left to keep their distance from Jimmy standing alone on the right. Only your mother, happy to make the most of any occasion, is smiling. All of the rest of you put on your sourpuss faces. Your mother put the photograph on the piano, but someone took it down."

The room remained in shocked silence until Kate spoke.

"You must tell both of them we all send our love, Papa."

"Jim, I will send a letter for you to take to Nell."

Gaudin waited a moment for others to speak. When even Mabel did not protest and remained silent, he spoke again with tears running down his cheeks into his white beard.

"Yes Inez, I will be pleased to take your letter with me when I go to see our boy. As a family we have left them out in the cold far too long. I have a chance to try to make it up to them and tell my son how proud I am of him. I hope to stay fit long enough to see them."

To end the silence that followed Agnes called for help packing for the move to the house on Hampshire Road. Gaudin's retirement forced the sale of the house on Craigflower Road and a move to a smaller house in Oak Bay, three miles east of town. The Gaudin daughter Mabel and her husband took over Gaudin's sense of obligation to keep his Chinese cook Charles Wing employed by hiring him for their new house north of town on Knapp Island. Gaudin called him *Charlie*, but everyone else spoke to him as *Wing*: All regarded the man with love and respect. The move also meant the boarder left to find a new place and the widow Nan Renouf Anderson and her young son left Victoria to move to Calgary, where she found work as a nurse to bring up her son, Harold Henry Caulfield (*Torchy*)Anderson.[11]

For some time past Agnes had been aware of her husband's earlier attachment to a woman he'd met in Chile 40 years ago and knew he'd seen her again when he carried coal to San Francisco in 1883. Later in bed that night, he spoke about it. "Inez, I hope you may have taken my words about Jimmy having chosen the life he wanted to apply to me, too. I am happy I stayed on my original course to come back to you from Chile. I am sorry if I caused you hurt, but it's past."

Agnes gave him a hug and whispered, "Do not worry, my dear husband."

****

[11] Torchy Anderson would become a noted Canadian Journalist and Editor of the Vancouver Province newspaper. In 1931 his newspaper published 'The Recollections of Susan Allison' in serial form, notably stating that Susan, as Susan Moir in Victoria before her marriage to John Allison, spent her spare time with Agnes Anderson and that thay became good friends. Some old-timers from the fur trade days knew Nan's husband Henry Anderson to have been the eldest son of BC Pioneer A.C. Anderson, and that Nan found a happy home with the Gaudins for 10 years after her husband died.

James Roderick Payn Gaudin, short and spare-of-build, greeted his father at the Skagway wharf. Agnes had told Gaudin their son's big nose and long ear lobes foretold good judgment and a fine future. Jimmy's Homburg and dark coat over a business suit and grey spats on shining black shoes fit the prediction.

"Jimmy, here I am!"

"Pater, I am so glad you have come north to see us. Nell has the house ready for you to stay with us."

"Oh that's good of both of you, Jimmy. I will be so happy to meet her."

"This get-up I wear to show you how I dress for the Directors and Shareholders from England when they visit."

"Jimmy, I am accustomed to see men in town who dress like that. Indeed, look at what I am wearing. I am not so much different."

Settled on board the train, and seated near the pot-bellied stove at the rear of the car, they talked.

"Nell wanted to come with me to meet you but I persuaded her to stay to keep the home fires burning. The sky farther north from here will be clear but snow remains on the ground, keeping temperatures down at night. How was your trip up?"

"Well, Jimmy, after going on after the stop in Vancouver, the old steamer *Victoria* had me back up in three days to the B.C. Central Coast, which I had come to know when I ran the Federal Government vessel."

"Did you feel well enough to get out to walk on deck?"

"Yes, I did that. In the cold night air I bundled up and stood on deck to see the flashes of light from lighthouses the Minister of Marine & Fisheries in Ottawa put in to mark the narrow channels of the whole length of the Inside Passage, Scarlett Point, Pine Island, Egg Island, Dryad Point, Ivory Island, and Boat Bluff Lighthouse to name some of my old friends located in the earlier parts of the route north. During the daylight hours I talked to other passengers, some of them interesting, some of them not, as you may imagine; or I stayed in my cabin and rested. I could have slept well enough when running through fog, but the steamer's whistle sounding a blast every few minutes to shake my cabin did keep me awake."

"Pater, I know enough history of the British Empire to say that General Scarlett led the Charge of the Heavy Brigade at the Battle of Balaklava in the Crimean War."

"Yes, you are correct; and of course, the Scarlett Point Lighthouse stands on Balaklava Island. I could not sleep until we passed the light at Pine Island. By that time the fog had lifted, and I could look out my open porthole on the starboard side to see the light at Egg Island ahead. We continued to steam north past low-lying Cape Caution in safety through remnants of ocean swell that would have been breaking on the shallows of the Sea Otter Rocks to port. A lot of open water here for the flood tide to come in from the ocean and to divide at Cape Caution to run north and south into the narrow channels. I set my alarm clock to get up later to see the lighthouse light at Dryad Point flashing as we turned past it. I stayed on deck for the often-rough passage across Milbanke Sound. The flood tide comes in from the ocean here, too, to push into all of the deep inlets and channels of the upper coast, but it returns with the next ebb tide to dump immense quantities of water back out to the ocean."

"Pater, I suppose that lessens the heave of the ocean swell?"

"Yes, sometimes that happens, but only until the next tide or the next storm incoming."

"You will have come soon to the narrow straight parts of the Inside Passage to Alaska won't you? I remember the calm channels there when I came north in '97."

"Yes, Jimmy, after passing the Ivory Island Lighthouse we turned north past a barren little island they say they intend to name after me. Soon we came up to Boat Bluff Lighthouse at the southern threshold of the Inside Passage. Then I went below for a long sleep. Nothing but heavy rain and a dreary slow passage the rest of the way. But enough of that_____, please tell me about the railroad."

"Whitehorse lies half a day's train ride beyond the *Divide*. The town stands on level ground on the western bank of the Lewes River, tributary to the Yukon. You will be in time to see the Ice Break-up, which will allow my stern-wheel steamers to run north downriver to Dawson City and beyond, carrying passengers and light freight."

"Troup told me your steamers must be lightly built with shallow draft so they can operate in shallow water."

"Yes, and that's why we push barges to transport the freight the steamers cannot take aboard. You will enjoy seeing the steamers hauled-out of the water in the shipyard at the edge of the riverbank and also some on the shore at Lake La Berge. If you will stay long enough with us I can take you as a passenger to enjoy steaming in the early summer weather. Unlike Victoria in the month of June, we have little rain at that time of year."

Jimmy went on to explain that the Ice Break-up would bring employment for the crews. They will be using jacks to make the boats slide down to the river's edge to float in the water. That work must be done with care not to damage the boats. The whole town stirs in parties and celebration: the cold winter will be seen to have ended and the sunshine will be coming from higher in the sky every day to bring good cheer.

"Jimmy, I will look forward to all of it."

"We hire men in winter to cut and pile cordwood on the shore for the steamers to pick up and use to fire their boilers to make steam. You can imagine how the ice breaking-up brings on a great buzz of activity to put the steamers in the water. The crews can then go on board. The break-up of ice downstream where the river widens at Dawson City and Fairbanks occurs in an even more dramatic manner."

"Jimmy, I will be happy to see it all. But let's talk about the railroad. Compared to the American trains I have traveled in, your rolling stock looks so miniature. This passenger car is much shorter than the American, but I can tell you the ride is just as smooth. The furnishings are superb. Your company has not scrimped."

"Yes, Pater, I am mighty pleased with all of it. I traveled by train south from Seattle to Portland to inspect the stern-wheel steamers running on the Columbia before I drafted the design papers for the stern-wheeler the *Anglian*. I saw for myself the excellence of some of the American railroads. The White Pass had good models to follow being run by a railroad in the Nevada-Colorado Mountains. Please tell me about your experience in riding American steam trains. You and your Chief Officer arrived back in Victoria from the Falkland Islands a half-year before the C.P.R. completed its railroad across Canada to Port Moody. Have I that correct?"

Before answering, Gaudin filled his pipe with fresh tobacco from the pouch he carried in his jacket.

"Yes, Jimmy, that's correct. Over 30 years ago I took trains east from San Francisco to New York, and five years later after the sinking of the *Rover of the Seas* off the Falkland Islands I came west from New York to reach Seattle through Portland on the new Northern Pacific Railroad. A lonely time your mother faced before I could get back to Victoria after the sinking. I could not send any word to her to say I was safe for such a long time. No connection for me to send a cable until I reached Montevideo, Uruguay, which I could reach only after a long 800-mile passage in the mail schooner from Port Stanley in January 1886, but enough of that. Please tell me why your company decided to build the track of this railroad as narrow gauge."

"The White Pass made a smart move to build the rail as narrow gauge," Jimmy said. "That saved the investors a tremendous amount of money by allowing the track to be laid with sharper curves, which reduced the amount of rock to be drilled, blasted, and hauled out of the way in construction."

Gaudin remarked on the small diameter locomotive driving wheels he had seen at the station, and that they were such a dramatic change from the high large diameter driving wheels on the American railroad locomotives, which run straight across country at speed with more gradual curves to the track.

"You saw the slow speed of our climb from the station this morning up the steep grade," Jimmy said. "The Americans can run their trains much faster cross-country than we can. But let me tell you about Nell. I made the right decision to marry her. Nell and I have a wonderful life here up North. I have a good job with B-Y-N with good prospects. She and I both get sent south to Vancouver every winter for me to attend to purchasing next year's supplies. The company is owned in England, and the Directors have confidence in me. While you are here I will show you our garden for vegetables and flowers. The short but intense growing season will begin soon."

"When I get back to Victoria your mother will want me to tell her all about the garden."

"Yes, Pater, I know how hard she worked to keep the garden growing, but I am afraid I did little to help her with it when I lived at home. Skagway, as you must know, is an American town in Alaska. Our train will soon cross the International Border. You will see your first red jacket police uniform there. The train will run beside Lake Bennett. We will stop for a stand-up lunch at the counter."

As the train gained speed on the higher level ground, both lit their pipes again as it sped on through occasional snow sheds to keep the tracks clear in winter.

"Farther along we will come to Carcross Station where our Lake Atlin steamer the S.S. *Tutshi* meets the train in the summer season," Jimmy said. We will have time to get out to see the steamer, hauled out on the shore of the lake for the winter. You will see for yourself the height her housework would be above water."

"TOO-SHY, you say it, do you, Jimmy? I will be pleased to stretch my legs and see her with my own eyes."

"Carcross is short for Caribou Crossing, nothing to do with the *Cariboo* country in the British Columbia Interior, which Grandfather Anderson, in his inimitable fashion with words, told Mater the name has *an obscure origin, little understood.* In any event the name *Cariboo* in B. C. has nothing to do with the big Caribou deer we shoot for meat, close in size to a small moose. Nell will roast us some cuts for dinner."

"If I can get back my appetite for food, I will look forward to a small helping of the well-done *niggly* bits, Jimmy."

"Pater, let's talk about what you have been doing. I want you to tell me about how your life changed after you left the sea for an upstairs office in a downtown building on the waterfront. At the time, I didn't think it would be a good move."

"That's a long story, Jimmy, but I will tell you."

"I have a feeling you must be happy not to be working any longer for such a hard employer."

"Jimmy, a job's a job. It was good at first moving from Pilots to work as ship's captain for the Federal Government. On a day I well remember because I now had a command with steady pay, June 4 1889, I steamed out as the Master of that fine near-new propeller steamer, the Federal Government vessel *Sir James Douglas* to service the Pacific Coast buoys and lighthouses. I had experienced mates and crew. She flew the dark blue ensign with a Union Jack inset in the top inside corner. Over the year we steamed the entire coast to service navigation buoys, lights, and lighthouses, bunkering at the coal dock in Nanaimo. After a few years in her they gave me the charge of the new and larger propeller steamer the *Quadra*, which Captain Walbran brought out from Scotland through the Straits of Magellan. The opening soon came with increased pay for the job of District Marine Agent, Examiner of Masters and Mates, and Receiver of Wrecks. I applied for the position to leave the sea for a desk in an office."

"Do you think you made a mistake leaving the sea?"

"Yes, God's teeth, yes. What a mistake I made turning to a job sending handwritten reports to civil servants in Ottawa whose budgets called for a pittance to be paid to lighthouse keepers for their work and little more than that for necessities."

"But what a wonderful move up you made to take command of the new larger vessel the *Quadra*. You must have enjoyed the new command?"

"Yes I did, Jimmy, but I should not gloss over my time in her. Nobody ever talks to me about it, which is just as well. I had the charge of the *Quadra* only for a month when I ran her onto an uncharted rock out in the middle of Houston Stewart Channel in the Queen Charlotte Islands. Had it been later in the year the kelp would have grown high enough to help me avoid the rocks it streamed up from. Or maybe the kelp didn't show in the wind-ruffled water? I am not sure which. I sensed critical eyes on me as I steamed the damaged vessel into Victoria Harbour with pumps running to keep the ship from sinking. Also I felt ashamed for not having done the job I had been sent to do in the Bering Sea. The opening of the position as District Marine Agent with the fine office in town soon came to give me an opportunity to focus on something new and to stop thinking about running on that damn rock."

A long silence followed.

"Pater, what were you doing in Houston Stewart Channel? I thought you wrote once to say you were sailing to the Bering Sea to support the Canadian sealing fleet sailing out of Victoria."

"That's correct, Jimmy. We were on our way to cross the Gulf of Alaska to the Aleutian Islands and beyond to the Bering Sea. We were to show the flag in support of our sealing schooners sailing out of Victoria. But first I had orders to make an inspection of the lay of the land at Rose Harbour in Houston Stewart Channel and report on its suitability for a harbour in support of a settlement on the shore. That done, I had it in my mind to take a short cut to the ocean past the remarkable collection of old Haida Indian Totem Poles and buildings on Anthony Island."

"You must have intended to use your deepsea navigation to take a short cut out over open sea in the North Pacific to the Aleutians?"

"Yes, I chose a good alternative to using up coal to steam the long way up the east coast of Moresby and Masset Islands to Dixon Entrance. My luck ran out. I placed too much reliance on the then-current edition of the Admiralty chart surveyed in 1854 by officers of the Royal Navy in Her Majesty's Ship *Virago* on rumours of gold being found in the Queen Charlotte Islands. I had the misfortune to find an uncharted reef out in mid-channel missed by the Navy in their survey. Soon afterwards I took the promotion to District Marine Agent with increase in pay to go ashore and let someone younger have a crack at it. In crowning insult, Ottawa will name the reef *Quadra Rock*, and they will name the side of the Houston Stewart Channel I should have taken on departing Rose Harbour as *Gaudin Channel* as a monument to my gaffe."

"_____Shall we talk about something else, Pater?"

"Yes, please go ahead with the story of building the first stern-wheel steamer in the Yukon, the *Anglian*. Please tell me more about it. People I know tell me the later stern-wheel steamers came upriver from a place in Alaska called St. Michael's."

"I am sad to say, Pater, the *Anglian* sank in the north before she reached the Yukon River. It's a long story that goes back to when you sailed us all from the Channel Islands to live in Victoria in late 1881. Two years later you moved us to the house on Craigflower Road on the shore of Selkirk Water. I remember the new place because I could play with my toy boats on the beach to get away from my bossy older sisters. Mater loved that house and garden."

"Yes, Jimmy, I am not too happy about now leaving it, but please tell me about your building of the steamer at Teslin Lake. That's what I want you to talk about. I have seen a map showing the lake placed a long distance north of the settlement at Telegraph Creek on the Stikine River. Please tell me how it all began."

"It began the day I decided I would not try to learn to be a solicitor in a law office in Victoria: you opened a door for me to apply at Victoria Machinery Depot and Albion Iron Works, and I never looked back. I learned the machinist's trade and I followed a long course of instruction and book learning to become an engineer. I learned the joy of operating a steam engine on land, but more particularly on the water to make a vessel come to life. I had turned twenty-one when Mister Gray put in the good word for me to The Canadian Development Company. Formed by investors from England, they engaged me as an engineer to design, build, and put into service a new stern-wheel steamer on the Yukon River. And I took on the responsibility to hire steamers to transport the men and all of the lumber, supplies, machinery, and equipment from Vancouver to Wrangell, Alaska."

"Jimmy, I know I am interrupting, but you had never done anything of the sort before. How could you know how to design such a vessel?"

"I had the Hudson's Bay Company steamer the *Enterprise* to go by as a larger model of what they wanted. My design came out with a registered length of 85 feet, beam of 21 feet, and a draft of 5 feet. The owners had money to pay a good builder to build the boat to my design at Lake Teslin at the place they selected for a sawmill and a shipyard.

They gave me instructions to supervise the building of the project at the Lake. I ordered and arranged for the transport and installation of the two horizontal high-pressure steam engines of 5.4 horsepower each and the boiler from Vulcan Iron Works in Seattle. I got the engines working to put the vessel in operation on the water at Lake Teslin. The captain had orders to take the *Anglian* down the Hootalinqua River to join the Yukon River and go to Fort Selkirk and Dawson City. No little task. From the beginning I made one good engineering decision after another. Others who knew the country decided on using the Stikine and the time of year for me to start, and they left me to carry it out. I knew nothing of the land up there, of course. My employers sent a sawmill to the Lake to cut the local trees into lumber, but I used none of it, having taken advice to use the best clear Douglas Fir for the hull planking and housework. I rented high-roofed shed space in Vancouver to lay out the lines for building. I gathered all of the timbers I would need for the bow stem, the frames, and the stern post, and with help of shipwrights who knew what to do with the wood, I saw to positioning them on the floor to build the hull of the boat before taking it all down, and packing it up for transport all the way up to Teslin for me to put together again in numbered pieces."

"Jimmy, how did the Americans at Wrangell look upon your *expeditionary force* entering their country?"

"No trouble because all goods and lumber shipped under bond. The American authorities allowed the army troops of the Royal Canadian Regiment from Eastern Canada and the Policemen of the Yukon Field Force to land at Wrangell to enter without payment of customs duty on their goods, kit, and gear. This extraordinary outcome only because all of us were bound two-dozen miles up the Stikine River to enter British Columbia. We were just passing through. I found this quite astonishing. I expected trouble. I learned that the U.S.A. and England had put an old agreement between the Hudson's Bay Company and the Russian Fur Company at Sitka into the form of a binding treaty: Britishers had the right to use the Stikine and the Taku River to enter Northern British Columbia from the sea."

"Jimmy, had you ever before managed a group of workmen?"

"Yes, I had a try at it at V. M. D. I must have been a good organizer of men from the moment the steamers came alongside the wharf at Wrangell. First off, rather than have them tarry in town to cause trouble, I sent the military off ahead on the river. I took advice from

Captain Sid Barrington who ran his steamboats and barges on the Stikine. He took everything 150 miles or more up the river at low water to a place on the north bank called Glenora. I had timed it to avoid both the late spring freshet from snow melting in the mountains and the later low water in the river. Also, earlier, we would have found the Teslin trail wet and muddy and the black flies doing their worst on the sweating skins of men. I found the mud on the trail hardened with frost. We moved the whole kit and kaboodle north to Lake Teslin on horse-drawn sleds a distance of 200 miles, none of it in a straight line or on level ground. Using shipwrights brought in by my employer to work at their shipyard on the lake, I took the most part of a year to get the steamer built to be ready to steam down the river in July 1898 bound for Fort Selkirk. I went in her as the Second Engineer. With captain and crew found by my employer, the *Anglian* took to life with a triumphant toot of her steam whistle at the end of June 1898."

"Jimmy, Fort Selkirk?"

"On the way down to Dawson City, where the Pelly River joins, not far from the Alaska Border, but as I said I must mention, the *Anglian* sank within a month of launching. We didn't get her as far down as the Yukon River. She sank after running into rocks in the Hootalinqua Rapids. I could only hope the owner had insurance against loss."

"Your steamer lasted only a month?"

"Yes, but she went out in grand style. In a madcap operation, the *Anglian* led a flotilla of scows and boats built at the Lake Teslin shipyard down the winding channels and rocks of Hootalinqua River in the Yukon's 24-hour-summer-daylight-days. Running the rapids, she crashed onto the rocks. Everything I had worked to build over the past year and a half sank, wrecked deep in a pool. But we all had a chance to get off. In a magnificent display of initiative and discipline the 40 soldiers of the Yukon Field Force took to the scows and boats, which had followed behind. Such a grand sight as they disappeared downriver to Dawson City to maintain order and to guard gold shipments. Some of them dropped off at Fort Selkirk to help keep the Union Jack flying in the Yukon against intrusion by American miners, who could enter the Yukon through the mountains from Alaska. I thought at first I faced career disaster with the loss of the *Anglian*, but I came out of it in splendid fashion. Within weeks, the British Yukon Navigation Company bought the River Division of the White Pass & Yukon Railroad from the Canadian Development Company. B-Y-N hired me immediately. By 1902 they promoted me to become Acting Chief Engineer of the River Division of White Pass & Yukon & Railroad to run bigger and better stern-wheelers, which joined the fleet coming up the Yukon River, a far better approach. A small part of my new responsibilities involved the salvage and re-building of the *Anglian*, now a B-Y-N asset."

"Jimmy, what a great story! As I have said, I am proud of you."

"Thank you sir. We haven't talked about Mater: how is she?"

"Jimmy, she is well, and she is happy I have come on this trip to see you and Nell. Your mother keeps busy with friends, our daughters and their children, St. Saviour's Church, and her garden."

"What do you hear of her brothers and sisters?"

"Rose Anderson plans to move to live in California. The Anderson property in North Saanich, long sold, and all have dispersed to live in various parts. Agnes finds it difficult to keep in touch with them, but her older brother Robert, who now wants to be called James, calls by often. He has found his office bookkeeping experience useful in obtaining work with the Provincial Government Department of Agriculture where he hopes to find quick promotion. He has made good friends with important people in town with his intellect and way with words like his father."

"This may be a difficult question for you to answer, Pater, but have you kept up contact with the Gaudin family in Jersey, or with your brothers?"

"I simply do not know where my seagoing brothers live, or if they live. With so many places to settle in the British Empire, I doubt any of them would have gone back to live on the Island of Jersey, which had such a downturn in the 1870s. Of course, the U.S.A. would have welcomed them. My father and mother never did write in reply to my letters sent some years ago. I never had the money to make a trip across Canada and the North Atlantic to visit them. It troubles me that we have lost touch with the people in Jersey, particularly now as we reach the end of our days and find ourselves outliving friends in town. But we can do little about that. All more the better Agnes and I are now making this contact with you and Nell."

"We will be in Whitehorse within the hour. You will find Nell to be a marvelous cook. I hope the two of you will enjoy each other. You will see I am a happy man."

****

People walking their dogs on Dallas Road in the early hours of a sunny Monday morning 19 June 1911 heard the blasts of the steam whistle of the night boat incoming from Seattle. The new Grand Trunk twin-screw propeller steamer *Prince Rupert*, hidden in low fog made her approach to Victoria off Clover Point. The tops of the snow-covered Olympic Mountains stood beyond in sunshine more than 50-miles distant south. Walkers on higher ground in Beacon Hill Park remarked on the sight of the tops of her two masts slicing through the low fog. Soon the steamer would pass Brotchie Ledge rocks in safety, a trap in fog for unwary vessels attempting to steer too close to shore on their way in from the east to Victoria's Inner Harbour. Any attempt to keep the shoreline in sight could lead a vessel into the rocks. In a few minutes people walking on Dallas Road, closer to the harbour entrance, would see the new Grand Trunk Steamer in plain view appearing out of the fogbank into early morning sunshine.

She and her sister ship, the *Prince George*, appeared to be identical, but coastal mariners prided themselves in spying out small identifying differences from a distance. Except for white housework and deck fittings kept clean and glistening, the two black-hulled vessels, each with three tall black smoke stacks, steamed under Grand Trunk Pacific Colours, and shone as veritable *Black Princes*. Even the black hull glistened.

The *Prince Rupert*, a three-stack ocean liner in miniature, steamed into Victoria with a stream of coal-fired black smoke slipping low aft from her tall smoke stacks, showing how fast she moved. Soon, her captain would sound her trademark whistle and wailing siren as she approached Ogden Point to enter the Inner Harbour_____, one long blast of her steam whistle followed by a long whooping wail of her siren to signal her arrival in port. The novel sound signal came as a surprise to coast dwellers. Quite different from the C.P.R. with its trademark steam whistle of a long and a short, followed by another long and a short, the letter C in the Morse code.

Some minutes later early risers in town standing at the edges of the Inner Harbour caught sight of the steamer emerging past Laurel Point into morning sunshine to slip in alongside the wharf in silence to disembark sleepy passengers going no further.

The Grand Trunk Wharf stood across from the C.P.R. wharf in

the James Bay part of Victoria's tiny Inner Harbour. The *Prince Rupert* would make only a short stop in town. Passengers will disembark and new passengers will board for the steamer to depart at 10 a.m. for Vancouver and other destinations on the B.C. Coast.

The new Empress Hotel at the head of the bay stood high bare brick, but sprigs of Virginia Creeper vine planted in the ground gave promise of a softer and warmer façade to come.

Agnes' older brother James Anderson met the steamer to take Gaudin home through streets that later in the day would become filled with pedestrians, electric trams, and noisy automobiles, but so early in the morning, stood silent.

"The Coronation of the King and Queen clearly occasions much interest. Just look at the telephone poles and lamp posts draped with flags and patriotic banners. I am surprised the people in this town take such an inordinate pride in the British Monarchy."

"Yes Gaudin, I tell you soon after you left for the Yukon in April, the wealthy and those high in the pecking order of the Establishment left town to travel to London for the Coronation. The Premier of the Province, Sir Richard McBride and his family will attend to represent the Province of British Columbia."

"I had no idea a Coronation in London would cause so much excitement. I suppose those travelling to be there will go across Canada by train and on across the North Atlantic by one of the big new four smoke-stacked steamships they call *Liners*."

"Yes, Gaudin, from Quebec City at this time of year instead of Halifax, but to change the subject: I meant to say to you at the outset, you are to be congratulated on the new home you chose before you went north. Agnes has had me over to see it. You will enjoy living on a quiet street close by the creek running out on the beach at Oak Bay. I'd say you will not miss the grinding noise of the Craigflower electric streetcar tram passing by your old home."

"We became used to it. I don't hear so well now, anyway. I plan to walk to the Oak Bay tram to get into town when I can. I see it a wonderful convenience."

"I doubt I will keep up my car, Gaudin. Far too much trouble as one gets older. Even Mabel's family on Knapp Island doesn't need a car. They go everywhere by boat and train from Sidney to town, and a steamer calls by to take them to the settlement at Ganges on Saltspring Island where her son attended Mister Tolson's boys school before becoming a boarder student at University School in Victoria."

Gaudin and Anderson came to the front gate calling out to Agnes. She ran to meet them from picking flowers at the sunny side of the house. She greeted them with warmth and affection.

"As both of you can see we are now happily settled in here. A nice quiet place, just a short walk from the new electric tram that Kate takes to town to work, Jim. Next year the pussy willows will come out for me to pick."

"I know we will make the best of it, Inez, but this place is a far cry from the house on Craigflower Road."

"Oh stop it, Jim, we are lucky to be alive to enjoy our family. James, please stay on to hear Jim tell all of us about Jimmy and Nell. Both of you please sit down. Have either of you had breakfast?"

"Yes Inez, thank you, I have eaten, but I think I need a nap before lunch. I stayed up half the night yarning with Chief Officer McLellan, and I am too tired to talk any longer this morning. Perhaps James will stay on to have lunch with us?"

Kate came out of the house to greet her father in the garden with a kiss and a big hug. She reported Captain Troup had tipped off Captain Robertson that her father would be coming home on the night boat from Seattle, and he gave her the day off work to be home when he arrived.

"That was a good-hearted thing for him to have done, Kate. James, you may not know that Ottawa put Captain George Robertson in charge on an acting basis when I left last April."

"Yes I did know Robertson put in charge. But Agnes, Jim didn't mention Jimmy or Nell or the trip north on the way here, which I found ominous, but I suppose I did most of the talking. Yes Agnes, I will stay for lunch, thank you. I have a bottle of scotch whiskey for you and Jim in this brown paper bag to have a wee dram later. As a Scot I spell the name W-H-I-S-K-Y, but the English spelling of the name appears everywhere, now."

Two hours later Gaudin came down from his nap to join the group.

"I will enjoy the wee dram before lunch, Anderson, thank you. Agnes, I can tell from the look on your face you think I should rest longer. I am NOT too tired to talk. The sandwiches will do fine, but I don't want tea, thank you."

Kate asked, "May I have a wee dram, too?"

And she did. They all did. After Agnes carried in a tray laden with peppery watercress sandwiches with just enough cold boiled salad dressing on the spicy greens to please her husband, Kate sat down with the others to join in the conversation, which began with Gaudin.

"My stay with Jimmy and Nell passed without me feeling I imposed on them."

"But, Jim, how are Jimmy and Nell making out?"

"They are just fine, Inez. I'm glad I went. As I said, they left me feeling I did not impose on them. I stayed for the noise and celebration of Spring Break-up of the Ice in the River and to see the shipyard men use jacks with great care to lift the steamboats on greased skids to float in the water. Jimmy took me on his stern-wheel steamers running down to Dawson City and return, truly a scenic river passage in the long daylight hours at his high latitude. I had a small cabin to sleep in. Earlier I had stood in open-mouthed amazement at the size of the B-Y-N shallow draft stern-wheel steamers hauled out on the banks at Whitehorse. They present a lot of upper housework windage to my seaman's eye, but I found the skippers handle them well. Many of them came steaming up the Yukon River from St. Michael's in Alaska to start work at Whitehorse. Nell asked me to stay longer, but I left to come home before I felt I had stayed too long."

"But Jim, how are Jimmy and Nell?"

"I'm getting to that, Inez. Please bear with me. As I had not connected with Nell's people on the way up, on Jimmy's urging I departed Skagway on a convenient Alaska Steamships sailing to land in Seattle to visit them. Jimmy made a present to me of passage home from Seattle to Victoria by Grand Trunk Pacific, and said he would send a wire to notify Captain Troup of my change of itinerary."

James Anderson interrupted, saying, "A good idea, so Troup could tell me."

Gaudin carried on after the interruption.

"Jimmy and Nell were good to me, but I am glad to be back with you, Inez. Parts of the trip I enjoyed but I was not feeling at all well a lot of the time. I feel better now that I am home."

"Oh, that you are feeling better is good to hear, dear husband, but please tell us about Jimmy and Nell. How ARE they?"

"They are both just fine, Inez. We do not have to worry about our Jimmy. I can see why he fell for Nell. She is a strong beautiful woman with a constitution full of energy and spirit. She reminded me a lot of you, Agnes, when we married. Rosy cheeks and lots of spunk."

"Oh that's good of you to say, Jim, but I am not the young one I once was."

"What about the story we heard a few years ago," Agnes' brother interjected, "that he married a dance hall girl from Michigan?"

"I will tell you what I know. Yes, she came with her parents from Michigan when prospects for the men in her family looked far better on the Pacific Coast, more particularly in Washington State. Many in Michigan migrated to Washington at that time, much as New Brunswick woodspeople came west to British Columbia. She decided to follow the Gold Rush north from Seattle to find employment."

In the silence that followed Gaudin raised the glass tumbler to his mouth and drank a sip of the whiskey before speaking again.

"Yes, Jimmy told me they met in a dance hall," he said. "She had arrived in Skagway on the steamer from Seattle. As he tells it to me, in a magical moment, his words, he decided to pursue and win her. More than ten years ago now. To my eye she still looks like a real catch. A wonderful cook, she fusses over him like a mother would, and he doesn't object to being told what to do. I heard no talk of children though, which I found a little disappointing. I'd be happy if the two produced some Gaudin grandchildren for us. The family strain has not yet been struck to my satisfaction."

"Oh Jim, that may come," Agnes said. "Jimmy is only 35. Did you get to see Nell's people in Seattle?"

"Yes, I did, on the return. I missed them in April. I hope I have made amends for any difficulty our family caused years ago. I told them I thought their daughter a fine choice for Jimmy's wife and, said to them with a laugh, her choice of Jimmy showed her good judgment."

"Oh I am so glad you did that, Jim."

Kate interjected after a long moment of silence.

"I do want to hear about the train ride from Skagway. Please tell us about that, Papa."

"Before I get to that Kate, all of you would have been impressed with the garden Jimmy and Nell will be planting."

"A garden!" Agnes exclaimed. "How surprising! Jimmy had no time for gardening when he lived at home with us."

"Yes, we must give Nell the credit for getting him interested. They assure me they will have an abundance of flowers and vegetables in the short summer growing season there. Whitehorse has little cloud and much sunshine during the long hours of daylight in mid-summer. They call it the *Land of the Midnight Sun*. Kate, you asked about the railroad. A remarkable piece of narrow gauge track laid after the Gold Rush to by-pass the steep slopes of Chilkoot Pass, which the miners climbed on their way north from Skagway. The narrow gauge steam locomotive and the rolling stock have every appearance of fine design and craftsmanship. The train made a slow climb up around sharp curves to mount high over Skagway. We stopped for a few minutes to look down to the harbour and our little steamer, which looked the size of a wood chip in the water, tied to the wharf. Nearing the top elevation we looked over to see the steep bare slope of Chilkoot Pass still covered with a blanket of snow. We could imagine the sight of Gold Rush men striving to climb up with their gear."

"How long did it take the train to get to Whitehorse, Jim?"

"Most of the day, Inez. The slow climb to the Divide took time and we still had a long way to go. Jimmy and I had lots of time to talk before the train arrived in Whitehorse."

"For the last part of your trip home how did you enjoy your cabin on the midnight steamer from Seattle? I have heard her passenger cabins are really quite wonderful."

"I must tell you that I found great enjoyment in the comforts aboard ship, electric light, steam heat in the cabins, and running water in cabin washbasins. I heard the sounds and felt the warmth coming up from the engine room, deep down in the ship. Such a change, Inez, from the times at sea I gave you in the *Lampson* and the *Rover*. I did like the look of the rake of the *Prince Rupert's* masts and the matching slope of the three slim tall black smoke stacks, which looked good to my seaman's eye. The cargo booms shipped forward showed she was no mere excursion boat for passengers. Captain Troup tipped off the steamer's captain I would board at Seattle. Captain Barney Johnson presented his officers to me. I remember particularly one of them, a remarkable young officer, Hugh Stanley McLellan. In introducing me to his officers Captain Johnson said I would be coming on this passage as far as Victoria; I had been to the Yukon by Alaska Steamships to see my son, a chief engineer in Steam, who is running Yukon stern-wheel river steamers; I had come up in Sail, a *Cape Horner*, he said, but I also knew this Coast from years of running Federal Government vessels to build and service the lights and the buoys; I have invited him, he said, to come up to the wheelhouse whenever he wants; I thanked him and said I would try to keep out of everyone's way and that I would go below to let him go about his business. Not just yet Captain Gaudin, he said, if you will permit, please go with my Chief Officer McLellan, who will take you on a quick inspection of the vessel. McLellan led me to my cabin on the starboard side of the vessel on the deck below the upper main deck, a cabin with its own porthole for me to stick my head out in the next morning's daylight, a quiet cabin distant from the passengers walking and talking on the upper deck. McLellan took a moment to say he came up in Sail as I had. On my face lighting up at the mention of Sail, McLellan suggested he could come to my cabin as soon as he came off-watch to yarn about it. Yes, please do that McLellan, I said. We won't have another chance like this to talk. You know my cabin, I said, knock on the door. The tour of the vessel done, I went up to the rail to see the crewmen use steam winches to take aboard the heavy rope lines from the wharf. Captain Johnson, standing on the flying bridge, reached up to pull the whistle cord for three distinct blasts of the steam whistle to signal to other vessels of his intentions to back the *Rupert* out into the harbour before turning to pass north in Puget Sound to Point Wilson, which lies near Port Townsend. The night trip began with the pleasing prospect of young Chief Officer McLellan coming to my cabin to yarn about his time at sea in Sail before he came to work in Steam on this coast. I called short my nap when the knock came on the door. I opened the door to let him after taking a hot wet cloth from the tap in the washbasin to wipe off my face and beard."

Anderson interrupted to say, "I cannot believe you did not stay sleeping."

"Jim, don't tire yourself. Tell us some other time."

"No, Inez, I want to go on while all three of you are together. I was so interested to hear McLellan speak of his years at sea. I missed such yarning in my time in the government boats since '89. McLellan brought a pot of hot coffee and a basket of fruit. He and I sat talking and smoking our pipes during the long stretch up to Point Wilson and beyond into the Strait. The seas of a fresh westerly wind didn't much affect the steamer as she ran at 16 knots. Just imagine such a speed for a heavy passenger steamer to make Victoria on time; but neither of us had trouble with seasickness as we sat talking in my cabin through to four in the summer morning. When we had finished talking I looked aft out the open porthole to see the light in the northeast sky put Mount Baker and the peaks of the Cascade Mountains in stark silhouette. But I intended to say McLellan, like our Jimmy, longed for a home life on land. I can tell you sailors do not really love the sea. It's coming back home from the sea that counts."

"Oh Jim, why do you tell us about this man McLellan?"

"Because I liked hearing him talk, Inez; and because in him I could see the man I might have been had I gone to sea later than I did. McLellan worked at the end of the finest days of Sail. He sailed in fine fast ships that could make their way across oceans so much faster than I could in my little barque. Don't you want me to go on?"

"Papa, please go on. With you away I have missed hearing you talk."

"I began by asking McLellan to tell me where he was born, what schooling he had, and where he served his time. I made my scribbled notes so I can tell you."

"Papa, I am so glad you did. I want to hear all of it, now. Such a different type of man than those I see coming into the office in town."

"McLellan told me he was born into a Scottish seafaring family 25 years ago at St. George's Bay, Newfoundland. He went to school in Halifax until 14. His father and uncle owned and sailed a large fishing schooner the *Highland Brothers*. They traded salt cod to the West Indies and South America, bringing back molasses and rum. He served two years in her as cabin boy and then shipped out of Saint John, New Brunswick in the Maritime Provinces as cabin boy in the full-rigged ship, the *Arctic Stream*, out of Glasgow, Captain Charles Dixon, Master. A real beauty, a long steel hull with wire rigging, square sails with yards crossed on all three masts, much longer than the *Lady Lampson* or the *Rover of the Seas*. I told him yes, I knew the kind of sailing vessel that seamen call a ship: I told him I sailed in three-masted barques. We called all of them our ships, regardless. In the *Arctic Stream* he ran first from Saint John with lumber 14,000 miles to Adelaide, Australia. Then a cargo of grain for England followed by a cargo of coal from Cardiff, Wales around Cape Horn to Acapulco for a bunkering station for the U. S. Navy and steamships running coastwise from California to Panama. Sailing vessels carried coal as paying cargo all over the world to put in piles at harbours for steamers to bunker from. The *Arctic Stream* carried coal in the Pacific from Newcastle, Australia to Peru and back for another cargo for the U.S. Navy; then another from Newcastle to Manila in the Philippines. Several more ocean passages ended in Sydney, Australia for orders that resulted in 60-mile tows by tug in boisterous winds to load more coal at Newcastle sometimes for Peru, sometimes for the Phillipines. One passage from Peru to Vancouver in ballast in

1904 to take on lumber for Sydney, Australia, then another load of coal from Newcastle to Manila. The passages from Sydney to Manila had them following the track of the clipper *Thermopylae* through the Solomon Islands and the equatorial calms belt to the North East Trades where they made fast sailing times. On one four-day stretch his ship averaged 300 miles a day, noon-to-noon, far more miles a day than I ever dreamed of in the *Lampson*. This would have been sailing at its best, and I envied him for it. They made several round-trip voyages between Manila and Newcastle, returning each time south through the Sunda Strait, which Captain Dixon knew from his earlier time sailing in the Canton trade past Java to the Cape of Good Hope. But the *Arctic Stream* turned south and east to come down around the south side of Australia to join the Roaring Forties to use the westerly winds in the Great Southern Ocean to best advantage on the return both times. A marvellous display of what a sailing ship could do. On arriving in Sydney for the last time, McLellan left the *Arctic Stream*. By that time he had built up sea time with Dixon for five years as an able seaman. Captain Dixon taught him navigation and prepared him to sit for his Foreign-Going Second Mate deep-sea ticket in New Zealand."

"Oh Papa," Kate said, "I remember you called us up to your office window to see the *Thermopylae* more than once being towed into the Inner Harbour to tie to the wharf close to the office on Wharf Street. You told me about her, the beautiful green-hulled clipper that came here to carry rice to her new owner's rice mill in Victoria and coal or lumber back to the Orient."

"Yes Kate, that's correct. We all saw her in Victoria's Inner Harbour when she came under local ownership, such a beautiful ship and bigger and faster than my old *Rover of the Seas*. She came on this run out of Victoria too late and too old, which is often the case for men, too. From Australia, McLellan signed on as Chief Officer in an American full-rigged ship the *Reuce*, which sailed with a cargo of coal from Newcastle, Australia to San Francisco, where McLellan left the ship and signed on the fast propeller-driven coastal steamer the *City of Puebla*, 326 feet in length, 38 feet beam, which had been sailing on a regular schedule between San Francisco and the Pacific Northwest. On that run she set a record of 48 ½ hours from San Francisco to Victoria. McLellan left the ship in Vancouver to sign on as a quartermaster in the Canadian Pacific Railway Company's fine-looking little steamer the *Princess May* to learn the British Columbia coastline and how to use echoes back from the ship's whistle sounded in fog to fix position, a trick I had to learn when I took command of the steamer *Sir James Douglas* for the Federal Government in '89. McLellan quickly became Second Officer and then Chief Officer working for Union Steamships in the passenger steamers *Cowichan*, *Capilano* and the larger *Camosun* for five years sailing the waters between Vancouver and Prince Rupert and as far north as the new mine at Stewart in Northern British Columbia. The Examiner who passed him for his Master's Certificate a year ago certified McLellan's supporting papers and credentials to be *exceptionally satisfactory*. McLellan pulled that letter out of his pocket with justifiable pride to show me. He applied to Grand Trunk Pacific, the new company on the coast competing with the C.P.R. and Union Steamships. They hired him as Second Mate and then Chief Officer for their steamer the *Prince John* on the North Coast. He continued to move up rapidly to ship out as Chief Officer in the new *Prince Rupert* with Captain Johnson on her maiden voyage. I asked McLellan how he liked working for Grand Trunk. He answered me in words to the following effect that told me so much, 'It's a good ship, sir, but the timetable is hard on a man. No time off, and the ship, herself, has no rest. Look at the weekly timetable Seattle to Skagway with stops in between in the summer season we are going to have to keep up. Captain Johnson and I have talked about a future together after leaving Grand Trunk running tugs on the coast out of Vancouver. Then each of us could have a home life.' McLellan looked at his timepiece and said he had to go on watch. He thanked me for talking to him. I bade him good sailing and farewell, and I went to have a short nap before coming in to Victoria this morning. I have never seen such fine quarters for passengers as those on the *Prince Rupert*. On the day you saw me off, Inez, did you get driven back to Craigflower Road?"

"Yes, Jim, I stayed to see the old steamship the *Victoria* leave the harbour before Captain Troup's driver took me home to finish preparations for our move to Hampshire Road-by-the-Creek, which is my name for our new home. Arthur Wilby and Marie helped organize the move."

"I must thank them for that," Gaudin said.

"Thank you for telling us about McLellan, Papa," Kate said, "I had no idea men had been leading such lives. Didn't we see the *Reuce* towed to V. M. D.?"

"Yes, Kate, and we saw her depart, towed out by tugs past the office loaded high with lumber from the C. P. S. mill in the Upper Inner Harbour at Victoria. Although I admire and respect McLellan, I don't envy him for the life he now leads, working for another under close supervision from men in an office in town. Looking back, I believe men in authority might have envied me for the independent life I led when I was out of their sight. He will be happier when he gets a vessel to command. My life at sea ended up well, considering the risks I took. It's not the ships that gave me the trouble: men in authority gave the trouble."

"Jim, you must be tired," Agnes interjected. "Perhaps you'd like another nap this afternoon?"

"Yes Agnes, that's a good idea. Don't wake me. I am not hungry so you and Kate go ahead with supper when you want. I want to sleep now, but first let me not forget to say McLellan told me something about the *Lady Lampson* that brought tears to my eyes: Captain Dixon told him of the pretty sight he caught of her in Sydney Harbour, still carrying the name of the *Lady Lampson*, flying the Stars and Stripes, and registered in Honolulu. Every sign of being well kept up, he said, but later he'd heard she had been run to her end on Kingman Reef 800 miles south of Honolulu in 1893.[12] The ship's two boats arrived there with the crew almost dying of thirst. I never had any doubt the Honourable Company should have accepted my recommendation to repair the *Lady Lampson* and keep her sailing. I often wondered how life would have been different had I been able to sail her back to London. I had been correct in saying the new owners would be American and that they would keep the name *Lady Lampson*. They gave her a new life I could not. What a wonderful time we would have had sailing her in the South Pacific to and from Honolulu if I'd had the money to buy her at auction thirty years ago. I would not have run her onto Kingman Reef. Thank you, James, for getting me home. Tomorrow, I want to walk down the low bank on this side of the creek to see the grass in the fields with the deep blue Camas flowers growing wild."

---

12 Reel 1A Potts Collection at the National Inland Waterways Library, a special library within the St. Louis Mercantile Library, at the University of Missouri-St.Louis University. See Missouri Waterways Journal index 1890-1910 May 6, 1893 page 7, re: story of Lady Lampson wrecked in 1893 on Kingman Reef in book Strange Sea Stories

In the last late night printing run of the Sunday Morning Victoria Colonist newspaper January 12 1913, editor Sam Matson stopped the presses to scoop the Victoria Times on the news of Captain Gaudin's death: -

DEATH OF CAPTAIN GAUDIN

It is with deep regret we chronicle the death of Captain James Gaudin for so many years connected with the Marine Department of this city. Few men in office have been as painstaking and conscientious as he. His whole heart was in his work. He combined with his great knowledge and efficiency, a fine courteous spirit, which made it a pleasure to have any official business to transact with him. He was a splendid specimen of a mariner, an excellent representative of the days when a seafaring life had its romantic as well as its practical side. Captain Gaudin had long been a resident of Victoria, where he leaves a widow and several children surviving him. He was socially very much esteemed. Indeed one may say he had none but friends in the whole community. To Mrs. Gaudin and her family we extend an expression of very deep sympathy.

The Victoria Daily Colonist newspaper printed six mornings a week including an issue for publication on Sunday but did not on Monday: the Victoria Daily Times did not print on Sunday but did on Monday.

The Daily Times newspaper on the street on Monday afternoon printed :-

Upon receipt of the news of the passing of Captain Gaudin, the officials of the Canadian Pacific Railway and the Grand Trunk Pacific and other steamship companies had the flags on their steamers and at their offices lowered to half-mast out of respect. Captain Gaudin was very popular with all of the seafaring fraternity of this coast. In the despatch of his duty as Agent Marine & Fisheries he showed a marked degree of courtesy and his decisions were always regarded as unbiased. Many of the old timers in the Province came to this port in the early days in the ships he commanded. He was known to be a skilful navigator who brought his vessels through storms that would have caused them to founder had they not been in such capable hands.

The Colonist did not print on Monday, but the following appeared in next-day's issue on Tuesday January 14 1913 :-

CAPTAIN GAUDIN CROSSES THE BAR-
Late Agent of the Marine Department passes away at his residence -a busy and honourable career.

Flags at half mast on the Marine Department Building and on every shipping office in the city and on all vessels in port yesterday bore testimony to the regret felt on news of the death of Captain James Gaudin by those with whom he had come most closely in contact during the years of his connection with shipping on the Pacific and later as the Agent for the Department of Marine & Fisheries. Interment will take place in the Ross Bay cemetery. **Attained Ripe Age:** Captain Gaudin was born in Jersey, Channel Islands, on January 28 1838 and thus would have attained his seventy-fifth birthday had he lived a few days longer. Like so many of the sons of the Channel Islands, he entered the mercantile marine service as an apprentice seaman, and during those years and in his younger manhood he was in vessels in the East India and Australian trade chiefly. Having secured his papers as a master mariner he was engaged after 1865 in the service between London and Victoria for the Hudson's Bay Company. He first came to this coast as first officer of the *Prince of Wales*. Possessed of great professional skill and being a careful navigator, he rose in the estimation of the company to be promoted to the command of the **Lady Lampson** and brought her to Victoria in 1869. **Served as Pilot** ___At first Captain Gaudin served as a pilot in British Columbia waters, continuing in that until 1888, when he took command of the Dominion Government's lighthouse tender *Sir James Douglas*. When the *Quadra* succeeded that vessel in April of 1892 he took charge of the new boat and was with her on the coast until September when he was appointed Agent Marine & Fisheries with his office on Wharf Street. For this new duty he was admirably fitted, knowing the coast as well as he did. When he took office very few lights or any other marks along the coast existed. The lighthouses and other aids to navigation on this coast came largely as a result of his doings. In 1911 he retired on the ground of ill health but retained two of his old positions as Examiner of Masters and Mates and Receiver of Wrecks.

Dedication

The writer dedicates this book to the memory of his late father Robert Oliver Dunsmuir Harvey Q.C. (1900-1958) who placed great stock in his Anderson and Gaudin family connection, and who commissioned the painting on the cover of this book by the noted Marine Artist Jack W. Hardcastle (1881-1980) of Nanaimo B.C. The painting depicts the Hudson's Bay Company's Barque the **Lady Lampson**, which Captain James Gaudin in the story sailed on nine roundings of Cape Horn 1869-1878. Contrary to the depiction, the **Lady Lampson** did not cross skysail yards, nor did her builder burden her with the weight of covering boards at the bow as shown in the painting.

ACKNOWLEDGEMENTS

-First and foremost to the long defunct General Register of Shipping & Seaman in Cardiff, Wales, which, in 1965 sent information no longer available without incurring heartbreaking effort and expense to examine records in depositories. Thereby the writer obtained a statement of all sailing vessels in which Captain Gaudin sailed from 1855, beginning with service as apprentice seaman.

-To Steve Schoenhoff and Matt Hughes, writing instructors at North Island College, Comox Valley Campus, for stimulating the author to write.

-To the microfilm copies of old Victoria newspapers that enabled piecing together the incomplete information from Cardiff on the voyages (1878–1885) of the barque **Rover of the Seas**. Captain Gaudin changed her port of registry from Sunderland to Victoria in the early 1880s with the result the Record Office in Cardiff received incomplete information during those years.

-To the late Donald Graham for the definitive writing about Captain Gaudin's work after his time in Sail in **Keepers of the Light** ISBN 0-920080-65-O and **Lights of the Inside Passage** ISBN 0-920080-85-5 (bound); ISBN I – 55017-060-O (pbk).

-To the Hudson's Bay Company Archives in Winnipeg, Manitoba for access to microfilmed 600 pages or more from the logbooks of the brig *Dryad* and the barques *Prince of Wales* and *Lady Lampson* and for the ready assistance provided in every respect.

-To the Royal B. C. Museum for permission to print photos.

-To Torchy Anderson for having published Susan Allison's recollections in the Vancouver Province in serial form in issues dated March 1st, 8th and 15th 1931, which can be seen in the microfilm collection at the Provincial Legislative Library in Victoria.

-To Captain John Anderson of Ladysmith for passing on some of his extensive knowledge of Deepwater Sail, which became invaluable in the early stages of the writing of the manuscript. Any mistakes that remain are not his.

-To Robin Percival Smith for his book "*Captain McNeill and his wife the Nishga Chief.*" ISBN 0-88839-472-1. His splendid book records historical facts relating to vessel movements along the coast in the early days. His book stimulated the writer to ascertain the locations of North Island (Langara Island) and *Kigarney* Harbour (north across Dixon Entrance (in fact, Kaigani Harbour on Dall Island in the Alaskan Panhandle) by reference to present-day marine charts and the *Dryad* 1833 logbook in the Hudson Bay Archives with respect to *Dryad's* track from the Columbia River to Fort Simpson on the Nass in 1833 and during the summer of 1834; and also by reference to Captain McNeill's logbook of the *Lama* in the year following, which the author found in the B.C. Museum.

- To Hudson's Bay Archives Fort Vancouver Post Journals Year 1826 – B.223/a/3 1826 fol. 65 for the substance of Lt. Amelius Simpson's Journal of his crossing of the Rockies with the Columbia Brigade in company with James Birnie.

-To Rob Morris, the editor of present-day Western Mariner Magazine for supplying a copy of the December 1992 Westcoast Mariner Magazine setting out at page 9 a letter to the editor from Captain Hugh Stanley McLellan Jr. of North Vancouver, which, with a photo of the barque *Arctic Stream*, laid out the story of his revered father's seagoing life: That letter to the editor, together with information from noted Marine Historian Mr. Frank A. Clapp of Victoria relating to the sailings of the T.S.S. *Prince Rupert* in 1911, formed the basis for the story of a meeting between Captain McLellan's father and Captain Gaudin told in Chapter 20.

-Last but not least, to the author's wife and family for their advice and encouragement to write.